SYNBAT

Other books by Bob Mayer

Eyes of the Hammer

Dragon SIM-13

SYNBAT

a novel by
Bob Mayer

LYFORD
Books

All the characters in this book are fictitious and any resemblance to actual persons, living or dead, is purely coincidental. The names, incidents, dialogue, and opinions expressed are products of the author's imagination and are not to be construed as real. Nothing is intended or should be interpreted as expressing or representing the view of the U. S. Army or any other department or agency of the government. All technical and tactical information presented is either drawn from unclassified sources or the author's imagination.

LYFORD Books
Published by Presidio Press
505 B San Marin Dr., Suite 300
Novato, CA 94945-1340

Library of Congress Cataloging-in-Publication Data

Mayer, Bob, 1959–
    Synbat : a novel / Bob Mayer.
       p.   cm
    ISBN 0-89141-416-9
    1. United States Army. Special Forces—Fiction. 2. Genetics—Research—United States—Fiction. 3. Military research—United States—Fiction. 4. Soldiers—United States—Fiction. I. Title.
PS3563.A95227S96   1994
813'.54—dc2O   93-28062
                                             CIP

Typography by ProImage
Printed in the United States of America

To all who've served.

SYNBAT

PROLOGUE
MONDAY, 6 APRIL

Eddyville State Prison, Eddyville, Kentucky
1:54 A.M.

The luminous minute hand slid one digit as the second hand rounded the twelve. Two more minutes. As beads of sweat formed on his brow, Chico Lopez's eyes and mind were totally absorbed by the march of time on his wrist. For the hundredth time he shifted uncomfortably on the state-issue mattress, careful not to dislodge the three hacksaw blades carefully hidden inside the back of his belt.

A flash of lightning flickered through the tall barred windows that lined the outside walls of Cell Block C, illuminating the building's Gothic architecture. Chico's cell was on the first level of the six-tier stack of eight-by-eight cubicles. Eddyville State Prison had been built at the turn of the century, when attractive surroundings for inmates had been an incomprehensible concept. The prison looked its task both inside and out: high gray stone walls with block turrets at all corners, perched on a hill overlooking the northern end of Lake Barkley. With the darkness of the thunderstorm adding to the blackness of night, only the occasional flares of lightning displayed the entire edifice. The searchlights from the guard towers fought a losing battle against the sheets of rain that pounded the Kentucky grassland outside the walls and the red dirt inside.

Another minute ticked off. Time. Chico quietly slid out of bed, taking his sheet with him, and stole over to the cell door. He'd been cutting the locking bolt now for a week, millimeter by millimeter. The last remaining fragment of bolt gave under his tug and he was out in the hallway.

Chico's cellmate continued to snore, unaware that the first and easi-
est door to freedom was open.

As Chico turned the corner where the long tiers of cells met a cross
corridor, two figures loomed out of the shadows. He pushed his ac-
complices into a dark recess in the outside wall where the main pipe
for the fire sprinkler system rose to the ceiling eighty feet above. By
crowding in, the three were out of sight unless someone walked directly in front of them and peered in.

"You're late," the larger of the two men hissed nervously, his eyes
glinting in the dark.

"Fuck you, Parson," Chico replied as he took the bed sheets from
the two men and tied them to his. "I'm on time. Give me your blades."

The other two convicts, Parson and Hill, handed over one hacksaw
blade each. Chico tucked them under his belt with his own three blades.
"When you see me go out, you climb up."

He looped the three sheets over his shoulder and grabbed the sprinkler
pipe. Wedging himself between it and the wall, he crabbed up. He didn't
look down as the dirty concrete floor receded. Thirty feet up he reached
the base of an old window, aligned with the third tier of cells fifteen
feet away.

Vertical iron bars eight inches apart ran from the masonry at the bottom
of the window, all the way up to the top, twenty feet above. Chico
tied off the end of the sheets to the closest bar and locked his right
leg over one of the stanchions holding the sprinkler pipe to the wall,
so that his hands were free. Then he slipped one of the hacksaw blades
out from under his belt and began cutting. The blades had cost Parson a hundred dollars each in a covert deal with one of the contract
workers building the new cell block. Half a grand for five pieces of
steel was the cost of freedom for Chico and his partners.

After ten minutes and two dulled blades, a foot-and-a-half section
of the first bar finally came free. Chico had planned to take out three
sections across, but it looked as though they might be a hundred bucks
short. He used longer strokes on the next bar, utilizing every part of
the blade, his fingers tearing as he tried to hold onto the sweaty metal.
He cut through the second bar in seven minutes, with some good teeth
remaining on the fourth blade.

Above the usual coughing and snoring that resounded through the
block at night, Chico could hear nervous rustling down below. It was
more than twenty minutes since they'd left their cells; they had less

than fifteen before a guard would make his rounds. If they were out by then, they might stay undetected until morning. If they weren't out, with Hill and Parson standing at the bottom of the pipe and Chico illuminated against the window, they would be spotted immediately. Chico cut faster, ignoring the blood that was now flowing from his slashed fingers.

Chico made the bottom cut on the last bar using the final good blade. He cut more than three-quarters of the way through the top of the bar before the blade was completely dull. Holding onto the remaining bars, Chico pressed both feet against the third bar and pushed with all his might. The bar bent ever so slightly, but that was all he needed. Wrapping part of the string of sheets around his fist, he punched out the bottom of the window; then he threw the cloth out into the pouring rain to hang down onto the slick outer wall of the cell block.

Hissing to let the other two know to come up, Chico forced his body in between the bars, his slight, five-and-a-half-foot frame making it through with little room to spare. He looked down at the wet mud forty feet below, then firmly grasped the sheets, which hardly covered a third of the distance. Hand over hand he lowered himself until he was hanging onto the very end. With a brief prayer, Chico let go and slammed into the ground, rolling over in the mud then onto his feet, all systems still functioning. He squinted up into the pouring rain and could see Parson's head pop out the window above.

Parson made it halfway out the window and then became stuck, the bar not bent far enough for his ponderous gut. Behind him, Hill put both feet squarely on Parson's rear and shoved. Parson let out a squeal of pain as the jagged edges of the cut pipe tore into his skin. Hill didn't hesitate and kicked again, popping Parson free. The fat man barely had time to grab the sheet rope before he was sliding down. The end of the sheets slid through his fingers and he was in free-fall for two seconds before landing with a loud plop in front of Chico.

"I broke my leg!"

"Shut the fuck up!" Chico warned, kneeling over him. He felt the indicated appendage. "It ain't broken. Get on your feet or I'll cut your fucking throat right here."

Hill hit on his feet and forward-rolled to absorb the impact of the fall. He popped up. "Let's go."

Together, Hill and Chico grabbed Parson and started dragging him toward the chain-link fence, the last physical obstacle between them and the outside. The searchlights from the guard towers, a hundred feet away on either side, were distant white spots against the blackness.

"To the left," Hill directed. The three men splashed to the low ground where the water poured under the fence in a rain-formed gully. Lying down, Hill went first, almost completely submerging as he slipped under the bottom links of the fence. Chico shoved Parson down and the fat man slithered through, the bottom of the fence tearing the shirt off his back and leaving long red gashes in his flesh. Chico easily followed and they were out.

Biotech Engineering;
Vicinity Lake Barkley, Tennessee
2:00 A.M.

The illuminated red numerals of the digital clock flickered to 2:00. Only four more hours. Stan Lowry had known when he'd applied for a security job this far out in the sticks that it would be relatively uneventful, but he hadn't suspected that it would be so thoroughly boring. Occasionally, when the empty nights got the better of him, Stan almost wished that a group of teenagers would come here to the hills and start hooting and hollering the parking lot. Anything would be better than the total lack of activity that Stan had experienced five nights a week, every week, for the last eight months.

He didn't even have to make rounds of the compact one-story building that was his nightly domain. Everything to be surveilled was displayed on the small TV screens stacked on the semicircular desk that was Stan's post in the building's front foyer. He listlessly scanned the twelve screens. Nothing on the three outside cameras other than the heavy spatter of rain sprinkling the darkened Tennessee countryside. The arc lights on the roof of the building barely penetrated the wet night, straining to reach the wood line on three sides of the building.

The parking lot out front was dimly lit by several light poles. The only present occupant of that lot was Stan's beat-up, old pickup truck, its drooping fenders a stark contrast to the clean lines of the modern building he guarded.

Stan shifted his gaze back to the internal cameras. Six screens showed empty offices. Two showed larger rooms that reminded Stan of the chemistry lab many years ago in high school. The last screen portrayed the main corridor that stretched the length of the building, accessed by double doors to his rear. That corridor ended in another double door with a boldly lettered restricted access warning painted on it.

Stan didn't know what was beyond those end doors, but he did know that everything the people in this building worked on was highly classified by the government. Whatever was behind those doors was something more highly classified than his secret clearance. Stan understood that, and asked no questions. One of the things that his twenty-four years as a noncommissioned officer in the army had taught him was the importance of security. If the feds said he didn't have a need to know what was back there, then that was fine with Stan. The name on the front of the building, and on Stan's paychecks—Biotech Engineering— meant nothing to him. Quite frankly, Stan wasn't overly curious about what happened here during the day. As long as they paid him on time, they could do any damn thing they pleased.

He lifted his feet off the desk and eased them to the floor. His knees constantly ached, the result of too many years carrying a rucksack in the infantry. Pouring a cup of coffee from his thermos, Stan glanced at the computer screen that was centered among the telemonitors. In all his time on the job, Stan had never seen anything come across the screen—just the cursor in the upper left-hand corner blinking like an eye that never slept.

Stan had been briefed that all the building's alarms were linked into the computer. If the warning light on top of the desk indicated an alarm going off, the location would be displayed on the computer screen along with instructions. If any alarm warnings came up on the screen, Stan was to call the staffer on the alert roster before doing anything. According to the instruction binder, under no circumstances were local law enforcement personnel to be allowed inside the building. The staff doctor whom Stan was supposed to alert would take care of anything occurring inside.

If Stan had been an imaginative man, he might have thought that was a little odd. Why were they more worried about internal alarms than external? Why the difference in response? And how could an internal alarm be tripped without an external one going off first? However, Stan wasn't very imaginative, which may well have been why he was hired for this job in the first place.

One thing Stan had noticed, though, was that if he mentally pictured the location of the restricted double doors against the dimensions of the building, there wasn't much room behind those doors. Stan suspected that they led to a staircase or an elevator and that there might be hidden, lower levels to this complex. The keys on the master ring on his belt were labeled, some of them for doors that were not on this floor. He had found that out during his first week on the job, when he had gone through the building. His curiosity had not led him to open the restricted double doors, though. Stan enjoyed getting paid to sit on his ass. In Stan's book, cold cash outweighed idle questioning every time. Curiosity had gone by the wayside on his first tour in Vietnam and had remained an unnecessary character trait throughout the rest of his time in the army.

Kicking his feet back and sipping his coffee, Stan returned to his favorite pastime of watching the numbers on the digital clock wind their way down to the end of his shift.

Vicinity Exit 40, Interstate 24, Kentucky
2:34 A.M.

"Where *is* that fucking bitch!" Hill exclaimed as the mud-soaked trio of escaped convicts struggled to the top of a grassy knoll overlooking the interstate.

"Watch your mouth," Chico muttered halfheartedly as he peered at the highway. "That's my sister you're talking about." He could see the ramp for Exit 40 illuminated as the occasional vehicle went by, so he knew that they were in the right place, but where was Leslie?

Hill had come up with the plan and prepared the way under the fence when on a work party; Parson had been the one with the money for the blades; and now Chico's contribution wasn't materializing.

"There!" he cried out as two headlights slid to a stop on the near side of the highway, just past the end of the ramp. A jag of lightning showed that it was a van. "That's her."

"Let's go." Hill was already running down the small hill and Parson and Chico struggled after him, their feet sliding out from under them on the slick grass. Parson's limp was gone in the excitement of the final piece falling into place.

The side door of the panel van slid open and the three tumbled in, Chico closing the door behind him.

"You all look like shit," the driver remarked nervously as she looked at her catch. The slender dark-complected woman anxiously sucked on the dying stalk of a cigarette as the three men caught their breath. Leslie "worked" Murfreesboro Road down in Nashville selling herself, and she was none too pleased to be involved in this operation. She'd had little choice, though, since Chico had made her an offer she couldn't refuse: Show up with the van or he'd track her down in Nashville and kill her. She knew that he was quite capable of the latter, since he'd already killed four men, and sibling love was an unknown entity in the Lopez family. "The alarm out yet?"

Chico shook his head, water flying out of his soaked hair. "We didn't hear no siren, so we're still good to go. Let's get the fuck out of here."

Leslie slid back behind the wheel. Chico climbed into the passenger seat next to her while Hill and Parson remained on the floor in the back.

"Take the ramp and head back south," Chico ordered. "You got the clothes?"

"In the bag back there."

Chico waited until they crossed over the cloverleaf and were heading southeast on I-24. "Take Exit 56 when we get to it and head south on 139 toward Cadiz. The first thing they'll do is seal up the interstate when the alarm goes out. We need to get out in the back country and head on down to Dover."

Biotech Engineering
3:05 A.M.

Stan sipped his coffee slowly. His thoughts centered on tomorrow's activities, or more accurately, as he again noted the digits on the wall clock, what he would be doing later today. He figured to catch a few hours of sleep after being relieved at six, and then head over to the Land Between the Lakes (LBL) and do some fishing. Lake Barkley, which marked the eastern boundary of the large LBL recreation area, was less than three miles west of Stan's present location. With the weather as wet and chilly as it was, he knew he'd have the lake to himself. He hoped the storm would have passed over by dawn and the fish would be biting.

As Stan was trying to decide on a fishing spot, the lights inside the building flickered briefly and then went out, replaced by the dim glow of the battery-powered backup lighting system. The video screens were dead, but the computer display still glowed. Stan leaned forward in

the chair and stared at the words etched there in eerie black letters against
the green background:

POWER OUTAGE / EMERGENCY POWER ON.
0:23 TO BACK UP BATTERY DEPLETION AND CONTAINMENT LIFE
SUPPORT SYSTEM FAILURE.
PRESS F1 FOR HELP.

What the hell did that mean? Stan wondered. He couldn't remember anything about a containment life support system in the instruction binder. The system had to be somewhere behind that locked double
door, on the lower level that he suspected existed.

Stan frowned as he pondered the problem. He knew that he was supposed to call the top name on the alert roster. He looked at the list.
Doctor Merrit's name was first. During Stan's numerous stints in the
army as staff duty NCO, he had received more than his share of butt
chewings from irate duty officers he had called up in the middle of
the night, as per instructions. He knew the perils that such interrup-
tions incurred for the caller.

Stan didn't like the idea of waking one of those doctors at two in
the morning over a power outage. Especially Merrit. He'd met her several
times when she had been working late, as she often did, and she seemed
very odd. Cumberland Electric ought to have the lines back up soon,
he figured. Maybe if he just followed the instructions on the screen,
he could cover everything until that happened.

Stan glanced at the screen again. The time was down to 0:21. As
he watched, the numbers changed to 0:20. Stan focused on the last line.
He didn't know much about computers, but he could connect the F1
prompt with the key on the top of the keyboard. Stan punched the plastic
button. The screen briefly cleared and then a new message appeared.

0:20 TO BACK UP BATTERY DEPLETION AND CONTAINMENT
LIFE SUPPORT SYSTEM FAILURE. TO EXTEND LIFE SUPPORT
SYSTEM OPEN CUBES. ACCESS CUBE OPENING SEQUENCE BY
PRESSING F5.

When a job paid minimum wage, it got talent commensurate with
the price. It didn't occur to Stan to ask himself exactly what "life" the

life support system was supporting. It also didn't occur to him to question the computer's instructions. Stan automatically reached out a stubby finger and pressed F5.

0:19 TO BACK UP BATTERY DEPLETION AND
CONTAINMENT LIFE SUPPORT SYSTEM FAILURE.
CUBE OPENING SEQUENCE ACCESSED.
OPEN CUBE ONE? (YES OR NO)

Stan's forefinger hunted over the keyboard and slowly answered the glowing question with three letters: YES.

0:19 TO BACK UP BATTERY DEPLETION AND CONTAINMENT
LIFE SUPPORT SYSTEM FAILURE. CUBE OPENING SEQUENCE
ACCESSED. CUBE ONE OPENED. OPEN CUBE TWO? (YES OR NO)

Stan answered again: YES.

The screen briefly cleared and a new message appeared.

CUBES ACCESSED.
1:19 TO BACK UP BATTERY DEPLETION.
CUBE CONTAINMENT SYSTEM BREACHED.
INNER CONTAINMENT DOOR SECURE.
OUTER CONTAINMENT DOOR SECURE.
ACCESS CONTAINMENT OPENING SEQUENCE
BY PRESSING F5.

Stan looked at the screen in concern. He didn't like the sound of "cube containment system breached." Made it sound as though he had screwed up somehow. Still, whatever he had done had extended the time to battery depletion and system failure. That had to be good. Curious to see if there was anything else he was supposed to do, Stan pressed F5 again.

1:18 TO BACK UP BATTERY DEPLETION.
CONTAINMENT OPENING SEQUENCE ACCESSED.
OPEN INNER CONTAINMENT DOOR? (YES OR NO)

(LEVEL FOUR SECURITY CLEARANCE REQUIRED
TO CONTINUE FURTHER)
ENTER LEVEL FOUR SECURITY CODE WORD

Stan looked at the prompt and shook his head. It didn't say anything about opening the inner containment door to extend the life support
system. Plus, even though he didn't know what a level four security
clearance was, he was damn sure of one thing: Since no one had told
him he had one, he assumed he didn't. He certainly didn't have a level
four code word, which obviously meant that he wasn't supposed
to open the inner containment door. Satisfied that he had done what
he was supposed to do, Stan picked up his thermos to pour himself another cup of coffee and wait for the power company to get
its act together.

Route 139, South of Cadiz, Kentucky
3:47 A.M.

Parson pointed over his shoulder. "There's got to be a place open in
Cadiz. We need to go back."

Chico shook his head, pivoting in his seat to look at the other two
men crouched in the back. "Yeah, right. Use your fucking brains, asshole.
We go to some Minit Mart there at four in the morning and you can
be damn sure the state troopers are going to be there right after us asking
if anyone seen anything. And then them guys are going to be right on
our ass. We got some people we got to see down in Dover before we
can head for Mexico. We got to get that money, and we can't have
the law thinking we're still in the area."

Hill slammed a fist into the back of Chico's seat, his eyes glaring
in the dim light of the dashboard. "Then your fucking sister should
have put some goddamn gas in the motherfucking gas tank."

Chico glared back as the van rolled down Route 139 at a steady forty-
five miles an hour. "We steal us a car."

Hill snorted. "Oh, yeah. That's fucking great, man. We'd be better
off going back to Cadiz."

"Naw, man," Chico argued. "They won't be able to make the connection with the van and a stolen car. We'll be all right."

Hill pointed out the window at the dark countryside. "Where the hell we gonna steal a car out in this place?"

"There!" Leslie spoke for the first time, anxious to try to contribute something positive. If they stole a car then they could get out of her life and she could go back to Nashville. She'd been silent ever since Hill had noted the gas needle flirting with empty, less than five minutes after they'd passed through the deserted streets of Cadiz.

The three convicts leaned forward as she braked the truck. The headlights came to a halt, illuminating the sign and the driveway that turned off beyond it.

Biotech Engineering
3:53 A.M.

Stan's attention was diverted from the glowing computer screen as a set of headlights carved into the darkness at the far end of the parking lot. About time the electric company got here, he thought as he hitched up his gun belt and strolled over to the front doors.

He frowned as the van pulled up next to his pickup truck and a man jumped out into the rain and started messing with his truck.

Stan unlocked the doors and stepped out under the front awning. "Hey! What are you doing?"

The voice startled Chico. The building had looked dark when they'd pulled in and he'd assumed that it was empty.

"Pull over to the building," he hissed at Leslie.

"Let's get out of here," she replied. Hill shoved her out of the driver's seat as Chico climbed in and picked up a tire iron.

"What'd you think you were doing?" Stan asked as they pulled up.

"Hey, man, I'm real sorry," Chico explained as he stepped out. "We're just about out of gas and, well, hey, there ain't no all-night stores on this road and I didn't want to run out before we got home."

Stan frowned, his eyes taking in the three disheveled men and the frightened woman. "You OK, miss?"

Leslie swallowed. "Yes, sir. I'm fine."

Stan stepped forward. "I got a can in the bed of my truck that I use for my boat. You can—"

The tire iron crushed the right side of Stan's skull and he sank to his knees, his hand reflexively trying to go for his gun. Chico swung again and again, the iron splattering bone and blood onto the wet pavement. After fifteen blows, Chico stopped, his arms covered with gore and his face beaming with a smile below two blazing eyes.

"What the fuck you do that for?" Parson was blubbering as Hill got out and unbuckled the holster and gun from the inert body.

"Help me put him in the van," Hill ordered. Parson reluctantly grabbed the guard's arms and helped Hill hoist the body into the van, dumping it on the floor.

"Let's see what we got in here," Hill said as he ripped the key ring off Stan's belt. He hopped out of the van and headed for the door of the building. As he stepped inside, the bright white overhead lights flashed back on. Startled, he almost dropped the gun, then realized what had happened. Chico, tire iron still gripped tightly in his hand, and Parson joined him. Leslie stayed in the van, scrunched up in the passenger seat, staring behind her at the body.

"You stay there, woman!" Chico yelled as the glass doors swung shut.

The flash of the red warning light on top of the console, compounded by the strident beep of an alarm, drew their attention to the desk where Stan's last cup of coffee sat, half-finished. A new message scrolled up on the screen as they gathered around.

POWER RESTORED.
SYSTEM MALFUNCTION
INTERNAL ALERT/ INNER CONTAINMENT BREACHED.
SECURE IMMEDIA

With the message still appearing, Chico swung the tire iron, smashing it into the screen. He pounded until the noise of the alarm stopped and the computer terminal was in shambles.

"See if there's anything we can use," Hill ordered, hitching the gun belt up to his belly, the weight of the pistol as comforting to him as the steel of the tire iron was to Chico. They went through the double doors into the main corridor. The sign on the door didn't indicate what was beyond, but did strongly suggest that whatever was in there was significant: WARNING: RESTRICTED ACCESS AREA. LEVEL FOUR CLEARANCE REQUIRED.

"What you think they got down there?" Hill asked out loud.

Chico's eyes still had a glazed look. "Let's check it out, man. Must be important. Maybe something we can sell."

Hill flipped through the keys until he came to the one labeled seventeen, matching the number above the lock on the side of the doors. He slipped in the key and turned it. The doors slid open, revealing a large freight elevator. Entering the elevator with Chico, he looked at the control panel. There were only two buttons: 1 and B.

"You coming?" Hill looked at Parson, who was still standing in the hallway.

"No, man. I'll check out these offices."

Hill looked the fat man in the eye. "Listen, motherfucker. You got any ideas of splitting with Chico's sister, you just better forget it. We'll track your ass down and blow your fucking brains out. You're in with us now. You killed that guard just as much as Chico did. Murder one, motherfucker. You got me?"

Parson nodded weakly. "Yeah, man, I understand."

Hill pushed B and the doors glided shut in front of him. The men felt their body weight lighten briefly, then settle as the elevator came to a halt. The doors parted open and they were facing a short corridor, ending in another set of sliding doors. Going up to the door, Hill read the number off the keyhole to the right: 18.

Hill slid in the appropriate key and turned it. The powered doors slid open and he stepped in, Chico right behind him. The room was dark. Hill's hand fumbled along the wall on the left before hitting the light switches.

As the fluorescent lights flickered on, the two men could see that they were in some sort of medical room. Two large tables covered with white sheets, with high-powered lamps looming over them, dominated the center of the room. Carts of sophisticated-looking machines ringed the walls.

Several doors led off to the side. Directly across from them, another set of double doors loomed. Unlike the other doors, these were solidly built of stainless steel. Squinting, Hill read the message painted on them: DANGER: OUTER CONTAINMENT DOOR. ENSURE INNER CONTAINMENT SECURE BEFORE OPENING.

Hill was checking out the medical equipment and cabinets of pharmaceuticals, judging their marketability, when he heard a noise from behind the far doors. It sounded as if someone had dropped some equipment.

Hill froze and pulled out the gun. "Anybody here?"

His words faded into the walls. Hill rubbed his forehead and considered the situation. Both men jumped as someone pounded on the doors. Hill edged up, signaling for Chico to move to the other side.

"Who's there?" he yelled.

He was answered with silence. The number above the keyhole on the control box to the right of the doors read 26. Hill found the corresponding key and slipped it in. He paused before turning it. For the first time, he felt fear. Some primeval sixth sense sent small tendrils of uneasiness through his stomach and tickled the hair on the back of his neck.

Fuck, ain't nothing to be afraid of, Hill decided. Not with Mister .38 in my hand. And there's no way I'm gonna show fear in front of Chico. He's one loco dude. Might as well turn the key and check it out.

"What the hell!" he muttered as the doors slid smoothly open. A short corridor, five feet long, appeared before him. The room beyond was strewn with equipment and papers. He stepped over the threshold between the open doors, Chico behind him.

Hill noticed movement out of the corner of his eye. He turned left, but much too slowly. Hill was still futilely trying to bring his gun to bear when he felt something ice cold rip into his gut. As the tear spread up to his chest, the coldness was followed by searing hot pain.

Hill still couldn't make out what tore into him as he was propelled onto his back, gun forgotten. His hands clasped his belly, fingers encountering something soft and wet. His unbelieving eyes saw intestines bulging against his hands.

That tableau stayed frozen for the long heartbeat of a second. A shadow loomed over Hill's right side and he could hear Chico screaming, as if from a very long distance away. Hill's own scream died in his throat as his trachea and carotid arteries were severed. Lying in a pool of his own blood, his last breath wheezed out of his slashed flesh.

Upstairs, Parson heard nothing. He was sitting at the security console, his hands trembling as he tried to figure out what to do. He was in for it now, he knew. Murder one. The big chair. Those dumb motherfuckers, he wanted to scream. The two had been idiots from the start— Chico's sister not having enough gas and Chico wasting the old man even though he said he'd give them some fuel.

Parson heard the doors to the elevator open behind him and spun around. He blinked and stared for a fatally long second, not believing what he was seeing. Then he screamed and leapt to his feet. He raced for the front door, but the figure jumped onto him from behind, the impact slamming Parson against the thick glass.

At the sound of Parson's scream, Leslie looked up from the guard's body. She watched the chase across the lobby with detachment, as if it were being played out on a movie screen.

The blood pulsing from Parson's cut throat splattered against the inside of the glass door, marking it with a cascade of bright crimson. Leslie finally reacted, jumping into the driver's seat and cranking the engine. The doors to the building were being opened and *they* were coming out. She pressed down on the gas pedal and tore out of the parking lot, the wheels almost losing traction on the wet pavement.

One of them almost caught up with her as the van roared onto Route 139, but she lost it as she turned left and desperately stomped on the accelerator. Low gas and the body on the floor behind her were forgotten as her eyes locked on the road ahead.

CHAPTER 1

Fort Campbell Military Reservation, Kentucky
5:37 A.M.

The BMW sprinted through the storm-lashed darkness, its headlights glinting off the wet pavement and the rows of trees blurring by on either side. Enjoying the sensation of speed, Doctor Glen Ward caressed the steering wheel. Military police cars were rarely out on this stretch of road so early in the morning, which is why he chose this route across the sprawling training areas of the Fort Campbell Military Reservation to get from his home in Clarksville to the lab. At this time of day, the only other traffic on the two-lane road was the few soldiers who lived on the western side of the reservation driving to their jobs in the opposite direction.

Ward tapped on the brakes as the edge of the military reservation slipped by and he was back on county road. He slowed further as he passed through the sleepy town of Bumpus Mills. He cruised along Route 139 until the road hit the tiny hamlet of Linton (population seventy-eight), on the banks of Lake Barkley, and then followed the road's sharp right turn to the north. The route now shadowed the shoreline of the lake.

After following the shore for four kilometers, Route 139 turned back east and climbed up into the low forested hills. The lack of people in this area had been one of the key reasons for building the lab here. Ward would have preferred someplace closer to Washington, D.C., since he seemed to spend most of his time there begging for funds, or even

Nashville, where he lectured occasionally at Vanderbilt University, but he'd reluctantly accepted what he was given. The isolated site allowed him and his assistants to concentrate on their work with few distractions. The nearby Fort Campbell military reservation also gave them convenient access to restricted training areas to field-test their project.

When Ward's headlights touched the small sign that indicated the private turnoff for the lab parking lot, Ward expertly spun the wheel and the BMW fishtailed onto the driveway. He rolled up the short incline toward the parking lot, satisfied with the trip. He wasn't as content with the thought of another day of writing up classified reports to justify the continued existence of his work.

It seemed to Ward that he spent more time on foolish paperwork than on his research. The few people in Washington who knew the true extent of the Synbat project—and the success it had already achieved—were behind Ward and his efforts. Unfortunately, the breakup of the Warsaw Pact and the Soviet Union, and subsequent head-hunting for peace dividends, put the Biotech Engineering project high on the list of classified projects heading for the chopping block.

General Trollers, head of the Pentagon's sixty-eight-billion-dollar-a-year secret Black Budget, which funded Biotech, was afraid to let even the congressmen on the intelligence oversight committee know what was really happening in the Biotech labs. Trollers felt that the project was much too sensitive and would never survive even classified scrutiny in Congress.

During the brief meeting the two had had in Washington three months ago, Trollers had indicated that it would be better for all if the project was simply dropped unless there were some immediate results, for both financial and political reasons. He had given Ward a final six-month extension on the research grant. That time was more than half over and the pressure for results was increasing correspondingly.

Ward shook his head as the car glided across the parking lot, past the night security guard's pickup truck. The tremendous advances he had achieved here in the last two years could all go for naught if the project was dropped. Just when things finally seemed to be going right, too, Ward thought bitterly.

Ward grabbed his briefcase as he unfolded from the car. He ran a practiced hand through his blown-dry hair. Ward prided himself on his appearance. His tanned face, framed by silver hair, made him look distinguished, in his own not-so-humble opinion. Fitting, he felt, for one of the top genetic engineers in the country, if not the world. His six-foot frame didn't show the wear of time to be expected in a man of fifty-eight years. An hour every day working out with Nautilus equipment in the basement of his house helped ensure that.

As Ward turned toward the building he froze at the red-streaked glass facing him. His eyes traveled down, coming to a halt on the mangled body lying just inside. His heart rate picked up and a trickle of sweat ran down his back.

The doctor threw his briefcase on the hood of the BMW and opened it, pulling out a Smith and Wesson 9mm automatic pistol. He inexpertly worked the slide, loading a bullet into the chamber and cocking the hammer. Gun held with both hands in front, the doctor made his way to the front door, unaware that the gun's safety was still on.

The fact that the front doors were unlocked barely registered as Ward stepped inside and his eyes flickered over the carnage in the lobby. He couldn't recognize the ravaged body, but he was certain from the tattered remnants of clothing that it wasn't the night guard.

Ward headed directly for the security console and halted in dismay at the smashed computer. He looked over the video screens. No sign of the guard. He knew that the screens covered the entire first floor. That left two places for the guard to be—either outside the building, beyond range of the external cameras, or on the basement level. Who, then, was the dead man up here?

Ward abandoned the security console and went to the first office behind the lobby. He unlocked the door and sat down at the desk inside. Flipping on the power to the computer terminal, he anxiously waited while the machine booted up.

Finally getting a cursor prompt, Ward typed in his override code word, accessing all data in the computer. Fingers flashing over the keys, he opened up the security status folder. The cursor was replaced with a message that confirmed Ward's worst fears:

ALERT/ ALERT/ *CONTAINMENT VIOLATION:*
INNER CONTAINMENT AND OUTER CONTAINMENT BREACHED.
INTERNAL ALARM/ DOOR 17 UNSECURE.
INTERNAL ALARM/ DOOR 18 UNSECURE.
EXTERNAL ALARM/ DOOR 1 UNSECURE.

Ward took a second to compose himself, then went back out to the hallway leading to the elevator. He keyed the elevator doors and stepped in. He punched B and the elevator descended. Just before the doors opened, he pressed up against the back of the elevator, pistol pointing at the doors. He took a deep breath and held it as the doors slid open.

The operating room had been ransacked. Equipment was strewn about the floor and several machines were overturned. After carefully scanning the room, Ward focused his attention on the open doors on the far side. He could see through both sets of containment doors. That confirmed the message on the screen. This was bad. Very bad. According to lab standard operating procedures, the two doors were never to be opened simultaneously.

Ward slowly made his way across the operating room, sliding around the tables and equipment. Broken glass crunched under his feet. When he was close to the outer containment doors, he saw a red slick of blood that had washed out into the short connecting corridor. Ward edged his way through the corridor, carefully avoiding the blood. Pistol first, he entered the containment area.

Two bodies lay just inside, staring sightlessly at the fluorescent lights. He recognized neither man, although their mothers would not have either. Their necks were severed almost halfway through from the front. Both had been eviscerated, and their entrails looped out onto the floor. Limbs had been torn down to the bone. Ward looked up; the doors to both Cube One and Cube Two gaped open. The square cells inside were empty.

Taking a deep breath, Ward made a conscious effort to slow his heart rate. He knew that there was only one thing that could make this situation worse. He crossed to the right side of the room to a large box freezer. The metal doors on top were flung open. He felt his stomach plummet. The two metal brackets inside were empty; the equipment they had held, gone.

Ward rapidly retraced his steps, securing the containment doors behind him. He rode the elevator up, ran down the hallway to his office, and grabbed a portable computer off his desk. He carried it to the security console, disconnected the damaged computer, and hooked up the laptop. Before doing anything else, he glanced out into the parking lot. Just his BMW and the old pickup truck. Luckily no one else had shown up yet. Biotech employed ten people, most of whom didn't arrive until the normal work hour of eight.

Flipping open his wallet, Ward pulled out the card he had been given two years ago and had never used. Grabbing the phone, his fingers rapidly punched in the designated numbers.

The other end was picked up on the third ring. "Site and code, please."

Ward followed the instructions on the laminated card. "Site seven. Code three alpha eight six."

"One moment, please."

Ward licked his lips as he waited. His mind went into overdrive as he tried to figure out a way to salvage his research from this disaster. Then it leapt to a more immediate issue—where were *they*? Nervously he glanced out into the parking lot again. For all he knew *they* were watching the building at this minute. He pulled the pistol closer on the desktop.

A deep voice came over the phone. "This is Agent Freeman. I'm the station chief here. Who am I talking to?"

Ward remembered Freeman from the man's few inspection visits to the lab. "This is Doctor Ward from site seven. I have a class-one security violation here."

There was a slight pause on the other end. Ward could barely hear the man talking to someone else in the background, then the voice came back on the phone. "Go secure."

Ward punched the red button on the STU III phone. "I'm secure."

He heard a hiss and beep as the other end went secure. Now, even if the phone line was tapped, the conversation would be unintelligible to anyone except himself and the man on the other end.

The agent's voice was calm. "All right. I'm going to ask you some questions so I can do an initial assessment. Please answer as succinctly as you can."

"All right, I'm ready," Ward said. He heard a rustle of paper on the other end.

"What's the status of the Synbats?"

"Gone. Present location unknown."

"How many other cleared people are aware of this incident?"

Ward looked out into the parking lot again. "Just me so far. No one else has shown up for work."

"Good. Is there anyone else, unauthorized that is, who is aware of this incident that you know of?"

"No."

"What's your best estimate of when this happened?"

"Sometime last night. I just discovered them gone a few minutes ago."

"What about the security guard? What does he report?"

Ward glanced about the lobby. "He's missing. I've got three other bodies here."

There was a pause on the other end. "Three bodies? Who killed them? The guard?"

"I think the Synbats did it."

Another pause. "Have you identified the bodies?"

"No. Just three males. One in the lobby and two inside the outer containment doors."

"Were they trying to steal the Synbats?"

Ward rolled his eyes. "How the hell am I supposed to know? If they were, they certainly didn't do a good job of it."

"Unless there were more than three, or the guard was involved."

Ward wasn't interested in this line of thinking right now. "Maybe they tried to steal the Synbats and underestimated what they were up against. I don't know, but the bottom line is that the Synbats have either been taken or have escaped."

Freeman obviously decided to stick with the immediate problem. "All right. Here's what I want you to do. First, secure the inside of the building."

Ward looked down at the computer screen and called up the building security program. All external alarms indicated that the building was secure except for the front door. He rapidly punched in instructions, electronically relocking that door, and was rewarded with a secure status on the external alarm. "I've done that."

"OK. Next, is there anyone on your staff you'll need to help in the search for the Synbats? Try to keep it to a minimum."

Ward considered that quickly. "Yes. I'll need my primary assistant, Doctor Merrit."

"There's one last thing you need to do. Abort the Synbats."

Ward stared at the phone. He'd been afraid that would be the decision. Actually, he knew that it wasn't a decision made by Freeman. It was required. "Can we hold off on that until we get a chance to track them down?"

"They've already killed. If they've been stolen, we need to get them terminated immediately. If they escaped we can't have them wandering around the countryside. According to standard operating procedure, termination is the next step. You agreed to it when you got your security clearance. It's right here in black and white in your project response plan."

Ward knew he needed to stall. Two years of his work couldn't be destroyed like this. "They're probably holed up somewhere right now. Or whoever took them has them secure. They couldn't have gotten far. Once we get the direction finder running, we can track them down in no time."

The voice on the other end didn't bend. "Blow the collars. I'll be there in forty minutes. I've got a chopper en route to my location right now to pick me up. I want you to send everyone else home as they arrive. Tell them there's a federal security inspection shutdown and they'll be called when it's over. Don't go downstairs again. Keep everything the way it was. My people will need to go over it all."

Ward wasn't overly worried about what had happened. He was more concerned with what was going to happen. "How about if I access the direction finder and run an azimuth on them? If I find they're in an area where they aren't likely to run into people, I really believe we should hold off on termination. We've invested more than two years and sixty million dollars in this project."

Ward glanced nervously toward the parking lot again. For all he knew the Synbats could be right out there in the tree line. They might even come back on their own. He didn't want to face that by himself, but he also didn't want to lose the results of his efforts.

Freeman was implacable. "I repeat, Doctor Ward: Get an azimuth on them and terminate now. I've got an alert started at Fort Campbell to get us some help tracking the bodies. Just hope they didn't run into anyone else before now. Hold in place and do as instructed. I'll be there shortly."

There was a click on the other end. Ward stared at the dead phone for a long time. He realized that he hadn't told Freeman about what had been taken from the freezer. Time enough for that when the government man got here. Ward glanced up. The rain had finally stopped and a car was pulling into the lot. He rose and scurried across the foyer. He recognized the driver as the day shift security guard. Ward ran out into the parking lot and waved him over.

The car pulled up next to Ward and the guard rolled down the window. "What's up, Doctor Ward?"

Ward stood between the guard and the building. "The feds have called a security shutdown. They've got people en route now to do one of their unannounced inspections. I'd like you to park over at the entrance to the lot and tell everyone to return home. We might be shut down for a while—today at least. Tell everyone I'll call to let them know when we're open again."

The guard frowned and tried to look around Ward at the building. "Security shutdown? What happened, sir?"

"Nothing happened," Ward snapped. "They're just running one of their damn tests and it's our turn to be checked. You can go home, too, after . . ." Ward glanced at his watch and estimated. ". . . after eight-thirty. Everyone should have come by then."

"Yes, sir." The guard could see the pickup truck. "What about Stan? Are you going to relieve him?"

Ward nodded. "Yes, I'll let him go once the test team from the feds are here." He started to head back and then remembered something. "By the way, let Doctor Merrit in. I'm going to need her to get the paperwork ready for the inspection."

"Yes, sir." The security guard drove off, back to the entrance of the parking lot.

Ward returned to the building and the security console. He accessed the security historical file and read the initial messages with growing concern. Using the cursor key, he scrolled the messages backward. The last message disappeared at the bottom of the screen as the previous ones appeared at the top. He ran through the file until he had a complete listing of everything the computer had logged the previous night. Then he went through once more in chronological order.

Ward shook his head as the import of the messages sorted out. Had the men who'd come into the lab cut the power? Was that why the guard had opened the cubes? Did they come in and open the inner containment from the computer and the outer containment when they went downstairs? But that didn't make any sense. Why not just come in and do everything from the computer themselves? Unless they had cut the power to get to the guard, Ward reasoned somewhat doubtfully. The computer controlled everything in the building, from security to power. When it went down, everything went down.

Ward cleared the screen and opened the termination program. Accessing the program automatically switched on the long-range antenna located on the roof. New words appeared on the screen:

TERMINATION REQUIRES LEVEL FOUR AUTHORIZATION.
ENTER LEVEL FOUR CODE:

Ward typed in his personal password: CASINO GAMBIT.
TARGETS ARE ON AZIMUTH OF 202 DEGREES MAGNETIC.
ENTER TERMINATION CODE WORD:

Ward licked his lips. Two years of painstaking work would be destroyed by typing one word. He slowly tapped in the code word, filling the eight spaces, and poised his finger over the ENTER key. It hung there for half a minute while a fierce internal debate raged in Ward's mind. Finally the doctor shook his head. Instead of the ENTER key, he hit the BACKSPACE key, erasing the code word.

Federal Building, Nashville, Tennessee
6:51 A.M.

Bradford Freeman ducked his head as the Bell Jet Ranger helicopter descended onto the landing pad that crowned the federal building in Nashville. He ran forward and entered the aircraft, settling into the left front seat. Freeman was a big man, almost six and a half feet tall. A former defensive lineman for Vanderbilt, Freeman still carried his weight well, fifteen years after his last tackle on the field. The light reflecting off the puddles on the landing pad highlighted the small beads of perspiration that glistened on the black skin of his face despite the morning's chill. The phone call from site seven had shaken him.

As Freeman buckled his seat belt, the pilot lifted the aircraft. The helicopter was from a local civilian company—one of several that Freeman's office kept on file for contract work and the one that had responded this morning in the shortest amount of time. Freeman was using the helicopter as the quickest means to go the sixty miles to site seven. Once there, he would have to go secure and use the military for any further transportation.

"Where we heading, sir?"

"Head north for Land Between the Lakes. I'll direct you once we get closer."

Freeman switched attention to his briefcase, opening it and pulling out the contingency plan for site seven. Freeman was the only man in the regional office who really knew what went on at the site. His position as head of the Nashville Regional Defense Intelligence Agency (DIA) section meant that he had to be a jack-of-all-trades. Not only was he the man responsible for emergency responses to any security problems at military installations in a four-state area surrounding Tennessee, but he had also been burdened with the immediate security response for thirteen classified federal research facilities in those four states.

The DIA was tied heavily into the security and operation of all of the Pentagon's Black Budget research projects. Since the DIA's inception in 1961, it had been involved in much of the shadowy work that appeared to be a requisite for maintaining national security. There were numerous DIA-supported research projects being conducted at the behest of the Pentagon, some more sensitive than others.

Freeman knew that the DIA had earned a bad reputation over the years when word about some of those classified projects had leaked. The use of LSD on human subjects to test its effectiveness as an interrogation device was one of the more glaring examples. From what Freeman was presently reading in the file, this could be another potentially embarrassing episode. There were two critical aspects to Freeman's job—prevention and then reaction. This was the first time he was in the reaction mode.

Fifteen years ago, there wouldn't have been a contingency plan for either mode. In a weird twist, it had been a Russian disaster that had spurred the development of this arm of the DIA. In 1979 an outbreak of anthrax in the Soviet Union was widely suspected in the intelligence community to have come from a breach in containment at the Sverdlovsk biological weapons facility. The specter of any such occurrence in the United States had driven the requirement for both tighter containment plans at all research facilities, regardless of the type of research, and the writing of DIA response plans to limit collateral damage for every facility funded by the Black Budget. An overall national DIA damage-control response force had also been formed and was headquartered in D.C.

Despite the plan, Freeman didn't like the present situation at all. His area of expertise was counterespionage. Who were the men who had entered the installation and how had they found out about the Synbat project? His predecessor had prepared the required contingency plan for reaction to a compromise at site seven, and Freeman had made the required quarterly inspection visits there, but reacting was uncharted territory, especially since Doctor Ward sounded as though he wasn't really sure what had happened.

From what Freeman had seen when he'd visited site seven, the escape of the Synbats could turn into a major disaster. Fortunately, with termination accomplished, it was now simply a case of tracking down the remains and then doing cleanup. The means to accomplish the first were already in motion due to a quick phone call that Freeman had made to the post staff duty officer at nearby Fort Campbell prior to departure. The means to the second had required a phone call to Washington.

CHAPTER 2

Biotech Engineering
7:10 A.M.

Ward was waiting at the front door when Robin Merrit's car rolled into the parking lot. The Volkswagen Beetle pulled into its slot next to his BMW and the engine died with a clatter and a few coughs.

Merrit was a small, young, mousy-looking woman with straight dark hair cut short. Ward had never seen her wear makeup, nor did it appear that she had any fashion sense. Her present outfit of loose-fitting jeans and a flannel shirt was typical of what she wore to work every day.

Although she was not worldly, Merrit was one of the most brilliant bioengineers that Ward had ever worked with—probably *the* most brilliant—which was one of the reasons that he had pressured the DIA watchdogs to grant her a security clearance and bring her into the program. Although Ward would never admit it publicly, Merrit had provided many of the keys to the breakthroughs that had enabled the Biotech Engineering project to make the jump from the theories in Ward's mind to the reality of the present generation of Synbats.

Ward knew that there were two reasons why Merrit was working for the government; they were the same two reasons he had. First, the Pentagon was one of the few institutions left that had the funds to do this type of research. Federal funding for research at universities and private institutions had all but dried up as the deficit noose tightened. Second, and even more important for Ward, working for the Pentagon released them from the stringent federal guidelines that severely

29

limited private research. It was ironic that federal research guidelines, especially for such things as experimentation with animals or dangerous viruses, applied only to non-federally funded, unclassified research. Biotech was one of the few places where the talents of as qualified and brilliant a person as Merrit could be fully used. It was a means to an end.

Ward greeted Merrit at her car, as he had the security guard. She looked at him questioningly as she got out.

"What's going on, Doctor Ward? The guard is at the entrance to the drive sending everyone else home. He said something about a security check by the feds."

"Someone tried to steal the Synbats last night."

Merrit blinked in surprise. "Who?"

"I don't know." He gestured over his shoulder at the blood-stained glass, and Merrit's eyes grew wide. "Whoever they were, they didn't do a very good job. There's two more bodies down in the lab inside the inner containment."

"Didn't the guard stop them?"

Ward rolled his eyes. Merrit had worked on this project as long as he had, but it was obvious that she had never really thought through the implications of what they were creating. "The people breaking in probably killed the guard, Merrit. Or the guard was in on it with them. Not only are the Synbats gone, but they took the backpacks with them."

Ward led her into the building, locking the door behind them. As Merrit caught her first glimpse of the eviscerated body, she gasped and staggered back, grabbing onto the security console for support. Ward led her to a seat on the far side of the console, out of sight of the body, while he sat down in front of the computer.

"But how did they get out?" Merrit asked in a weak voice.

"I don't know yet," Ward replied.

"I should have been called," Merrit mumbled. She looked up. "We have to terminate them immediately."

Ward shook his head. "That's two years of work down the drain."

"We can rebuild. We can't let someone have the Synbats or let them run free, especially with the backpacks."

Ward leaned forward in his chair. "We can't be sure we can rebuild. It took us more than twenty thousand transgenic attempts to get this generation as viable results. Without the Synbats we'd have to start all over again from scratch except for the data we have in the computer. And with the effect that this escape and these deaths are going to have, we probably won't get that chance. With the Synbats still alive we have a slim chance of keeping this project going. Without them, we're sunk. We have to catch them alive."

Merrit was obstinate. "But they killed and they'll do it again unless we terminate them."

She *still* didn't understand, Ward realized angrily. "Damnit, of course they killed! The goddamn Pentagon ought to be happy that their toy worked."

Merrit gazed at Ward with a level, almost dead stare. "We need to terminate immediately."

Ward jumped to his feet and leaned his face into Merrit's. "They're a weapon! Weapons kill! That's all Trollers' Black Budget people care about. We gave them what they wanted! It isn't our fault they escaped. The security setup is the government's responsibility."

Ward took a deep breath and sat back down. He looked Merrit in the eye. "We can still keep this going if we get the Synbats back. We need them to work on the refinements."

Merrit's tone was softer but her message wasn't. "We can find out all we need to know from postmortem work on the bodies and the data we've already collected. Plus we had the aberration with this generation that was unacceptable. We've *got* to terminate."

Ward stuck to his position. "You know as well as I do that the information we need is in the nervous system and the brain. Any postmortem brain material needs to be frozen and preserved within fifteen seconds of death in order to do any sort of valid analysis. And we'd have to have injected the tracers prior to death." He shook his head. "We aren't even fifty percent done with our live work on the four of them."

Ward remained firm in his decision. "Let's get the map from downstairs and see which way they went. We need to retrieve the direction finder and get the azimuth."

Fort Campbell Post Headquarters
7:14 A.M.

The phone call from Agent Freeman of the Nashville Defense Intelligence Agency regional office had been logged in by the Fort Campbell staff duty officer (SDO) at 6:46 A.M. Since that time, the SDO, Major Johnson, had spent twenty-five fruitless minutes trying to track down someone who could act on the message he had been given. This Freeman fellow could not have picked a worse time to call, Johnson fumed. At the present moment, almost every soldier on Fort Campbell was out doing morning physical fitness training.

Fort Campbell was home to almost twenty-three thousand soldiers, including the 101st Airborne (Air Assault) Division, the 5th Special Forces Group (Airborne), and the Headquarters for the 160th Special Operations Aviation Regiment. Straddling the Tennessee-Kentucky border, the sprawling 105,000-acre military reservation was fifty-five miles northwest of Nashville. The main post was on the eastern end of the reservation; the western end of the Fort Campbell training area came within nine miles of site seven. Because of the fort's location, it had been designated by the DIA to supply the emergency response force for any incidents involving site seven along with several other sites in Tennessee and Kentucky. At the present moment, it wasn't doing a very good job of fulfilling that mission.

Major Johnson knew nothing about the alert code words that Freeman had relayed to him. Johnson was a field artillery officer who pulled SDO every few months on a rotating roster. His SDO instruction book directed him to contact someone at the post's Directorate of Plans and Training Management (DPTM) in response to such a call from the DIA. Unfortunately, no one was answering the phone. Johnson knew that the military members of DPTM were out doing physical training and probably wouldn't be in until about nine. The civilian workers were still making their way onto post for their 8 A.M. work call.

Johnson kept ringing the DPTM number every three minutes, hoping that sooner or later—hopefully sooner—someone would answer. Until then there was nothing else he could do. He had already rung up the on-call person listed in his instruction book, only to be told by a grumpy wife that her husband had left home for physical training a half hour ago.

Johnson looked at the message he had written in his duty log: *Site Seven. Priority One Alert. Reference DIA Contingency Plan One Seven.* Johnson was smart enough to realize that anything labeled "Priority One Alert" had to be serious, which was why he swore every time he called DPTM and didn't get an answer. Finally, at 0716, the line was lifted on the other end.

Biotech Engineering
7:18 A.M.

Ward checked the azimuth on the portable computer screen one last time, then drew a pencil line across the topographic map. The mark went west from the lab site toward Lake Barkley and the Land Between the Lakes recreation area on the far side of the lake.

"They're along this line, which means that they weren't taken or else they certainly would be farther away. They must have killed all the men who were trying to take them."

Ward pointed at the map. "They're in an uninhabited area. There's nothing between here and the lake. They aren't in a position to hurt anyone. I was right not to terminate them."

He looked up at Merrit. She looked more pale than usual. The sight of the two dead men, seen when they had gone downstairs to pick up the transponder, had stunned her into sickness. She responded quietly to Ward's reasoning. "As long as they stay where they are, they most likely won't be a problem. But we still must terminate them."

Ward ignored her and focused on the green screen of the computer. The antenna on the roof was picking up the signal emitted by the small radio transceivers built into the collars that the Synbats wore. Since only one azimuth was being displayed, the four Synbats were together. The number had not changed at all, which meant that they were either sitting still or moving in an exact straight line away from the lab. Ward suspected the former. Based on the strength of the signal, the computer estimated that they were within five kilometers of the lab.

Ward was confident that once Freeman got here with some of his people, they would be able to track down the Synbats. Of course, that would be after he got through explaining to Freeman why he hadn't terminated as ordered. Confronting Freeman didn't worry Ward very much. He was more concerned about whoever flew in later today from D.C. representing General Trollers. Then there would probably be some questions asked that Ward didn't particularly want to answer. The only thing he could use in his defense was the argument that security was the DIA's responsibility, not his.

With that thought still foremost in his mind, Ward heard the distant chatter of helicopter blades pulse through the walls of the building. He got up from the desk, gesturing for Merrit to take his place. "Monitor the computer. Let me know if they move."

He made his way to the front door and unlocked it. A small civilian helicopter swung around and slowly descended into the parking lot. A tall black man with a briefcase got out and ran over to Ward's location. The helicopter immediately lifted and flew off to the south.

The site chief stuck out his hand. "Doctor Ward."

The DIA agent returned the handshake. "Agent Freeman. Let's go inside."

As soon as they stepped inside, Freeman walked over to the body and knelt down. He stared at it for a while, then finally stood, going with Ward to the security console. Merrit stood up to meet the two approaching men and Ward made the introductions. "Agent Freeman, this is Doctor Merrit. She's my primary assistant here at Biotech."

Freeman briefly shook her hand and then looked at Ward. "Give me an update on what you have."

Ward gestured at the desktop. "We've got their azimuth. I've hooked up the portable computer to the cable from the roof antenna." He pointed at the topographical map. "They're somewhere along this line, between here and the lake and not moving. Less than five kilometers away."

Freeman nodded, a slight look of relief softening his face. "So they're still in the vicinity. Good. All we have to do now is go in and scoop up the bodies."

Ward briefly glanced at Merrit, then returned his attention to the DIA agent. "I've got tranquilizer guns down in the lab that we've used to—"

Freeman cut him off. "What do you mean, tranquilizer guns? They're supposed to be dead."

Ward faced the larger man. "I didn't terminate them. They're too valuable to waste." He held up a hand to forestall Freeman's reaction. "They're one of a kind. I'm not sure we could ever produce such creatures again. We need data we can only get from them alive." He stabbed a finger at the map. "They're in an uninhabited area. We go out and tranquilize them and bring them back."

"I told you to terminate." Freeman pulled a folder marked top secret out of his briefcase and slapped it on the desktop. "This is what you agreed to with my predecessor when you set up this place. It was one of the security stipulations behind this project. It's not a decision you and I can make. It's a requirement." Another thought struck Freeman as he remembered something from the file he'd read on the flight here. "What about the backpacks?"

Ward sighed. "They're gone. The backpacks need to be kept below freezing to remain static. As soon as they get above freezing they will begin to initiate. Outside the controlled environment of the lab, I doubt that will happen successfully. Which makes it even more imperative that we get the Synbats back alive."

Freeman was working himself into real anger. "You didn't tell me that the backpacks were gone too! That should have been in your phone call. That makes it all the more important you terminate." Freeman took a step closer to Ward. "Terminate them now."

Ward stood his ground. "No."

"I'll do it." The two men swung around in surprise. Merrit sat in front of the portable computer.

"You can't!" cried Ward, reaching toward her.

Freeman reached out one massive hand and grabbed Ward's arm in a vicelike grip. "Leave her alone."

Merrit looked at Ward, her face set. "After seeing those bodies, we can't allow them to run around out there. We don't know what they're capable of. We can't take the chance."

Ward and Freeman looked over Merrit's shoulder as she entered her level four authorization and the screen glowed with the final termination prompt.

TERMINATION REQUIRES LEVEL FOUR
AUTHORIZATION.
ENTER LEVEL FOUR CODE:

Merrit's fingers flashed across the keyboard: PARLOR CRISIS. The screen cleared and then new words formed:

TARGETS ARE ON AZIMUTH OF
202 DEGREES MAGNETIC.
ENTER TERMINATION CODE WORD:

Merrit looked up briefly and then tapped in eight letters, replacing the empty spaces one by one: CAULDRON.

*   *   *

Her right index finger slid over the keyboard and hovered above the ENTER key. Merrit never even looked up at Doctor Ward as she hit the key. The electronic message was beamed from the antenna on the roof to the radio transceiver in the collars. The transceiver tripped a fuse that ignited the explosive charge built into the radio collars. The azimuth on the screen disappeared as the homing devices were destroyed along with the collars.

Freeman released Ward. The Biotech chief slumped wearily down into a chair. It was all over now. Nothing left to do but collect the pieces.

Freeman headed out to the front door. "Let's get the lobby cleaned up before we start receiving visitors."

Fort Campbell
7:34 A.M.

Once the alert reached the full colonel in charge of DPTM, the reaction process speeded up. The colonel, still wearing his sweat-soaked PT uniform, opened up his office safe and pulled out the classified DIA contingency files. He leafed through until he found plan 17.

There wasn't much information—just a few basic instructions. The plan called for a small armed reaction force to be airlifted to a grid coordinate just to the west of the Fort Campbell Military Reservation. The colonel frowned at the requirement for all personnel involved to have security clearances. That ruled out sending a squad or platoon of infantry from the 101st.

The colonel picked up his phone and dialed five numbers.

The commander of the 5th Special Forces Group answered the phone on the first ring. "Colonel Hossey," the stocky officer growled into the phone.

Since breaking his left arm on a parachute operation a month ago, Hossey had been using the PT hour to finish some of his daily paperwork. That freed up time later in the day for physical therapy at the hospital, but it didn't do much to improve his normally gruff temperament.

"Karl, this is Mike Lewis over at DPTM. I've got a priority alert from the Defense Intelligence Agency in Nashville and I need to borrow some of your soldiers."

Hossey frowned. "What for?"

"We're not cleared to know that. All I've got is the alert and a contingency plan tasking for a squad-sized element—all of whom must have at least secret level clearances—to get on helicopters as soon as possible and be airlifted to a set of coordinates. I'm also not cleared to give you the location. We're behind the power curve timewise reacting to this because of screwups on my end, so I'd appreciate it if you could put this together as soon as possible. I've already alerted a couple of choppers and they'll be at PZ twelve by 0800."

Bullshit, was Hossey's unspoken reaction. In his book DIA meant dumb insolent assholes because of previous encounters over a twenty-four-year career. Bullshit, but he knew that there was nothing he could do about it. His men had been used on more than one classified reaction mission since he'd been in command, and one of the banes of commanding a Special Forces unit was that even the commander sometimes didn't know what his own men were doing. And Hossey had firsthand knowledge of what could happen when a commander didn't keep personal track of his men. He had learned that harsh lesson in his previous command of the Special Forces Detachment in Korea; memory of that fiasco made his blood pressure rise every time he got a message like the one that had just been relayed.

"All right. I'll get you a team." Hossey looked at the clock and calculated. "I'll have them armed and at PZ twelve in twenty minutes. Anything special they need to know?"

"Not as far as I know. The plan says just that they need to be armed with live ammo."

"All right. Out here."

Hossey slammed down the phone and thought for a second. He picked up his phone again and dialed the headquarters of his 3d Battalion.

CHAPTER 3

Fort Campbell Operations Shop, 3d Battalion,
5th Special Forces Group (Airborne)
7:35 A.M.

"Shit," the burly soldier muttered, stretching out his left leg straight from the seat. In spite of the pain, he worked the knee—bending and straightening it—for twenty more seconds as beads of sweat dotted his forehead. The doctor had told him not to move the knee for another two weeks, but he was damned if he'd sit here on his rear any longer than he had to.

The buzz of the secure STU III phone interrupted the regime. A large gnarled hand shot out and curled around the receiver. "3302. Sergeant Major Powers. This line is unsecure, sir."

"Powers, this is Colonel Hossey. Go secure." There was a pause as Powers pushed the button on his phone, then the colonel's voice continued. "Dan, I want a team at PZ twelve in nineteen minutes. They need to be armed and ready for a deployment. Have them draw a basic load of live ammunition from the arms room. Got that?"

"Yes, sir."

"There'll be two choppers landing at that time to take the team to an LZ where they will be opcon to someone from the DIA. That's all I have, so don't bother asking any questions."

Powers smiled briefly. He liked Colonel Hossey; he was old school army, not one of this new breed of ass-kissing political officers whom he seemed to be encountering with more frequency. "Yes, sir. One team, armed, basic load, PZ twelve, eighteen minutes, opcon to DIA at the LZ."

"Good," Hossey's voice rumbled. "And Dan . . ."

"Yes, sir?"

"I want you to send good people and I don't want to lose track of whoever you pick. You understand what I mean?"

"Yes, sir. I stay in contact with all my teams. It's SOP."

"Good. Out here."

Powers put down the phone. He looked out the window next to his desk onto the large field that stretched behind the headquarters and separated the buildings housing the team rooms for 2d and 3d battalions. Despite the wet ground and moisture in the air, Powers could see several teams out there doing exercises in clumps of eight to twelve men each.

Powers scanned the groups until his eyes came to rest on one where the men were lined up in two rows of five, paired off facing each other. The men were wearing fatigues; their rucksacks lay on the ground nearby. One of the soldiers stepped forward toward his partner and, with movements too quick to follow, swept his opponent off his feet, slamming him into the ground. Powers smiled for the second time this morning. He knew who had done that move and he knew he now had the perfect choice for this tasking—a choice that Colonel Hossey would definitely approve.

Powers focused in on the man, who was now kneeling on the other soldier's chest. He was talking to the soldiers gathered around, making a point. Powers didn't have to be any closer to recognize that figure. Back when Powers had been a master sergeant on a 7th Special Forces Group A Team at Fort Bragg, that man, Dave Riley, had been his team leader for two years. Not only had the two served together, but Riley had also been his best friend. During a mission to Colombia against the drug cartel, Riley had saved Powers's life. Powers wasn't an overly emotional man, but he had a special place in his heart for the wiry, half Irish, half Puerto Rican warrant officer.

Powers yelled for the battalion staff duty NCO and gave some quick instructions. Then the sergeant major jerked to his feet and limped for the door, ignoring the crutches that the doctor had ordered him to use. He slammed open the heavy metal door to the rear of the building and stood on the loading platform.

His knee on Doc Seay's skinny chest, CWO2 Dave Riley finished his open-hand strike a fraction of an inch above the medic's neck. Riley glanced around at his team. "Always finish the man off while you have the chance. There's no such thing as a fair fight. Your goal is . . ." He paused as he recognized the voice that rumbled across the parade field, calling out his name.

Riley popped to his feet. "Doc, take over. Practice leg sweeps."

The warrant officer turned and jogged toward battalion headquarters, where he could see the sergeant major leaning against the back wall, favoring his bad leg. Riley shook his head. Dumb son of a bitch wasn't using his crutches like he was supposed to. Riley loved the old NCO like a brother, but the guy sure could be pigheaded at times.

Riley had once heard the 5th Special Forces Group surgeon hold forth on theories regarding Special Forces soldiers and their various injuries. The man had compared being in Special Forces to playing professional football with regard to frequency and severity of injuries, particularly to joints. Knees were usually the first victims of an intense lifestyle that included such activities as parachuting, rucksacking with hundred-pound packs, hand-to-hand combat, and physical training seven times a week when not deployed, not to mention the potential of getting wounded or killed on a mission.

As Riley drew near his former team sergeant, he reflected on the fact that a professional athlete was considered ancient if he or she was over thirty. Yet here was Powers, forty-seven years old, and coming off his third major knee operation, still trying to get back in shape so he could return to the real world of operational missions rather than filling time working in the battalion operations shop. It certainly wasn't because Powers was making four million dollars a year like Joe Montana. It was because Powers was like the majority of Special Forces men— a dedicated professional who believed in what he was doing.

As he lightly sprinted up the metal steps to the platform, Riley felt a twinge from the puckered scars on his lower right abdomen and upper right back: entry and exit holes from two AK-47 rounds. They were reminders of a classified mission years ago on the other side of the world—his own physical sacrifice.

He came to a halt in front of the sergeant major, who towered over him. "What's up, Dan?"

Powers didn't waste any time. "You've got sixteen minutes to have your team ready to board two inbound birds here at the PZ. Rucksacks ready for deployment, personal weapons, and basic load. I already got the SDNCO tracking down the armorer, so the arms room will be open in a couple of minutes. The birds will fly you to an LZ where you'll be opconned to some DIA weinie. I got that straight from the group commander on the secure line two minutes ago." •

"Anything else I need to know?"

Powers leaned forward. "Just remember our SOP about staying in touch." He reached out a hand and shook Riley's. "I'll take care of this end. Good luck, compadre."

Biotech Engineering
7:46 A.M.

Ward followed Freeman through the wreckage of the basement lab. The DIA man stared at the two bodies, then turned to look hard at Ward. "You didn't want to terminate those things after seeing this?" He didn't give Ward a chance to answer as he continued. "We're going to have a hell of a time keeping this under wraps."

Earlier, they'd taken the body from the lobby, put it in another room, and cleaned up the glass. The stain on the carpet they'd covered up with a rubber mat.

Ward was antsy. He'd already lost his prized creations. He wanted to find out if he'd lost everything. "When are we going after the remains and the backpacks?"

Freeman was examining the cubicles. "We wait until we get reinforcements. I've got a reaction force team coming from Fort Campbell. When they get here we'll go looking. My headquarters in Washington is also sending a team, but it'll take them a little longer to arrive." He pointed to the carnage. "They'll handle this."

Freeman swung the cubicle doors back and forth. The doors could be opened either manually from the outside or electronically by the computer. There was no sign of the doors being forced from the inside. "How did these get opened? And the inner containment doors?"

Ward summarized what he had gleaned from the computer log. "Those were opened by the guard in response to computer prompts when the power went off. We keep the environment inside the cubes controlled—mainly for monitoring purposes—and without power the Synbats would have eventually suffocated. Opening them increased the amount of oxygen, since they had access to all the air inside the inner containment. If the guard hadn't opened them, the Synbats would have been dead within twenty-five minutes." Ward shook his head. "The guard was supposed to call the doctor on duty before he did anything, but I guess he reacted to the computer prompts."

"What about the containment doors?"

"I'm not sure we'll ever be able to piece together exactly what happened with those. The guard's key is still in the outer one, so that was used to open them. I'm not sure how the inner one got open. As I said, that idiot was instructed to call me or Doctor Merrit if something like a power failure occurred, yet he never did."

Freeman looked at Ward pointedly and then at the bodies. "I guess that 'idiot,' as you call him, either was in on what was going on or he never had the time to call. Who was on call last night?"

"Doctor Merrit."

Freeman looked up. "I assume she didn't get a call?"

"She didn't mention anything and I'm sure she would have." Ward was already thinking ahead. "What are we going to tell the army people when they get here?"

"We'll stick with the cover story in the contingency plan."

"That will work until we come upon the bodies. Then what?" Ward asked.

"With the charges in those collars, there won't be much in the way of bodies. As soon as they spot them, we have them back off. These guys are just the most immediate response we can get, and they all have security clearances."

Fort Campbell
7:51 A.M.

The chatter of helicopter blades reverberated off the buildings surrounding pickup zone (PZ) 12. Before the aircraft came into sight, Riley could identify them from the sound as UH-1 Huey transports. As he split the team into lifts, he spotted the two helicopters coming from the east in the thin line of clear sky between the ground and low-lying gray clouds.

Riley pulled off his patrol cap and stuffed it into the cargo pocket of his lightweight camouflage fatigues. As the aircraft settled down on their skids, he moved forward toward the right side cargo door of the lead bird. Throwing his rucksack in ahead of him, he slid over on the gray web seats until he was facing forward on the left side. Four other members of the team clambered in behind. The crew chief slid the doors shut and the Huey lifted.

Riley reached over and tapped the crew chief, signaling for a headset. The young specialist indicated that there were no extra sets on board. Riley pointed at the rig that the crew chief wore. The man shook his head. Riley smiled benignly at the young man, pointed at his own subdued collar rank insignia of two black dots on a green bar, versus the young man's specialist rank, and signaled that he wanted to use the headset only for a minute. The crew chief reluctantly handed over the set.

Riley settled the two ear cups in place and then pushed the ON switch for the boom mike. "This is Chief Riley. I'm in charge of the guys back here. Can you all tell me where we're going?"

The pilot in the right front seat glanced over his shoulder. "I'm Captain Barret. I've got a grid out near Lake Barkley. There's supposed to be a building there and we're to land in the parking lot. I've been told there'll be an officer named Freeman who we're to take orders from. That's all we've got. Do you know what this is about?"

"No, sir. What you just said is about ten times more than I know. We were just told to get on board."

The pilot returned his attention to the front. "Then just relax and enjoy the ride. I've got an ETA of fourteen minutes."

Riley handed the headset back to the crew chief. For the first time since he had been briefed by Powers outside the headquarters, he had a chance to really think about the present situation. This whole thing was unusual. Riley knew that his team had been picked simply by virtue of its being in the right place at the right time in the right uniform. Riley didn't mind that too much. He was tired of sitting around in the team room. He liked action.

His thoughts flickered to the most recent real action he'd been in and the woman who'd been with him. When he'd returned with Kate Westland from Colombia after the mission against the drug cartel, Riley had thought that he was ready to settle down—at least for a while. Kate and he had entertained serious thoughts of marriage, but then the realities of their professional lives had kicked in. The CIA—grudgingly acknowledging Kate's crucial role in the successful completion of the mission, but seething over her disrespect for authority—had banished her from Langley to a field office in Atlanta, where she did little more than process paperwork. The army high command had shuffled Riley out of Fort Bragg as quickly as they could print the orders and had sent him to Fort Campbell.

Kate and Riley had kept a long-distance relationship going for a while, but Riley found himself absorbed by the demands of commanding his team. In addition, Kate had been getting very moody over the downward spiral of her career. The talk of marriage had disappeared from their conversation more than six months ago, and it had been two months since Riley had last driven across Tennessee down to Atlanta to see her. Kate had shown little interest in making the reverse drive. He'd talked to her on the phone two weeks ago and had been vaguely bothered by the lack of spark and her pervasive depression. Riley was concerned about Kate and her unhappiness. He was bitter at the CIA for treating her so poorly after she'd put her life on the line to save both him and Powers.

As the blades cut through the air above his head, Riley resolved that the first chance he had he would go down to Atlanta and see her. Their future as lovers might be over, but he knew that she needed a friend and he had not been a very good one lately. He hoped he wouldn't be deployed too long on this mission, whatever it was; he wanted to be there to support her while she sorted out her life.

He also was somewhat concerned about his team. Riley had been in charge of Operational Detachment Alpha (ODA) 682 for only four months. The team was currently two personnel short of its authorized strength level of twelve. They lacked a commissioned officer as team leader, which explained why Riley—a warrant officer who would normally be the team's executive officer—was in charge. They also lacked a junior commo man. The personnel shortage in itself was no major problem; almost every team that Riley had been on had been short personnel. The thing that truly bothered him was the personalities of some of the team members, particularly the team sergeant.

Riley glanced across the cargo bay at the overweight figure of MSgt. Joe Knutz. The man was what Riley would define as R.O.A.D.: retired on active duty. Knutz had twenty-four years in the army, and in Riley's opinion he just didn't give a shit anymore. He was marking time, earning a larger pension percentage with each year he hung around. Once upon a time Knutz might have been a good soldier, but since his attitude had gone down the tubes, the rest of his abilities had followed suit, making the team sergeant more of a burden than an asset. Over the past month, Riley had been consulting with the B Company sergeant major, trying to work out a way to ease Knutz off the team into a relatively harmless slot. Riley was tired of doing the work of team leader *and* team sergeant.

The ranking enlisted man on the other helicopter would be the man whom Riley would pick to be team sergeant if he had his say. Doc Seay was the opposite of Knutz. A senior sergeant first class, Seay had recently turned down an offer to be team sergeant on another team. Seay enjoyed being the senior medical sergeant, and he was the most knowledgeable medic with whom Riley had ever worked. Seay was also an extremely competent NCO. If the shit ever hit the fan, Riley wanted the doc to be his right-hand man.

The presence of two cans of 5.56mm ammunition and one can of 9mm that senior weapons man Mike Trovinsky had carried on the aircraft made Riley wonder if this mission could possibly be one where the training ended and the action became real. It had been awhile since he'd gone anywhere with real bullets. Of course, this also could be a test alert run by Group or by the Special Operations Command (SOCOM) to test their readiness to deploy. Riley had been on many of those too.

Having done as much figuring as he felt was appropriate given the lack of information, Riley leaned against the seat back and watched the low, rolling terrain of the Fort Campbell Military Reservation slide by beneath them. The rain had stopped, but the clouds still hung low, threatening to deposit more moisture. The temperature was in the high fifties, normal for April in Tennessee.

The helicopter was flying at a hundred feet above ground level (AGL). Despite the lack of leaves, Riley could barely see the earth through the deciduous trees and tangled undergrowth. The pilots were following a paved road to their destination. The aircraft did a hard bank to the right and Riley could see mist-covered Lake Barkley through the left window. Pushing up against the door, he could make out an isolated low-lying building and a parking lot with three vehicles in it. The helicopter came to a hover over the lot and began to descend.

Biotech Engineering
8:11 A.M.

Freeman glanced at his watch. A little more than an hour since he had first called Fort Campbell for the reaction force. He wasn't sure if that was a good time for them or not. It really didn't matter now, since it was just a matter of going out and policing up the bodies and backpacks. He turned off the computer terminal where he'd been looking at the scant data from the night before.

The two helicopters landed and the side doors slid open. Soldiers got off, carrying rucksacks, and quickly ran toward his side of the lot. The whine of the helicopters declined as the pilots rolled off their throttles. A short Latino soldier in camouflage fatigues threw his rucksack down with the others and then came over to Freeman.

"I'm Chief Warrant Officer Riley, sir, team leader for ODA 682, 5th Special Forces Group."

Freeman stuck out his hand. "Major Freeman, Defense Intelligence Agency. I'm in charge of . . ." He paused as another soldier came up. The newcomer was an overweight man, almost as big as Freeman, with a balding head.

Riley did the introductions. "This is Master Sergeant Knutz. He's the operations NCO for the team."

Freeman shook the team sergeant's hand and then gestured for both men to follow him. "Let's go inside and I'll fill you in on what's going on. Your men can wait out here."

Riley and Knutz followed Freeman into the lobby. Riley had already noticed the sign on the front of the building that read Biotech Engineering. That, plus the man from the Defense Intelligence Agency, made for an interesting combination. Riley could see two other people waiting inside: A tall, distinguished-looking man in a white lab coat and a frumpy dark-haired woman seated at a large desk.

Riley had spotted the remote cameras on the roof of the building as they landed, so he assumed that the television screens here were the terminus for the cameras. That pointed to a pretty extensive security setup for a place in the middle of the woods. The only thing Riley could figure from this sketchy visual data was that some sort of security leak had occurred.

Freeman introduced the two groups to each other. "This is Doctor Ward, who is in charge of this lab, and his assistant, Doctor Merrit. This is Mister Riley and Sergeant Knutz. They're from the 5th Special Forces Group over at Fort Campbell and are here to help us with our little problem."

After all parties shook hands, the two Special Forces men pulled over some plastic chairs. Riley unbuckled his load bearing equipment (LBE) and laid his M16A2 across his knees. His first impression of the two doctors was that they were very upset by something, especially the woman, but trying hard not to show it. He pulled a small note-book from his pocket and prepared to take notes.

Freeman shook his head. "No notes. Everything that you do, hear, and see here is classified top secret. It shouldn't take us long to take care of things. You all should be back at Fort Campbell by dinner."

Riley shrugged and put the notebook away. He'd go along with them. He'd played the secret game longer, and in more real situations, than this DIA major had.

Freeman turned to Ward. "Doctor, perhaps you could give these men a quick rundown on what this lab does, without getting into anything too classified. Enough so they understand the background."

Ward turned and faced the two men. "Biotech Engineering conducts research into mutating various viruses in an attempt to find cures for the effects of the original viruses. We work mostly for the National Institutes of Health, doing some of their more sensitive projects. Right now, we're working on various forms of the known biological weapon viruses, hoping to find a mutated form that might act against the pure form as an antidote. We conduct live experiments on monkeys to stimulate the growth of the mutated viruses in a host organism and examine the results against the original virus."

Freeman cut in. "That's the reason you gentlemen are here. Four of the lab's monkeys escaped last night. These four were infected with a mutated form of the biological agent VX."

Riley frowned. VX was a biological agent that was in the Soviet inventory. What the man was saying was serious, but why was he using the past tense? The female doctor, Merrit, was curiously quiet and looked uncomfortable. Before Riley had a chance to ask a question, Knutz jumped in, anxious, Riley supposed, to show that he was still work-ing for a living.

"How did they escape?"

Riley noticed a glance between Ward and his assistant as Freeman answered. "How they escaped isn't important. What is important is that we find their bodies as quickly as possible."

Knutz cut in again. "What do you mean 'bodies'?"

Freeman gestured at the portable computer. "The animals were wearing collars that contained both a homing beacon and an explosive charge. When we determined that they really had escaped, we electronically triggered the charges in the collars. The charge was more than suffi-cient to kill the animal. Prior to firing we got a direction fix on them."

These people were certainly serious about not letting those animals run free, thought Riley. Freeman slid a map over to the edge of the table. Riley and Knutz got up to look at it.

Freeman pointed at the penciled-in line. "The bodies must be somewhere along this line, which is the last azimuth we had prior to detonation. The range is less than five kilometers. What we need you and your men to do is move along this line and find the bodies for us."

Riley frowned. "Why'd you kill the monkeys? Why not just capture them?"

Freeman fielded that question. "We couldn't take the chance of their running into people. Even though the possibility was low, we didn't want to expose anyone to this new, mutated virus. We felt we had to kill them in order to stop them."

Riley noticed that the male doctor didn't seem too thrilled about having terminated the monkeys. He traced his finger along the line on the map, noting where it ended at the lake. "All right. It shouldn't take us long to move three klicks along an azimuth from here. Mind if we use this map?"

Freeman gave it over. "It's all yours."

Ward held up a hand. "There's something else. When one of your men spots the bodies, he must be sure to immediately back off and call us in to take care of the remains. The virus might still be active in the corpses and we don't want to take any chances. Your men are not to get any closer to the bodies than they need to for identification purposes."

Riley shrugged. He doubted that any of his men would want to get close after they heard what the monkeys had been infected with. "Sure. I'll brief them on that."

"How contagious is this virus?" Knutz asked.

Freeman answered. "As you know, in the weapon form, the VX is sprayed or deployed by airburst. Here they injected it directly into the monkeys' blood, so as long as you don't make contact with the blood, you'll be all right. Just do what Doctor Ward said."

The female doctor spoke for the first time. "Are you at least going to tell them about the backpacks?"

Ward turned toward her angrily. Riley noticed that the senior doctor restrained himself with great difficulty.

"What's she talking about?" Riley asked.

Ward turned from glaring at Merrit and spat out the words. "The monkeys took two pieces of equipment with them."

"What's in these backpacks?" Riley demanded.

Freeman cut in. "That's classified. Your men are also not to touch the backpacks if you see them. They should be with the bodies."

"Well, what do these backpacks look like?" Riley asked.

"About the size of a large ALICE rucksack," Freeman answered. "But instead of nylon, the whole thing is plastic and painted gray-green. The bottom line is that you find the bodies and back off immediately. Call us in and we'll do the recovery. Doctor Ward and I will be moving along with the center of your search line. Doctor Merrit will remain here."

Riley had had enough of the "I've got a secret" game. "All right, sir. Is there anything else we need to know?"

Freeman looked at Ward, who shook his head; then he turned back to Riley. "No. That's it. Tell the helicopter pilots to stay here until we're done. This shouldn't take too long. We need to get body bags from the lab downstairs and some other equipment, and we'll join you in the parking lot in a few minutes."

Riley headed outside, closely followed by Knutz. The team had dumped their rucks near the wall of the building. Trovinsky had broken open one of the cans of 5.56mm and the 9mm and was passing out the ammunition. Each team member was loading magazines.

Riley got their attention. "All right, guys. We won't be needing the ammo. Go ahead and put what you've got in your ammo pouches, but I don't want anything live in your weapons. I don't want to see any magazines in."

Riley spread out the map that Freeman had given him. "Here's the deal. They had—"

"I'll brief the team, chief."

Riley looked up in surprise at Knutz's interruption, but stepped back, handing over the map. It was the team sergeant's prerogative as operations NCO to brief the team, something he should have been doing long ago. Riley was glad that Knutz finally appeared to be taking his job seriously, but to be honest, he was also a little miffed. He was used to doing things his way.

Knutz used a pen to point at the map. "They had four monkeys escape from this lab last night. The monkeys had collars on that had a radio-detonated explosive device built in. The people working here fired the devices, so now there are four dead monkeys out there. Before they blew the devices, the direction finder on the collars gave an azimuth, which you see marked on the map. We're going to move along that azimuth in a search line and find the bodies.

"Once you spot anything that resembles a monkey's body, you're to back off and call in the doctor who will be traveling along with us. There's also something they call backpacks that the monkeys took with them—the size of a large ruck and gray-green in color. If you see these you're to back off and call in the doctor.

"We'll move with fifteen meters between each man. That gives us a hundred and fifty meters of frontage. Since the signal was good for only five k's, it shouldn't take us too long to find the bodies." Knutz looked over the team. "Any questions?"

He sure was direct and to the point, Riley thought, but uninspired. Knutz would never be a leader. Riley decided that he'd better elaborate a bit. People worked better when they knew the why behind the what. "I'd like to highlight the reason we're not supposed to go near the bodies. According to the doctors here, these monkeys had some sort of variation of the VX biological agent injected into them. They don't want you to mess around with the bodies, and I'm sure you don't either. They say the only thing that is contagious is the monkeys' blood, but make sure you be careful. Let's let the doctor earn his pay."

Riley could see the men giving sidelong glances at each other. Doc Seay raised a hand. "Hey, chief. What's in these backpacks?"

Riley shook his head. "They wouldn't say. Let's assume the worst and figure that it might be some sort of container for viruses or other types of biological agents. So let's not mess around with this stuff. You see something that nature didn't put in the woods, you yell out and we'll let these people deal with it. We're just the spotters on this operation. We'll let them pick up their own garbage." Riley looked around the gathered men. "Everyone got that?"

Eight bobbing heads indicated assent.

"We'll leave rucks here with the helicopters." Riley glanced over at the two silenced aircraft. He turned to the team's intelligence sergeant. "Bob, I want you to tell the pilots to cool their heels. The man in charge said they're to wait until we get done. Hopefully we'll be back at Fort Campbell today."

Sergeant First Class Bob Philips, a lanky New Englander with a massive hook nose that was often the butt of jokes, strode over to the two aircraft where the crews were still sitting inside.

Riley pointed at the open cans of ammunition. "T-bone, I want you to close those up and put them on one of the aircraft. We'll account for all the rounds after we get done."

Sergeant "T-bone" Troy, the junior weapons man, clamped shut the lids. Troy had picked up the nickname T-bone during a survival training exercise when he'd spent the last five days gnawing on the bones of a squirrel he'd caught on the first day. Since his real first name was Bob, same as Philips, the distinction had caught on. Riley's philosophy for the team was that nothing on ODA 682 was sacred, so he'd ignored Troy's protests about the nickname. The man was going to have to learn to live with it. Troy was a solidly built, six-foot, blue-eyed, blond-haired Viking. He spent most of his off-duty time working out and lifting weights. Unfortunately, in Riley's opinion, the man had the personality of a rock, to match his muscles. T-bone's lacking a sense of humor made the other members of the team pick on him that much more.

Riley's musings on T-bone Troy were interrupted by Ward and Freeman coming out the front door of the building. Ward was carrying a day pack with something stuffed into it. Freeman, wearing a suit and dress shoes, didn't look ready to go traipsing through the woods, but Riley figured that was the man's own problem. Ward had changed into slacks and a short-sleeved shirt under a windbreaker, along with a pair of sneakers. Slightly better to go beating the bush, but not by much in Riley's estimation.

The men of 682 were wearing the same uniforms they'd had on for their PT ruck march this morning prior to the close-quarters combat training: lightweight battle dress camouflage fatigues, jungle boots, load bearing equipment, and patrol caps. The only addition was the M16s. On their LBE each man sported two canteens, two ammunition pouches, a butt pack containing survival equipment, a first-aid pouch holding two dressings on the nonfiring shoulder, and at least one knife. A shoulder holster was strapped on beneath the LBE, holding each man's 9mm Beretta semiautomatic pistol.

Riley pulled his Silva compass out of its case on the LBE. He laid the Silva down on the map, then rotated the fixed arrow in the compass base to line up with the penciled-in azimuth. By keeping the north arrow aligned with the outer ring, all he now had to do was follow the arrow to stay on the desired azimuth.

At the present moment the arrow pointed straight from the lab toward Lake Barkley. Since the map sheet was the same as the one they used for Fort Campbell, Riley knew the declination difference between magnetic north and grid north. His compass was preset to compensate for that difference.

Riley looked up and called out to the team. "Azimuth is two-oh-two degrees magnetic." He waited while the rest of the team set their compasses. "It's three klicks from here to Lake Barkley, so that's our far limit." He designated personnel with quick jabs of his finger: "I want you five to my left and you four to my right." He checked with Freeman. "Ready, sir?"

"Let's do it."

Riley swept his free hand overhead and they started. The team moved around the building and then spread out on the indicated azimuth. To Riley's immediate left, Chief Knutz beat his way through the undergrowth; to Riley's right, Doc Seay was the closest man. Ward and Freeman followed several paces behind Riley.

Immediately behind the building the terrain dropped off into a creek bed running southwest. Riley selected a tree on line on the far side of the ravine and used that as his aiming point.

As he went down into the creek bed, he wondered what the remains of the monkeys would look like. An explosive charge in a band around the neck was pretty nasty. Riley could understand the concern, though, about letting any sort of biological hazard get free. Stringent control measures did seem necessary.

Despite that, a few things about the operation didn't fit, in Riley's opinion. Knutz's question about how the four had escaped was a valid one. The lab seemed to have a good security system, and if those Biotech people had gone to the trouble of rigging homing beacons and explosive collars, they must have taken other strong steps to prevent an escape.

Another thing that bothered Riley was the lack of any security personnel at the building. He very much doubted that one of the doctors had been on the guard shift last night when the escape had occurred, yet there had been no sign of a guard. Riley had noticed the old pickup truck in the lot: It had a retired enlisted sticker on it, which authorized the driver to enter the closed Fort Campbell main post. He wondered who that belonged to. Obviously not to Ward, Freeman, or Merrit.

Riley was a suspicious and observant person. Harsh experience had imbued him with those characteristics. His boyhood, growing up on the streets of the South Bronx, had taught him the value of observation. A person who couldn't learn to notice the warnings of various developing situations didn't stay healthy very long on those streets.

Riley had survived the Bronx for seventeen years, threading a delicate path through the demands of a rough environment and avoiding the kind of trouble that would end any hope he'd had for getting out of the cesspool that lapped at him. Earning a high school diploma under those conditions had been a major achievement and had allowed Riley to enlist in the army.

Riley's introduction to Special Forces had reinforced those early lessons. He remembered his first team sergeant in Special Forces: MSgt. Frank Kimble, Okinawa, 1981. Riley was a young E-4, fresh out of the Qualification course, when he ran into Kimble. Kimble had tried hard to pass on to the younger man knowledge earned in three tours in Vietnam and nineteen years in Special Forces.

Kimble had constantly honed Riley's powers of observation. They'd be sitting in a bar on a Saturday night getting drunk, and the veteran would suddenly ask Riley to describe all the people behind him without turning around. After six months of that, Riley had learned to be much more observant—just in time for his first live mission to Thailand, running classified border operations. In the years since, Riley had sharpened his skills, always trying to notice any anomalies in the environment. Right now, his instincts were buzzing from several anomalies he had picked up at the lab.

Riley pushed his way through the thick undergrowth that lined the watercourse. He carefully extracted his arm from a thorny bush and high-stepped through the storm-swollen creek. Behind him, he heard Ward curse as the man became caught in the brambles. Riley stepped out of the water and halted, listening carefully, tuning out the man-made sounds. Looking to his left he spotted Knutz, who gave him a quick nod. To his right, Seay took a few more seconds to appear.

Riley was pleased that his team was moving silently and staying on line. Riley's philosophy was that the members of 682 had to travel like ghosts through the woods. Despite the fact that there was no need to be quiet here, the team was reacting that way because they knew what Riley expected. To him, every moment was training.

Riley dug in his feet and pushed himself up the far side of the ravine. His eyes were constantly scanning back and forth, searching for any signs of the bodies or the backpacks. When he reached the tree he had designated, he pulled out his compass and selected another target along the azimuth. From his pace count, confirmed by a studied look at the map, he estimated that they had progressed six hundred meters from the lab.

He crested the incline and paused a minute. The terrain flattened out slightly. Looking back, he waited as Ward and Freeman clambered up the slope. Knutz and Seay gave Riley a thumbs-up from fifteen meters away on either side, indicating that everyone on their respective sides was on line. Riley waved his arm, signaling for them to move out again.

After another hundred meters they crossed an old dirt road. Riley knelt and looked carefully at the ground. There were no recent tire tracks or any other markings on it. He moved across and pushed into the woods on the far side. The trees were getting thicker and the cloud-filtered midmorning light was barely penetrating. The men moved through a dripping, dimly lit brown and gray cathedral. Vines looped from trees, forcing Riley to duck his head. Prickly bushes grabbed at his fatigue pants. Yet Riley maneuvered his way smoothly through the woods, his years of practice showing.

Riley glanced at his watch as they walked across a small knoll that he could locate easily on his map: 10:02 A.M. The knoll placed the search line approximately one kilometer from the lab.

Looking up through the trees, he could see that the sun was struggling to break through the clouds. Hopefully, that would take away some of the morning chill. On the far side of the knoll, the terrain descended to another creek running from northeast to southwest. According to the map, this watercourse, labeled Williams Hollow Creek, ran into Lake Barkley, a little more than a kilometer and a half away. Checking to his left and right, Riley began the descent. This slope was steeper than the last, and he divided his time between looking for the bodies and searching for secure footholds.

Riley was startled by a yell from behind him. He wheeled, instinctively swinging his empty M16 around, pointing toward the source. He was greeted by the sight of Doctor Ward tumbling down the slope. Riley slammed his rifle, butt first, into the ground along Ward's path and with his other hand he grabbed hold of a tree. As Ward slid by, he reached out and grabbed the rifle, almost pulling Riley's other hand from its grip on the tree.

The doctor cautiously stood up, cursing. He was streaked with mud and leaves. His small day pack continued the trip downhill without him. Riley continued on his way down. Reaching the bottom, he picked up the day pack and waited for Ward. He silently handed it to the doctor and then led the way across the lowland. Knutz and Seay indicated again that the rest of the team was on line. They were two-thirds of the way to Lake Barkley. Riley hoped they would find what they were looking for soon. He also hoped that none of his men had passed by anything, although he imagined that the results of the explosions ought to stand out pretty strongly. Blood, popped-off heads, and torn bodies was the logical guess of what they would find. Despite the thick undergrowth, that sort of gory spectacle ought to be noticed rather easily.

Williams Hollow Creek was swollen from the previous night's rain. Riley didn't give it a thought as he splashed out into the swiftly running water and pushed his way across. Discomfort had been a constant companion during his years in Special Forces. The ability to put up with a minor irritation like being wet and chilly was more mental than physical in his opinion.

Riley had survived, and operated in, environments ranging from a windchill of minus sixty degrees at 14,000 feet of altitude, to sweltering jungles. He had learned to adapt rather than fight nature. During those six months in Okinawa, Frank Kimble had taught Riley that a man could never win a fight against the elements. Nature was unchanging and unforgiving, just as the enemy was. Instead of making the environment the enemy, Riley had learned to make it his ally. He embraced the terrain and weather's hardships because it made his enemies weak.

In martial arts training during a tour in Korea, Riley had worked with a Korean master who had not believed in checking the weather before starting an outdoor workout. The two had practiced in six inches of snow, barefoot and bare chested on top of a mountain in the Korean countryside, using snapped-off branches as kicking targets. Riley had quickly learned to focus on the training and ignore the environment as he worked his way toward his first-dan black belt in tae kwon do. During his Korean tour he added that black belt to the one in Hapkido he had earned years earlier in Okinawa.

Riley's wet pants stuck to his wiry legs as he pushed his way up the far side of the creek. One more stretch of high ground and then they'd be at Lake Barkley.

Behind Riley, Ward was wondering when they'd find the bodies. They'd been scrambling through this forest for more than an hour and a half now. He had no idea how far they had come or how far they had to go before reaching the lake. His legs and arms smarted from the tiny scratches that thorns had inflicted upon him. On top of that he was wet, cold, and hungry.

Ward felt uneasy working with these army people. The Special Forces soldiers were moving so quietly through the woods that it was eerie. The man named Riley, whom Ward was following, had not said a single word since they'd left the lab. Ward was used to people who spoke and made their thoughts known.

Even the DIA man was quiet. He was probably figuring out how he was going to write this up, Ward thought. Ward himself had spent most of the time during the move trying to figure out how he was going to keep the Biotech project alive. The major problem was how the Black Budget people, particularly General Trollers, reacted to this incident. Ward had to admit to himself, as he slapped a branch out of his face, that the security breach looked bad. But Ward also figured that the Synbats' killing of the three men was good, in a perverse sort of way. It demonstrated that his creation could do something that the army should surely appreciate.

Ward bitterly regretted Merrit destroying the Synbats. Genetic engineering was more often a case of trial and error than precise calculations—a case of building on previous efforts. This last generation of Synbats had represented a key step in the direction the project ultimately needed to go. Their loss was a tremendous setback, even without the potential of the program getting shut down.

That fucking bitch Merrit, Ward thought angrily to himself. Who the hell did she think she was going against him like that? Ward was determined that if nothing else happened after this, he would definitely send Merrit packing. The woman had indicated several times before that she wanted out; this time Ward would see to it that she went. But he'd also see to it that she never worked in the bioengineering field again.

Ward was so immersed in his thoughts that he almost walked into Riley's back. The team sergeant was halted at the edge of a drop-off. Riley turned as Ward and Freeman blundered up next to him and spoke the first words in almost two hours. "There's the lake. No sign of your monkeys or the backpacks."

Riley looked down at the tranquil surface of the lake five feet below. "Is it possible they might have been in the water when you blew the collars?"

Ward considered that. "I doubt it. Monkeys don't care to swim. They barely have the capability, and certainly not the inclination. I'm pretty sure they would have stayed on land."

Riley signaled to Knutz and Seay to have everyone bring it in. The two passed on the gesture. Riley looked at the map and then at the terrain. After the team was gathered, he looked around the small circle of faces. "Did anyone see anything unusual? Anything even remotely resembling the monkeys or the backpacks?"

He was met with a negative response. Riley decided to try to make some peace with Knutz. "What do you think, Top?"

Knutz pointed at the two civilians. "They're the experts." He passed the question off to the DIA officer. "What do you want us to do now, sir?"

Freeman rubbed his chin. "I guess we turn around and do a sweep on the way back. We must have missed them. Maybe we were off course."

Riley stabbed a finger at the map. "We're exactly where a two-oh-two degree azimuth from the lab meets the lake, sir. No more than twenty meters off either way. How accurate was this beacon on their collars?"

Ward didn't have the data on that. "I'm not sure. But we've got to find the bodies."

Riley looked back the way they had come. "The choppers wouldn't do us any good. It's too thick down here." He addressed Freeman. "How about calling in some more help from Fort Campbell, sir?"

Freeman knew that wouldn't go over well at his higher headquarters. "I'd like to keep the number of people involved to a minimum as long as possible. Let's try a sweep on the way back. If we don't find anything, I've got some of my people flying in from Washington; they should be here soon."

Riley shrugged; sometimes it was better to be the follower rather than the leader. "All right, guys. Let's reverse it. Keep your eyes open. We'll go a little slower. Check out any clumps of bushes. Maybe they crawled under something before they got blown up. Let's do it."

Biotech Engineering
11:20 A.M.

Robin Merrit punched up the security log one more time and stared at it. Being an expert on computer systems was just one of the necessary skills that had made her a top genetic engineer less than four years after completing her doctorate. If the malfunction lay with the security setup the DIA had imposed, that might allow Ward to point some fingers and give the project some breathing room. Merrit knew that Ward was fighting the Pentagon to keep his conduit of funds flowing. In an era of reduced world tensions and budget cutbacks, even the anonymous Pentagon Black Budget was going to take a beating.

Merrit had long ago recognized the reality of her situation. She didn't like it here and she hated working for Ward. All her knowledge and work was siphoned off by the older man and she knew that she would get little, if any, credit for their research advances. Initially, her deepest regret was not being able to publish any of their results because of the security requirements. It was a catch-22. Working for the federal government allowed them to bypass the stringent procedural limitations on research imposed by law, but it also kept their findings from being acknowledged or replicated by the rest of the scientific community. Thus even the scant satisfaction of knowing that their work might be used productively somewhere else was denied to her.

Merrit's colleagues from college would be dismayed and shocked to learn that she was working for the government—the Pentagon no less. It had not been an easy choice, but the alternatives had been bleak. After graduating with her doctorate in bioengineering, Merrit had worked briefly as a lab researcher at the University of Texas at Austin. That job had lasted for four years, during which time she had started earning a closed-circle reputation for brilliance, supported by the ability to do the thorough, tedious work to back up her ideas.

Initially, for personal reasons, she had spurned several offers from various government agencies to put her talents to work for them. It was only after the university lost its federal research funding for farm animal genetic engineering that she was forced to consider government work. She finally took stock of the current state of scientific research in the United States, and was dismayed by what she found. Pure research in America was at a level less than 10 percent of what it had been thirty years before. A budget-conscious Congress had seen to that.

The ability, or desire, of universities and corporations to fund such research was also very low if the research did not point to an immediately usable solution to a problem—a profitable solution at that. The nebulous goals of pure research made it an undesirable field for investment of capital. This was despite the fact that pure research laid

the foundation for the more immediate and practical findings. Like a
slow-acting leukemia, the lack of funding for pure research was deteriorating the lifeblood of American industry, which relied heavily on
research and development to be competitive in the international arena.

Despite her blossoming reputation, Merrit had had difficulty in her
search for a new civilian workplace. Compounding the problem was
the fact that stringent animal experimentation requirements, forced upon
the research world by animal rights groups pressuring the government,
made it almost impossible to conduct the live-animal research necessary to genetic engineering.

Faced with the dual challenges of lack of available research sites
and the federal limitations, Merrit gave in and listened seriously to
Doctor Ward when he came to her with a pitch for a job.

The concept for the project at Biotech Engineering sounded relatively harmless but fascinating and challenging. The proposed budget,
lab setup, and freedom from federal limitations were strongly attractive. Merrit had long nourished a radical concept in bioengineering,
and Ward's proposal seemed to open the door to pursue that dream.

Only after she had signed on and started working at the lab did Merrit
realize that Ward had twisted the truth. Yes, she was doing quite a bit
of interesting theoretical work and valid applied experimentation. And,
yes, this work was on the cutting edge of genetic engineering. But Merrit
did not feel comfortable with the end result.

The purpose of the Synbats repelled her. Still, the advances they
were achieving fascinated her. They were beyond the current scope
of biological engineering, exploring uncharted territory. If Ward had
ever stopped to see what they had truly achieved, Merrit thought he
would realize, as she did, that they had moved beyond the realm of
present understanding and, she felt, far beyond the requirements imposed by the Pentagon.

For the past year Merrit had lived on an emotional edge regarding
her work. On the one hand, she knew that the theoretical findings would
be invaluable once released to others in the field under the Freedom
of Information Act. On the other hand, she also knew that the actual
practical work done at Biotech would never be released to the public.
The fact that they had initially been so far from the specifications desired
by the Pentagon had given her false comfort. She had no way of knowing
that Ward was falsifying his reports to General Trollers to keep the
project going. Naively, she had waited for the budget plug to be pulled.

It was only after she had tapped into Ward's personal files in the computers that she discovered his deception to both her and their military bosses. She saw then that the Synbat project would not be terminated anytime soon.

Merrit felt that they had stumbled onto something very significant in the Synbats—significant in a way that no one else in the project truly understood, or even cared to. Ward was too concerned with keeping his funds flowing and meeting the statement of requirements dictated by the Pentagon. Merrit alone had focused on what they had developed, and in doing so she had noticed some strange quirks in the data and, even more important, in the actions of the Synbats.

The situation had come to a head less than three months ago when Ward had gone to Washington for a week-long conference. Up to that point, they'd kept the Synbats heavily sedated to make them more compliant. The extreme aggression of the creatures had always been a major concern. Without sedation they were not trainable or controllable. Even with it, they were extremely dangerous, as evidenced by the events of last night. As Merrit had discovered from the computer, Ward had not reported that problem to the Pentagon; he was hoping that they could do something in the next generation to make the animals more tractable yet capable of performing as the Pentagon expected—an almost impossible set of contradictory requirements.

During those five days that Ward was gone, Merrit had held back the sedatives to see how the Synbats—now full-grown adults—would react without its numbing effect. The results had been startling and disturbing. She'd shown Ward the videotape, but he'd insisted that they keep it quiet or else face the loss of funds from the Black Budget.

At that point, Merrit had tried quitting. Despite her limited job options outside of the government, she had had enough. At last, she admitted to herself that she was terrified of what was happening in the lab.

Unfortunately, she had found out that quitting was not as easy as making an announcement. Ward felt her to be indispensable to the project, and the Defense Intelligence Agency had sent a representative to Merrit to clarify her position in no uncertain terms, pulling out the original work agreement she had signed when starting at Biotech.

The agent had explained it succinctly. The DIA would see to it that she didn't work for any research facility receiving federal funding. That meant she would either continue to work here or not work in the field at all. Additionally, any work she did on her own would have to be processed through the DIA's Research Supervision Office to ensure that nothing in it was related to any of the classified work she had done for the government. In other words, she could do nothing on her own. With that brief one-way conversation, the DIA had effectively nailed her to the job at Biotech.

Yet for the first time in many months she felt hopeful. Ward had upset the DIA by not blowing the collars on time. That and the three bodies had probably sounded the death knell for Biotech Engineering and correspondingly freed Merrit from her prison.

But three people were dead! The project should not have turned out this way. If they'd only listened to her. The world had enough problems without adding this unholy experiment, the exact ramifications of which not even its creators knew.

Vicinity Lake Barkley
11:43 A.M.

Riley was preparing to recross Williams Hollow Creek when he halted. Something on the far side caught his attention. He squatted down and scanned the bank, trying to focus. The sun had finally broken through the clouds and he was sure he had seen the light reflect off something. He heard the two nonteam members of the party come up behind him, breathing hard.

"What's the matter?" Ward puffed.

Riley put up a hand to silence him. Something metallic lay underneath a small bush on the far side. Riley stood up and waded across the creek, climbing up the far bank. He signaled for Ward and Freeman to stay back and then gingerly moved toward the bush. He scanned the ground beneath him. In the damp earth he could see some unidentifiable tracks.

Riley's questions about the entire operation hit him with more force on seeing those strange tracks. He pulled a magazine out of his ammo pouch and slid it into the well of the weapon. Seating it with a tap, he pulled back the bolt and slowly let it ride forward. He pushed on the M16's forward assist to make sure that the round was seated properly, then he rotated the selection switch to semiautomatic. Out of the corner of his eye he could see Doc Seay mimicking his actions with his weapon.

Riley crossed the last few meters to the bush, taking care not to trample the tracks. He could now see what was under the bush. He scanned the far side of the bush and the far slope. Nothing. If there had been anything else, they would have spotted it on the first trip.

Riley took a deep breath, then signaled the team to assemble nearby. He turned and gestured for Ward and Freeman to move up.

"Don't step in the tracks," Riley warned as the two came forward across the creek. He pointed at the bush. "There are your collars, or what's left of them."

CHAPTER 4

Freeman held the remains of the collars in his hands. "What's going on, Doctor?" There were four half pieces of metal, the ends cleanly cut.

Ward took the pieces and examined them. "These had to have been sawed off prior to getting blown. It looks like the part with the fuse and transceiver in it was destroyed but the other side was okay."

"How did they get sawed off?"

Ward shook his head. "I don't know."

"Whoever took the Synbats had to have done it. Most likely the security guard, if he was in on it."

Ward didn't believe that Stan Lowry had been part of the escape, but Freeman was right: The fact that the collars had been cut off increased the possibility. Maybe someone had even been behind the power failure. Ward reminded himself to look more closely at the computer records when he returned to the lab.

For the moment, Ward was simply glad that the Synbats were apparently still alive. He told Freeman: "It doesn't matter how they got out and who removed the collars. The problem is that we still have to track them down and catch them as soon as possible. I've got the tranquilizer rifles at the lab. We can use those to put them to sleep and bring them in. The army guys can take care of whoever stole them and took off their collars."

Freeman frowned. "I'll let you tranquilize them if you can, but I'm going to tell these men to shoot if there's any danger of the creatures getting away."

Ward realized that this was the best compromise he was going to get; he nodded his acceptance.

Thirty meters away, at the side of the stream, Riley was fielding questions from his curious team. "What was under that bush, chief?"

Riley glanced over where Ward and Freeman were still arguing, then swung his attention back to the team to answer Doc Seay's question. "There's four half circles of metal that look like they were part of the collars Doctor Ward told us about. There was also a small blackened area. From what I could see, it looks like the collars were cut off the monkeys before they were detonated."

Riley addressed Trovinsky, the team's senior weapons man. "Ski, take a look at those tracks where they come out of the creek there and tell me what you think."

Trovinsky walked over to the bank. He was a wiry man with a hatchet-shaped face framed by short black hair. Since Trovinsky spent most of his off-duty time hunting or fishing, Riley figured that he might have some idea what had made the tracks.

After a few minutes of examination, Trovinsky came back, shaking his head. "I don't know, chief. Never seen anything like them. From the impressions, I'd say you got something big—about a hundred thirty to a hundred fifty pounds, walking on two legs. I've never seen monkey tracks before, but I imagine that's what they are. There's four distinct sets, two larger, two smaller.

"From the condition of the edge of the impressions, I'd estimate they were here about eight to ten hours ago. It's rained since they were made, so we're talking prior to dawn."

Riley considered the information as he waited for Ward and Freeman to finish their hushed discussion. The two appeared finally to agree on something and came over to where the team was circled up. Riley noticed that both men were more nervous than before. Things weren't so clean-cut now, Riley thought. Plan A was down the tubes. Time for plan B, whatever that was.

Freeman spoke first. "It looks like somebody removed the monkeys' collars. Since there are no bodies here, we have to assume that the collars were cut off before the charge was initiated and the monkeys are still alive."

"I thought you said they escaped," said Knutz. "Are you saying now that someone stole the monkeys and cut off the collars?"

Freeman sighed. "From the original data at the lab we didn't think so, but based on this I'd have to admit there is a possibility that someone did break in and steal them. It's the only thing that makes sense."

Well, that certainly changes things, Riley thought. Still, something didn't sit right. He decided to point out the obvious. "If they were stolen, why aren't there any human tracks here?"

Ward slid his tongue over his lips. "We don't know what happened, so we can't answer that. The important thing now is that we find the monkeys as quickly as possible. I need to get back to my lab and get the tranquilizer guns so we can capture them."

Riley shook his head. "These tracks were made before dawn. That means they've got at least a six-hour lead on us. If someone stole them, they would have had a vehicle nearby and already be long gone. Maybe their plans went to shit and they're on foot for some reason. Maybe these monkeys escaped from the people who broke them out. I don't know, but whatever the reason, we can't afford to wait for you to go back to the lab. If you're serious about catching these monkeys, we've got to move after them *now*."

Riley wondered why Doctor Ward was so anxious to get these particular monkeys back alive. Surely they would have other samples of the modified VX virus back in the lab. Riley waited for a response to his suggestion. He could tell that the DIA agent and the doctor were at odds regarding the best way to handle this.

Riley was surprised when Doc Seay's quiet voice cut in. "If those monkeys are carrying a laboratory-manufactured strain of the VX virus, we can't afford to let them run around. There isn't even a working vaccine for the old strain, never mind a new one. We've got to go after them before they get too far. If someone has stolen them, the only reason I can figure is because that person wants the new strain. I have some worries about that person's motives. Maybe something went wrong and the monkeys escaped from whoever freed them. I don't know. All I do know is that I agree with the chief—we can't waste any more time."

Riley nodded his agreement. Seay was a good man, and on the few occasions he gave advice, Riley paid attention. The slightly balding, skinny medic was one of the smartest people Riley had ever met. And Seay had common sense, a more important commodity than pure intelligence, in Riley's opinion.

Freeman proposed a compromise. "How about if I go with the team after the monkeys and Doctor Ward goes back to the lab with one of

your men to get the rifles? Then they can fly out here on one of
the helicopters."

Riley gestured around at the forest. "There's no place for a helicopter to land around here, sir." He pulled out the map and looked at
it. "But the bird might be able to touch down where this creek runs
into the lake. The map shows an open area."

Riley turned to his team. "T-bone, you go back with the doctor. When
we hear the bird coming in, I'll send someone down to that open area
to meet you and guide you back to wherever we're at." He pointed at his
senior weapons man, Trovinsky. "Mike, check out that area where the
collars were and see if you can find the monkeys' tracks leading away."

Trovinsky walked over to the bush, and Ward and T-bone took off
to the east. Riley waited until they were out of sight before he turned
to Freeman. "What were you two arguing about, sir? This whole thing
is getting kind of flaky."

Freeman shook his head. "It doesn't make much sense to me either.
That's what I was talking to Doctor Ward about. We don't know whether
the monkeys escaped or if they were stolen. Who would have done
that and why they would still be in the area, I don't know."

"Maybe one of those radical animal rights groups did it," Doc Seay
suggested. "When I was going through the med lab portion of the Q-
course at Bragg, some of those people tried to break in and free the
goats we were using to study wound trauma."

Freeman shook his head. "The presence of monkeys at this lab is
classified, as is everything that goes on there. I doubt if any animal
rights group could have found out about it. Regardless, if you see the
monkeys, you're authorized to shoot to stop them from escaping. Attempt
to detain any people if they are involved."

Riley addressed the team standing around him. "I want everyone
to lock and load. A round in the chamber and the weapon on safe. Like
the man said: You see the monkeys and they try to get away, you shoot
and stop them."

The air filled with the sound of magazines slamming into weapons
and the slap of bolts being released.

Trovinsky yelled from his position, about ten meters behind the bush.
"I've got tracks moving upstream. Same as the ones going in."

Riley led the team over. "Any sign of human tracks?"

Trovinsky shook his head. "Nothing. With the rain we had last night,
there should be some sign if people were with the monkeys."

Riley gestured for the men to spread out in a wedge. "Let's move out."

Following Trovinsky, the team began moving up the east side of Williams Hollow Creek.

Biotech Engineering
12:56 P.M.

After reaching the dirt road, Ward had turned south, heading down to Route 64 and then following that up to the lab. Going that way instead of cross-country had saved a considerable amount of time. Ward had ignored the few questions that the Special Forces soldier asked when they first started out, and the rest of the trip had been made in silence. He was busy thinking, trying to figure out how the collars could have been cut off. He had to acknowledge the growing possibility that someone had survived the break-in. It would explain several of the more unusual factors they'd discovered so far. But the Synbats must have gotten away from that person, since there were no human tracks where they'd found the collars. But if no humans were present, how were the collars cut off?

Ward was still grappling with that problem when they turned into the lab parking lot. Two plain white vans with government plates had joined the other three vehicles there. The vans were unmarked and had tinted windows in the front, preventing him from looking in the vehicles. Ward told the soldier to stay with the helicopters and he entered the building.

Merrit was still at her position behind the counter. A tall man wearing unmarked khaki pants and shirt was with her. Ward didn't recognize the stranger. The man had dark hair flecked with gray, and a patrician face. His bearing and stance immediately suggested to Ward that this man was military. Merrit and the stranger turned from the portable computer and faced Ward as he strode in.

Merrit stood up and gestured. "Doctor Ward, this is Mister Lewis. He's—"

The man interrupted in a voice accustomed to command. "That's *Colonel* Lewis. I'm the DIA chief of CONUS security. I just flew in from Washington to Fort Campbell by military flight along with my team and our vans. My men are downstairs right now sweeping up."

Ward wondered what Lewis meant by "sweeping up." But he didn't have time to waste—he needed to get back out into the woods.

Ward stuck out his hand. "Nice to meet you. You'll excuse me if I don't have time to talk with you right now. I have to get our tranquilizer rifles and go back out."

Lewis didn't shake the offered hand. "Slow down, Doctor. I thought the creatures were terminated by remote detonation."

"We did do that, but we just found the collars out in the woods and no bodies. It looks like the collars were somehow cut off prior to detonation. The Synbats are still alive. The soldiers and your man Freeman are tracking them. Now, if . . ."

Ward paused. Four men carrying a body bag pushed open the doors to the corridor and walked by with their bundle.

Lewis watched as the two men went outside and threw the bag into the back of a van. One of the men got into the pickup truck and the two vehicles drove off. Lewis turned his attention back to Ward. "Doctor Merrit has filled me in on what she knows. Perhaps you'd better give me your version, and then tell me what's presently going on out there in the woods."

Ward shook his head. "I've got to get back out there. The—"

Lewis held up a hand. "Doctor, let me explain something to you. This may have been your lab but I'm in charge here now. You've got a fuckup on your hands and my job is to clean up the mess. Freeman knows to kill those things if he spots them. In fact, he made a mistake by even allowing you to think we'd let you tranquilize them. Those things have already killed. If they attack some civilian, it will make the situation that much worse. Just their existence being discovered is unacceptable."

The colonel poked a finger in Ward's chest. "Listen closely. This is the way it's going to work from here on out. I've already explained it to Doctor Merrit. *I* ask the questions. *You* give the answers. I tell you what to do. You do it without question."

He stared hard at Ward. "If you have a problem with that, you can pick up the phone and call General Trollers. Let me warn you before you do that, though, that you're not a very popular person with the general right now. Congress is looking to kill the Black Budget programs, and your screwup here could hand them the scalpel they need."

"This wasn't my fault," Ward defended himself. "Those people— whoever they were—broke in and tried to steal the Synbats. The security—"

"Those *people*," Lewis interrupted, "were three convicts from Eddyville State Prison who escaped last night. We have a positive ID on the remains.

We're holding that information from the local authorities because they're our ace in the hole in case your creatures do some more damage out there in the real world. Those bodies not being discovered gives us a very convenient cover story."

Ward seemed stunned. "But what about the security guard?"

"I don't know about that yet," Lewis admitted. "Those convicts had to have gotten down here from Eddyville somehow. Maybe they had someone else with them. I don't know. I've got people checking on that right now.

"We haven't had a chance to analyze everything yet, so we don't know what happened, but we'll worry about that when we get this thing under control."

Lewis sat on the edge of the desk. "Now. That helicopter isn't going anywhere until I say so. And I'm not going to say so until I know what's happening. So. Fill me in."

Route 139, North of the Tennessee Border
1:08 P.M.

Kentucky State Trooper Mike Truscott had his service revolver lying in his lap ready for use as he slowly cruised down the road. The manhunt for the escapees from Eddyville was concentrated along the interstate, but Truscott had been detached to check out the area in the vicinity of the Land Between the Lakes. All morning he'd cruised the entire length of the Trace, the road running up the middle of the LBL, and now he was moving east, closer to the suspected path of the escapees. People in the local area were very nervous, because two of the three escapees—Billy Hill and Chico Lopez—were convicted murderers.

As Truscott topped a small rise, he spotted tire tracks rolling off the hard tar into mud on the right side of the road. He slowed and pulled to a halt, peering off to the left where the back side of a van was visible through the trees. He called in his location and the situation, grabbed his shotgun, and exited the patrol car.

The back doors of the van were shut and the windows blacked out, so he edged around the driver's side, muzzle of the shotgun leading. He stepped up, pointing the gun directly at the glass, and stared in. A woman was in the driver's seat, staring directly ahead, her hands gripping the wheel. Truscott would later tell his buddies over a few beers that it appeared she was still driving the van in her mind, because her hands were twitching on the steering wheel, trying to maneuver as if she saw a turn in the road.

Truscott tapped on the glass with the shotgun; the woman ignored him. He'd seen many victims in shock after accidents but never anything quite like this. Putting down the shotgun, he grabbed the panel door and slid it open. He lunged for his shotgun as the body of an overweight man rolled out the door onto the wet grass.

Vicinity Lake Barkley
1:23 P.M.

Williams Hollow ran northeast from Lake Barkley. After twenty minutes, the team had reached the end of the draw, where the tracks had turned north. They'd been following them in this direction for fifteen minutes.

Riley was impressed with the tracking job Trovinsky was doing. The wet ground obviously helped, but in places the trail traversed old leaves or rocky areas and Trovinsky was still able to stay on track.

They were walking along the edge of a ridge when Trovinsky halted. He turned and signaled for Riley to come up.

"What do you have?"

Trovinsky indicated some matted grass at the base of a tree. "They must have slept here for a while."

Trovinsky edged around the tree with Riley following. He pointed at some droppings. "Now we'll get an idea of how long ago they were here."

Trovinsky poked at the feces with his knife and the lumps broke apart. "I'd say they were here not more than two hours ago. This hasn't had a chance to harden much yet. I've followed deer when I bow hunt and use the same method to tell how far behind I am." Trovinsky cleaned his knife on some leaves and resheathed it. "I would assume that monkey shit works pretty much the same as deer shit."

Riley signaled for the team to come in. "Looks like they rested here. They're less than two hours ahead. Let's tighten it up a bit. I want to move in an inverted V with Trovinsky at the point. I'll be his swing man."

Riley pointed at Freeman. "You follow right behind me, about ten feet back."

Riley was a little nervous about his men having live ammunition. He trusted them, but he also knew from hard experience that it's just as easy to get killed by friendly fire as enemy. Bullets didn't care if you were a good guy or a bad guy. Riley was encouraged that eight of the men had seen duty during Operation Desert Storm and knew how to play the game for real.

Riley addressed the team before starting off again. "Make sure if you shoot that you have a clear field of fire. I don't want anyone firing on three-round burst. Semi only. I know I probably don't have to say this, but do not fire across the formation." He peered around the group. "Any questions? All right. Let's move out."

At that moment a distant chattering in the air grabbed his attention. Shit, Riley thought. Terrible timing. He gestured. "Philips and Carter. Head on back to the stream and follow it to the lake. There should be an open area there. Bring the bird down and then guide the doctor and T-bone up here. On the double."

The two men backtracked at a trot. Riley was now down to seven men, eight counting Freeman. He turned to the DIA agent. "You armed, sir?"

Freeman pulled a snub-nose Colt from under his jacket. Riley was tempted to tell the major to be careful not to shoot himself. He contemplated taking his 9mm automatic from its shoulder holster under his fatigue shirt and giving it to the agent but decided against it. Instead he simply signaled for the team to move out.

With Trovinsky in the lead, the team broke through the dense undergrowth. The great monkey hunt, Riley thought sarcastically. Riley had worked with some DIA people in Thailand in the early eighties on some so-called intelligence-gathering missions; he didn't have much respect for the military men in civilian clothes trying to play superspy.

The DIA was the Pentagon's pooper-scooper. Too many of the men and women in the DIA came from regular military intelligence circles and, in Riley's opinion, lacked the flexibility in thinking necessary to conduct intelligence operations. They might be good working a desk, but some were disasters out in the real world. Traditional army mentality didn't jive with the curvilinear, inductive thinking often required to do good intelligence work. Certainly the DIA must have many good people, but Riley had had the misfortune to work with some of the bad ones.

The DIA also tended to overemphasize security at the expense of operational necessity. This Freeman fellow wasn't giving them the whole story, and Riley didn't like that. Experience had taught him that uninformed people made mistakes.

Riley diverted his attention from Trovinsky to briefly scan the rest of the team's positioning. Doc Seay was a comforting presence on his right. Riley could make out Barret, the junior engineer, breaking brush to the right of Seay. On Riley's left, Knutz was moving solidly through the woods, bulling his way through the undergrowth rather than slipping through as Riley was. Beyond Knutz, out of sight, Sgt. Martie Trustin and SSgt. Lou Caruso finished out the left wing of the wedge.

Riley turned his attention back to Trovinsky in time to see the man stop abruptly and signal a halt. Riley raised his fist and passed the signal to the rest of the team. He patiently waited as Trovinsky quartered the ground in front, gradually increasing the radius of the search pattern. After ten minutes, Trovinsky turned to Riley.

"The trail ends here."

Riley looked around. "Then where are they?"

Trovinsky pointed up. "They took to the trees."

2:14 P.M.

The party from the helicopter had tramped up from the beginning of Williams Hollow to the point where the monkeys had gone vertical. Ward seemed very subdued and Riley took an instant dislike to the DIA colonel. Lewis's first comment after Freeman's quick recount of events was to demand to know why they had stopped looking. Riley decided to step in at that point.

"Look where, sir? There's no trail to follow up in the trees, and none of my men are Tarzan qualified. We need to bring in a bunch more bodies if we're going to sweep this area. Those monkeys could have gone in any direction once they went up."

Lewis leveled his hard gaze at Riley. "You have any other brilliant observations to make, mister?"

Riley held his temper. From behind him, Freeman interceded. "What about thermal imagery from the helicopters?"

Lewis nodded. "That's a good idea. I'm sure some of the infantry units at Campbell have thermal sights that we'll be able to use."

Lewis obviously is going to do whatever he wants, Riley thought. He'd be damned if he'd get into an argument with the man. Warrant officers didn't win many pissing contests with full colonels.

Lewis made his command decision. "I'm going to have one of those helicopters go back and get some thermals. It's worth a shot."

Trovinsky offered another alternative. "If we could get some search-and-rescue dogs, we might be able to find them."

Lewis frowned. "If the monkeys are up in the trees, how can the dogs follow their trail?"

Trovinsky shook his head. "Not all search-and-rescue dogs are trailing dogs, sir. Some use what's called winding. We put them downwind of the last known position, which is here, and the dogs do a search pattern until they pick up the scent, and then work upwind to the source. It's actually a lot quicker than trailing, because the dogs can head straight for the source once they pick up the scent rather than following a winding trail. The Montgomery County Sheriff's Department over by Clarksville has some dogs trained in that."

Freeman threw in his two cents' worth. "We can call the sheriff's department and ask for their assistance."

Riley could tell that Lewis didn't like the idea of calling in anyone else. The colonel seemed to be holding an internal debate. Lewis made his decision. He pulled out a Motorola radio from a shoulder holster and keyed the send button. "Search Base, this is Search Six. Over."

The radio hissed. "This is Search Base. Over."

"Call the DPTM at Fort Campbell and have him get some thermal sights ready for pickup. Then send Jameson back with one of the helicopters to get them. Also, contact the Montgomery County Sheriff's Department to get us some tracking dogs. Use the other bird to pick them up. Have Gottleib go on that one. I want the thermals brought back to the lab and the dogs brought straight out here. Over."

"Roger. What should I tell the sheriff's department is the reason for the dogs? Over."

"The goddamn federal government needs them, that's why. Out."

CHAPTER 5

While waiting for the dogs to arrive, CWO Dave Riley spent forty-five minutes trying to sort through the day's events. He was a methodical thinker who scrutinized every aspect of a situation, examining each detail from various perspectives. Then he'd try to reassemble the details so that the entire situation fit together and appeared clearly in his mind's eye. Except it wasn't working here.

Riley could understand the concern about the possibility of a new strain of the VX virus getting loose via these monkeys. But he was puzzled by just about everything else he had seen today. The collars, the security setup at the lab, the vehicle in the parking lot with a re-tired enlisted sticker, the—

Riley's thoughts were interrupted by the sound of an inbound Huey. He held his patrol cap in place as the helicopter settled down onto the knee-high grass bordering the terminus of Williams Hollow Creek. The side doors slid open and two county sheriffs hopped off, each one controlling a German shepherd on the end of a short chain. A third man got off, dressed in what Riley assumed to be the DIA's field uniform of khaki pants and bush jacket over a khaki shirt. The man was armed with an MP-5 submachine gun slung over his shoulder. The bird lifted and winged back in the direction of the lab.

After briefly greeting the two law officers, Lewis gave the order for Riley to lead the entire party back to the last ground tracks of the monkeys, where Trovinsky and Caruso were standing by. Riley quickly led the way, his team automatically fanning out on either side of him. The dogs, their handlers, Lewis, Freeman, the third DIA man, and Ward tramped behind in the center.

Once they reached the tree, the two sheriffs allowed their dogs to spend some time sniffing around the base and along the monkey tracks leading up to the tree. As soon as they got the scent, both dogs immediately started an agitated whining.

"What's wrong with them?" Lewis demanded.

The senior sheriff, identified as Douglas by his nameplate, shook his head as he tried to control his dog. "I don't know. I've never seen them like this. I guess it's because they've never smelled monkey before."

"Are they going to be able to do the job?"

Douglas nodded. "Yeah. They'll be all right."

The two officers spent a few minutes calming their dogs, then both switched the short chain leashes for longer nylon ones.

"All right. Let's go," Douglas called out. "The wind looks good, coming from the west, and the dogs are picking up the scent that way. Just keep your people downwind from us."

Riley positioned his men with a few quick hand and arm signals. He followed as the two handlers moved the dogs out in a series of S-shaped movements, always coming back centered on a west-northwesterly heading. Riley pulled out his map as they moved. Another klick and they'd hit Lake Barkley. Nowhere for the monkeys to go then. He glanced around, making sure that his men were spread out and alert.

Suddenly the left dog halted and started yipping furiously, straining backward on its leash. Riley slid the selector lever on his M16 to semiautomatic and signaled for the rest of the team to stay in place. He moved over to Douglas. "What's the matter?"

Now the other dog joined in the same shrill barking. It made the hairs stand up on the back of Riley's neck.

Douglas was pulling on the leash. "Don't know. They're smelling something they don't like." He yanked the dog forward. It slinked along, hackles raised.

Riley scanned the bushes and trees in the immediate area. He gestured for Caruso and Philips to keep their eyes up in the trees as he moved with Douglas.

The lead dog stopped, its nose pointed at something dark on the ground. Riley knelt next to it. It took a second for his brain to register what the object was: A few pieces of fur and a skull with tatters of flesh on it identified the carcass as that of a rabbit.

A few feet away lay some dark lumps. Riley recognized them and signaled for Trovinsky to come forward. "That look the same as the last pile you found?"

Trovinsky knelt down next to the feces. "Yeah. Same color and texture." He stood up and tapped them with his boot. "About two to four hours old, I'd say."

"What do you make of the carcass?"

Trovinsky reached forward to poke it with his finger.

"I wouldn't do that," Riley advised. "Remember that if those monkeys ate this thing and they're carrying the virus, their saliva might be on the body."

Trovinsky quickly pulled away his hand. He slid out his knife and poked with it. "Guess around two to four hours, like I said. Maybe more. Hard to tell. The body—what's left of it—looks cold. The blood is pretty dry."

Riley looked around. Lewis, Freeman, and Ward, along with the other DIA agent, were clustered behind the team's skirmish line. The three DIA men had their weapons drawn and were looking around a little nervously. Seemed a bit of an overreaction to Riley. He noticed that Lewis had a massive .44 magnum revolver for his personal weapon; the new DIA man had the MP-5 in the ready position. Hell of a lot of firepower for a few monkeys.

Riley turned his attention back to Douglas and nodded toward the dogs. "They always get like this over a dead rabbit?"

Douglas shook his head and looked at his partner, Sheriff Lamb. "Pete, you ever seen these dogs act this way? They acted funny when they first got the scent."

Lamb spit out a wad of tobacco. "Only time I seen Jake get stupid like this is when we ran across some panther tracks up in the Smokies last summer."

Riley considered it. "Think it's just like you said earlier—they've never smelled a monkey before?"

Douglas shrugged. "Could be. Don't know." He jerked the chain. "Come on, Caesar. Let's get going."

Lamb shook his head. Riley overheard him mutter to himself, "I'd say it's cause they're scared shitless." The sheriff forced his dog forward.

Riley walked back to Ward. "We've got more feces and the body of a rabbit that looks like it's been stripped clean of almost all the meat. I didn't know monkeys ate meat."

Ward glanced about nervously. "Monkeys are omnivorous. They eat whatever they can get."

"You all probably want to scoop up that body to make sure that none of your virus is in it," suggested Riley. "Wouldn't do to have some other animal feed on it."

Ward and Freeman put on surgical gloves and delicately placed the remains in a large freezer bag, then put the bag into Freeman's backpack. Once they were done, Riley gave the signal to move out again.

They crossed an old dirt road and started heading downhill. According to the map, Riley could see that they were within a hundred meters of the lake. Through the trees he could make out small patches of sparkling light as the sun briefly broke through the heavy clouds and reflected off the water. He signaled for his team to tighten up the formation.

With a final plunge, the dogs were out of the tree line and standing on the thin grass strip that bordered the lake. Both dogs were poised in the same position: nose up, leaning forward, pointing straight at the lake.

The men assembled on the bank and collectively looked at Doctor Ward. Knutz voiced the thought they all seemed to have: "I thought you said they couldn't swim."

Ward seemed preoccupied, staring across the dark water at the far bank, almost a kilometer and a half away. "They can't. At least I didn't think so. We never tested them on swimming. There's no way they could have made it over there by themselves, though."

"Well, where are they then?" Lewis demanded.

Riley went into his slow and steady thought mode. He wondered what Ward meant by never having "tested" the monkeys on swimming. "All right," Riley announced. "Everyone just back up off the shoreline. Trovinsky, I want you to take a look along the bank and see if you can find where they went in the water. If the dogs are smelling them across the water from here, they must have gone in either here or maybe somewhere upstream."

Riley eyed the shimmering surface of the water. Lake Barkley was actually a dammed-up portion of the Cumberland River. The water didn't appear to be flowing in either direction, but from looking at the map, he could see that the Cumberland ran into the Tennessee River, which meant that the water in the lake was flowing from left to right.

Riley gestured at Seay. "Doc, you and Caruso head down that way along the bank and see if you spot anything."

As Riley waited for Trovinsky and the others to finish their search, he noticed the DIA men having another heated discussion with Doctor Ward. This is getting more and more curious, Riley thought. His reverie was interrupted by Doc Seay's call.

Riley jogged the thirty meters to where Seay and Caruso were standing. "Check this out, chief."

Riley followed Doc's finger. Someone or something had pulled a log off the bank into the water. The indent where the log had laid was clear, as were the drag marks leading down into the water. Tracks identical to the ones they had followed up to the tree were clearly impressed in the mud.

"Pretty fucking smart monkeys," Caruso muttered.

"You know what they say," Doc Seay offered. "Lock fifty monkeys in a room with fifty typewriters for fifty years and sooner or later one of them will write a play by Shakespeare."

Riley shook his head. First the collars and now this. "Yeah, well it's been only twelve hours and we have only four monkeys. Let's see what the brain trust over there has to suggest now."

Little goodwill was evident between Colonel Lewis and Doctor Ward. The two stood, separated from the others, staring out over the water. Lewis's radio beeped and he removed it from his belt. "Search Six. Over."

"This is Search One. We've recovered the guard's body. We've also got a survivor from the attack at the lab. Kentucky State Police found them both in a van south of our location about three hours ago. A captain from the state police showed up here a half hour ago wanting to know what's going on. I took over both the woman and the body but they're plenty pissed at the secrecy. Over."

Lewis gripped the radio tightly. "Do the locals have any idea what happened? Over."

"Negative. The woman's in shock and out of it. Hasn't said a word. I told them she must have been with the escaped convicts and that they ransacked the lab here and must have taken the guard's body with them. I suggested that the guard getting killed in front of her is what put her into shock. I also told them we had nothing more here that could help them and that the facility was classified so they couldn't enter. I think they're satisfied that the convicts have moved on and left the woman behind. Over."

Lewis relaxed slightly. "All right. Find out from the woman what happened. You know how to do that. I'll get back to you when I figure out what's going on out here. Call me immediately if any more locals show up. Out."

Lewis slipped the radio back into his belt and looked at Ward. "Our cover is barely holding. If the Synbats are in this area, they're relatively isolated. We need to get back to the lab and get reorganized."

CHAPTER 6

Land Between the Lakes
7:32 P.M.

Bill Hapscomb checked out Mrs. Werner's figure in the glow of the firelight. Man, what I wouldn't give to have a piece of that, he thought. Not that it was likely, the way her old man hung around her, like a moth around white light. That Werner fellow was one pussy-whipped dude, Hapscomb figured. Rich, though. Shit, you didn't get women like that if you weren't.

Bill Hapscomb sure hadn't gotten anything resembling the blond-haired woman who was patiently braiding her daughter's hair. Despite her years, at least forty Hapscomb estimated, Mrs. Werner still had what it took to register on his old pecker meter. Hell, give the daughter a few more years and she'd be the spitting image of her mom except younger and better.

Hapscomb glanced over toward the dome tent that the head of the Werner household was trying to set up. The man was having trouble with the telescoping poles, which had to be bent and slid and tucked. Hapscomb was damned if he'd help that pompous son of a bitch. His boss, McClanahan, the chief wrangler for the Land Between the Lakes Wrangler Camp, had told him that Mister Werner was some big shot down in Nashville. Something to do with country music recording and all that. Hapscomb couldn't give a rat's ass. The guy was lucky he could find the ground when he was on a horse. The critical thing was that the man was willing to pay.

At that moment, Mrs. Werner happened to look across the fire and catch Hapscomb in his mental perusal of her body. Hapscomb could have sworn that she gave him a half smile. Damn, he thought. That bitch had been teasing him all day long, brushing her body up against his every time he was close. Give him half a chance tonight and he had a feeling he might be getting some drawers off that woman. Hell, he knew he looked a hell of a lot better with a hundred and ninety pounds of muscle filling out his six-foot frame than her short, balding, potbellied old man.

Usually Hapscomb's job was to chaperon a group of twenty to thirty screaming prepubescent kids out of the Wrangler Camp in the LBL Campground. But for a weekday in the early spring, he took any traffic that came along. Werner sure was willing to put out the bucks to have a personal guide along—not that a guide was needed in this area. Surrounded on three sides by water, you'd have to be a damned fool to get lost in the LBL. The Trace, the only two-lane tarred road in the area, ran up the center of the peninsula, neatly splitting the park in half.

Hapscomb knew that he wasn't along as guide but as joe-shit-the-ragman to handle the horses when the Werners got bored. Although Mrs. Werner obviously knew her way around horses—and what he wouldn't give to have those legs wrapped around *him*—the old man and his daughter were lucky they hadn't gotten their asses busted riding around today.

Hapscomb slipped a leather bota filled with throat-burning, high-grade Tennessee whiskey out of his saddlebag, figuring that he was done for the day. The horses were picketed along the wood line, about twenty feet away. The campsite that Hapscomb had picked for the Werners was a good one. Hell, he had almost the whole damn park to choose from. As far as he knew there was no one within ten miles. The site was a level clearing about thirty by forty meters on top of a knoll. The ground sloped off on all sides. To the east the dark line that represented Lake Barkley could barely be discerned through a few breaks in the trees.

The only problem was the weather. It had been misting all day; although stars were poking through here and there, the sky still hadn't cleared. This morning's long-range forecast had hinted at the possibility of a nasty storm moving in behind this front of rain. If it did, Hapscomb was sure that the Werners would call it quits tomorrow morning. Then he'd get paid for the next two days and not have to work. That would be a good deal.

Damn, there she was giving him the once-over again. Hapscomb gave her the long slow smile he used on the local girls in Waverly when he went down there on his Friday night snatch hunts. Hot damn! Tonight could turn out to be all right, Hapscomb thought.

Biotech Engineering
7:45 P.M.

Riley felt the skids leave the ground as he pulled his Goretex rain jacket tight around his body. The wind swirling in the open doors of the helicopter dropped the night's chill a notch into the cold category. Riley could feel Doc Seay's legs bumping against his. They were both lying on the floor of the helicopter, facing out opposing cargo doors. Restraining harnesses were cinched about their bodies and the nylon strap that ran out of the back of the rig was firmly snap linked into an eyebolt on the floor of the helicopter's cargo bay.

The aircraft swooped across Lake Barkley toward the Land Between the Lakes park. Riley twisted the ON switch for the thermal sight. After a few seconds of warming up, the screen on the inside of the eyepiece glowed with an eerie representation of the outside environment. Instead of the normal human light spectrum, the screen showed the varying degrees of heat in the range of vision. Tiny blocks represented different temperatures and outlined the objects below. While Riley and Seay were using the thermals, the pilots up front were wearing ambient light–amplifying PVS-6 night vision goggles to fly at an altitude of two hundred feet.

After Colonel Lewis had insisted that they continue the search despite nightfall, Riley had worked out a grid search pattern for the helicopters over the Land Between the Lakes. In his opinion they didn't have much chance of picking up the monkeys, but Lewis was a colonel and Riley was just a warrant officer. Riley had been around long enough to know when to say "yes, sir" and drive on.

The rest of the team was staying in the lab, rolling out their sleeping bags and pads on the floor of one of the rooms off the main corridor. There were now at least eight DIA men on the scene, with two vans. The DIA men were all staying on a lower level that Riley had not even known existed this morning. His men weren't authorized access to that floor, and a DIA man stood guard at the security console to ensure that one of the Special Forces men didn't wander down there or any other unauthorized place.

As the aircraft flew over the shoreline that marked the beginning of the peninsula of the Land Between the Lakes, Riley talked into the hot mike that linked him with the pilots and Doc Seay. "All right. Let's hold it here till we get oriented, OK, sir?"

Captain Barret's laconic voice crackled in Riley's headset. "Sure thing, chief. What's the big deal anyway? My orders are to stay out here as long as needed and do whatever Colonel Lewis says, but he sure hasn't told me *why* we're doing all this. My battalion commander was all over my case when I flew back to Sabre Army Airfield this afternoon to refuel and pick up the thermals and our night vision goggles. Apparently no one's told him what's going on either."

Riley sympathized with the pilot. "Got me, sir. I just do what I'm told." Riley knew that the pilots were probably not thrilled about having to spend the night out here. Aviators tended to like living comfortable lives and were used to having a nice bed to curl up in at night. Sleeping away from home was not high on their list of desirable activities.

Riley had their position now. The dim light at the lake's Bacon Creek boat access ramp was off his door. "OK, sir. We're north of where the monkeys probably landed if they pushed that log all the way across."

The unspoken question Riley had was whether the monkeys had even made it across, or had they headed up or down the lake and relanded on the same side, or slipped off the log, dropped into the water, and drowned? Or maybe they still were on the log, floating down toward the dam. In addition, Riley wondered, why were they hauling around those backpacks? For that matter, did they still have the backpacks, or had they abandoned them on the other side of the lake or even dropped them into the lake? There were too many unknowns in this whole operation.

Riley dismissed those thoughts for the moment. Time to handle the known before trying to tackle the unknown. "Let's follow the shore for about five miles and then come back up. We'll go in about four hundred meters on each sweep. Take it slow, sir, so we can do this right."

"Roger that." The helicopter nosed over to the left and Riley settled in for what he felt was going to be a wasted two hours of burning fuel.

The trees below were a dark mass in the thermal sight. What are we supposed to do if we spot the monkeys? Riley war-gamed. There were very few landing places for the helicopter in the area. When they'd returned to the lab after losing the trail at the edge of the lake, Doctor Ward had been uncertain about whether the monkeys would be moving at night. He'd said that baboons—the type of monkey they were after—normally were diurnal, which meant active in the daytime. But, Riley reminded himself, Ward had also said that the monkeys probably wouldn't cross the lake.

Colonel Lewis's orders had been simple and direct: Get a fix on them and land if you can; if you can't, we'll hunt them down from that spot in the morning.

Fort Campbell
8:29 P.M.

Segeant Major Dan Powers drained the beer, crushed the can, and deftly pitched the empty into the garbage. He checked the PRC-70 radio set one last time, ensuring that it was on and tuned to the proper frequency. He traced the cable running from the radio to the digital message data group device (DMDG). All set to go. The DMDG was designed to either send or receive Morse code messages at accelerated speed. To receive, the DMDG took the burst from the radio, slowed it down, and transformed the dots and dashes to readable alphanumeric form on a small screen.

At exactly 2030 local or, as commo men preferred, 0230 Zulu (Greenwich mean time), the radio's speaker crackled briefly, followed by a two-second squealing hiss. Powers leaned over and checked the DMDG's screen. It read: "Message Copied." Despite that positive information, Powers leaned back in his chair with a notepad on his good knee and pencil at the ready.

After a moment of silence, the speaker issued forth a series of dots and dashes at the rapid speed of twenty-three words a minute. Powers's pencil floated over the page, his mind automatically translating the Morse into letters. After a brief pause, the message started over again. Powers stopped writing and checked his first copy against the repeat. When the speaker finally went silent, Powers allowed himself a small smile. Despite not having served as a primary communications man on a team for more than fourteen years, he could still keep up to speed on manual Morse.

Powers tore off the top sheet and rewrote the message in six-letter blocks onto a new sheet. The result was unintelligible:

AORELD	FJWMPR	EKTPCS	AQPZMC	ALWOXM
WJTNDW	TIWNSK	QSXPTK	RHTIGM	ACVZZS
QPRJFN	QWJRUA	QOELSM	QLEPNV	RHTNDM
TIHDFN	PILVNF	DFJRUE	EHDBCN	FNDHFJ
UOTYKW	SJWURH	WKCMSK	ZXCVBN	WELKJH
EDCVUJ	UJNHYT	EFVIKM	EDCHYN	VBNMKJ
ASDFGH	HJKLPO	SDFGHY	RTYUIO	OIUYGB
EDFVRT				

Powers pulled out a copy of the pocket-sized battalion field SOP, which every team was required to carry when they departed post on a training mission. He turned to page one and matched the letters from the message with the corresponding letter from the first page. Powers didn't need a trigraph; he had long ago memorized the standard three-letter groupings. Combining the original Morse letter with the letter from the page in the Bn SOP gave him the third letter on the trigraph, which made the message readable.

Swiftly his pencil ran down the page, making the message intelligible.

ZEROON	EXXODA	SIXEIG	HTTWOX	XSITRE
PXXSPE	NTDAYS	EARCHI	NGWOOD	SFORES
CAPEDM	ONKEYS	XXGOVE	RNMENT	LABHER
EGRIDO	NESIXS	DRONES	EVENTH	REESIX
FOURNI	NEXXXO	NESIXS	DRONES	EVENTH
REESIX	FOURNI	NEXXDI	AXXXDI	AINCHA
RGEXXS	HOULDB	EHOMES	OONXXA	MIGOXX
XXXXXX				

Used to dealing with the six-letter groups, Powers's mind assimilated the message:

> ZERO ONE (indicated that it was the first message the team sent)
> ODA SIX EIGHT TWO (designated the team that sent the message)
> SITREP (situation report)
> SPENT DAY SEARCHING WOODS FOR ESCAPED MONKEYS
> GOVERNMENT LAB HERE GRID ONE SIX SDR ONE SEVEN
>   THREE SIX FOUR NINE
> DIA (repeat) DIA IN CHARGE
> SHOULD BE HOME SOON
> AMIGO

Amigo was ODA 682's code word to ensure that the message wasn't being sent under distress. A message sent without the code word was assumed to be compromised. Powers wasn't worried that Riley might be encrypting the message under duress on this mission, but it was good training to always do it properly.

Powers set the message down on his desk as he popped another beer. He focused in on three letters: DIA. That had worried him from the beginning. He didn't trust anybody who ran around in a three piece suit and called himself an agent instead of a soldier. Still, the message said they'd be home soon. That was good news. He took a deep chug and started working his bad knee. Pain was weakness leaving the body.

Biotech Engineering
8:32 P.M.

Colonel Lewis accessed the secure satellite communications net that his men had brought with them to contact General Trollers in Washington. He wasn't looking forward to the report he was going to have to make. He glared across the desk at Doctor Ward and Doctor Merrit. The two had been nothing but irritants since he'd gotten here. The local DIA representative, Freeman, was doing his best to appear inconspicuous. The transcript of the interrogation of the drugged woman found with the van and guard's body was lying in front of him.

The whole situation was a mess and Lewis knew that Trollers wasn't going to like it. Lewis was career army, West Point class of '73, and didn't like the positions in which he occasionally found himself because of his job. The West Point honor code had definitely taken a beating from the requirements of life in military intelligence. He'd long ago learned to come on as a hard-ass when starting out a mission because that way people complied more quickly. Except that technique didn't seem to be working well with the Special Forces men.

The speaker on the desk crackled. "Trollers here. Give me a situation report."

Lewis allowed himself the indulgence of a small sigh and then jumped into it, good news first to soften the blow. "I've got the lab swept clean, sir. The guard's body has been taken care of also. We're blaming it on the escapees. In fact, the woman we've got says that the guard *was* killed by one of the cons. The local cops have bought off on it. We've kept the other bodies secure so there won't be any inquiry into that. The locals think the convicts are still on the loose."

"What's the status on the Synbats?"

"We tracked them from where we found the collars to the shore of a lake. Apparently they used a log to float across the lake. I've got a helicopter with thermal imaging up right now searching for them."

"You mean they're still unsecure? How populated is this area they're loose in?"

"It's a park area called Land Between the Lakes, run by the Tennessee Valley Authority. The park is bounded on three sides by water and there are only four ways in by road. This time of year there's hardly anyone there. We're lucky in that regard. We couldn't have picked a better place for them to run to. Unpopulated, and—"

"Goddamnit, Lewis! Stop trying to make it sound so great."

Lewis took another deep breath. "Sir, I'd like to seal off the park. We can say we've discovered that some sensitive equipment was stolen by the escapees and we're helping the locals track them down."

The general's reply was brief and to the point. "Negative. Even with the cover story, we'll have the media up our ass to our eyeballs."

Lewis wasn't at all happy with that response. "Then, sir, I'm going to need more men for the search. I'd like to bring in some more troops from Fort Campbell. I've already got all the men from our Washington response team here."

"Negative. Goddamnit, Lewis, don't you understand? We've got to keep this under wraps. It's bad enough you got those soldiers involved. You keep those Special Forces men and you use them."

Lewis rubbed his forehead. He felt the beginnings of a massive headache forming like a thunderstorm in his forehead. "Sir, I really feel I need more men if I'm going to find them soon."

General Trollers snorted. "Let's not go overboard here, people. We're talking about some animals, for chrissake. This is a major fuckup, but we don't want to make it a world-class one by letting word get out about what Ward's doing in that lab. No one is going to miss those three escapees. The death of the security guard is unfortunate but had nothing to do with our project anyway. If this area is as unpopulated as you say it is, the odds are that the Synbats will never run into any people. You keep your search going and track them down. You've got a Special Forces A team and helicopters. That should be more than enough to get these things."

Lewis shook his head. He thought that Trollers was seriously under-estimating the situation. The general hadn't even heard the worst of it yet. "Sir, there are two aspects to this I think you need to be aware of."

"What?"

Lewis shot a dirty look at Ward and then started. "It wasn't in any of the reports, but the last two generations of Synbats have been kept under control by the use of depressant drugs from infancy on up. The Synbats you saw on the videos for the demonstrations that Doctor Ward arranged were sedated. Apparently they were uncontrollable without the use of the drug. That drug will be out of their systems completely in four days. God knows what they'll be capable of doing when they're *not* sedated compared to what they've already done."

"Then we goddamn make sure they don't last four days" was Trollers's succinct reply.

Lewis sighed and moved on. "Sir, the Synbats also took the two backpacks that Doctor Ward had prepared for the fifth generation phase four test."

"So what? Your initial report said that. It also said that the backpacks would go bad outside of the controlled environment of the lab."

Lewis threw another withering look at Ward. If the son of a bitch had terminated immediately as the plan had directed, they wouldn't be in this mess. And if he had filed accurate reports on the Synbats, then things might never have gotten to this point.

"Yes, sir. That's what will most likely happen. But apparently they were further ahead here than we realized. There is a very slight pos-sibility that the backpacks may work outside of the lab."

There was silence on the other end. The low hiss of static echoed lightly in the office.

The general's voice came back, the argumentative tone gone. "The backpacks barely worked before under lab conditions. What makes you think they'll work now, Ward?"

Ward cleared his throat. "I don't think they will."

Lewis cut back in to clarify. "It's Doctor Merrit who thinks they may, sir."

The general switched tactics, his voice reaching out to the other scientist in the room. "What about you, Doctor Merrit? What do you think is the chance of the backpacks working?"

Merrit was gratified to be called on. Obviously the general had lost some of his faith in Ward. "To be honest I couldn't say. But I think it's foolish to say that the odds are low. We designed them to work under these types of conditions, and we trained the Synbats to carry them and guard them. Even if it's a one percent chance that they'll work, we can't afford to take it. It would start something that could easily get out of control if we look at a geometric progression."

"Is this true, Ward?"

Ward was glaring at Merrit. "Well, sir, like Doctor Merrit said, it's only a very slight possibility. We made some improvements on the series seven pods and we were going to run an operational phase four test on them in about three weeks. I really think the chances of them working outside the lab are very, very low."

"How long do we have if they do work?"

Merrit handled that one. "They were designed to complete initiation in seventy-two hours. Considering that they started out frozen and not at ambient temperature, I'd say we have to add a couple of hours. We're looking at Thursday morning."

There was another long silence on the other end. Finally, General Trollers's voice came back. "All right. I need to know the odds. Ward, I want a number. What are the chances of the pods working?"

Ward ignored Merrit. "I'd say no more than five percent of success."

"What about you, Merrit?"

She didn't hesitate. "I'd say twenty-five to fifty percent of at least a few successful initiations."

"No way!" Ward was standing. "They weren't designed with—"

General Trollers's voice silenced him. "Thank you, Doctors. That will be all for now. Colonel, you keep looking. You've got twenty-four hours before I have to run this up the flagpole. If that happens you can kiss Biotech and your careers good-bye. I hope you can give me good news before then. Out here."

The radio went dead. Merrit looked accusingly at Lewis. "You didn't tell him about the videotape when they weren't drugged."

Lewis rubbed his forehead. "Listen, Doctor, I've got enough shit on my hands. I don't need to be giving the general some half-assed theory of yours." He pointed at Ward. "Your boss doesn't even buy into it. It really doesn't matter anyway because we're going to get these things either tonight or tomorrow, so we won't have to worry about the backpacks or the drugs wearing off or your theory."

CHAPTER 7

Land Between the Lakes
9:03 P.M.

Hapscomb cracked his eyelids and watched as he lay on the ground pretending to be asleep. Mrs. Werner was getting out of the tent. In the dim starlight, his eyes followed her as she made her way toward the wood line. Hapscomb smiled to himself. A call of nature most likely, but he felt his own call of nature. He rolled off his sleeping pad and lightly stepped across the clearing toward the trees where the woman had disappeared.

She hadn't gone too far into the woods. Hapscomb gave her some time to finish her business and then stepped up as she was still buttoning her tight-fitting jeans.

Mrs. Werner looked up, startled at the noise. "What are you doing here?" she whispered.

Hapscomb let loose his winning smile, apparently unaware that it was wasted in the dark woods. "I just wanted to see if those looks you gave me all day were just a tease or whether you were willing to follow through."

The lack of an immediate negative response prompted Hapscomb to pull her over next to him. She looked up at him with large dark eyes as he reached out for her.

9:05 P.M.

"I've got two heat sources. Two legs, two arms on each. Due west."

All right! Riley thought on hearing Seay's report. This was their second

93

rotation back up the search area. "Guide us in, Doc. I'm going to put the goggles on to see what we have."

As Doc Seay directed the pilots in a banking left-hand turn, Riley carefully stowed the thermal sight in its tied-down case and pulled out a set of PVS-5 night vision goggles. He slipped the bulky goggles over his head and turned them on.

The ambient light was immediately computer enhanced and he saw as if it were daylight. The only drawbacks were that everything was represented in varying shades of green, and there was a certain lack of depth perception. As Riley slid over to the left side of the helicopter next to Seay, he wondered how the pilots could fly using the things; even though their PVS-6s were an upgraded model, it was still very difficult to operate with them on. Riley had a hard time walking while wearing them. On the other hand he supposed it beat flying without any sort of night vision device.

"Where's the target?" Captain Barret asked.

"See that clearing about four hundred meters to our left front on the hilltop?" Doc Seay directed.

"Roger that."

"It's off to the north of that clearing about ten meters inside the tree line. I'm also getting a heat source from the clearing. Real hot. Looks like a campfire."

"Damn," Riley cursed. "I see a tent in that clearing. If your heat source is our monkeys, they're close to that tent. I can't spot the other heat source you see in the thermals. The trees are too thick."

The pilot pointed the nose of the aircraft straight for the clearing. "I'm going to put us in the center of the clearing and let you guys off."

Riley grabbed his M16. The pilot flared the helicopter and Riley hopped out as soon as the skids touched the ground. He could see someone crawling out of the large dome tent, hunched against the blast of wind from the blades.

"U.S. Army. Stay in place, please." Riley ran past a confused man who was yelling, "What's going on?"

Riley ran into the tree line where Seay had indicated. Immediately he spotted a white shape to his left front. Riley drew down on the target, his finger easing over the trigger.

Whoa! Riley said to himself, forcing his arm to relax.

"What's the meaning of this?" the woman demanded, squinting into the dark as she struggled to button her blouse. The man was trying to buckle his belt.

The older man who had crawled out of the tent showed up, shining a huge flashlight. Riley shut off his goggles to prevent them from overloading. He slid them off his head, allowing them to dangle on their dummy cord around his neck.

"Marjorie, what were you doing?" the man demanded.

Riley watched as the woman squirmed under the glare of the flashlight. Whatever he had interrupted, it looked as though he wasn't the only one who was going to catch some shit. Riley decided to do some quick explaining and get the hell out. Doc Seay had run up and was taking in the spotlit scene.

"I'm sorry, ma'am . . . sir," Riley said, indicating all three people. Out of the corner of his eye he could see a young girl of nine or ten standing next to the tent, staring at the still running helicopter in the middle of the clearing. "I'm Chief Riley from Fort Campbell. We're out here investigating reports of some rabid animals and we spotted your campsite through our thermal sights and landed to investigate. I apologize if we caused you any inconvenience. We'll be taking off now and won't bother you again."

Riley headed for the chopper. The man from the tent was obviously torn between jumping on Riley for landing on top of them and confronting the woman, who apparently was his wife, about her little liaison in the woods.

"What did you say your name was again?" the balding little man asked as Riley brushed by him.

"Uh, that's Chief Ryan. R-Y-A-N, sir. I'm with the 101st Airborne Division at Fort Campbell."

Riley rapidly left the little man behind and jogged toward the bird, followed by Seay. They hopped on board and Riley grabbed his headset. "Let's get the hell out of Dodge, Captain."

"Roger that." Barret applied cyclic, pulled in collective, and the aircraft was airborne.

Riley was treated to the sound of Doc Seay laughing as the other man put on his headset. "Chief *Ryan*, huh? 101st, eh? You silver-tongued bastard. What was going on down there anyway?"

Riley allowed himself a laugh, too, now that they were out of there. "Looks like we caught a lady with someone who wasn't her husband, doing something she should have been doing only with her husband. I don't think they're going to be happy campers tonight."

It took them a minute or two to regain their composure, by which time the helicopter was about four kilometers away from the Werners' campsite.

"All right. Let's resume the pattern. Back to the thermals," Riley ordered.

9:15 P.M.

Hapscomb could hear the angry hiss of the Werners arguing inside their tent. He felt a bit sorry for the little girl having to witness all that. He felt nothing but contempt for Mister Werner. The little worm hadn't even had the balls to confront him. After the helicopter lifted, Werner had simply grabbed his wife by the arm and dragged her over to their tent, completely ignoring Hapscomb.

What a wimp, Hapscomb thought. And what was going on with the army landing like that? The fellow wearing the funny-looking goggles had scared the living shit out of Hapscomb, especially when he pointed that M16 at them. The man looked like he was ready to blow them both away in a heartbeat.

Rabid animals, the soldier had said. That was a bunch of bullshit, too. They wouldn't call in the army for that. Sons of bitches had ruined a good piece of ass for him. Hapscomb pulled out his bota and took another drag. A great night ruined 'cause of some fucking army cowboys. He'd be damned lucky if Werner didn't complain to McClanahan and get his ass fired. Son of a bitch sure wouldn't—

Hapscomb's thoughts froze in place as he heard the horses whinny. His eyes narrowed as he looked over to the tree line where he had picketed them. In the dim starlight he could make out all four horses pulling tight against the picket line, straining to get away from the line of black that indicated the edge of the clearing.

What had spooked them? Hapscomb rolled off his sleeping pad and threw on a shirt. One of the horses starting bucking. Hapscomb broke into a jog to reach them.

He ran a hand along a quivering flank. "Whoa, girl, easy. Easy." He looked at the darkened forest that seemed to be the source of the horses' terror. What was out there? Hapscomb had heard old stories of an occasional bear in the area, but there hadn't been any spotted for the last ten years or so.

"What's the matter with them?" Mister Werner demanded as he strode angrily across the clearing, waving the flashlight.

"I don't know. Something's spooked them."

"Well, you'd better calm them down and let my wife and daughter get some sleep. You've caused enough trouble as it is."

Hapscomb wanted to laugh at the sight of the little bald man standing there, looking so righteous in his pajamas. At that moment, however, the horses swung around, catching Hapscomb off guard. They jumped to the left, pushing him out of the way.

Hapscomb looked to the right. Whatever was spooking the horses was moving around the outside of the clearing toward the tent. For the first time, Hapscomb felt a small knot of uneasiness begin to bind his guts. Something was wrong. He'd seen spooked horses before, but not like this. Whatever it was had to be damn close if it was moving that quickly around the camp.

Hapscomb forgot about his problems with Werner. He spoke tersely. "Mister Werner, I think it might be a good idea to get your wife and daughter out of the tent. We'll build up the fire a bit. I don't know what's got the horses all riled up, but I don't like it."

Werner, however, wasn't so quick to forget recent events. "You're just trying to make it seem like you know what you're doing—like you're protecting us to save your job. Don't think I'm not going to report what you did. Don't try to make a little scene here to—"

Hapscomb caught a brief glimpse of something—damned if he knew what it was—moving in the tree line, about fifty feet from the tent.

He ran past the flabbergasted Werner, yelling, "Mrs. Werner! Christie! Get out of the tent!"

As if his yelling was the cue, all hell broke loose. In the space of less than a second, several different facts registered on Hapscomb's various senses.

Two figures broke from the trees, making a beeline for the tent. They were about five and a half feet tall and ran with an unusually swift loping stride. Hapscomb caught a shadowy glimpse of them in the starlight and his heart froze. They had to be demons from hell.

Mrs. Werner stuck her head out of the tent and asked puzzledly, "What?" Mister Werner had started after Hapscomb, yelling, "You son of a bitch, what do you think—"

Hapscomb felt that time had slowed down. His brain was screaming at him to get to the tent, but it seemed as though he was running in slow motion. Mrs. Werner still hadn't spotted the two figures heading for her when, to Hapscomb's consternation, the figures turned and headed toward *him*. He screeched to a halt in the knee-high grass and switched direction. An old joke he'd once heard ran insanely through his mind as he reversed course: Two friends are camping and one comes racing back to camp yelling that he's being chased by a bear. As the man goes by, the friend asks: "Do you think you can outrun a bear?" The first man answers, "No, but I can outrun you."

Hapscomb glanced over his shoulder. Dear God, they were moving fast. They were only ten feet behind him when he passed Mister Werner.

Poor Werner never knew what hit him. One of the demons went high and the other low. Werner let out a surprised grunt from the impact of almost three hundred pounds of flesh. The grunt was replaced by the most terrifying scream Hapscomb had ever heard. He stopped and looked back. Werner's body made a few spastic jerks and then was still, one of the figures straddling the body, the other off to the side, all in the course of less than five seconds.

In the sudden quiet, Hapscomb's breathing sounded loud in his own ears. That sound was split by the scream of Mrs. Werner. At the noise, the two intruders swung their gaze over to the tent, where Mrs. Werner stood, her daughter beside her.

Oh sweet Lord! Hapscomb thought. Please help us. He wanted to yell at Mrs. Werner to shut up, but he was too scared. Any noise and they might head his way, and God knows he didn't want that.

As if on cue, the two figures swung away from Werner's body and casually loped toward Mrs. Werner and her daughter. They seemed to know that this new prey wasn't overly dangerous and they could take their time.

Distract them! one part of Hapscomb's mind screamed at him. Get the fuck out of here! the stronger, self-preservation side ordered. As quickly as he could, without attracting attention, Hapscomb sidled back toward the quivering horses. He kept his eyes on the scene being played out before him. It was like some bad horror movie, except that it was happening for real and he knew he was letting it happen.

The two creatures moved smoothly. One circled right and the other left. Mrs. Werner was frozen, her arms clasping her daughter. In tandem the two beasts accelerated their lope into the terrifying charge that had killed her husband.

Mrs. Werner finally reacted, stepping in front of her daughter in a last gesture of maternal instinct. They took her down quickly; she didn't even have a chance to scream as her throat was torn out.

Hapscomb untied and mounted his horse as he watched Mrs. Werner die. Christie now did the smartest thing that any of the Werner family had done that evening. Instead of screaming or running, the girl started slowly moving away from the scene of her mother's dismemberment. Hapscomb was touched by the girl's pathetic bravery and common sense. He checked his horse, which was trying to bolt. If Christie could make it halfway across the clearing, he'd try to pick her up.

Come on, Christie, Hapscomb prayed silently. The two demons still had their snouts stuck in Mrs. Werner. Bastards must like fresh meat, Hapscomb thought wildly. He watched the girl pick up speed as she got farther away from them.

She was halfway across the clearing, yet Hapscomb didn't act on his earlier silent promise. His conscience railed at him, but his ego told him that those things were too damned fast. They'd get both the girl and him if he moved now. Another ten feet and then he'd—

One of the creatures lifted its head and swung a dripping snout in the direction of Christie and, just beyond, Hapscomb. He felt the hairs on the back of his neck stand up. Christ, no, he thought. I don't want to die like that. He dug his heels into the horse and turned for the trail off to his right rear. At that, the two leapt off the body of Mrs. Werner.

Hapscomb hit the trail at a full gallop. No way could they outrun Angel—she was damned fast. Hapscomb wasn't going to stop until he hit the goddamn Golden Pond Visitor Center, where he knew that there was a twenty-four-hour attendant. Lock the fucking doors and call the goddamn cops. Call the fucking army—

Hapscomb's entire body went rigid as Christie's scream pierced the night. She wailed again and again. Finish her! you demons, Hapscomb prayed as he rode away. Why were they taking so long? After ten long seconds Christie's cries abruptly ceased.

Hapscomb shut Christie out of his mind. The fucking army, he realized. Those things are why that helicopter landed tonight. Rabid animals, my ass. Whatever those things are, they have never been in this area, rabid or not. They aren't anything he'd ever seen before.

As he rode, Hapscomb weighed going directly to the Wrangler Camp, which held the closest phone, but he decided against it. He might be able to make a phone call, but he was afraid that the demons would trail him there and attack.

In another mile he'd hit Lick Creek Road. He'd turn right on that, then in another eight miles or so he'd hit the Golden Pond Visitor Center. He wondered if the attendant there had a gun.

Hapscomb slowed Angel just a bit. Nice and steady, girl, he thought. Just get me there. I sure don't want to have you come up lame on me now.

The horse settled into a steady canter and a quarter mile of road flew by. Soon Lick Creek Road. Hell, there might even be a late night car on the road, although that was extremely doubtful, Hapscomb knew.

Suddenly Angel halted and whinnied. She shook her head from side to side and skittered sideways, almost into the drainage ditch at the side of the dirt road.

What the fuck? Hapscomb wondered, and then he knew. He couldn't see or hear or smell anything, but he just knew, *they* were coming.

God Lord Jesus! Hapscomb wanted to cry. Didn't they have enough back there at the camp? Why'd they have to come after him? In answer, the side of the brain that Hapscomb had overridden in making all his decisions so far this evening whispered its indictment: Because you left the girl to die, asshole, that's why.

Aw, fuck. It ain't fair! Hapscomb gouged his boots into Angel's sides. The horse unexpectedly bucked and, without a saddle, Hapscomb slid off and slammed into the dirt. The horse wasn't stupid. Without the extra weight it took off, sprinting into the darkness away from the bad spirits.

Hapscomb shook his head groggily and rolled to his knees. His right leg throbbed with pain. Must have busted something, he thought idly. He peered back down the road. Where were they? He could see little in the dark. He started crawling down the road, his bad leg dragging in the dirt, eyes peering backward, waiting for those two forms to appear.

They leapt out of the trees above his head. Hapscomb's last thought as his throat was crushed was to pray to God that he be forgiven for leaving the girl to die. But his conscience told him to expect the gates of hell.

Biotech Engineering
9:45 P.M.

Riley yawned as the Huey settled down into the parking lot. In the glare of the building's arc lights he could see Colonel Lewis standing there, waiting for the blades to stop turning. Riley was in no rush to face Lewis. He sat back on the web seat as the pilots slowly decreased throttle until the transmission disengaged. For the next two minutes the massive blades whooped by overhead, slowing slightly on each revolution. Finally they halted.

Riley stepped off, followed by Seay, as Lewis strode up. "Well?"

Riley rubbed his aching eyes. "We spotted quite a few deer, lots of smaller creatures, and one campsite where two people were screwing each other out in the woods—but no monkeys."

Lewis shook his head. "Not good enough. You all need to go back up."

Captain Barret overheard and interjected from where he was tying down the blades. "Sir, with all due respect, we've just put in two hours of goggle time. We also flew for four hours today on and off. That puts us over our limit for crew rest. The—"

"I don't give a shit about your crew rest, Captain. I want you back up in the air *now*."

Barret faced the irate DIA colonel. "Sir, you're not authorized to make us break flight regulations. We don't need crew rest just because we feel a little tired. We need it because we're not too far away from putting this bird into a tree. My eyeballs feel like someone's turned them inside out. I'm not safe to be flying now. Besides that, there's a front coming in and I don't think we're going to be able to do much more flying for a while. At least not at night."

Lewis stabbed a finger at the other helicopter. "What about them? That crew has been sitting on their ass inside the building all evening. They've had plenty of rest. I want them up in the air now."

Barret shook his head. "Sorry, sir. Neither of those pilots are current in NVGs. They're not authorized to do that kind of mission."

Lewis shook his head. "Jesus fucking Christ. What a bunch of wimps." He turned and stalked off toward the lab building.

Riley grinned at the captain. "You sure know how to piss off the colonel, sir."

Barret shrugged. "I'm not going to corkscrew one of these birds into the ground looking for a couple of monkeys in the dark. If it was something important I'd do it, but this is bullshit."

Amen to that, Riley thought. He respected the captain for being safety conscious. He'd seen too many men overextend themselves needlessly and get themselves and others killed because of it. You pushed yourself to the extent that the circumstances justified. If this was a combat mission, he'd have been the first to get on the pilot's ass.

The night sky was rent by a mournful howl echoing from the west. Riley turned and looked out in that direction. Next to him, Doc Seay muttered, "What was that, Dave?"

Riley shook his head. "I don't know." It was something Riley couldn't recall ever hearing, and it sent a chill down his back. He was glad that whatever had made that noise was on the far side of the lake. His next thought was to wonder if that noise had anything to do with their mission. Could monkeys howl like that?

After entering the building, his first act was to grab SSgt. John Carter, the team's lone commo man. "Did you get the message off?"

Carter grinned. "Roger that, chief. Went into the woods, out of range of the cameras on the roof, to send. I imagine that old Sergeant Major Powers was back there copying my manual code to check on it."

Riley smiled back. "Yeah, I'm sure he was. Makes him feel useful. All right. Make sure you get our receive tomorrow morning, and don't let these people know."

"No problem."

Riley tapped him on the shoulder as he passed by. "Good job, John."

10:35 P.M.

Riley rolled off his camping pad and slipped on his boots. The noise of his team members sleeping on the floor of the large office produced a low rumble of mingled snores. Riley carefully stepped over bodies and made his way out the door into the main floor hallway.

He glanced to his left. The elevator leading to the basement was unguarded, but Riley also knew that a DIA man was on duty at the front security console, which monitored this hallway. He was tempted to flip the bird to the camera perched above the far door, but refrained. Riley didn't trust any of the DIA men, and Lewis probably wouldn't see the humor in it.

Riley turned right to make his way to the men's room. As he did so, a door opened almost directly across from him and Doctor Merrit stepped out. She looked surprised at his presence in the hallway.

"Excuse me, I hope I didn't startle you," Riley told her softly.

She shook her head and then, with a quick look down the hallway, gestured for Riley to follow her back into her office. Curious, Riley obliged, shutting the door behind him. He wasn't sure if the guard had seen the brief encounter on the monitor, whether he'd been looking at that particular screen at that particular time. Riley had a feeling that Colonel Lewis wouldn't approve of him talking to either Ward or Merrit without his presence.

As soon as he stepped into Merrit's office, Riley realized that it really didn't matter if they had been seen on the hallway monitor; there was also a camera in this room.

"What's up, ma'am?" Riley inquired. He estimated that it would take the DIA man at the console about half a minute, maybe less, to get someone down here.

Merrit grabbed his arm and looked up into his eyes. For the first time Riley noticed that she had dark green eyes behind those thick glasses. Those eyes were open wide now and had a wild look. Her voice shook and the skin under one eye jerked with a tic. "There's some things that Ward and Lewis didn't tell you about this lab and about what you're doing."

No shit, Riley was tempted to say. Let's go, let's go, Riley thought, watching the doorway out of the corner of his eye. "Like what?"

"You need to be very careful when you're going after the so-called monkeys. They're much much more than that. They're—"

The door swung open and Freeman, the black DIA agent, stood there. "I'm sorry. You two are not to be talking without supervision. Doctor Merrit, you should know better. You were instructed not to interact with any personnel here without permission. Mister Riley, I'm going to have to ask you to leave."

Riley nodded good-naturedly, although inside he was seething. Fucking spooks and their goddamn games. People got killed because of their little secrets. He wondered who the real enemy was here.

Riley headed toward the door. As he brushed by Freeman, he turned and looked back over his shoulder at Merrit. "Good night, Doctor. Hope you sleep well."

As Freeman pulled the door shut, Riley turned and faced him. "With all due respect, sir—and to be quite honest the only respect I hold for you or your partners right now is based purely on rank—what is going on?"

Freeman looked uncomfortable. "What do you mean?"

Riley let out a low incredulous laugh. "Come on, sir! What's the big secret? Why don't you want us talking to Ward and Merrit? A blind man could tell that you all aren't leveling with us. Why don't you trust us? I've been on more classified missions than you've read about."

Freeman shook his head. "There's nothing more that you have a need to know."

Riley leaned toward Freeman, his short, lean body causing even the hulking ex–football player to back up slightly. Riley's amiable appearance was gone, replaced by the intense fury of a man poised on the edge of violence. "Just between you and me, Major, I want you to understand something. If one of my men gets hurt because you all didn't fill us in on what's going on here, I'm going to have your ass. I don't give a shit about your fucking rank or the fucking DIA. That isn't a threat. That's a promise written in blood."

Riley stared hard at Freeman until the bigger man dropped his gaze.

"There's nothing more you need to know," Freeman muttered.

Riley nodded. "Just as long as you know where we stand."

CHAPTER 8
TUESDAY, 7 APRIL

Land Between the Lakes
6:24 A.M.

Pete McClanahan threw the rusty Ford Bronco into neutral, turned off the ignition, and rolled to a halt as the engine sputtered into silence. The eastern sky was just beginning to acquire a dull gray tinge, heralding the coming of dawn. To the west, the horizon was an ominous pitch-black wall, threatening nasty weather. McClanahan eased himself out the door of the truck. After stretching his old aching back, the head wrangler slowly made his way over to the stables, gingerly sipping on a plastic cupful of hot coffee.

Halfway to the one-story wood barn, he stopped and looked around, sensing that something wasn't quite normal. McClanahan slowly scanned the entire Wrangler compound, looking for anything strange.

The horses that had been left out in pasture overnight were all gathered together in the center of the fenced-in field. McClanahan couldn't remember ever seeing them standing that tightly bunched. His forty-three years of horse experience told him that something had spooked them bad.

Better not be those damn kids coming out with their pellet guns again, McClanahan thought angrily. Some teenagers had driven out here a couple of months ago and fired shots into the pasture, hitting two of the horses. McClanahan had seen them from the Wrangler Camp shack and chased them, but their hopped-up road car had outrun his old four-wheel-drive truck.

McClanahan was still shaking his head over the memory when he saw Angel. The mare was standing in the shadows next to the stable doors. McClanahan hurried over. The horse was covered with dried sweat, indicating that she'd made a hard run sometime during the night. But there was no saddle or bridle. McClanahan peered about. No lights were on in the two-room shack that served as headquarters for the Wrangler Camp. Hapscomb's Dodge truck and the Werners' Volvo were still sitting in the parking lot, the only other vehicles there except his truck.

McClanahan's first thought was that Angel had broken the picket line last night and returned home. But that didn't explain why the horse had been in one hell of a hurry. Shit, he hoped nothing had happened to Hapscomb. The young son of a bitch drank too much, but he was one of only two men whom McClanahan could count on to work weekdays during the off season, and he needed Hapscomb to guide a private school group coming in next week. The damn fool better not have gotten drunk and had an accident.

"Guess I better return you to your man, girl," McClanahan whispered as he scratched Angel's neck.

It took him ten minutes to get his own horse saddled and ready to go, and a few more minutes to let Angel finish some hay and water. Then he put a halter on her and tied her off on the horn of his saddle. McClanahan knew that Hapscomb liked taking campers up to a clearing on a knoll above Lick Creek, about three miles away. McClanahan glanced at his watch and estimated. He set off at a gentle amble to meet them there for breakfast, or at least before the storm broke.

Biotech Engineering
7:02 A.M.

"What's on the agenda for today?" Doc Seay inquired as he sipped instant coffee out of a canteen cup.

Riley gestured at one of the government vans. The dogs were tied to a door handle and the two sheriffs were feeding them. "We take the dogs across the lake and pick up the trail on the other side. Ought to be able to run them down today if the weather holds. *If* they're over there." Riley glanced at his watch. "We move out in twenty minutes."

Seay swallowed the last of his MRE issue ration, a less than sumptuous breakfast. "This whole thing is pretty flaky. You know that, don't you, chief?"

Riley agreed. "Yeah. The pieces don't add up. There's something going on that they aren't telling us. I mean besides the obvious stuff that they aren't telling us, like what's in those backpacks."

He watched the other members of the team eat their breakfasts out in the parking lot. The helicopter crews and two sheriffs had been upset the previous evening when they were told they had to spend the night out there. Riley had asked his men to share some food with them. The pilots and crew chiefs were currently preflighting their aircraft.

Seay gestured at the sign in front of the building. "Biotech Engineering. That could mean damn near anything. If they were experimenting with strains of the VX virus on those monkeys, I'd make it a better than even bet that there might be some form of the virus in those backpacks. That would explain why they're so hyper to get those backpacks and monkeys back."

Riley considered that. "Maybe. That would also explain why they haven't notified the local and state police to lend a hand. I mean other than just these two sheriffs, who seem to have been told even less than we have."

Seay leaned toward his team leader from his perch on top of a rucksack. "I'll give you my theory, chief. I think they aren't researching the VX virus here for an antidote. They're researching it to use as a weapon. The Russians developed the original VX. So there's a good chance that the Russians—or the Confederation of Independent States or whatever the hell is left over there—have a vaccine or antidote for it already. Now these people are working on a U.S. version that the original antidote won't work against."

A similar theory had crossed Riley's mind. He disliked the thought that the U.S. government might consider such an operation, but he also was realistic enough to know that a lot of shady activity went on behind the veil of national security. Riley particularly didn't like it because he had every soldier's abhorrence of both chemical and biological weapons. No matter what training they'd received and how good their equipment was, the thought of the invisible threat of chemicals or viruses was much more terrifying than the more brutal and direct ones of the conventional battlefield.

Riley hadn't told Doc about the encounter with Merrit the previous evening. She was a strange woman. What had she meant by "so-called" monkeys? What had she wanted to let him know? And why were Lewis and Freeman determined not to let her communicate?

Riley considered her tone of voice and the tic under her eye. She was a person on the edge; people like that made him nervous, especially on live missions. If they didn't get those monkeys tracked down this morning and finish this thing, Riley decided to try to somehow get hold of her and find out what she was so nervous about. In the meantime, he would repeat his warnings to his men to be extra cautious.

Riley raised his voice so that the entire team could hear. "Listen up. I want everyone to have a magazine in your weapon, round in the chamber, selector switch on safe. I don't want you to take any chances if you run into the monkeys. Shoot first and let the scientists pick up the pieces. Don't get any closer to the bodies than you have to in order to kill them."

Riley pulled out the miniaturized battalion field SOP from his right breast pocket. Using a trigraph, he encoded a sitrep directly from his mind onto a piece of notepad paper. He wanted it sent this morning. The requirement for any deployed team to make contact with the battalion headquarters at least every twelve hours had been implemented by Powers when he was forced up into the S-3 sergeant major slot after his knee injury. It wasn't very popular with most of the teams in the battalion. They felt that it was just another administrative requirement imposed upon them.

Riley thought it was a good idea, not just because the sergeant major was his friend. Riley firmly believed that a team could never have enough training in maintaining a long-range, high-frequency link with higher headquarters. Powers had made the requirement an even more valuable training experience by requiring radio operators to not only burst their messages, but also to send the messages in manual twice after the burst. This kept the operators up to speed on their Morse knee keys. Dating back to the beginning of the OSS (Office of Strategic Services) in World War II, the grandfather of modern-day Special Forces, the ability to send and receive Morse code manually had been an integral part of special operations. The 5th Group standard was 18/18 for communications men, which meant being able to send and receive Morse at eighteen words a minute. The standard for all other team members was 5/5. Unfortunately, even that low standard was difficult for some to attain.

Riley himself felt insecure trying to send and copy Morse. He seemed to have difficulty hearing and translating the dashes and dots. If push came to shove, he would have to write out the dashes and dots and then translate them on paper. It was a weakness in his Special Forces abilities, and he knew that it could be a critical one. His life had been saved three years ago on another mission by one of his old team members from DET-K (Special Forces Detachment Korea) who was able to send out a manual message requesting exfiltration from a dangerous situation in a country where they weren't supposed to be.

For now, though, Riley was content to write out the encrypted messages and give them to his commo man to send. He had too many other things on his mind. He had just about finished the message when Captain Barret strode up.

"I've got bad news, chief. Just got the weather forecast over the FM from Campbell Army Airfield." The pilot pointed to the towering black clouds that had been creeping ever closer during the past hour of gray daylight. "We got a whopper of a storm front headed this way. Should be here in about two hours. Once it hits we're going to be grounded for the duration."

Riley gestured toward the building behind him. "Have you passed the good news on to the colonel, sir?"

Barret shook his head. "Not yet. After last night I'm not too thrilled about talking to Colonel Lewis."

"I'll tell him."

Riley considered the information. Before he went to advise the colonel, he figured that it was best to have an alternate plan to continue the search. With a maximum of two hours of blade time left, they had to make the most of it. Riley didn't think the helicopters were all that much help anyway. They were going to have to catch the creatures from the ground. They'd already been outmaneuvered on foot once. It was time to use a little technology.

Meanwhile, inside the building on the basement level, Colonel Lewis had the misfortune of having to tell General Trollers that the search last night had turned up nothing.

"Goddamnit!" the general roared over the SATCOM net. "The Old Man isn't going to like this. He wasn't ever briefed on the Synbat project, and I have a feeling he's going to be very upset about that, never mind the fact that we lost your little toys. I've got a 0930 meeting tomorrow with the national security advisor. I'm going to have to brief him on this."

"We'll get them today, sir. I'm sure of it. We're sending the dogs across the river."

"It's getting close to being too late. Is this situation still secure on your end?"

"Yes, sir."

"How are you going to proceed today?"

"I'm going to have my people on the ground with the two vans in radio communication with the two helicopters. Five Special Forces people on each bird along with a dog team each. We're going to set the dog teams down, one team north of where we think the Synbats are and one south, along the shore. We'll have them move in; the wind is out of the west so both should pick up the scent. My people will stay on a tarred road called the Trace, which divides the park. Between the four groups we should pin them down pretty quickly."

Lewis nervously fingered the weather report that Gottleib had handed him five minutes ago. The impending storm could spell disaster for any hopes of conducting a search. He wasn't about to inform Trollers of that, though, at least not until he gave it his best shot. He wasn't that confident about the plan he had just briefed either.

"How much have you told the Special Forces people? Do they understand the situation?"

Lewis considered his answer. Freeman had told Lewis about finding the Special Forces warrant officer and Doctor Merrit together, but the tapes from the video and the audio monitors showed that she had been stopped before she revealed anything critical. "I haven't told them any more than the VX antidote cover story. I don't want to change the story now. I think that would cause them to lose confidence in us. They've been instructed to shoot on sight."

"All right. You'd better finish it today. And you'd better recover those backpacks. Call immediately if anything new develops." The radio went dead.

Lewis sighed and leaned back in his chair. He was lost in thought when Gottleib cautiously knocked on the door.

"What is it?"

"Sir, that Special Forces warrant is here to talk to you."

Just what I need now, Lewis thought. "Send him in."

Riley entered the room and faced the colonel at a modified position of parade rest. "Sir, the head pilot, Captain Barret, has informed me that we've got a front heading this way that's going to ground his birds. It's also going to knock out any scent for the dogs while it lasts."

Lewis nodded irritably. No shit, Sherlock. "I know that."

"Sir, I've got an idea of how we can still search over there even without the aircraft and cover a lot more ground than we would on foot."

Lewis leaned forward in his chair. At last someone with answers instead of just problems. "What's your idea, Mister Riley?"

Land Between the Lakes
7:14 A.M.

McClanahan was two miles up Wrangler Trail when his horse, Ginger, in concert with Angel, started acting nervous. "Whoa, girl. What's the matter?"

McClanahan peered up the trail. The two horses were smelling something they didn't like, that was for sure. Wisps of early morning fog still drifted across the trail, obscuring the view. It would be at least another hour before the fog cleared, if it did at all with this front heading in. McClanahan didn't like the sight of the clouds in the west. He figured that the Werners would probably have to cut short their vacation. It wouldn't be any fun in the nasty weather that was coming.

McClanahan spurred Ginger and the horse grudgingly obliged. Angel was much more reluctant, pulling against the lead line.

"I ain't never seen two more stupid horses than you idiots," McClanahan muttered. He was uneasy himself. For the first time he noticed that it was too damn quiet. No birds chirping, no insects, no nothing. Maybe it was just the storm coming. Then again, maybe it wasn't.

McClanahan wondered if Angel showing up at the Wrangler Camp wasn't more than just a busted picket line. Maybe something had happened to Hapscomb. But then why hadn't he seen the Werners or their horses heading back to camp?

As they came to a bend in the trail, Angel stopped, and no amount of tugging or coaxing by McClanahan could get her to move forward. "Goddamnit, girl. You ain't got the sense God gave a rock."

McClanahan looked up the trail, trying to see what was scaring Angel. The dirt road curved left around a solid tangle of growth. He dismounted and tied the two horses to a tree on the side of the trail.

McClanahan had just started walking forward when he heard the distant whop of helicopter blades in the air. The sound carried easily across the blanket of quiet that had settled over this part of the forest. The noise of something man-made caused McClanahan to stop and think for a second. If there was something up ahead that had the horses spooked this bad, then maybe he didn't want to run into whatever it was either. On the other hand, McClanahan's rational side told him that there was nothing in the forest in the Land Between the Lakes area that he should have to fear. The last bear had been sighted almost ten years ago. A rabid animal was about the worst thing he could think of. McClanahan revised that thought—the worst thing he could think of would be humans bent on mischief. He recollected the news he'd heard on the radio this morning about the escaped convicts from Eddyville.

"What the hell am I going to do?" McClanahan muttered to himself; it was a phrase he repeated when under pressure. His wife had chided him about the expression more than once. "Go back and sit on my butt in the shack while Hapscomb is out here without a horse? Maybe the damn fool fell and busted his leg or something. Those music people from Nashville sure wouldn't be much help." Then again maybe the party had run into some criminal-type people. Whichever, he needed to get going.

Having verbally rationalized his decision, McClanahan started walking around the bend, scanning the woods on either side of the trail. He cleared the bend and stopped in his tracks, his eyes growing wide at the sight that greeted him.

Something was lying in the trail—something that looked worse than the worst road kill McClanahan had ever seen. The warning buzzer that was his survival instinct started a low ringing in the back of his mind, telling him that this heap of mangled blood, bones, and muscle was Hapscomb.

McClanahan took a few steps closer, to a point about ten feet from the remains. A custom-made snakeskin boot, drenched in blood, at the end of what McClanahan assumed to be a leg, confirmed his fear. It was Hapscomb.

"Lord help me! What the hell could have done that to a man?" The buzzer in the back of McClanahan's mind started ringing louder, telling him that whatever had done this to Hapscomb might still be around.

"Hellfire—it must have been a damn car." No way, McClanahan's rational mind told him. You want to believe that it was a car, but it wasn't. No car could tear a man apart like that.

At that moment, the horses whinnied loudly. The head wrangler needed no further urging. He turned and ran back to the horses as fast as his old, out-of-shape legs could carry him. Both horses were pulling back on their lead ropes, trying to get loose.

It took all McClanahan's strength for him to untie the horses and mount Ginger. The animals needed no urging to head back the way they came. McClanahan was looking back over his shoulder for whatever had spooked the horses when, with a rush of wind and noise, an army helicopter roared by overhead, perhaps ten feet above the treetops. Both horses bolted and it took all of McClanahan's skill to stay with Ginger.

CHAPTER 9

Land Between the Lakes
7:23 A.M.

Riley's Huey flew straight toward Lake Barkley, while its partner banked right and shot an azimuth back toward Fort Campbell. Riley watched the other aircraft fade into the distance as the dark waters of the lake rushed by below. Four members of his team were on board the other aircraft heading back to home base to implement the idea he had presented to Colonel Lewis.

Riley spotted the easily identifiable inlet at Lick Creek. That jig of shoreline was designated as center of sector. Where the inlet ended, the aircraft—Search One—broke south, to drop the team off at the designated point.

Riley was sitting with his feet dangling over the edge of the aircraft, toes a few inches above the skids. Behind him was the sheriff's deputy, Lamb, holding tight onto his dog's leash. Riley scanned the terrain flashing by beneath them.

As they flew over a small trail, something caught Riley's eye. "Turn back," Riley spoke into the headset he wore. "There was someone on that trail back there with two horses."

"Roger," Captain Barret acknowledged and pulled the Huey around in a steep right-hand bank, reducing airspeed at the same time. In a few seconds the helicopter was in a hover at fifty feet above the ground.

Riley leaned out the left side and peered down at the ground. He saw a man trying to control two runaway horses, and waving one arm as though he was signaling them to land. Riley looked around the immediate area.

"Sir, you think you could set us down in the small clearing about fifty meters off our left side? This guy looks like he wants to talk to us. Maybe he saw something. Radio Search Base and tell them we'll be a few seconds late getting started."

"Roger, no problem."

Riley turned to the sheriff next to him and yelled in the man's ear: "Doc and I will take a look and be right back." Riley signaled to Caruso, Trustin, and Trovinsky to stay on board the helicopter.

The Huey sidled over and Barret lowered his collective, allowing the aircraft to settle straight down into the clearing. As soon as the skids touched, Riley jumped off, followed by Seay. He pushed through the undergrowth toward the trail, the whine of the helicopter behind them dropping down a notch as the pilot reduced throttle to idle.

Riley inspected the man on the horse as he got closer. The old fellow looked terrible; his face was pale and he was looking over his shoulder as if something were behind him.

"Thank God you're here." The man jumped off his jittery horse and tied it to a tree along with the other horse.

Riley looked around the immediate area. Nothing unusual that he could spot. "What's the matter?"

"One of my men's bodies is up there on the trail. Something tore the shit out of him. I don't know what the hell could have done it. He was guiding for a family from Nashville and I don't know where they are. I don't know what the fuck happened. What could do that to a man?"

"Are you sure he's dead?" Doc Seay asked.

The old man was close to going into shock, but he hadn't totally lost it. "I've seen dead people before in the war and Hapscomb is *dead*. He's torn to pieces. Only way I recognized him was by the boots he was wearing. Snake skin. He loved those goddamn boots. Thought he looked good in them. Damn, I never—"

"How far away is the body?" Riley cut in.

"About three hundred feet down the trail. Round that bend there. I was taking his horse back out—came back on its own last night, you see—and I knew my man needed it and then the horses got spooked and wouldn't go around—so I got off and walked around and then I saw him—and then I figured maybe I better get the hell out of there 'cause the horses, they wouldn't go that way anyway—so—"

Riley stopped the old man's ramblings by grabbing his arm. "You stay here. We'll go take a look. My friend here is a medic, so if your man isn't dead we can take care of him." He turned to Seay. "Let's go."

The old man wasn't impressed. "Medic ain't gonna do no good. He's tore up bad. There's blood all over the place, I tell you. There ain't—"

Riley left the old man behind. He flipped the selector lever on his M16A2 to semiautomatic. Seay slipped into place on the right side of the dirt road. They automatically adjusted the muzzles of their weapons to cover across each other's front.

Riley rounded the bend and came to an abrupt halt at the sight of the mangled body. He did a slow scan of the surrounding area— including the trees—before moving any closer. Satisfied that there was no threat in the immediate vicinity that he could see, he nodded for Doc Seay to follow him forward, up to the body.

"Well, he's dead for sure," Seay commented.

"Is that your expert medical opinion?" Riley returned, his words belying the surprise and shock he was feeling.

The sight was sickening, but Riley had seen similar ones. Most people were used to the clean killing shown on TV cop shows. In reality, the human body has a plethora of blood and guts packed into it, which tend to get thrown all over the place when hit with devastating physical trauma. The odor of emptied bowels competed with the sweet, sickly smell of blood and internal organs exposed to the air.

The man, if it was a man, had had his throat almost completely torn through. The chest and stomach cavity had been slashed to ribbons. The face was unidentifiable due to the cuts. If Riley didn't know any better, he'd swear that something had been dining on the man, since there were large chunks of muscle missing.

Doc Seay squatted down next to the body and poked at it with his knife, lifting up the few scraps of clothes. "It's a man. Looks like something wanted to make sure he was dead."

"What could have done that? Bear?"

Seay looked at some of the wounds. "I don't know. Possibly. Probably more than one of whatever it was."

Riley checked the ground for tracks. His eyes narrowed as he spotted one clear print in the dirt. "Son of a bitch." He pointed. "Check that out, Doc. Remind you of anything?"

"These are the same tracks we followed on the other side of the lake. Whatever we were tracking killed this guy. No monkey I ever heard of could do this."

Several thoughts struck Riley in a series of worsening implications. The old man had said something about this man guiding a family. Riley's thoughts flitted to the encounter last night. This had to be the same man they'd run into at the campsite. Which meant that this guide had been killed sometime after 9 P.M. Which also meant that this fellow had been going somewhere in the dark, running away from the campsite. Riley pulled his map out of his cargo pants pocket. The place they had landed the previous evening was less than half a klick away to the southeast.

Riley remembered the little girl he'd seen standing by the tent when he ran back toward the helicopter the previous evening. His face was drawn tight as he addressed Seay. "Doc, we need to get up to that campground ASAP."

Riley started running back down the trail, Doc Seay in hot pursuit. McClanahan was still standing around the bend with his two horses.

"Follow us," Riley yelled at the man as he sprinted by. Riley pushed through the trees into the small clearing where the Huey squatted, blades slowly turning. Riley halted short of the arc of the blades and signaled for Caruso and Trustin to get off the aircraft.

The two men responded to Riley's summons and ran over. Riley yelled into Caruso's ear. "Got the body of a man up the trail through those trees. I want you and Trustin to stay here with the old man. There's a campground we're going up to in the bird. You two hold in place here until someone comes back for you."

Caruso nodded. Riley increased the pressure of his grip on Caruso's arm. "Listen, Lou. I don't know what killed that man, but whatever it is tore the shit out of him. I think it's the same things we've been following the last two days. Whatever they are, they aren't monkeys. Don't hesitate if you see anything strange. Fire first."

"Roger that, chief."

Riley ran toward the helicopter, followed by Seay. He jumped on board and grabbed a headset. "Sir, this is Chief Riley. Remember that campground we landed at last night?"

A short laugh preceded Barret's reply. "How can I forget? You two came running out of there like chickens with your heads cut off."

"We need to get up there as quickly as possible."

"Roger."

The whine of the turbine engine increased and the aircraft shuddered with the increase in power. The skids separated from the ground. Barret increased altitude until he was clear of the trees and then nosed over to the southeast. In less than thirty seconds the clearing appeared dead ahead on top of the knoll.

Riley leaned out the door, peering down as Barret brought the aircraft in. He heard Barret over the intercom. "Sweet Jesus! What the hell happened here?"

The helicopter settled down. Doc Seay raced over to the first body. Riley blinked in the cloud of grass blown up by the aircraft's blades. He leaned back into the helicopter and grabbed Barret. "Sir, I think you need to shut down here. Call Search Base and tell them to get their asses over here ASAP!"

Fort Campbell
7:55 A.M.

Powers heard the helicopter land and limped his way over to the battalion headquarter's back door. Four figures piled off the aircraft and the bird immediately lifted, heading west toward Sabre Army Airfield. Powers could make out the large form of Master Sergeant Knutz leading three other members of ODA 682 in his direction. Powers tenderly shifted his weight to the good leg and waited until Knutz came up. "Where's the rest of the team?"

Knutz shook his head. "Can't tell you that, Sergeant Major. We're on a classified mission."

What an idiot, Powers thought to himself. Obviously Knutz didn't even know that Riley was making commo back; Powers had just been waiting for the 0800 contact. "Then what are you all doing back?"

"Chief sent us back to dispatch our humvees and return."

Powers frowned. He'd hoped that this whole thing was over. "Anything else I'm supposed to know?"

Knutz shook his head. "Nope, Sergeant Major. We're under orders not to talk about this mission."

Powers stuck a large hand into Knutz's chest. "Wait one. If you all are drawing your humvees, are you also drawing your fifties?" he asked, referring to the .50-caliber machine gun that could be mounted on each vehicle.

Knutz obviously hadn't thought of that. "I guess so."

"What about ammunition for the guns?"

Knutz shifted from one foot to the other. "I don't know. I mean, can we get some, Sergeant Major?"

Powers pulled his hand away. He was disgusted at having to do the team sergeant's thinking for him. "Bring your vehicles around to the back of battalion after you draw them and I'll square you away. I'd also suggest that you dump some extra chow in the humvees."

"Thanks, Sergeant Major."

With that the team sergeant headed off for the three-story building that housed the battalion's team rooms to get the keys for the humvees.

The sergeant major limped back to his desk and put on the headphones for the radio. The burst came through and then the manual, very slowly. Since Carter had come back with Knutz, that meant a noncommo man was sending this second message. Good training, Powers thought absently as he checked the man's dots and dashes. When it was done, Powers took off the headphones and swiftly decoded the message.

ZEROTW	OXXODA	SIXEIG	HTTWOX	XSITRE
PXXNEE	DINFOO	NBIOTE	CHXXXB	IOTECH
ENGINE	ERINGX	XDOCTO	RSXXWA	RDXXXW
ARDXXM	ERRITX	XXMERR	ITXXAS	KKATEF
ORHELP	XXFOUR	DEADCI	VILIAN	SBYESC
APEDMO	NKEYSX	XTHISI	SCLASS	IFIEDT
OPSECR	ETNEED	TOKNOW	XXECHE	LONSAB
OVEXXM	ETOYOU	ONLYJU	STINCA	SEXXWI
LLMONI	TORALL	SCHEDU	LEDREC	EIVESX
XAMIGO	XXXXXX			

Powers made sense out of the message groups:

ZERO TWO XX ODA 682 XX
SITREP XX
NEED INFO ON BIOTECH XXX BIOTECH ENGINEERING XX
DOCTORS XX WARD XXX WARD MERRIT XXX
MERRIT XX
ASK KATE FOR HELP XX
FOUR DEAD CIVILIANS BY ESCAPED MONKEYS XX
THIS IS CLASSIFIED TOP SECRET NEED TO KNOW XX
ECHELONS ABOVE XX
ME TO YOU ONLY JUST IN CASE XX
WILL MONITOR ALL SCHEDULED RECEIVES XX
AMIGO

Powers leaned back in his seat and sighed. He'd had a bad feeling about this mission. How could monkeys kill people? Powers hadn't heard anything on the news on the way in to work about any dead civilians, although he had seen the story on the escapees from Eddyville. Upon a moment's reflection, Powers realized that didn't mean anything except that the DIA was doing its job of covering up. Maybe even making up the Eddyville story as a cover for something else.

Powers knew that Riley sending this message, and the previous one, was a security violation. Which would mean deep federal shit for both him and Riley if they were found out. Now Riley wanted to bring Kate in on it. Powers didn't hesitate. He picked up the phone and dialed.

Atlanta, Georgia
9:08 A.M.

Kate Westland signed off on the memorandum of understanding between her Agency and the local FBI office on some minor drug case and threw it into her out box. Another challenging day of pushing paper. The most exciting thing she did here was read local FBI reports on domestic industrial spying and condense them for forwarding to Langley.

She hadn't been overly surprised at the reaction of her bosses upon her return from Colombia the previous year. Despite having successfully completed the assigned mission against one of the largest drug dealers in the world, *and* helping Dave Riley rescue Dan Powers after he was captured during a failed raid on a drug lab, her reception in the hallowed halls of Langley had been extremely chilly. They hadn't appreciated her *technique,* the Latin American station chief had explained. An acrimonious exchange between the Department of Defense and the CIA over the use of Special Forces soldiers in covert actions hadn't helped much either. In the end she'd been swept under the rug to Atlanta, where the only reminders of her days at Langley would be her signature on the weekly report from that field office.

At least Dave had been able to stay in his job, even though the army had moved him out of Bragg as quickly as she'd been exported from Langley. Kate leaned back in her seat and sighed. She was so tired of all this busywork. She even longed for the days when she'd been an analyst deep in the bowels of CIA headquarters; at least there had been worthwhile applications to her work. She thrived on challenges, and this job definitely wasn't one. She wasn't sure what she was going to do. Maybe with a change in administrations the Agency might be overhauled and she could breath some life into her stagnant career, but most likely not. The CIA still was an old boys' network and she was not only a girl, but a maverick one at that. She knew her own capabilities, and the fact that she couldn't use them fully in the present situation was tearing away at her day by day.

Damn! Her mind shifted gears. She owed the local DEA official a reply today on a routine request for information. She had typed it into the computer the previous afternoon but hadn't printed it out. She spun around in her seat and turned on the machine. As the main drive booted up, the phone rang.

"Westland, this line is unsecure."

"Kate, this is Dan Powers."

Kate smiled slightly. It had taken almost a year to get Powers to call her by her first name. She knew he had great difficulty accepting her as an equal, and she wasn't sure if his apparent friendship with her was based more on his relationship with Dave than on true feelings toward her. "What's up, Dan?"

There was a pause. "Uh, well, this is an unsecure line and—"

Kate's heartbeat accelerated. "Has something happened to Dave?" Even as she spoke the words she was surprised at the feelings that had coursed through her in that brief moment—feelings she thought had died months ago.

"No, no. It's just that I need to talk to you and I really can't do that over the phone."

Kate frowned. It sounded like Dan had some classified information to pass to her. But what could he have that she needed to know? "I can go secure. You on a STU III?"

"Yeah. Wait one." She heard a beep, and a button on her phone glowed green, indicating that the conversation was now safe from eavesdropping.

Land Between the Lakes
8:10 A.M.

Colonel Lewis had taken charge as soon as he'd arrived. Riley had the four remaining members of his team spread out in a security perimeter around the knoll.

Down the road, the DIA had relieved Caruso and Trustin of their guardianship, spiriting away McClanahan in one of their vans. The other van was parked near the remnants of the tent and the body of the woman. The girl's body was covered by Riley's poncho. All the corpses had been cut up pretty badly. Teeth had obviously made most of those wounds, but some of the cuts were clean, as though an edged weapon had been used, which didn't make any sense at all.

Riley had seen some bad scenes before, but the sight of the dismembered young girl had penetrated his professional detachment. That, in combination with the realization that he and his team had been lied to since leaving Fort Campbell, raised his anger and disgust to the boiling point. No monkey had done that to those people. The tracks up here were the same as those by the body on the trail and the ones they'd followed on the other side of the lake from the site of the collars. It didn't take a genius to figure out the connection.

Even more galling than the lies, though, was the fact that Riley realized he had made a mistake the previous evening, a mistake that might well have cost these people their lives. After taking off from this location last night, he and Doc Seay had not turned on the thermals again until they were a distance away from the campsite. And the helicopter had not flown back over the campsite during the subsequent search patterns. That had left a gap in the search grid. Whatever did this obviously had been in that gap.

Riley did one last check to make sure that all avenues of approach to the knoll were covered as well as they could be given the few men he had. He warned his men to watch the approaches in the trees. He wasn't going to take any chances.

The weather was swiftly deteriorating. The wind was gusting, carrying traces of rain with it. The sky was a boiling sea of dark clouds. Flashes of lightning lit up the western horizon, slowly followed by the rumble of thunder. Soon the chopper wouldn't be able to fly. Riley was also worried that when the storm broke, the dogs would not be able to get any scent.

Riley glanced back to the center of the knoll. Some of the DIA men were taking pictures of the scene. Lewis and Ward were standing by the man's body, discussing what to do next. The two had said nothing to Riley when they arrived. Riley figured that he'd give them another ten minutes; then they'd better tell him and his men what was going on.

Atlanta
9:14 A.M.

The message that Powers had relayed to Kate from Dave wiped away the depression she had been feeling all morning, replacing it with a churning anxiety. "When did you get this?"

"0800 receive. Four of the guys flew in about fifteen minutes ago. They're drawing the team's humvees right now and are going to head back out toward west of post. I don't think they even know what was in the message."

Kate looked over the critical parts of the message she had written on a notepad on her desk. Biotech Engineering. Doctors Ward and Merrit. "What killed four civilians?"

"The first message Dave sent said that they were hunting down some monkeys that had escaped from a government research facility. Dave's team is opcon to the DIA, so that means there's some shady shit going on. The DIA runs interference for a lot of government research. I'm even thinking that this thing on the news about the escape of those cons from Eddyville might be a DIA cover story."

Kate's mind was already racing ahead, trying to figure out who she could call back in Langley to research this for her. The fact that the DIA was involved, and that there had already been some deaths, didn't deter her, although she was smart enough to realize she had to be extra careful. In fact, the latter matter—the deaths—made her more than willing to put her neck on the line to find out whatever she could. She didn't know what Dave and his teammates were up against, but she wanted to see them all come home in one piece.

"I'll have to do some digging to find out anything. It will take time."

Powers gave her a phone number. "I'll be here until I hear back from you."

Land Between the Lakes
8:24 A.M.

Lewis and Ward stood in the middle of the clearing, surveying the wreckage of their individual plans. Ward knew that these deaths effectively killed his project. The DIA would undoubtedly create some sort of cover story to whitewash this. But Ward had been around the bureaucratic mind-set of the Pentagon and the Black Budget long enough to know that someone was going to take the fall, and that someone was most likely going to be him and his project.

Lewis was viewing the bodies in a different light. General Trollers's insistence on keeping this entire operation secure, and not allowing him to shut down the park, had come back to haunt them. Lewis was at a loss about what to do—a rare experience in his military career. His men had sequestered the old wrangler, McClanahan, and would keep him quiet for a few days. They would then feed him the cover story to explain all the bodies, with a dire warning about national security. But before this was over, Lewis was afraid that the convict cover was going to wear mighty thin.

Lewis shifted gears in his attempt to find a direction for action. The glaring problem right now was that the Synbats were still loose. Not only that, but the backpacks were missing also. The weather was looking decidedly worse by the minute. If the helicopters were grounded, his options would be reduced, although the plan Riley had suggested would help. Lewis looked nervously at his watch. Less than forty-eight hours before the time bomb ticking away in the backpacks was initiated—if they worked.

He spoke to Ward. "Well, your creatures did what they were supposed to, Doctor. I don't know if I should congratulate you or knock the shit out of you. If you had aborted when you were supposed to, we wouldn't be in this predicament."

Even as he said it, Lewis knew that he was wasting his breath. They were in this situation and he had to find the quickest way out of it. It was obvious that some of his own men were spooked. The Special Forces men were acting professionally, and their team leader had set up a secure perimeter around the knoll—something that had not occurred to Lewis until the Green Berets had already done it.

He could see Riley glaring at him from thirty feet away. Lewis knew that it was time to brief the soldiers; the virus story would no longer hold up. The question was, how much should they be told? He would have to answer to Trollers for any security breach.

Regardless of what he told the Special Forces people, Lewis had to keep the two sheriffs in the dark. The two were currently waiting at the Wrangler Camp with one of Lewis's men. Lewis threw off his uncertainty with a decision. He called over one of his aides. "Gottleib, I want you to sweep this site. As soon as you get it as clean as possible, I'm going to bring the dogs to the edge of the camp to get the scent. We'll track these things down and kill them. I don't want the sheriffs to know about the bodies here, though."

Gottleib, an aspiring young captain in the DIA, frowned. "How are we going to keep all this under wraps, sir? We've got four bodies, and that fellow McClanahan who saw one of the bodies on the trail. And the wounds, sir! We're going to have to release the corpses, and no one's going to believe that humans did that."

Lewis turned a cold gaze on his subordinate. "Vehicular accident. The bodies were burned beyond recognition. We have the two vehicles down at the Wrangler Camp—this fellow Hapscomb's pickup and," Lewis checked his notepad, "the Werners' Volvo. I'd say a head-on collision between the two would work very well. We use our own doctors for the autopsies and seal the caskets. And if McClanahan doesn't want to play along for the sake of national security, we can always arrange for him to have been in the pickup truck with Hapscomb. This is the big leagues, Gottleib. We're talking a major national security issue here." Lewis could see his own hidden disgust mirrored in the face of his subordinate. But what the hell else could he do?

Gottleib swallowed and nodded weakly. "Yes, sir. I'll take care of everything."

Lewis turned back to Ward. "I'm going to have you brief the Special Forces men on the Synbats. The only things you need to tell them are . . ."

Atlanta
9:31 A.M.

The sharp buzz sounded twice before the receiver was lifted on the other end. "Research and analysis. Patterson here."

Kate smiled wistfully at the businesslike voice on the other end. She had worked with Drew Patterson back in '89 during the invasion of Panama. Considered one of the best data analysts in the building, Drew had also been deemed a social loser by most of his colleagues. A lonely man with more than twenty-five years' experience in sifting through information and making intelligence out of it, he didn't appear to have much personality when Kate first met him.

After a few weeks, however, Kate had found that he was really a fascinating and caring person beneath his cold intellectual exterior. There had never been a hint of romance between them: Kate was still too bitter over her divorce, and Drew, twenty years her senior, had treated her more as the daughter he'd never had.

"Drew, this is Kate Westland."

The voice on the other end was rich in sincere warmth. "Kate! I haven't heard from you ever since—well, since you know when. Where the heck are you?"

"I'm calling you from Atlanta. Listen, could you do me a favor and go secure? I'm on a STU III."

Patterson didn't seem fazed by her request. There was a brief silence followed by a beep. The line was now secure. Then Patterson's voice came back with a different tone. "Since you asked me to go secure I have to assume that this isn't totally a social call."

Kate looked up at the closed door of the office. She didn't have time to chat. She hoped Drew would come through. "Drew, I need a favor."

His voice was guarded. "Favors are dangerous here."

"I know that."

"Do you have a good reason?"

Kate was sincere in her answer. "I think a friend may be in trouble. Potentially life-threatening trouble."

There was no hesitation on the other end. "All right. You know the ground rules. I'll deny everything if they track this back, but it will still screw me. But I don't have much more time left here anyway. They're going to put me out to pasture in a year or two. Be nice to have a friend I could call up and ask for a favor then. What is it?"

"I need anything you can find out about a research facility in Tennessee run by a firm called Biotech Engineering. I think they're working under a government contract, watched over by the DIA. I've also got two names from that company." She paused to make sure that Patterson was getting all this.

"Shoot."

"A Doctor Ward. And a Doctor Merrit. I think that's M-E-R-R-I-T but I can't be sure of that."

"All right. How do I get hold of you?"

Kate gave him her number.

"How quickly do you need it?"

"Something's happening as we speak, Drew. Something that has already involved death, so the quicker the better."

"All right. I'll do what I can."

CHAPTER 10

Riley's ten-minute limit had passed long ago and Lewis was still fixed in his position at the center of the knoll with Doctor Ward. Riley harnessed his anger and strode over to the two men.

Lewis held up a hand to forestall Riley: "Chief, I know there are some things you want to know and I'm prepared to tell you everything."

"I don't like being lied to, sir. Especially about something that kills people."

"I'm sorry about that," Lewis said smoothly. "Bring your men in and we'll brief them."

Riley gestured around the hill. "What about security?"

Lewis looked at Doctor Ward. "Do you think they'll return?"

Ward shrugged. Since he realized that the curtain had closed on his project, his enthusiasm for the entire operation had waned. There would be no tranquilizing now. "I don't know. I doubt it."

Lewis pointed to where his men were rolling the Werners' remains into body bags. "As soon as we get this place cleaned up, I'm having the dogs brought up and we're going after these things. I think we can take a chance on bringing your men in to find out what they're up against."

Riley whistled, circled his left hand above his head a few times, and then pointed down. His men abandoned the perimeter positions and made their way to his location. After all were present, Riley gestured at Lewis. "The colonel is going to fill us in on what's going on. I want you to listen to him, but your eyeballs can still be watching the tree line."

Lewis assumed a modified position of parade rest as he began. "I apologize for not informing you men from the start, but that wasn't my option. I assure you that decision was made at the highest levels and there was a reason for it. It was felt that this situation could be handled rather easily and quickly."

Lewis gestured around the clearing. "As you can tell, it hasn't turned out that way. Security of the Synbat project was our highest designated priority on this mission. Our number one priority now is to stop these things before they kill again. I'll let Doctor Ward tell you about his project and the creatures you're tracking."

Just great, Riley thought. Now it wasn't monkeys anymore but "creatures." What had Ward been doing in that building?

Ward began hesitantly. "You heard the colonel refer to the Synbat project. Synbat is an abbreviation for synthetic battle forms. At Biotech Engineering we were working on a prototype for a creature that could partially replace the soldier on the battlefield."

Ward glanced around as six sets of unbelieving eyes briefly focused on him. He licked his upper lip. This wasn't a group of staff officers sitting in an air-conditioned room in the Pentagon. He backtracked slightly. "Not in terms of handling sophisticated weaponry or in terms of killing the enemy. Basically, this research was a variation of a project that the navy has been working on for years—training dolphins to recover equipment underwater and also to carry equipment."

Lewis realized that Ward's words weren't going over very well, and he interjected: "There was felt to be a need for a similar form of expendable creature for the army. A creature that could carry equipment or weapons into an environment where we wouldn't send men."

Lewis continued. "We were looking at the possibility of transporting equipment across chemical- or radiation-contaminated areas using an expendable platform."

Is that what he calls these things, Riley thought incredulously, a platform?

"There are all sorts of situations where a living creature capable of cross-country movement would prove valuable and useful if it wasn't an appropriate situation in which to use human beings," Lewis continued.

Riley couldn't think of many combat situations where using human beings *was* appropriate.

Ward picked up the story. "What we did was take a normal baboon and conduct various types of genetic engineering procedures on its growth processes. The baboon is the largest of the simian or, as commonly called, monkey species, which gave us a good base.

"We worked on increasing the size of the creature. The Synbats you are tracking are the fourth generation we have grown. They no longer closely resemble the original body type. The males are about five foot five and weigh between one hundred forty and one hundred fifty pounds. The females are smaller, about five foot two inches in height and one hundred twenty to one hundred thirty pounds. Despite the fact that they are somewhat smaller than you, they hold the advantage in unarmed combat by being quicker and being armed with integral weapons."

"What the hell are integral weapons?" Trovinsky asked.

"Their fangs. The males' fangs measure nineteen centimeters, or a little over four inches. The females' are about sixteen centimeters. As you could see from the bodies here, those fangs have the capability of crushing a grown man's throat. You must remember that their main killing weapons are their fangs. Additionally the creatures are very strong.

"They are extremely quick and aggressive. They can travel on the ground or through the trees. Their movement across Lake Barkley caught me by surprise, since baboons are normally leery of going into water. On the ground they can reach speeds up to twenty-five miles per hour for quick bursts."

"They can't outrun a muzzle velocity of a thousand meters per second," junior weapons man T-bone Troy offered.

Ward showed a spark of life hearing his prized creations questioned for the first time. "No, they can't. But first you have to find them and then you have to hit them before they get you. You all haven't done a very good job of that so far, have you?"

"We haven't known what we were up against either, Doctor," Riley replied heatedly. He gestured around the now-cleared campsite. "So far your Synbats have managed to kill a couple, their daughter, and a guide. Pretty impressive."

"That's enough," Colonel Lewis interceded. "Now you know what you're up against. As soon as the dogs get here we're going after them, and we're going to finish it, this morning. The dog handlers are not to know the information you were just briefed."

"So these creatures aren't carrying any sort of virus?" Doc Seay asked.

"No."

"What about the backpacks?" Seay pursued.

Lewis looked at Ward to answer. "The backpacks are just a training device we worked on with the Synbats to get them used to carrying equipment. The backpacks are rigged with two straps that the Synbats can slip over their arms."

"Then why were we warned to stay away from them?" Seay wasn't going to let this go.

Ward exchanged a look with Lewis that made Riley a little nervous. They still weren't giving the full story. He also wondered about some of the clean cuts on the bodies—he doubted that those were made by fangs.

Lewis fielded the question. "That's not really important right now."

"I have a feeling it might be," Riley interjected.

In response, Lewis reverted back to his standard defense. "Mister Riley, you know enough now to complete your job. From here on out you do what I tell you to do. Right now, I want you to get your people ready to move."

Riley glared at the colonel for a few seconds. He was tempted to say fuck it and walk away from this whole thing. He didn't need this bullshit.

Doc Seay touched Riley's elbow and leaned close, whispering in his ear. "Come on, chief. Don't lose it now. There's nothing you can do about this anyway."

Riley still hesitated, his eyes burning at the senior officer. Despite Doc Seay's presence at his elbow, Riley didn't want to back off. He'd backed off from too many people like Lewis before. He was fed up with it.

"Sir, and I use that term loosely, you can—" Riley was interrupted by the rumble of the other DIA van pulling into the campground with the dog teams on board. Riley bit off his remark, realizing that if he completed that sentence, Lewis would relieve him on the spot and then Knutz would be in charge, which was akin to leaving no one in charge. This was a very dangerous situation. It wasn't the time to let emotions interfere.

As the dog teams got out, Lewis walked away, apparently feeling that in this case discretion was the better part of valor. Riley took a deep breath and came down off his toes. He turned to his men, who had been watching the confrontation with avid interest.

"All right. You know what we're up against. Let's do it. On line, round in the chamber, weapons on safe."

Lewis briefed the sheriffs and then had them get the dogs going again. The animals had no trouble picking up the scent, and the procession moved off the knoll, Riley and Seay in the center, trailing the two sheriffs and their dogs. The rest of ODA 682 was spread out in a wedge-shaped formation, with Riley at the point leading the way. Lewis, Ward, and three other DIA men, including Freeman, brought up the rear. They left the helicopter in the middle of the clearing with the DIA vans parked near it. The knoll would now be the center of operations.

As they passed under the trees, Seay sidled over next to Riley and spoke in a low voice. "Hey, chief, there's something else that was funny about that campsite."

Not taking his eyes off the terrain ahead, Riley asked, "What?"

Seay was also keeping his watch to the front. "The horses."

"What horses?" Riley replied, sparing Seay a brief questioning glance.

"That's what I mean. Where are the Werners' horses? Hapscomb's horse made it back to the Wrangler Camp, but not the Werners', according to the head wrangler. And they weren't at the campsite. What happened to them?"

"Probably broke free."

Seay shook his head. "Then they should have gone back to the Wrangler Camp; horses always head back to the barn."

"Maybe these Synbats got them out in the woods somewhere on their way back."

"I guess so," Seay agreed in an unconvinced tone. "Seems like they would have stayed on the road, though. Woods here are kind of thick for cross-country movement."

Seay's tone of voice made Riley ponder the situation for a few seconds. Doc had a point. Where were the other horses? The area where all four horses had been picketed had been easy to find, along with the trail that Hapscomb had left when he had taken off running. The bridles for the other three horses had been slashed—not untied. He had assumed that Hapscomb had cut the other horses free prior to running.

Riley thought again of the clean cuts on the bodies. Could the Synbats have cut the horses free? Besides being a little chilled at the intelligence level needed to do that, Riley asked himself what their motivation would have been. For a moment he had a vision of monkeys riding off on horses—something right out of *Planet of the Apes*. This is getting too bizarre, Riley thought. The missing horses were another question to heap on top of all the others making up this confused, classified puzzle. It was a question that Riley decided to shelve for the moment.

The Synbats' trail moved south off the knoll. Riley checked his map when they were less than four hundred meters away from the hilltop.

If they continued in this direction, in another half a klick they'd hit Fords Bay, an inlet off Lake Barkley. According to the map, the terrain there dropped off abruptly into the water.

Soon, however, the dogs started drifting west of south and then almost due west. Suddenly both dogs halted and began jumping about.

Riley pushed forward to the handlers. "What's up?"

After a few moments of discussion with his partner, Lamb answered with a question. "You said there were four monkeys, right?"

Riley nodded.

The sheriff pointed south and west. "Well, looks like they split up. The dogs are getting scents from two different directions and are confused."

"Can we follow both?" Riley asked.

The handler shook his head. "We need to go with the stronger of the two first. We work as a team. Then, once we track that one down, we'll let the dogs loose on the other one. Plus we're truly downwind of only one trail now. We'd have to backtrack to get the other one." Lewis and Ward appeared from behind, and the sheriff repeated his explanation.

"How far away do you think they are?" Lewis asked.

Douglas shrugged. "Hard to tell."

The colonel made his decision. "All right. Let's get at least two of them."

Ward seemed troubled. "I'm surprised they separated. They're very group oriented."

Lewis had more important things to worry about. "Maybe they know they're being chased. I don't know and I don't care. Let's get a couple of the sons of bitches. Go after the stronger scent first."

The two sheriffs nudged their dogs off to the west and the party moved out. Soon they hit a dirt trail heading in that direction and the dogs stayed on it.

During a short rest halt, Riley called Trovinsky over. "Mike, check the road a little bit ahead of where the dogs are and see if you can spot any tracks."

Trovinsky moved ten feet past the two policemen. He spent a minute there and then returned. "Roger that, chief. Two sets of tracks, moving right up the center of the trail to the west. One set larger than the other."

Riley unfolded his map and peered at it, holding it steady against the wind that threatened to rip it out of his hands. They were almost a kilometer from the Werners' campsite. This trail was marked on the map and joined up with Lick Creek Road in another five hundred meters. He had a feeling that the creatures were deliberately leading them this way. Every move the animals had made since escaping from the lab seems to have been made for a reason.

Colonel Lewis gave the order to move and they picked up the trail again. Within fifteen minutes they arrived at the single-lane hard-topped road, labeled Lick Creek Road on the map. The dogs moved unerringly straight down the road for four hundred meters to where an improved gravel road headed off to the west and Lick Creek Road turned south. The dogs took the gravel road, eagerly pulling their handlers along behind.

Riley consulted his map again. They were now on Fords Bay Road, still heading almost due west. The Synbats were making no attempt to hide their trail or take to the trees, and they'd already covered almost three kilometers from the site of the Werner massacre. They were moving in practically a straight line. This was all too easy in Riley's opinion.

It occurred to Riley that the creatures might be outrunning them, but it obviously hadn't occurred to either Lewis or Ward. Riley was tempted not to say anything, but the thought of one of those things running into some innocent civilians negated his antipathy toward Ward and Lewis. He slowed slightly, falling back to Lewis's party, signaling for Seay to take the lead.

As they tramped down the road, Riley looked over at Ward. "Doctor, how fast can these Synbats move? I mean at a steady pace."

Ward shook his head. "I don't know. We've never field-tested them on that parameter."

Riley decided to clarify what he was asking, since it was obvious that the doctor had not understood the implications of his question. "What I want to determine is whether we're gaining ground on these things. They may be staying a set distance ahead of us or even pulling away."

Riley could see the question sink home on Lewis. The colonel abruptly stopped. "Tell your men and the sheriffs to hold up, Riley." He unclipped a Motorola radio from his belt. "Search Base, this is Six. Over."

Riley couldn't hear the reply, but he could follow Lewis's side.

"Have the Special Forces people gotten back from Campbell yet? Over."

Pause.

"All right. Give me a call the minute they do. What about the helicopter? Over."

Riley could tell by Lewis's expression that the answer wasn't a good one.

"OK. Have them secure the helicopter there. I want you to move Base Two out to our location here. We're presently—hold one." The colonel paused and raised his eyebrows inquisitively at Riley.

"Fords Bay Road, about three klicks from the camp."

"Fords Bay Road. We're about three kilometers west of your position. I want you here ASAP. Out."

As the squelch on the radio went out, the rain began pouring down in earnest. Riley shielded his face from the blasts of water that the westerly wind threw at him. This was going to complicate things quite a bit. He made his way over to the two sheriffs, who were taking meager shelter under a large oak. He couldn't tell who looked more unhappy: the wet dogs or the two soaked sheriffs. "Can you guys do anything now?"

"Hell, no. Dogs won't be able to smell and we can't even see. Why don't we call it a day and pick this up tomorrow?"

Because we got four bodies and we don't want any more, Riley answered silently. Still, if the dogs were ineffective now, it seemed pointless to keep the handlers out here. Unfortunately this wasn't Riley's decision to make. He hunkered down with his team in a loose security perimeter, waiting for Lewis to give further instructions.

Atlanta
10:06 A.M.

Kate grabbed the phone on the first ring. "Westland."

"Kate, it's Drew. Go secure please."

"I'm secure. What have you got?"

"First off, you need to know we're dealing with Red Level Two, Q clearance information here. You know what that means. Do you still want me to tell you?"

Kate indeed knew what that meant. Heavy shit if they got caught digging around. Red Level Two was the next to highest security level possible. "Go ahead."

Patterson was all business as he laid out the few facts he had dredged up. "Biotech Engineering is working under direct contract for the Pentagon."

Kate had figured as much. "Black Budget?"

"Yes. Trollers's people. I couldn't get too much out of the computer. They're still being smart over there and keeping all their files in paper copy and on disk—nothing incriminating in their central data base hard drive. I got more from running the two names you gave me through the unclassified data base.

"Ward—that's Doctor Glen Lowell Ward. Graduated Harvard in 1968 with an M.D. Then earned a doctorate in genetics in 1974 from Stanford. He's considered one of the top men in the field. His specialty is animal growth. He was one of the developers of the porcine growth hormone."

Kate interrupted. "What's that?"

"It's something they inject into pigs. Makes them develop faster, more efficiently, with leaner meat. The animals reach market size approximately ten days earlier. That doesn't sound like very much until you multiply the number of pigs by the overhead for those ten days, then it comes out to quite a bit of money."

"Why's he working for the government?"

"I don't know, Kate, but if I had to make a guess I'd say for the research money and more importantly the ability to work without as many restrictions. I also found some news reports that he was involved in work with human fetal tissue that caused a bit of a stink several years ago."

"Do you have anything on what he's working on now?"

"No. The other name—Merrit. That's Doctor Robin Merrit. Graduated University of Tennessee with a doctorate in bioengineering in 1985. Worked for four years at the University of Texas at Austin as a lab researcher. Her specialty is recombinant DNA."

Kate considered the information along with Riley's message. "Drew, if you add those two people in with four bodies and monkeys, what do you come up with?"

Patterson's words were chilling. "I'd say they've been doing something to those monkeys. In fact they may no longer be monkeys."

"Whatever they are, they've escaped, and my friends are involved in the security response."

Patterson's voice changed from professional to personal. "Listen, Kate. You know that these people play hardball. If there are deaths involved there's going to be a cover-up, and some very high-level and powerful people will be behind it. Although your friends are caught up in it, there really isn't much we can do. And I'd say that whatever your friends are being told probably isn't the whole truth either. I'd suggest you lay low on this."

Kate knew that Patterson had made a valid point. There really wasn't much she could do to help Dave, other than relay the information to Powers. "Is there anything else, Drew?"

"No. Do you want me to keep digging? I'm really not sure there's anything more I can find out without raising a red flag."

Kate considered the offer. "If you can't get anything on the program itself, maybe you can dig up some more information on those two people. Anything that could possibly indicate what's going on. How about checking their clearance investigations?"

"All right. Be careful."

"I'll do that. Out here." She pressed the OFF button briefly, then turned the phone back on and called Powers.

Land Between the Lakes
10:13 A.M.

The DIA van finally pulled up and Lewis got in the back, gesturing for Ward and Riley to join him. The inside was packed with electronic equipment and smelled of wet clothes. There were no windows and the driver's compartment was separated from the rear by a thick black curtain. Lewis commandeered a swivel seat facing a communication system. Riley sat down on the floor and leaned his back against the door. Two other DIA men sat in their own chairs looking at the colonel expectantly. Ward slumped into another seat, managing somehow to look more miserable than everyone else.

"What did the sheriffs have to say about the dogs?"

Riley ran a hand across his forehead, trying to stop the water from dripping into his eyes. "The dogs are done for until this storm stops."

"You have any suggestions?"

Riley was slightly surprised to be asked that by Lewis. He realized that the colonel must be at the end of his rope. He considered his reply. The Synbats, or at least two of them, were somewhere not too far ahead. Although the dogs were no longer useful, and visibility was down to about fifty feet, they couldn't just drop this and go back to the lab. He checked his watch.

"My men should be back here with the humvees in a little while—I'd say anywhere from fifteen minutes to a half hour. Without them, we'd just be blundering around. I suggest we wait for them to get here and, while we're waiting, work out a search pattern so we can get started the minute they arrive."

Lewis got up from his chair and stepped over to an acetated map stapled on a board. "Let's do it."

In fifteen minutes they had worked out the rudiments of a plan that would allow them to quarter as much of the area as conditions and trails would permit. Riley wasn't optimistic about their chances of finding the Synbats in this weather without the dogs, especially if the creatures kept moving, but he knew that they had to give it their best shot.

Someone pounded on the door and Riley slid it open to the whipping rain. Knutz stood there wearing a Goretex rain suit.

"Got the vehicles, chief."

"All right." Riley took his waterproof case containing the map of the area and tied it with a length of cord to the buttonhole on his right cargo pocket, then zipped up his rain jacket. Ignoring the weather, Riley gathered his team around the hood of the humvee on the right. The other three vehicles were parked next to it, their squared chassis held high above the mud by the beefed-up suspension.

Humvee is the nickname for H.M.M.W.V.: high-mobility, multipurpose, wheeled vehicle. The humvee started coming into service in the mid-eighties, replacing not only the venerable jeep, but also the gamma goat cargo carrier and the mechanical mule used by airborne units. The vehicle had become particularly popular during the Persian Gulf War. The basic design was a four by four, powered by a 6.2-liter V-8 diesel engine. Its rated top speed was sixty-five miles an hour, but members of 5th Group had broken that barrier several times. It was capable of climbing a sixty-degree embankment, fording five feet of water, and could run for thirty miles with all four wheels flat.

The 5th Special Forces Group had taken the basic-issue humvee and modified it for operations in Southwest Asia, the group's area of operations. Each vehicle mounted either a .50-caliber machine gun or 40mm automatic grenade launcher in an open hatch in the center of the roof: sort of an armed sunroof. The gunner stood with his chest out of the vehicle, and the pedestal-mounted gun was capable of firing 360 degrees. The humvees also had FM radio capability. Each team in the group had four vehicles assigned.

After outlining the various areas of responsibility to the vehicle commanders, Riley added some final words. "We'll go with team SOP for breakdown on crews. I want the guns manned and all quarters scanned. I know that the weather conditions aren't the greatest, but we're dealing with something that has killed and will do so again until we stop it.

"Don't underestimate these things. Just because you have weapons, don't think you hold the advantage." He looked around at the wet faces and felt a slight unease. He was leading men into a potentially life-threatening situation, and he felt a strong sense of responsibility for each of them.

"We'll search until dark. Stay in contact on your FM radios according to schedule. The van back at the campsite will be called Search Base. Colonel Lewis's call sign is Search Six in that van there. You know our call signs. Everyone make sure you check the headspace and timing on your fifties before moving out. Any questions?"

Doc Seay raised a hand. "What if we come into contact with any civilians? What authority do we have over them?"

Riley turned to Colonel Lewis. "Sir, can you give us something on that?"

Lewis had come out of the van to watch the briefing and now he pushed his way in next to Riley. "Technically we don't have any authority over civilians. I can't even get permission to seal off the area yet. But let me tell you all something. These things have already killed. I don't want any more deaths. You come across anybody, you tell them to get the hell out of the area. If they ask you why, tell them it is a federal security exercise. They might not believe you, but at least you've given it your best shot."

Riley was surprised for the second time that day by the DIA man. Obviously, he did care somewhat about what he was doing, and about people as well. Riley sensed that in a way Lewis was as upset as he was about what had happened so far. One of the greatest drawbacks of military service was that sometimes you didn't want to be involved in a particular situation but you had to do your best anyway.

Everything that needed to be said had been said. Riley put his map away. "Let's move out."

The ten men of ODA 682 broke down into four groups and hopped into their respective vehicles. Ranger One was Riley's humvee and call sign. He had the team's only commo man, John Carter, as his driver. Riley would man the gun and radio.

Ranger Two was commanded by Knutz with T-bone as driver. Ranger Three was Doc Seay's with Bartlett as driver and Caruso along for the ride. Bob Philips was in charge of Ranger Four; Trustin was the driver and Trovinsky was also part of that crew.

The four humvees rolled out, vehicle commanders standing in the top hatch manning the .50-caliber machine guns. The drivers were scrunched up in their seats, noses pressed against the flat pane of glass that served as a windshield, as the wipers struggled against the pounding rain. Both drivers and commanders wore headsets with boom mikes that allowed them to work both the radios and intercom. It looked as though it was going to be a long, wet day driving around in the mud.

Fort Campbell
11:23 A.M.

Colonel Hossey drummed his fingers on the desktop. The door across the room opened and Powers stepped in. The NCO stopped at the appropriate two steps in front of the desk and snapped off a brisk salute.

"Sergeant Major Powers reporting as ordered, sir."

"Sit down, Dan." Hossey waited until Powers was settled. "You have contact with six-eight-two?"

"Yes, sir."

"What's going on?"

Powers considered his answer carefully. "As far as I know they're doing some classified work for the DIA in the vicinity of Land Between the Lakes, sir."

"When will they be back?"

"I don't know, sir."

"When was your last receive?"

"Zero eight this morning, sir."

"Anything interesting in the message?"

Powers hesitated. "No, sir."

"Then why did they draw their humvees and fifties this morning? With live ammunition?"

Powers knew he couldn't keep something like that a secret. "I don't know, sir. I saw Master Sergeant Knutz when he came back in and he wouldn't tell me. He said it was classified."

"Do you have any idea what they are involved in?"

"No, sir."

Hossey looked long and hard at the sergeant major. "Dan, I know we're dealing with classified material that we don't have a need to know. But I also know that you and Dave Riley are very tight, and I have a strong suspicion that he has at least given you an idea of what's going on out there. My primary concern is the safety of my men. I want to know if they are in a dangerous situation."

Powers sighed. He reached into his right cargo pocket and pulled out the hard copies of all the sends and receives for 682. He handed them across the desk to the group commander.

It took Hossey only a couple of minutes to go through them all. "I don't like this, Dan. Four deaths, yet there was nothing on the news other than that prison break stuff. Nor have I been informed of anything by the DIA. What did Riley's friend find out?"

Powers was surprised that Hossey hadn't gotten upset over that part. "Just some information on the doctors working at the lab." He handed over the draft of the message he was going to send to Riley later in the day.

Hossey looked at it. "This is some bad stuff. Genetic engineering. God knows what they're messing with out there." He grabbed a notepad and wrote on it. "I want you to add this to your next message."

Powers took the slip of paper along with all the messages. "Yes, sir."

"Now, get out of here and let me get some work done."

CHAPTER 11

Land Between the Lakes
2:30 P.M.

"Look at them damn rebels," Jeremiah muttered. "I thought they was supposed to be setting up yonder along the holler."

"It don't start till tomorrow, Jer." Louis, the elder of the Sattler brothers, locked the brake on the tractor trailer truck and turned off the engine. "I guess they're setting up here for tonight and are leaving their trailers and such in the parking lot for the duration. I'm sure they'll be gone tomorrow."

"I don't want to be spending no night this close to rebels." Jeremiah spit a large wad of tobacco out the window on his side, then opened the door and followed it out. Louis exited his door and met his brother in front of their rig.

Four men on horses splattered by in the rain and tipped their hats. Louis returned the gesture while his brother pointedly ignored the riders. The men wore the light gray and butternut of southern cavalry. Jeremiah noted the insignia on their belt buckles—3d Georgia Cavalry.

Jeremiah and his brother were dressed in the dark blue coats and light blue pants of Union soldiers. Their insignia designated them as members of the 7th Cavalry—the Garry Owen Regiment. Louis was wearing the rank of a lieutenant; Jeremiah only fifteen years young, was a private.

"There's the colonel. Let's see where we picket the horses."

The two brothers had just driven seven hours from the regiment's hometown of Waukegan, Illinois, a moderate-sized city on the north

side of Chicago. A truck driver in his other life, Louis hauled the trailer
containing eight of the regiment's horses whenever the unit traveled
to a reenactment. The rest of the men should be arriving later in the
day and on into the evening in several cars. The long weekend's fes-
tivities would start this evening with a formal mustering of the Confederate and Union forces on the large open field three miles to the
south of the LBL Wrangler Camp. Then the two groups would sepa-
rate and conduct mock battle for the two days before heading home
Sunday evening.

Louis was looking forward to this camp. It was predicted that there
would be units from almost every state east of the Mississippi. A visitor
wandering through the area would have felt transported a hundred and
thirty years to an era of citizen-soldiers who waged the bloodiest war
the world had seen up until that point.

Every detail was painstakingly exact, from the horses' rigs to the
wire-rim glasses the men wore. No modern tents were pitched in the
campground; rather there were canvas tarps stretched between trees,
and men cooking "sloosh" on their ramrods over open fires.

At every reenactment, Louis felt himself sent back to a time when
he should have been born. In his heart he was a cavalryman in the 7th
Cavalry. His other existence as a truck driver for Red Ball Lines was
just to provide him the means to explore his real life on these weekend trips.

The colonel directed them to picket the horses on a rope between
two trees on the edge of the field and throw some feed to the animals
for the night. Wisps of fog and the light, misty rain combined to reduce visibility to less than a hundred yards.

That task done, the two brothers looked for a spot to string up their
tarp. Jeremiah was adamant about not setting up within sight of any
rebel camps. Sometimes Louis worried about his little brother; he took
the whole thing way too seriously.

At Jeremiah's insistence, the two set up their camp the farthest east,
out in the woods. After getting their gear settled in, they headed over
to the main encampment to join in an afternoon and evening of au-
thentic Civil War camp merriment. The only thing lacking were the
camp followers.

Jeremiah was carrying his brother's rifle in addition to his own. Louis
took charge of the canteen full of "Oh-be-joyful," which he had started
sipping when they'd crossed the Illinois-Kentucky state line. He was

feeling no pain and didn't even notice the light rain. They had just reached the edge of the forest when Jeremiah halted, his brother bumping into him.

"Whassa-matter?" Louis slurred.

"Listen."

"To what?"

"It's quiet." Jeremiah's fifteen-year-old mind was in tune with the forest and the creatures in it. And the creatures were lying low and quiet. From ahead, the sounds of the main encampment could be faintly heard.

Louis just wanted to get there and share his canteen with the others. He tugged on his brother's arm. "Come on."

"Shh!" Jeremiah didn't know what was happening, but if all the woodland animals were being still, it might be good for the two humans to do the same. He strained his eyes, trying to see, turning his head from side to side. Something was coming. He wasn't sure what it was or from where, but it was coming.

"Here," he whispered, handing his brother his musket. "It's charged. Ain't got time to put a ball in it."

Visibility was poor. Jeremiah put his musket to his hip, muzzle pointing out. The part of him that went to school every day told him he was being foolish, but the part of him that spent the afternoons and weekends in the forest told him to beware.

His seriousness had finally gotten through to his brother, who matched his position. "What are we waiting for?"

"I don't know, but there's—"

Something large flickered across his field of vision—up, above their heads in the trees. Jeremiah swung the muzzle up and pulled the trigger. The rifle roared and a tongue of flame licked up toward the branches. There was a loud screech and suddenly the branches were alive with movement. Louis blindly followed suit with his musket.

The noises in the branches moved away. Jeremiah quickly reloaded, his hands running through the twelve steps with the ease born of thousands of practices. This time, though, he included the one step they never did at reenactments: He inserted the .60-caliber minié ball. He wished he'd had a round in the weapon instead of just the powder charge on the first shot. He didn't know exactly what he had glimpsed in that brief second, but there was no doubting it was bad.

"What was up in the trees?" Louis was fully alert now.

Jeremiah pointed his loaded weapon, listening. The woodland sounds were coming back slowly. Whatever had been in the trees—it or they— was gone. The younger Sattler felt a chill hand settle over his heart. He didn't know why, but he knew.

"It was a demon." He turned to look at his brother. "It was here to claim us."

Louis wanted to laugh out loud at his brother's words, but he'd long ago learned that Jeremiah was a different sort of person who sensed things that others didn't. Instead of laughter, he felt a sense of unease wrap around him. He pulled his brother by the arm. "Come on. Let's get over to the main camp."

2:34 P.M.

In his humvee two miles to the northeast, Riley shook the rain off his goggles and looked at his map. They'd covered a lot of ground in the last several hours with no results. The Synbats could be hiding forty feet off the road and they'd never spot them. They were going to need a lot of luck to run into them as long as the weather stayed bad. The rain had let up quite a bit, but using the dogs was still out of the question.

Something was nagging at Riley and he couldn't quite put his finger on it. He had a feeling that no one knew exactly what was going on anymore. The Synbats' escape was a mystery, and they had picked up no more clues. The removal of the collars also muddied the picture. What bothered Riley the most, though, was the way the whole thing had been handled. If he had been told what the Synbats truly were in the beginning, he would have pushed the search harder, especially last night. The vision of that young girl lying in the wet grass was seared into Riley's memory.

If the Synbats were just altered baboons, Riley couldn't blame the creatures. He blamed the system—and the people who made up the system—that designed such things with no regard for the consequences, then lied to the people trying to bail them out.

There had been no sound reason for Freeman and Lewis not to tell him and his men the truth about the Synbats. Yet Riley wasn't surprised. Secrecy was more of a habit than anything else. A maxim of the intelligence community was to never say anything unless absolutely necessary. In addition there were still too many loose ends, too many things that didn't fit. They *still* hadn't been told everything.

Riley watched the woods roll slowly by, shifting his gaze from right to left. The rumble of the engine and the moisture-filled air deadened any sounds. If they hadn't found the Synbats by evening, he wondered what Lewis's next step was going to be.

2:57 P.M.

At the campsite Captain Barret watched the rain run off the helicopter's Plexiglas windshield in shallow rivulets. Through the earpieces in his helmet he could hear the Special Forces soldiers in their humvees talking to each other as they searched. Sitting here dry in the helicopter was one of the perks of being a pilot rather than a ground pounder— almost as good as the extra $650 a month in flight pay.

The captain pulled back one of the ear cups and turned to his co-pilot. "How long before you think we'll be authorized to take off, Steve?"

Steve Vergil, the Huey's copilot, popped his gum and put down the magazine he'd been reading. "Awhile. Last weather report said it might clear up a little in a couple of hours. We might get a brief window of no rain and mist, but we can't count on it for long." He gestured out the front. "The wind seems to have died down a little."

Barret looked over his shoulder into the back. The crew chief, Specialist Fourth Class Klohen, was stretched out on the web seats sleeping. Another exciting day in airborne country. They'd been sitting there all day, and Barret had no idea if they were going to spend another night out here.

He returned his bored gaze to the front. The government van was parked about forty meters away and shut securely. Barret didn't know who the spooks in the van were, but they had whisked away the bod-ies from the clearing in record time. Whatever was going on was some bad shit and Barret wanted to keep his feet as far out of it as possible.

Inside the DIA van—Search Base—Doctor Ward was also listen-ing over the radio's speaker to the intermittent reports from the search teams. One of the two DIA men was using a grease pencil to mark the movements of the humvees on the acetate cover of an area map. The vehicles had already searched a large square around the knoll and were beginning to move westward toward the Wrangler Camp. Ward thought that they had little chance of finding the Synbats. There had never been a provision for finding the creatures if the collars were removed.

The other DIA man, Gottleib, was sitting in front of the radios reading a novel. Ward felt uneasy and claustrophobic in the darkened interior, with no window to view the outside world. He thought about climbing up to the driver's seat to look out the front window, but decided he'd rather go outside.

He stood up, pulling his windbreaker tightly around himself. "I have to take a leak."

Gottleib ignored him, and the other man simply nodded. Ward slid open the side panel door and was greeted by a light but steady downpour. At least it wasn't as windy as before. Ward stepped out and shut the door behind him. He was damp all over anyway so the fresh rain didn't bother him.

Actually, now that he was out, he really did have to urinate. He walked over toward the tree line, stopped about ten feet shy, and unzipped his pants. His urine mingled with the raindrops splattering the ground. As he stood there, he casually scanned the forest. His gaze froze on a pair of golden eyes glaring intently back at him.

Ward's bladder was already voided, but the overwhelming fear that gripped him caused his sphincter muscles to loosen. Wet shit slid down the inside of his trousers. Ward knew that he was dead; it was just a question of how quickly. He couldn't even summon the strength to turn and look back toward the van or the helicopter to see how far away they were.

In the helicopter, Barret had watched the doctor climb out of the van and walk to the tree line. He was the sole witness, other than Ward, to the events of the next ten seconds. He could see the doctor stiffen and freeze. He was just beginning to think how odd that was when a large brown blur flashed across the ten feet of open area from the tree line and knocked the doctor to the ground.

"Jesus Christ!" Barret yelled as he shot bolt upright in his seat. He considered going out to help, but quickly vetoed that idea. Hell, they didn't have a weapon bigger than a survival knife between the three of them on the aircraft.

Outside, Ward was flailing his arms futilely at the Synbat. Barret keyed the mike and screamed into it. "Search Base, this is Search One! We've got one of those things outside and it's attacking the doctor! Over." Even as he finished, Barret realized that he could have phrased the message more clearly.

The reply lacked the urgency the words should have ignited. Gottleib was confused. "This is Search Base. What things are you talking about? Over."

Barret could see that Ward had stopped moving. The captain tried to clarify his first message, speaking slowly into the mike. His copilot and crew chief, alerted by his yell, peered out the glass with him, mesmerized by the scene being played out in front of them. "One of those creatures has got the doctor down on the ground right outside the van. I think the doctor is dead."

Gottleib apparently had the IQ of a gnat. "Are you bullshitting me?" The DIA captain kept the mike keyed as he talked to his partner. "Pete, check on the doctor outside. The people in the chopper say he's been attacked."

As a squelch came on indicating that the mike had been released, a new party broke in: Lewis from the other van. "This is Search Six. What's going on back there? Over."

Barret yelled into the radio, "No! Don't go out." But it was too late. The creature left the body and headed for the van. Barret had a side view as the door to the van slid open. The Synbat was on the DIA man before he even got a foot on the ground.

"Let's get the hell out of here!" Barret's words broke the copilot and crew chief out of their spectator modes.

Vergil reached for the checklist on his kneeboard and started reading it off.

"Fuck the checklist!" Barret screamed. "Generator switch to start. Fuel on." At the same time, the pilot rolled the throttle to the start position and pulled the start trigger. The turbine engine slowly whined to life. In the rear the crew chief was securing all the loose equipment.

Barret watched the N-1 gauge, the indicator of the engine's RPMs, slowly rise. At 15 percent the blades overhead finally began moving. Since he had been listening to the radio, the battery was down and the whole process was taking slightly longer than it normally would have. A minute at least, Barret calculated, before he could get them into the air.

Inside the van, Gottleib whirled in his seat as Pete crashed to the floor with the Synbat on top of him. Blood was spurting from a wound in the man's neck. As Pete's screams echoed off the panels, Gottleib reached for the MP-5 lying on the radio console. Sensing the new threat, the Synbat sprang off the downed man with startling speed and lashed forward.

Barret heard the roar of a submachine gun and a dying scream from the live mike in the van. The gun roared again.

"What the fuck is going on? Over." Lewis's voice crackled in the headset.

Barret keyed the radio. "I heard gunfire from inside the van. I think they shot it." Nevertheless, he was going to get into the air just in case.

"Search Base, this is Search Six. Report. Over."

No answer.

Forty seconds since starting and 40 percent power. The copilot turned on the inverter switch. "Straight to full power, watch the gauges," Barret commanded, ignoring the usual safety check.

The whine of the engine increased. Only ten, maybe fifteen seconds at the outside before they'd be in the air. Barret wondered why the men in the van didn't answer.

The Synbat appeared in the door to the van, MP-5 in hand. Long arms awkwardly held the weapon's stock to its body. The bowed legs were spread apart in a grotesque replication of a firing stance. Matted brown hair hung limply over the entire body and the protruding jaw dripped blood. The eyes scanned the clearing and focused on the source of all the noise.

"Jesus Christ! It's fucking armed!" Barret yelled as rounds slammed into the Plexiglas below him. Large cracks appeared as the bullets ricocheted off the nose of the aircraft. The Synbat pulled the trigger again, but the gun was out of ammunition. Throwing down the sub, the creature sprinted toward the helicopter.

Screw the safety requirements and the possibility of overtemp! Barret slammed the throttle to full on and hauled in an armload of collective. The chopper shuddered.

The Synbat came in for its attack, aiming for the exact point at which it had fired. It hit headfirst and the Plexiglas shattered. "You have the controls!" Barret screamed as he pulled his feet off the tail-rotor pedals, getting them out of reach of the two powerful hands that scrabbled blindly at him. Barret could see blood pouring from wounds in the creature's head as two golden eyes stared up at him.

The copilot repeated Barret's efforts at the controls, and this time the aircraft slowly lifted. Grasping for a hold, the Synbat snatched Barret's right pedal, causing the tail of the aircraft to swing violently to the right. Vergil desperately pressed on his left pedal to counteract. Barret stomped down on the creature's hand. That, in combination with the swing of the helicopter, caused the Synbat to lose its grip. A jagged edge of the windshield tore deeply into its left arm as it released its hold.

Barret sighed with relief as the creature fell off the aircraft onto the ground twenty feet below and lay there stunned. The copilot finally regained control of the wildly careening helicopter.

Vergil screamed a curse as the tail rotor tore into a tree behind them and seized up. They didn't even have time for an emergency reaction as the helicopter inverted and went down. One blade of the main rotor struck the ground first, twisting the other blade; it slashed into the cockpit, cutting both Barret and his copilot in half. The crew chief in the back was slammed against the rear bulkhead as the aircraft came to a tangled rest.

Bouncing in his humvee, Riley heard the screams of the pilots over the radio headset, then silence. Colonel Lewis's voice came on. "Search Base, this is Six. Report. Over. Search Air, this is Six. Report. Over."

Silence.

"Break. All search units head for the base camp. We're going to get this bastard. Out."

Riley had already turned his vehicle around and was heading for the base camp. Another minute and he'd be there. He swung the barrel of the .50-caliber machine gun in an arc. To be extra sure he recharged the gun, ejecting the round that had been in the chamber. He held the dual grips of the gun tightly against his chest, rolling with the bounces of the vehicle.

Carter spun the wheel and the humvee slid around a steep turn. Riley scanned the hilltop as it appeared before him, keeping the muzzle of the machine gun following the arc of his eyes. He could see the helicopter lying on its side at the edge of the clearing; amazingly enough, there was no fire yet. Riley checked the rest of the hillside. No sign of the Synbat.

"Go to the helicopter," Riley ordered. Carter drove to it.

"Man the fifty." Carter took his place; Riley hopped out and ran over to the helicopter. He could smell leaking fuel and knew that it was probably only a matter of seconds before the wreckage would erupt in flames. He peered into what remained of the cockpit. It was a jumble of blood, flesh, Plexiglas, and machinery.

Riley moved around to the side. The cargo door wouldn't budge. He opened the access for the emergency entrance and pulled the lever; the Plexiglas popped out of the side window. Riley slid in and

grabbed the crew chief, hoisting him up through the window. He followed the body out, then threw him over his shoulder and ran just as
the helicopter burst into flames.

Riley put the body down on the backseat of his humvee and quickly
did a primary survey. The man was breathing and wasn't bleeding, other
than a few scratches. He'd survive for a while without attention.

Riley replaced Carter at the fifty and put on his headset. Out of the
corner of his eye he could see another humvee roar into the clearing.
Riley circled his right hand over his head, pointed at his eyes, and then
gestured for the vehicle—with Doc Seay standing in the hatch—to move
to the left and take up security there.

A brown figure appeared to Riley's left front, stumbling toward the
van. Riley depressed the butterfly trigger and the fifty roared. His first
tracers were short and he was arcing the rounds up when the Synbat
disappeared behind the cover of the van. Riley released the trigger.

"Ranger Three, do you have it in sight? Over."

"Negative. Over." Riley knew that Doc Seay would have seen the
creature if it had made for the far wood line.

Riley switched to intercom. "John, move to the right so we can see
the other side of the van."

The humvee moved at almost a walking pace. Riley kept the muzzle
of the weapon trained on the van, expecting to see the creature hiding underneath or huddled on the far side.

Riley could now see another body lying near the wood line. Then
the side door to the van came into view, gaping wide open.

"Hold here." Between his position and Doc Seay's, Riley knew that
they had the van completely covered. There was only one place the
Synbat could be.

Riley keyed the radio. "All stations this net. This is Ranger One.
The helicopter is down and on fire. Both the pilot and copilot are dead.
We've got one body that we can see lying near Search Base. The Synbat
is hiding in the van. Over."

"This is Search Six. Wait until I arrive. I'll be there in about five
minutes. Over."

Philip's humvee now rolled into the clearing. Riley directed the driver
to take up position to his right.

An eerie scream wafted through the damp air, echoing out of the
open door of the van. Riley had heard that howl once before. The scream

was repeated. They had the Synbat trapped and there was no rush to move in. Riley checked to see where his fourth humvee was.

"Ranger Two, this is One. What is your ETA at Search Base? Over."

On board Ranger Two, MSgt. Joe Knutz was dodging low-hanging branches, trying to prevent the barrel of the .50-caliber machine gun from getting caught up. They were less than a quarter mile from the campsite. He activated the radio to answer Riley's question. "I'll be there in two mikes. Over."

"Roger. Out."

Ranger Two hit a turn on the trail. The left wheels of the humvee lost traction and the vehicle slid sideways, slamming the driver's door against a tree.

Knutz cursed down through the hole as T-bone spun the wheels in the mud. "Put the fucker in four-wheel drive!"

T-bone let up on the gas briefly and yelled back: "It is, Top! We're stuck."

Knutz took off the headset and hopped out of the hatch to push.

On the knoll, Riley called Seay on the radio. "Ranger Three, do you have any movement in that body near the van? Over." He wasn't about to order anyone to go on foot that close to the van.

"Negative. I checked it with my binos. It's Doctor Ward and he looks very dead. Over."

"Roger. Break. Search Six, this is—" Riley paused as another howl split the air. This one came from the west, not from the van. He listened for a few moments, ignoring the squawk of the radio, but the cry wasn't repeated.

"Ranger Four, I want you to move and cover the western tree line. Sounds like another one is heading this way. Over."

"Roger."

"Search Six, this is Ranger One. Over."

"This is Six. Over."

"How many people were in the Search Base van? Over."

"Two of my men and Doctor Ward. Over."

That meant two people, probably very dead people, were still inside the van. Riley wished that Lewis would get here quickly so they could deal with the animal in the van. He suspected the DIA van was

having trouble maneuvering in the wet conditions. And where was
Ranger Two?

Knutz was slipping in the mud, trying to push, as the humvee's engine
whined, fruitlessly spinning the wheels. The team sergeant slammed
his fist on the back hood of the humvee to get the driver's attention.
T-bone stuck his head out the window.

"Rock it. Reverse and forward in short bursts," Knutz yelled. He
put his shoulder on the back end and pushed forward as T-bone shifted
gears. Knutz's left foot slid out from under him and he fell in the mud,
just as T-bone reversed gear. The humvee rolled back. Knutz screamed
as the bottom of the back bumper pinned his leg against the wet ground.

"Stop it! Stop it!" Knutz yelled as he levered a shovel into the mud,
trying to push the rear end of the vehicle off his leg. T-bone must have
heard him because he turned off the engine. In the silence T-bone could
hear Knutz's labored words.

"Don't move it. I think my leg is busted."

A howl sounded almost on top of them and Knutz turned his head.
A Synbat stood in the road staring at him, less than ten feet away. The
two locked eyes for almost three seconds. Then the Synbat moved.

Riley heard the new howls again. The other one was damn close.
Lewis's van came rolling up the hill and stopped about ten feet to the
left of Riley.

The colonel got out and splashed over to Riley. "Is it still inside?"

Riley nodded.

"Fire it up."

"What about your men inside?"

"I said fire it up, mister."

Riley knew that the men inside were almost certainly dead. He pushed
the send on his radio. "This is Ranger One. I'm going to fire into the
van. I want everyone else to hold their fire unless the creature makes
a break for it. Over."

"Three, roger."

"Four, roger."

Riley let go of the transmit switch and made sure that he had a good
grip on the machine gun. He lay the muzzle directly on the opening
and pushed down on the trigger. The first rounds flew right in the door
of the van.

Riley kept the trigger depressed as he shifted the string of bullets slightly left and right, smashing into the sides of the van. The half-inch-diameter bullets were tearing holes in the sheet metal and rocking the van on its suspension.

The Synbat exploded out the front passenger door and sprinted for the woods. Riley let up on the trigger as he swung the muzzle to follow. The creature was screaming and moving more slowly than Riley had expected. It was about thirty feet from the tree line.

"Get it! Get it!" Lewis yelled. His men were moving out in front, fanning toward it.

Riley fired over the DIA men's heads, forcing them to duck. His first rounds were slightly low, but he walked the bullets up into the creature. The Synbat flew sideways like a rag doll as the steel-jacketed projectiles sank into its body.

Riley let up on the trigger. The DIA men sprinted toward the body. "The north! To the north!"

Riley recognized Bob Philips's voice on the radio and turned to look in the indicated direction. The second Synbat must have circled around the camp, bypassing Philips's defensive sector.

Riley could see that this Synbat was carrying something as it moved swiftly toward the body of its comrade. Riley turned the fifty to track, but he didn't depress the trigger because the DIA men were now in the line of fire. One of the DIA men let loose with a wild burst from his MP-5. The healthy Synbat stopped, swung up an M16, and let loose a sustained burst. Two of the DIA men tumbled down as the others hit the dirt.

Riley was stunned by what he had just witnessed. The armed Synbat retreated into the wood line and disappeared.

CHAPTER 12

Land Between the Lakes
3:12 P.M.

"Go after it!" Colonel Lewis ordered.

Riley looked down from his perch on top of the humvee. "No, sir." He keyed the radio. "Ranger Two, this is One. Over." He waited a few seconds. "Ranger Two, this is One. If you can hear me, break squelch twice. Over." The low hissing of the radio continued unabated. Nothing.

Riley looked at his other two vehicles. Doc Seay had driven over to the DIA men and was working on the two bodies while Caruso manned the fifty, pointing it at the woods where the armed Synbat had fled. Philips had moved his vehicle close to that tree line, also providing security. Riley felt a hollow weight in his chest as he pondered various courses of action. He quickly made his decision and hopped off the vehicle, Carter replacing him on the gun.

Colonel Lewis placed himself in front of Riley as he jumped to the ground. "I'm ordering you to pursue that Synbat, mister."

Riley looked him in the eye. "No, sir. I'm not going after that thing until I know exactly what I'm up against. You've lied to me from the beginning and have continued lying throughout. Right now, as far as I'm concerned, you don't have any credibility as an officer." Riley brushed past him and moved over to Doc Seay, Lewis trailing him.

"How are they?"

Seay stood up slowly and shook his head. "Both dead."

"Take care of the crew chief from the helicopter."

Riley turned and addressed Lewis. "That's two more. Because of these things eleven people are dead—that I know of. I don't know how many more you haven't told us about. I've also got two men missing, and I think that might be where the Synbat got the M16. In which case, two of my men are probably dead too." Riley turned to his team members.

"Bob, take your vehicle and try to find Knutz. Check the roads leading up here from the southwest. Be careful. These things are armed now. Give me radio checks with your location every five minutes."

"Roger that, chief." Philips hopped on board his humvee and it roared out of sight. Riley walked away from the bodies and Colonel Lewis. He poked his head in the door of the van. The rounds from his machine gun had torn apart the interior. The two DIA men's bodies had not been spared either, the bullets compounding the wounds the Synbat had caused, producing barely recognizable corpses. The story was told by the empty MP-5 submachine gun lying in the mud outside the door and the 9mm brass on the floor of the van and in the dirt outside.

Riley splashed over to where Ward's body lay. The doctor's sightless eyes stared up into the light, misty rain, his throat torn out. Riley felt no compassion.

Riley walked over to Doc Seay's humvee. Doc had the crew chief in the back, stabilized. The man was semiconscious, obviously on some sort of strong painkiller.

"How's he doing?" Riley asked Doc Seay.

"A couple of minor breaks. Nothing too bad. I've splinted the leg, which is the worst. We need to take him back to post to get X-rays and let them set the broken bones."

Riley checked his watch, then went over to Lewis, who was supervising his men as they put the Synbat's remains into a body bag. Riley found it disgusting that they gave top priority to the creature's remains while the human bodies still lay in the mud.

Before the DIA men had zipped the bag, Riley pushed them aside and lay the flaps open, looking at the creature. He was shocked by what he saw. It looked more human than monkey, as if a man had been given some simian characteristics rather than the other way around. Large fangs protruded from the thrusting jaw, but otherwise the shape of the head was manlike, with a high forehead suggesting intelligence. The eyes had golden irises and, even in death, spoke of something more than animal cunning. The body was covered with thin brown hair. The hands were totally human, with just a smattering of coarse hair on the backs.

Riley's gaze scanned down the body. There was a powerful-looking tail, and the muscled legs were bowed. The toes were longer than human toes and looked capable of gripping.

A crude bag made of torn cloth was tied over the creature's left shoulder. Riley untied the knot and looked in. It contained several scalpels and medical saws. At least now he knew how the collars had been removed and what had made the clean cuts on some of the bodies. No sign of a backpack.

The way the Synbat had used the rifle indicated both intelligence and training. Riley felt a chill as he considered the implications of what he had just experienced. No wonder Merrit said "so-called" monkeys. What were these creatures?

Riley looked up at Lewis, struggling to contain his rage and deal with the matters at hand. "Sir, we need to send the crew chief from the helicopter back to the hospital at Fort Campbell."

Lewis licked his lips. "Is it critical?"

"No, sir. Simple fracture of the leg, but there's nothing more we can do for him out here."

"We can't move anybody until I get word from Washington on how to handle this thing."

Riley wasn't thrilled, but he held his tongue. Lewis was an errand boy. Right now was the time for damage control. Riley's first priority was to find Knutz and T-bone, and he had sent Bob Philips to work on that. He went back to his own humvee to start on the second priority.

Carter had the vehicle's antenna hooked into the PRC-70 radio to receive the morning's message from Powers. Carter had just finished transcribing the six-letter groups off the DMDG.

Riley sat in the driver's seat, glad to finally be out of the rain. "Got the receive?"

Carter handed Riley a piece of paper.

Riley pointed at the FM radio. "Hear from Ranger Two or Four yet?"

Carter indicated negatively. "Nothing from Two. I've been trying to call them every two minutes. Maybe their radio is down. Got a sitrep from Philips. Nothing yet."

Riley felt the knot in his stomach grow.

Carter looked at Riley. "What do you think happened to Knutz, chief?"

Riley pointed in the direction of the dead DIA men. "Well, that M16

the thing had came from somewhere. I've got a bad feeling it might
be Knutz's or T-bone's." In fact, Riley held little doubt that it was,
and that Knutz and T-bone were dead. This whole operation had gone
to shit in a matter of ten minutes, all because they hadn't been told
the truth. Obviously the Synbats had been designed and trained to be
more than beasts of burden. Riley's fear for his men equaled his disgust for Colonel Lewis and Doctor Ward, and all they represented.

Riley took out the field SOP and quickly decrypted. Obviously Powers
had contacted Kate and gotten the requested information.

ZERO TWO XXX
FOB THREE XXX
BIOTECH ENGINEERING WORKING PENTAGON CONTRACT XXX
PROJECT UNKNOWN BUT IN FIELD OF GENETIC ENGINEERING
XXX
HIGHLY CLASSIFIED XXX
WARD SPECIALIST IN GROWTH HORMONES AND GENETIC
ENGINEERING XXX
MERRIT SPECIALIST IN RECOMBINANT DNA XXX
HOSSEY SAYS TO CALL FOR HELP IF NEEDED XXX
HE KNOWS AS MUCH AS I DO XXX
NOTHING MORE XXX
WILL TRY TO FIND OUT MORE XXX
BE CAREFUL XXX
COMPADRE

Too little, too late. Riley hoped that Kate and whoever had passed
this information to her had not jeopardized themselves because of it.
The fact that Colonel Hossey knew what was in the messages was
dangerous for Kate, but Riley wasn't overly worried. Colonel Hossey
had been the commander of Special Forces Detachment Korea (DET-K)
when Riley had run the Dragon Sim mission into China three years
ago. Hossey had stood by Riley's team when everyone else had abandoned them. Riley was willing to trust him now.

Riley slumped back in the cargo hatch behind his fifty and thought
about what to do next. This whole thing sickened him. He had no
doubt that those creatures had been designed by the Pentagon to attack
and kill. The way they had returned to this campsite indicated a high
degree of tactical sense. They had counterattacked their pursuers at

the most vulnerable point and almost succeeded in wiping out everyone who had been left here, at the loss of only one of their own. The use of the M16, the tools, the bag to carry equipment—all were highly disturbing.

Riley felt drained and disappointed. He was well on his way to losing faith in the U.S. government and the military. This was the third time that he had run a classified mission where people had died. And what had been accomplished? The mission into China in 1989 had achieved nothing, as far as Riley could tell from watching the news over the subsequent years. The raids into Colombia had briefly hurt the cartel, but the drug trade seemed to be thriving, and there had been no follow-through on that effort. And now it was damage control for a military experiment that he didn't think should have been going on in the first place; it was probably illegal and most certainly morally wrong.

All these deaths for what? Riley could understand soldiers dying and the necessity to cover it up for security reasons—albeit poor ones—but the death of civilians was another matter entirely. He knew what would happen, though. There would be a lot of ass-covering and finger-pointing in classified circles about this incident and then it would be business as usual.

He could see the DIA men wrapping up Ward's body. The doctor's death would be very convenient for the others involved. They could all point fingers at a dead man.

Riley realized that he was bone tired of this type of operation. He wasn't sure he wanted to play this game anymore. None of that mattered now, though, not with three of the Synbats still loose.

The FM radio speaker came alive. "Ranger One, this is Four. Over."

Riley grabbed the handset. "This is One."

"We've found Ranger Two. Both dead. Their M16s are missing. Over."

Riley closed his eyes and leaned back against the rear of the turret. "Bring them to Search Base. Out." He let the handset slip from his fingers.

3:27 P.M.

In the remaining van, Lewis had finally made contact with General Trollers over the secure SATCOM link. Lewis decided to get all the information out in one fell swoop and let Trollers pick over it.

"We've terminated one of the Synbats, sir. Doctor Ward was killed prior to that. I also lost four men. One of the helicopters from Campbell crashed and the pilot and copilot were killed. The crew chief was injured and is in stable condition right now. The Special Forces have lost two of their men."

There was a long pause. "What about the other three Synbats?"

"I don't know, sir. One of them was here and escaped, so they can't be too far away."

"Will you be able to track them down?"

Lewis rolled his eyes. The general was talking about looking for three animals in such a vast area that it was the proverbial needle in the haystack, except in this case the needle had the ability to turn around, prick the searcher, and then disappear again.

"Sir, the Synbats have weapons now—at least two M16s that we know of. It's war out here. We need to seal off the park."

"I have to run that one by the Old Man."

Lewis glanced at the clock on the wall of the van. "Sir, we need immediate help."

"I'll get things rolling. Out."

Lewis threw down the handset in disgust, bouncing it off the console.

3:52 P.M.

The bulk of the Union and Confederate forces arrived during the day. More than eight hundred Civil War enthusiasts now crowded the fields to the west of the Wrangler Camp, cleaning gear, feeding horses, and swapping stories. Of the eight hundred, seventy were mounted; the rest would fight as infantry or artillery. The youngest participant was an eight-year-old drummer boy from the 8th New York. The oldest was the honorary ninety-one-year-old commander of the 6th Michigan.

In eight minutes they would form under their various battle flags; the blue across the north end of the main pasture and the gray symbolically across the southern end. After the muster, the two groups would spend an evening preparing for the mock battle that would commence the next day. Some units would march out this evening to assume their battle positions.

In the midst of blue ranks were Jeremiah and Louis Sattler. They had almost forgotten the events of the previous night, although Louis

was a bit worried about Jeremiah's moodiness. But soon the reenactment would begin, and Louis was confident that it would shake his
brother out of the funk he'd been in all day.

The dim echo of firing off to the east had been heard not too long
ago. Louis wondered if firing from the ranges on Fort Campbell on
the other side of Lake Barkley could carry this far. He didn't think
so, but he couldn't come up with any other explanation for the sound
of machine guns. He quickly forgot about it as the order was given to
fall in.

Fort Campbell
3:56 P.M.

Powers looked at the message one more time, preparing himself for
the storm that was to come.

> ZERO THREE ODA SIX EIGHT TWO XXX
> SITREP XXX
> TOTAL THIRTEEN DEAD MILITARY AND CIVILIAN XXX
> KNUTZ AND TROY DEAD XXX
> MONKEYS ARE GENETICALLY ALTERED CREATURES
> CALLED SYNBATS XXX
> SYNBATS ARMED AND CAN USE WEAPONS XXX
> ONE SYNBAT KILLED THREE STILL LOOSE XXX
> NEED HELP XXX
> WILL MONITOR FM VOICE ON THREE SIX ZERO ZERO XX
> THREE SIX ZERO ZERO XXX
> FILL IN GROUP COMMANDER ON SITUATION XXX
> AMIGO XXX

Powers couldn't believe what he had just read. He punched in the
number for Colonel Hossey's office. The phone was picked up on the
first ring.

Chapter 13

Land Between the Lakes
4:00 P.M.

Knutz's and T-bone's bodies lay on the backseat of their humvee. Both men were smeared with mud and blood. Knutz's throat had been cleanly cut. T-bone had obviously had the opportunity to put up more of a fight. His face and arms were slashed, in addition to his throat. Knutz's pistol was still in its shoulder holster, indicating that he'd been taken unaware. T-bone's holster was empty.

"Knutz was caught underneath his vehicle," Bob Philips explained. "It was stuck in the mud and Top must have gone back there to try and push it out. We had to winch it out to get it off his body. T-bone was lying near the driver's door." Philips handed over a Beretta 9mm. "His pistol was in the mud next to him. No rounds fired."

Riley silently took the pistol and stuffed it into his pants cargo pocket.

"Both M16s were gone, along with their LBE."

"Cover them up," Riley ordered. "Trovinsky, I want you to move that humvee to cover approaches from the east, and man its fifty."

"Yes, sir."

"Bob, I want you to cover the south."

"Roger that, chief."

The rain had finally stopped, leaving a damp fog in its place. Riley walked to the van where Lewis was ensconced. He slid open the door without knocking and stepped in.

Lewis looked up as he spoke into the phone. His face was haggard. "I'll get back with you in a little bit." He hung up. "Mister Riley, I apologize about everything that has happened. I'm very sorry about the loss of your men."

Riley sat down and laid his M16 across his knees. He stared at Lewis for a long minute. The other men in the van were very quiet. Freeman was squirming in the corner, trying not to be noticed, a difficult thing for a man his size.

When Riley spoke, all emotion was out of his voice. "Tell me the truth now. What are those things?"

Lewis rubbed his eyes. "I really don't know what the Synbats are or what they're capable of." He held up a hand to forestall Riley's outburst. "No. Listen to me. I don't know. Probably the only person still alive who does know is Doctor Merrit, and I've got her on the way out here to brief us. I can tell you what they were *supposed* to do and how far along Doctor Ward reported they were. But other than that, you know as much as I do.

"What I told you earlier was mostly true. The Synbats are genetically altered creatures designed to be soldiers. But not just haulers of gear. They were supposed to be infantrymen. Grunts. Expendable ones. Ones that we could give a weapon to and send out, and not have a public outcry when they got killed. Not only that, they were supposed to be even better than the present infantryman. More aggressive. Stronger. Faster. More adaptable to harsh environments.

"It was a long-range project. You've seen what they can do now. In a few years they would have been even better."

Riley broke in. "What about the weapons? Where'd they learn to use them?"

"At the lab. We sent in some paramilitary folks to work with them. I know that Ward had them out at ranges on Fort Campbell a couple of times."

"How'd they control the animals to take them to the ranges?"

"Ward drugged them constantly, making them more complacent. We just found that out ourselves. The Synbats went to the range only a couple of times and were at a rudimentary level with the weapons."

"What other training have they received?"

"That's about it. The initial goal was to simply have them fire a rifle with a certain degree of accuracy."

"They've achieved that," Riley acknowledged sarcastically. "Do they know how to reload?"

Lewis shrugged. "As far as I know, they can point a weapon and pull a trigger. That's it. If there's more, Merrit can tell you when she gets here."

"Why didn't you tell me before about the weapons capability?"

"They didn't *have* weapons until they took them from your men," Lewis answered weakly.

"Your men in the van were killed with their own weapons," Riley reminded him. "The helicopter was shot at with that MP-5 we found lying outside. You heard the pilot's radio call that the creature was armed." Riley shook his head. Trying to discuss what had already happened was futile.

The sound of an incoming helicopter pounded through the walls of the van.

"That should be Doctor Merrit now." Lewis stood. "You can find out what else you need to know directly from her."

Fort Campbell
4:00 P.M.

The alert for the 5th Special Forces Group started in Colonel Hossey's office. It went to the battalion commanders, who in turn called each company commander. The company commander notified his sergeant major and five team leaders. The team leaders passed the word to the team sergeants.

There are three battalions in 5th Group, three companies in each battalion, five teams in each company, plus service and support units: almost a thousand men and women all told. By 4:15 P.M., arms rooms were being opened and humvees were being dispatched.

The soldiers of 5th Group were used to alerts, but one on a Friday afternoon that encompassed the entire group was somewhat out of the norm. Alerts were usually called in the early hours of the morning under some strange theory that all crises would happen at 4 A.M. The last time that anyone could remember the entire group being called out was the initial alert for the Persian Gulf crisis. But then, after the alert, it had taken almost a month for the whole group to deploy because of limited aircraft capability.

This afternoon, though, was different. The only word coming down the chain of command was for the teams to mount up and be prepared to move out by ground vehicle, locked and loaded. No word of movement to the airstrip or inbound aircraft.

Hossey, satisfied that his own unit was getting ready to roll, now moved on to his hardest task. He'd already called the post chief of staff and scheduled a 4:10 P.M. meeting with the post commander, Major General Williams, at the Fort Campbell headquarters. As his driver dropped him off in front of the old World War II–era building, Hossey tried to figure out the best way to present what he had.

"Sir, Colonel Hossey reports."

Williams was wearing camouflage fatigues and was seated behind his massive desk. "Afternoon, Karl. Have a seat." He waited until the Green Beret colonel was settled. "Now, perhaps you can tell me what the crisis is."

As calmly as possible, Hossey started with the dispatch of the team yesterday at the behest of the DIA. Williams nodded when he was done. "All right. But what does that have to do with right now?"

Hossey then launched into the sequence of events described by Riley in his messages, concluding with 682's present position in the Land Between the Lakes, the discovery of the downed helicopter, the deaths of Knutz and T-bone, and the fact that three of the creatures were still on the loose.

Williams looked at Hossey long and hard. "You expect me to believe this? Killer monkeys running around murdering people?"

"Two of those people were my men," Hossey replied. "I believe it."

Williams frowned. "But monkeys using weapons?"

"Altered monkeys, sir. We don't know what was done to them in that lab. You can verify that the alert from the DIA was phoned in here yesterday morning."

Williams drummed his fingers on the desktop as he collected his thoughts. "You realize, of course, that your man has broken security, and that you yourself have broken security by telling me all this?"

"Yes, sir."

Williams thumbed his intercom. "Mary, get me General Trollers at DIA on the secure line and speaker phone, please."

"Yes, sir."

They waited fifteen seconds, then the phone buzzed.

"4602. This line is unsecure."

Williams reached forward and pushed a button on his phone. "Go secure, please."

There was a hiss from the other end. "Secure."

"This is General Williams calling from Fort Campbell. I need to talk to General Trollers."

"Wait one, sir."

After almost half a minute a deep voice came on. "Trollers here."

"General Trollers, this is General Williams from Fort Campbell. I've got a problem here and I'm going to take care of it with or without your help."

Clarksville, Tennessee
3:04 P.M.

"Don't you touch me!" Emma Plunket screamed as she ducked.

Her husband's fist smashed into the wall barely three inches from her head, denting the side of the trailer. Emma moved with remarkable dexterity for a woman who stood five foot six and weighed almost two hundred pounds. She faked right, then darted left. Eight Milwaukee's Best had left Billy Joe a little slower than normal, and Emma made it out of the trailer, the torn screen door flapping behind her rapidly scuttling butt.

"You get your ass back here, you fucking bitch!" Billy Joe bellowed as he tore the door off its hinges and stomped out in the parking lot. He was just in time to see the taillights flash briefly on his '75 Ford pickup as Emma squealed out onto 41A, narrowly missing a car.

Billy Joe was really livid now. Not only had she taken his truck, but he hadn't had dinner yet and there was nothing on the stove. In fact, now that he thought about it, that was how the fight had started. He'd come home after earning a bust-ass day's pay to find that worthless bitch sitting in front of the TV with no goddamn food on the stove and sporting a smart-ass attitude. Billy Joe popped a brew and sat down on the wooden steps, letting the cold beer fuel his anger. He'd bust her ass for sure when she came whimpering back home.

Whimpering home wasn't high on Emma's list of choices as she took the left-hand fork where 41A and 79 split, ending up on 79 West to Dover. With the sun in the western sky glaring into her eyes and Clarksville receding behind her, Emma considered her options. She knew one thing for damn sure: She was tired of Billy Joe busting her up every time he felt like it. She'd put up with that shit for six months now and enough was enough.

It took her thirty minutes to reach Dover. Emma rolled through the town and then turned left into a neighborhood of beat-up old houses.

She pulled into the driveway of a two-story dwelling, got out, and headed up the walk. An old man sat on the porch, newspaper in hand. He lowered the paper and watched her approach without a flicker of emotion.

Emma's voice crackled with apprehension. "Hi, Dad."

"What are you doing here?"

"Is Mom inside?"

"I asked you a question, girl."

Emma didn't answer, shifting her considerable weight from one foot to the other.

"Billy Joe know you're here?"

Her voice moved up an octave into the whine range. "He been hitting me, Dad. I just couldn't take any more."

The old man moved for the first time. He threw down the paper and reached Emma in two swift strides. The force of his open right hand left a smudge of red on her face. "He's your *husband*, girl! He can hit you any damn time he wants. What'd you do?"

Emma's voice sank to a whisper. "Nothing."

"Don't you lie to me. What did Billy Joe say you done?"

Emma looked up, over her father's right shoulder, and saw her mother standing there, in the dimness of the foyer. She caught her mother's eyes, imploring her to come to the rescue. Her mother turned and disappeared into the shadows.

Emma did an about-face and headed back to the pickup. Her father stood on the stoop, hands on hips. "You go back to Billy Joe and you do what you're told to do. I don't want to see your ass out here again unless Billy Joe is behind the wheel of that truck."

Emma threw the pickup into reverse and spit gravel as she backed out into the street. She drove back up to 79 and hesitated there at the stop sign. Turn right, back to Clarksville and Billy Joe?

"Uh-uh," Emma whispered to herself. At least not tonight. Maybe by tomorrow he'd have cooled off a little. At the very least he wouldn't be as drunk, she hoped.

Emma turned left onto 79. Stopping at a Minit Mart, she bought a twelve pack of Busch—her favorite beer. Billy Joe wouldn't let her drink it at home. He said it was too expensive. Emma figured that it didn't matter what she bought, she was in trouble anyway—might as well go first class.

She took the poorly marked right turn onto the Trace, the tarred road leading to Lake Barkley. A small parking area by the lake was her old high school hangout. This time of year it was empty, but in a month or so there would be several cars out there on weekend nights, full of teenagers with surging hormones.

Emma parked the truck facing the water and turned off the engine. She got out and climbed into the bed of the truck, twelve pack in hand, the shocks squeaking as she moved about. Sitting on the right wheel well, she popped the top on the first beer. She slammed the entire thing down in one long gulp—a quality that had endeared her to Billy Joe early in their relationship. She tossed the empty out toward the water.

Seven beers later Emma felt a certain pressure in her lower abdomen. She belched and lumbered off the back of the truck. Another couple of brews and she'd be ready to crash. Emma finished her call of nature in the woods and then headed back to the truck, straining to button her jeans at the same time. Twenty feet from her steel bed she halted and blinked.

Someone was messing with the driver's door. Billy Joe sure as shit wouldn't like that. Emma's voice was saturated with drunken indignation. "Get your ass away from my truck!" She picked up a rock and threw it.

There was no answer. Then the shadowy figure turned and Emma felt her stomach plummet. It was no person.

Something moved off to her left—another figure, this one with a rifle in its hands. What little higher-level cognitive functioning Emma had left shut down. She turned and ran; the creatures kept their distance, herding her to the east up an incline.

Emma pushed blindly through the undergrowth, bouncing off trees, thorns tearing at her skin. The drive went on for almost fifteen minutes. Every time Emma tried to stop and turn, one of *them* would be there, heading her in the desired direction.

Finally, Emma broke through some undergrowth and there was nothing beneath her feet but space. Her last thought as her legs pinwheeled in the air was relief that the running was over.

CHAPTER 14

Land Between the Lakes
4:08 P.M.

The skeleton of the helicopter smoldered on the side of the knoll. The riddled DIA van sat on four flat tires, the interior full of smashed equipment coated with blood. All the corpses were in body bags and laid out in a row. ODA 682, augmented by the surviving DIA men, maintained a thin perimeter around the top of the hill.

Riley, Lewis, and Merrit all clambered on board the other helicopter to fly back to Biotech, where Merrit insisted she had something to show them if they were truly going to understand the threat posed by the Synbats. Riley thought that the battlefield they were leaving was ample proof of the creatures' destructive capabilities. He couldn't imagine anything worse.

They landed and walked into the building to an office where Lewis's men had set up a radio hookup. A VCR and TV stood in the corner. Lewis took the radio controls from his man and gestured for him to leave the room, then he looked away from his machines for a moment and addressed the others. "I've got a speaker box and room mike set up. We're going to have a conference call so all of us get to hear what Doctor Merrit has to say. Then we can work out a course of action. The other people who will be on the line are General Trollers, my boss, who is presently in the air en route to Fort Campbell; General Williams, who commands Fort Campbell; Colonel Hossey, the commander of the 5th Special Forces Group; and the duty officer at our headquarters in Fairfax."

Lewis flicked a switch. "This is Search Base. We are prepared on this end."

A loud voice boomed out of the speaker. Lewis scrambled to turn down the volume. "This is General Trollers. On line."

A new voice. "This is General Williams from Fort Campbell with Colonel Hossey. On line."

"This is Colonel Statmore at Home Base. On line."

"This is Colonel Lewis. I've got Doctor Merrit with me here, along with Mister Riley from the 5th Special Forces Group. Doctor Merrit is the most knowledgeable person we have concerning the Synbats. Mister Riley has been in charge of the team that was part of the initial response to the escape of the Synbats, so he's our expert as far as fighting them."

"Doctor Merrit, this is General Trollers. What we need from you is information."

Riley wasn't surprised by the anger in Merrit's voice when she spoke. "I thought you had all the information you needed from Doctor Ward's briefings and status reports."

Trollers made a vain attempt to speak in a soothing voice. "I do have quite a bit of information, but I need you to give General Williams and Colonel Hossey a briefing on the Synbats. Their troops are in the process of being alerted and will be responsible for the neutralization of our problem. I have the overview of the Synbat project, but we need details now. We need to know the extent of the threat and how we can destroy the animals."

Merrit leaned forward and closed her eyes in concentration as she organized her thinking. Then she spoke. "Synbat stands for synthetic battle form. We were attempting to use artificial processes to develop an organic form that could function on the battlefield.

"We were working with baboon and human genes using transgenic manipulation, more commonly known as splicing, to produce a large and quick-growing mutation. We came up with a creature that, upon maturation, was approximately forty percent larger than a normal baboon and grew at a factor of roughly fifteen times faster.

"The creature retains some of the phenotype of the original baboon species but we—"

General Williams's voice cut in. "Could you please define phenotype?"

Merrit thought for a few seconds. "Phenotype is the observable appearance of an organism as determined by genetics and environment. There is also genotype, which is the genetic constitution of an organism, which may or may not be expressed physically."

Trollers's voice was tinged with impatience. "That's all fine and well, Doctor, but we're just concerned with what we have to face and how to kill them."

"You need to understand the concepts, General," Merrit shot back at the radio, her voice rising almost out of control. With visible effort, she continued. "I'll explain why in a little while. The Synbat is both human and baboon. We don't know the exact extent it is of either one. In reality it is a totally new species."

"You've created a new species?" Williams exclaimed in disbelief. "How could you do that?"

Merrit backtracked. "Biotechnology is a relatively new field. In terms of history, 1977 is considered year one, the year when scientists first coaxed microorganisms to manufacture insulin for humans, and first produced somatotropin, which is a growth hormone, as well as interferon and some oil-eating microbes. The capability to manipulate genes has been around for more than a decade."

"Then why has no one done it yet, other than your lab?" Williams asked.

"People have done it, just not with human genes. Federal regulations released in June of '86 prohibited that, except under controlled and approved guidelines. The possibility of mutating a microorganism inimical to man was too great. A technology that deals so directly with the basic life processes is fraught with great dangers and is very tightly controlled.

"To get back to what we did. As I said, the technology and knowledge to do it have been in place for more than a decade. With a—"

"Excuse me, doctor," General Trollers interrupted. "Getting back to General Williams's question, I think everyone should know that there is a very strong belief that the Russians worked on their own version of the Synbat project as early as 1983, although our best intelligence estimates put them years away from achieving any sort of success. With the breakup of the Soviet Union we're not sure what the present status of their project is."

Riley had expected some sort of justification to be offered for the project. Even though the world had changed greatly in the last few years, it was interesting to see that the Russian boogeyman was still alive and well, even if in a diminished form. Riley was tempted to point out that in these circumstances they had met the boogeyman and it was ours.

Merrit tried again to pick up the story. "With a waiver from the Pentagon, we worked directly with human and baboon genes, splicing them. The splicing was easy. What wasn't easy was getting a viable splice. The Synbats you are after are the fourth generation of our first viable splice, which occurred after approximately twenty thousand attempts.

"Physically, again referring to their phenotype, the results are obvious. The Synbats are slightly smaller than the average human but far larger than the average baboon. Their feet are prehensile, which means they can use their toes for grasping and climbing. The hands, however, are mostly human, facilitating use of equipment designed for humans. They have a tail that is functional. Their skin is covered with a thin layer of brown hair.

"Their heads are perhaps the most unique part. They have extended jaws, retaining the fangs that baboons have. However, the forehead is not sloped back as in most primates. And that, General, is why you need to understand when I speak of what is visible and what isn't. We don't know the true capabilities of the Synbat. There are several reasons for that."

Colonel Hossey spoke for the first time. "Why don't you tell us about the capabilities you do know about, and then we can get into the speculative area. I'm particularly interested in their facility with weapons."

Merrit's voice settled into a dull monotone as she recited the facts. "The purpose of the project was to produce a replacement for the individual soldier on the battlefield. There were several base requirements given the project by the Pentagon. One, obviously, was the physical size and capability. We achieved that using genetic manipulation. Another was the ability to reproduce or grow these creatures rapidly. The theory was that we could create an army out of a laboratory given a limited time constraint—in effect having a test tube army always on standby. 'Minimal cost for maintenance with rapid potential' I believe was the phrase Doctor Ward used. We partially achieved that through manipulation of those genes that affect growth. That was Doctor Ward's area of expertise.

"The most critical factor, though, was intelligence. It was accepted from the start that we could not produce a creature capable of operating sophisticated machinery, such as missiles or aircraft, but we felt we could develop one that could handle an individual weapon. We wanted a creature that could follow a few simple commands and would fight. To do that, we needed a higher degree of intelligence than was currently present in the animal world or had ever been produced in genetic experiments. That is where the human factor entered. We used fetal tissue as the human gene source in the transgenic splicing. As I said—"

"Wait a second," General Williams interrupted. "Isn't that illegal?"

Riley considered the question rather foolish, considering the scope of the entire Synbat project. What was one more bending or breaking of the rules?

"We received a waiver—or at least Doctor Ward said we did," Merrit continued in the same dead voice. "As I said, it took a lot of time and effort to find a viable match. It was as much a matter of luck as skill. On each generation, we continued to manipulate and improve. This was the area I focused on.

"We did achieve a high level of intelligence, but along with it an extremely high level of aggression. To deal with the aggression, Doctor Ward used depressant drugs in various combinations. I strongly felt that those drugs had a corresponding effect on the Synbats' capability to think, and I'll show you very shortly what happened when the Synbats were off their sedation.

"The Synbats' current weapons capability is very limited. They practiced handling mock-up weapons in the lab. This was the first generation that was ever actually taken out to the range. All four Synbats have spent three days on the range under the instruction of military people, practicing firing."

Lewis spoke now. "I've checked our records on that training. They can shoot; we've seen ample evidence of that. However, they don't seem capable of much else with a weapon, such as reloading or cleaning. When they empty a magazine, as far as they are concerned, the weapon is finished. Since the creatures were drugged when they were trained, there was some question as to whether the training would even hold."

"How about if they learn how to reload?" Riley asked.

"Someone would have to teach them," Lewis answered.

"Did someone teach them how to escape or cut off their collars?"

Riley inquired quietly. "The two men I lost had their load bearing equipment taken off them, which had their extra magazines in ammo pouches. There must have been a reason why the Synbats took those."

There was a brief silence as everyone considered that, then Merrit continued. "Mister Riley brings out a good point. We can't be sure what the Synbats are capable of. I don't think we should underestimate them. Just because we didn't teach them something doesn't necessarily mean they don't know how to do it.

"You have to understand reality from the Synbats' perspective. All they've ever known is the lab and the few trips to the ranges at Fort Campbell. Their instinct and sole goal right now will be survival. They attack for three reasons: their innate aggressiveness, a search for food, and what they view as defense against your attempts to track them down.

"Concerning the first two factors, the Synbats, by virtue of their rapid growth, are extremely aggressive and have a high metabolic rate. They have to eat at a rate equal to their accelerated life cycle. They are almost constantly ravenously hungry."

"If they grow quickly, then won't their life span be shorter?" Riley asked.

"Yes. These adult Synbats have only four more months left before their anticipated life span ends."

"We can't wait four months," Trollers commented.

"No, we can't," Merrit agreed. "They'll still want to survive, just as much as you or I would want to survive. They'll fight to live if they perceive a threat. You've already seen an example of that. The ones that came back attacked and tried to destroy what they viewed as a threat."

Merrit looked around the room, animation finally coming back into her voice. "My greatest concern, however, is that we have something out there totally unexpected."

"What do you mean?" Lewis asked.

"I mean there is a possibility that we've never really understood the true mental functioning of the Synbats. They are intelligent creatures— I don't think there is any denying that. I believe they are much more intelligent than Doctor Ward gave them credit for. Without the constraints of the laboratory, there's no telling what capabilities they may develop on their own or may already have that we didn't test for."

"Such as?" Riley asked.

In reply, Merrit walked over to the VCR and turned it on. "I'll describe what we're seeing, so those of you not with us can understand. This is a videotape made about three months ago. Whenever we worked in the containment area, we kept a person monitoring the video outside containment to check on what was going on inside. On this particular day I was inside and one of our assistants, Mark Donovan, was watching the monitor.

"To give you the background on this particular day, Doctor Ward had been gone for five days to a conference in Washington. As soon as he left, I withdrew the drugs from the Synbats' diet. I wanted to see what happened when they were operating at what might be called a normal functioning level."

Riley's eyes followed the figure that appeared on the screen and stood in front of the two cubicles. The creatures inside were sitting, simply staring straight ahead.

Merrit described her actions. "I just stood there for a while. We'd noticed no real change over the five days since drug withdrawal and I was going to reintroduce the drugs in their next meal. You could say that this was their last opportunity to do anything different."

Merrit stayed silent for about thirty seconds, then the Merrit on the screen stepped forward toward the cubicle on the left.

Merrit's voice was tight as she tried to explain what was happening on the screen. "You can see the male Synbat in Cubicle One turn on his mate and attack her. We'd never seen aggression between the mated pairs, which was why we allowed them to be together. I thought he was killing her."

On the screen, the larger Synbat in the left cubicle had the other down and appeared to be banging her head against the far wall. Merrit's hand was on the combination lock for the cubicle, manipulating the numbers. A voice could be heard in the background, asking her what she was doing.

"As you can see, I was trying to set the combination for opening. I was going to try to save the female. Luckily, Mark reacted quickly. You can hear him in the background trying to find out why I was doing that. He overrode my attempt, using the computer."

The camera shifted back to the cubicle as Merrit stepped back from the door, letting go of the lock. The male Synbat stopped his attack and turned and looked at her. The female also stood, with no apparent damage done.

"Later, when we had sedated them, I checked out the female completely. There were no marks on her—nothing to indicate that she'd really been attacked."

"So what?" Lewis asked. "You're saying that the Synbats were trying to trick you into opening the door?"

Merrit looked at him, her eyes wide, the tic on the left side of her face flicking every few seconds. "I realize you'll find it hard to believe, but I know they were trying to set me up to do exactly that. You have to believe me!"

"Cut to the chase, Doctor," Trollers's voice interrupted. "How smart are the damn things when they're not sedated? Can they communicate with each other?"

Merrit closed her eyes and took a few deep breaths. Riley noted that her hands were balled up into fists, the knuckles white. "Do any of you know anything about the bicameral mind?" Riley's and Lewis's blank expressions gave her ample answer. "All right. I'll try to make it as simple as possible."

Merrit began. "The key question is the difference between man and animal—the baboon, for example. Most people would say thinking, but that's not true. All the manifest examples of thinking are present in various degrees in the animal world: learning, concepts, even rudimentary language. The baboon has approximately eighty signals or commands that it uses—communication, in effect. This ability was another factor in our choosing the baboon as part of our genetic base to make the Synbats.

"Humans started out in the same way. There is a theory that humans truly broke away from the animal world only when we were able to communicate extensively with a verbal language and act as individuals rather than as part of a group. There is also a theory that prior to having an extensive verbal language, Homo sapiens could communicate at some sort of telepathic level. Although that made for an effective group defense in a harsh environment, it also retarded progress because it required the group to stay close together and also think somewhat alike. Once we developed verbal language, we were able to explore and have more initiative as individuals.

"The interesting thing is that the development of language wasn't dictated as much by external factors as by the evolution of the brain itself. That's where the bicameral mind comes in. The human brain consists of two halves that are almost identical but have very little connection to each other.

"The speech centers in the brain are present to almost the same extent in both hemispheres, yet they are functional in ninety-seven percent of people only in the left hemisphere. What happened to the speech center in the right hemisphere? It is still there but is nonfunctional in almost everyone. Some feel that this is the place where a simplistic telepathic ability resided. Initially, man's brain was more connected between the two sides and the speech centers worked together.

"The Synbats' speech centers are developed equally in both sides of the brain. They are not capable of actual speech—at least not that we have been able to determine—yet they do have that part of the brain present in both hemispheres. The two hemispheres of a Synbat's brain are also more connected than a human's. I think there is a possibility that the Synbats have an ability to mentally communicate among themselves to some extent. They're at that point in evolution between ape and man."

"Oh, come on now, Doctor!" Trollers exploded. "Next you're going to be telling us that they read minds. They're just goddamn animals."

"They're more than animals!" Merrit blurted. "They're—" She suddenly paused and her eyes became unfocused.

"They're what?" Colonel Hossey prompted.

Merrit blinked and looked at Riley. "They must be destroyed," she said as calmly as if she were reporting that the sun would come up in the morning. "They must all be destroyed."

"Back to the intelligence question," Riley said, trying to get the meeting back on a useful track. "I can confirm that they're smarter than any animals I've ever seen." He touched Merrit lightly on the shoulder. "Can you give us an idea of how smart they are?"

Merrit's head barely nodded. "There is no doubt that they are extremely intelligent—cunning would probably be a more appropriate word. I don't think they have the ability to do much abstract reasoning, but they are extremely capable of formulating some basic plans. And I think the events of the last twenty-four hours back that up. We may never know exactly how they got out, but they have taken advantage of the situation, and they will continue to do so until we stop them."

The chatter of helicopter blades slicing the air drowned out Merrit's quiet voice. Riley stepped out into the hallway and glanced outside. A UH-60 Blackhawk helicopter settled onto the parking lot. The doors slid open and ten armed soldiers jumped out. Riley recognized several of the men. It was a team from A Company, 3d Battalion. The helicopter lifted with a surge and roared off, back to the east for another load.

"The first lift of reinforcements has arrived," Riley announced to the others.

General Williams spoke. "We've got lifts of men from 5th Group landing at the bridges leading into the Land Between the Lakes, sealing off the park. Task Force 160 is also launching some helicopter gunships to cover the water, to make sure they don't try getting out the way they got in."

"I'm going to put three teams into Lake Barkley in your vicinity," Colonel Hossey added. "They should be in the air with their boats in fifteen minutes."

Trollers continued the update. "I've already been in contact with state authorities in both Kentucky and Tennessee. As soon as we seal off the park, we're going to clear it."

Riley was relieved that the wheels were finally turning. Colonel Hossey then asked the question that had been on Riley's mind since this mission had started. "What's in the backpacks I was told about?"

Merrit took a deep breath. "The backpacks contain fifth generation embryos along with nutrients for surviving the birth process. As I told you, with every generation, we were working on a way we could rapidly produce more of the creatures. One of the requirements for the project was to be able to keep these creatures in a sort of hold status until they were needed. What we used were frozen embryos. We removed the embryos from the females at the start of their third trimester and then froze them. We kept the Synbats in cubicles as couples and allowed them to breed at will, always removing the embryos.

"The theory was that upon removal from the static cold environment, the backpacks would provide a suitable environment for the completion of the birth and growth process. It was what we called a Phase IV trial.

"In our last Phase IV test, out of fourteen possible live Synbat births, we had four successful ones. And that was under lab conditions."

Trollers cut in. "How many embryos are in the backpacks?"

Merrit's math was chilling. "Two in each single pod. Seven pods to a backpack. Two backpacks stolen. Twenty-eight embryos."

"You mean we could have twenty-eight of those things running around out there?" General Williams was incredulous.

"I doubt very much that even fifty percent of them will survive the birthing process. It's not a normal birth. They are hooked up to enough nutrients in the pods to get to normal birth size in about forty-eight hours. Then the plan was for the mature Synbats to take care of the newborns, bringing them food until they could hunt for themselves. That was an additional reason we made them a backpack configuration—in order for the mature ones to carry their young until birth."

"So we're going to have ten to twenty more of these things if we don't track them down before the process starts?" Williams asked.

Merrit pulled out a piece of paper and began calculating as she spoke. "If you don't catch all the Synbats, it could be much worse than that, General."

"What do you mean?"

"I told you we had a growth factor of fifteen over normal; for reproduction we use the baboon normal for the Synbats, since that is the way they have turned out. The normal baboon is capable of mating in about a thousand days, or a little more than three years of age. The Synbats can do that in sixty-seven days."

"So?"

"So these Synbats start growing in two days when the pods initiate. Sixty-seven days from then the new generation will reach puberty."

"You mean they're capable of producing more?"

"Yes. And with a gestation period of only ten days we could be seeing another generation of Synbats three months from the birth of the first generation." Merrit was rapidly putting numbers on the page. "The geometric progression is staggering. Also remember that the first generation of adults—the three still alive, two females and a male— can reproduce again, with the same rapid gestation, even as the backpack generation is growing up to its own mating age."

There was a brief silence. Then General Trollers spoke. "We won't have to worry about that. We're going to get them in the next forty-eight hours. Even if the backpacks activate, we can still sweep up all the Synbats inside the park. There's no way they'll make it to mating age."

Riley thought that was pretty confident talk considering the damage already wrought. The Synbats had done a very good job of staying alive and hidden so far. Still, though, with the addition of the forces from Fort Campbell, and with the park sealed off, they ought to be able to track them down.

"I'll be landing at Campbell Army Airfield in thirty minutes," Trollers announced. "We'll move out to your location in the park and set up headquarters. In the meantime, we'll seal off the park. Out here."

Lewis turned the radio off. "Let's head back over to the park."

Riley looked at Merrit. The nervous tic was at work under her left eye. He'd have to keep close tabs on her. The important thing was that the Synbats were trapped inside the Land Between the Lakes, and they were finally bringing in an adequate force to deal with them.

Atlanta
5:15 P.M.

Kate grabbed the phone on the first ring. "Westland."

"Go secure."

Kate switched on the scrambler. "I'm secure, Drew."

Patterson was businesslike as he gave her what he'd found. "You've got two strange people working on this Biotech project. Which one do you want first?"

"Start with Ward," Kate said.

"I found out why he's working for Trollers. He got caught four years ago working with fetal tissue—that was after the president put the ban on it. He was working for one of the top bioengineering firms in the country; when Trollers's people latched onto him, they used what they found to lever him out of there. He claimed he was innocent, but apparently they had a good case on him. The firm kept quiet because they didn't want the bad publicity, and Ward went along because he didn't want to go to jail."

"I wonder if he got set up by Trollers," Kate said.

"There's nothing to indicate it from what I found, but I wouldn't put it past him. You do have to remember, though, that there's a hell of a lot of money involved in bioengineering."

"So we know why Ward was at Biotech," Kate said. "What else?"

"That's it on Ward. I found some very interesting stuff in the classified intel background check on the other one, Merrit. I'll start with the most recent and work back.

"Three months ago Merrit tried to quit working out there at Biotech. It's not really clear what her reasons were, but the DIA locked her in with one of those 'we'll make sure you never work again for anybody else' speeches.

"Backing up from that, she was cited at the University of Texas at Austin, where she worked, for conducting unauthorized experiments on cats. Seems she had some strange theories about their brains and was running her own little experiments. She got caught and was almost fired. The faculty member they interviewed down there stated that Merrit had an unstable personality.

"The real interesting thing about her, though, is her family—more specifically her father. He was one of those caught inside when a government nuclear plant making materials for weapons malfunctioned in Idaho in the early seventies. It never made the news, but they damn near had a meltdown out in some place called Cedar Creek. One of the rods blew, killing four men. The place was too hot to even try to get the bodies out, so they just brought in loads and loads of concrete and covered the place up with the four bodies still inside. Merrit's father was one of those four."

"Damn," Kate commented. "That might account for an unstable personality. But what does it have to do with this stuff that's going on now?"

"Well, first off," Patterson replied, "the investigating officer on Merrit's clearance recommended disapproval. He said that he'd been told by several people that she still harbored great resentment toward the government for not only her father being killed, but the fact that his body was never recovered."

"I would have had to agree with his recommendation," Kate said. "So why did she get clearance?"

"Ward pushed real hard for it and Trollers backed him up. She was just too good at her job to pass up. I guess they felt they had nothing to worry about. Nothing in her background suggested that she might be a security risk, just a flaky person."

"Did they do a psychiatric evaluation on her?"

"Yes. I managed to take a look at the psych eval they gave her before she went to work out there. Nothing significant other than that the doctor felt she was extremely idealistic while at the same time very paranoiac. A strange combination. But . . ." Patterson paused.

"What?"

"But I think part of the eval's missing. It's not complete."

"Why would someone have pulled part of her psych eval?" Kate asked.

"Maybe because the complete report would have caused Merrit to have been terminated from the project. Maybe Ward convinced Trollers that Merrit was too important to the project and that he could control her. I'm not sure if this information is any help, but it's always good to know who you're working with."

"I agree," Kate replied. "I really appreciate everything you've told me. I'm not sure any of it matters now anyway. They've alerted 5th Group and some other units on Campbell to deal with this problem, so at least Dave won't be out there alone anymore."

"That's good. Let me know if you need anything else."

"All right, Drew. Thanks a lot. I owe you one."

"Out here."

As she put down the phone, Kate considered what she'd been told. It really didn't amount to much useful information. She wrote a summary of it and picked up the phone. She had to get it to Powers before he deployed, so he could pass it on to Dave.

CHAPTER 15

Lake Barkley
5:34 P.M.

"Slow. Slow. Lower." Sergeant Major Powers was leaning out the side of the UH-60 helicopter, looking at the surface of the water as he spoke into the headset, guiding the pilot down. The dark water of Lake Barkley was being churned by the downdraft of the blades as the helicopter glided along slowly at an altitude of ten feet and a forward speed of ten knots.

Powers glanced at the other three men in the aircraft. He received thumbs-up from all. "We're launching," he announced to the pilots.

"Roger." The left pilot was looking over his shoulder at the men in the back while the right one flew the aircraft.

"Releasing!" Powers yelled as he slammed his open palm on the quick release for the Zodiac slung beneath the helicopter. The boat separated and dropped.

Powers pointed at the two forwardmost men sitting on either edge of the cargo bay. "GO!" They threw their waterproofed rucksacks overboard and immediately pushed off, following the rucks.

Powers slid his legs over the edge of the aircraft. "GO!" he yelled over his shoulder, and the other man went as he did. The four men were all out within six seconds.

As Powers had exited the aircraft he threw his ruck—attached with a fifteen-foot safety line—out ahead, then pushed himself off, tucking his head into his chin and putting his hands behind his neck. The shock of the cold water as he speared into it took his breath away. The air that was trapped inside his dry suit popped him to the surface. He put on his fins, pulled his ruck in close, and, lying on his back, stroked toward the Zodiac.

He clambered on board, his injured knee protesting the contortion. Two of the other members of the team were already putting the forty-horsepower engine onto its mounting and priming it. They were from the B Company, 3d Battalion, scuba team. The team sergeant had been on emergency leave all week, so Powers had quickly volunteered to be acting team sergeant for this operation. In the confusion of the alert and deployment, the battalion commander had not discovered the move.

The engine roared to life, and Powers directed them to their designated position. As they moved, Powers had one of the men unzip his dry suit; he peeled it off, then returned the favor.

A second helicopter flashed by overhead and another boat was dropped along with four men a hundred meters farther up the lake. Within ten minutes there were nine boats in the water, spread out in a loose line from the Bacon Creek Boat Ramp, south to below Fords Bay. Overhead, an OH-6 gunship from Task Force 160 flitted by, minigun slung off the right skid, pilots scanning the water.

Powers slid a round into the chamber of his M16 and smiled. He was back in action. The pain from his injured knee was a dull ache submerged in the rush of adrenaline.

Land Between the Lakes
5:56 P.M.

Riley watched the bustle of activity going on around him: Helicopters landed and took off and a secure communications network was set up so that General Williams could control his forces. A colonel from General Williams's staff was giving an updated operations briefing on the situation, and Riley was hanging on the fringes of the command group, listening in. His disheveled appearance and the glare in his eye kept the young lieutenant flunky from shooing him out of the area.

"Both bridges over Route 68, traversing the LBL area, are now sealed. We have Special Forces soldiers from 2d Battalion, 5th Group, guarding the exit routes, and Kentucky State Police on the far sides keeping people from coming in." The man slapped a pointer on a map tacked to an easel. "The only other bridge, twenty miles north, here where the Trace exits the park, is also in the process of being closed off. We are allowing traffic out but none in.

"We are primarily using 5th Group soldiers on this mission because of their security clearances. However, the southern perimeter to the park is entirely land and will require more troops to secure than 5th Group can provide. Because of that, two battalions from the 101st Division are currently loading out to deploy along the length of Route 79 from where it crosses Lake Barkley to Kentucky Lake. They will use the road as their picket line, orienting north."

The pointer slid up along Lake Barkley and then bounced over to Kentucky Lake. "In addition to the Special Forces' Zodiacs in the water, helicopters from Task Force 160 are overflying both lakes, searching for any movement in the water. In all, we are surrounding almost one hundred seventy thousand acres of forest."

That seemed like a heck of a lot of forest for three creatures to hide in, Riley thought. He was glad that they were finally bringing in what seemed to be an adequate force to deal with the problem, but he wished it had happened twenty-four hours ago.

"How are you going to find the Synbats once you get the perimeter secure?" General Trollers asked.

"We will use OH-6 helicopter gunships from Task Force 160 against the Synbats. The integrated thermal sights on the aircraft should be able to find the creatures, even under the trees." The briefer paused. "Unfortunately, there are still civilians in the park and the heat signature from a Synbat and a human is too similar. We have to hold off until we get the park clear.

"The basic concept is to use the remaining daylight today to seal the park and use tomorrow to clear the park of all civilians. Then Saturday night, the OH-6 gunships will overfly the park using thermal sights to aim their miniguns. We also have a Spectre gunship en route from Hurlburt Air Force Base right now, which will give us a platform that can stay on target for a continuous period of time and use its low-level-light television to supplement the helicopters. Anything that has two arms and two legs will be gunned down and the location marked. Teams from 5th Group will be in the air on UH-60 lift aircraft and immediately land at all shooting sites to investigate the remains."

Riley's team was one of those designated. There were two other A teams at the headquarters site with the same mission. Riley agreed with the decision to go after the Synbats from the air. He didn't relish the idea of going after them on the ground again, even with dogs, especially now that the creatures were armed.

"If you don't get them tomorrow night, the pods will initiate the next morning. It doesn't leave you much slack." Merrit's comment caught the briefing officer off guard.

Trollers stood to reply. "We know that. We don't have much choice. The weather is still too bad to use the tracking dogs. We have no other means to go after them tonight. We could try the thermals, but there is a Civil War reenactment group just four miles from here, which means almost a thousand people, and they're spread out, getting ready to play war tomorrow. There are also a few campers and hunters in the park area. We're in the process of getting those people out of here, but I don't think we can find them all before dawn. Tomorrow we'll go along all the trails with loudspeakers. That ought to get everyone alerted and out.

"Also we do have to be concerned about security. The cover story being used with the civilian authorities is that we've had some armed military prisoners escape from Fort Campbell and we are tracking them down."

Riley wondered how that cover story was flying. The DIA was obviously scrambling to keep the lid on, even though the temperature on the pot had been rising for the last two days.

Colonel Hossey asked the question that had just occurred to Riley. "How can we be sure we get all of the Synbats if we miss them tomorrow night and the pods do initiate?"

Doctor Merrit stood. The tent full of army men turned and listened as the diminutive doctor spoke, her voice cracking from the strain of the past few days. "There's a maximum of twenty-eight Synbats possibly being born Thursday morning. Although not that many will actually survive, I can't give you an exact number. If we could find the location where the backpacks initiate, then we should be able to find the remains of those that don't survive, and that would give us an accurate number. The most dangerous possibility is if we cannot account for a mating pair."

General Trollers held up his palm to forestall any more ominous words. "We'll find them before the pods initiate." He stood up, signaling that the briefing was over. "Let's get to work."

6:13 P.M.

Louis was bothered by the helicopters flying overhead. How could he pretend to be living in 1863 with a constant reminder of the modern age intruding on his senses. The 7th Cavalry was deployed in a line along the north flank of the Union lines in preparation for the battle tomorrow.

Louis was throwing sticks in the fire he'd built, waiting for the coffee in the pot to boil. His brother, Jeremiah, was still acting spooked. Damn kid spent too much time in the woods back home, and he listened to that preacher way too often.

Between those strange things in the trees earlier in the day, the helicopters, and the lousy weather, Louis was beginning to lose his enthusiasm for this reenactment. He longed for the warmth of his home and wife back in Illinois.

Lake Barkley
7:12 P.M.

High overhead a large buzzard had been circling Fords Bay for ten minutes. Finally it swooped down, wings spread wide against the tricky air currents that played along the cliff face. Talons splayed, the bird passed through some branches and landed on a large pile of rotting flesh. Pay dirt. The buzzard's pea-sized brain registered elation. Its beak plunged into the carrion. The bird was working on a second swallow when its senses were alerted to a threat. Expanding its wings, it lifted in one swift sweep.

Too late. One of its legs was grasped from below. For a moment there was a curious balance between the wildly beating wings and the weight from below. The grasp tightened. The buzzard made one last surge to break free, squawking loudly.

On the water Powers had been watching the bird circling in the waning daylight. He heard the desperate squawk echo across the water and waited for the buzzard to reappear in the sky. After five minutes and no sign of the bird, he pulled out his map.

The northern shoreline of Fords Bay showed tight contour lines representing a cliff. They'd been briefed that the creatures they were hunting could climb trees, so it made sense that they could climb rock. It looked like there were only two ways to get into the small sliver of shoreline at the base of the cliff: climbing down from the top or coming in from the water.

Powers waved his hand above his head at the other two boats, signaling for them to stay in place and cover his area. He turned to the other men in the boat. "We're going into that bay over there. I want you to keep your eyes open. I saw a buzzard go down there not too long ago and I want to check it out. Let's go."

In a minute they reached the entrance to the bay. Powers pushed a low overhanging branch out of the way as they passed through. After the tight entrance, the bay opened up to about a hundred meters wide. It looked like a long green cathedral as the setting sun angled through the high trees on either side. The ground on the north gained in altitude, rising to become cliffs. On the south side was a relatively level tree-covered bank.

The navigator—Cartwright—had the engine idled down low, the boat moving along slowly. After a couple hundred meters, Powers signaled a temporary halt. "Do you smell that?"

Cartwright nodded. "Something died in there."

"Move in along the shore. I'll watch for depth and obstacles."

Cartwright edged the boat closer. The Zodiac drew only a few inches of water, but the propeller went almost a foot deeper. Powers kept switching his gaze from the shoreline to the water directly in front of the boat. Trees were crowded in the thin spit of land between the cliff and the water, with thick undergrowth choking the space between the trunks.

Finally the smell was so strong that Powers signaled Cartwright to halt, and they took cravats from their first-aid kits to use as makeshift face masks. Powers had smelled death before; whatever was rotting up ahead was no squirrel. It was big.

They moved in closer. An uneasy knot formed in Powers's gut. He flicked the selector lever on his M16 to semiautomatic.

"Hold it!" His voice was muffled by the green cloth wrapped around his nose and mouth. Cartwright killed the engine and joined him in the front of the boat. The other two men had their weapons at the ready, covering the flanks.

Ten feet away on the shore, they could make out piles of white bones in the undergrowth.

"I'm going ashore. Cover me."

Powers slid over the side of the boat into the surprisingly chilly water. The dark surface lapped around his waist until he got close to shore. Pushing aside branches, he began to take in the scope of what he'd just found.

"Bring in the boat," Powers yelled. He scanned the trees and the cliff face for any movement, the muzzle of his weapon following his eyes. As far as he could tell, the bones were from animals, but he didn't want to make a personal contribution to the ghastly pile.

After the Zodiac was beached and tied off on a tree, Powers deployed the three men in a skirmish line facing the cliff. He didn't need to give them any warnings. The signs of death were present everywhere.

"Take a look around. Make sure you keep checking out the trees."

Less than five seconds later, Cartwright's voice broke the silence. "Over here, Sergeant Major!"

Powers pushed through to where the man was standing. Large bones were covered with tattered flesh and mingled with rotting internal organs. Powers could recognize the three skulls: horses.

Powers looked up the cliff face. They'd fallen off the edge of the cliff and landed here. He didn't think horses were stupid enough to do that on their own—not three, one after another. Something had run them off the cliff. And then that something had dined on the carcasses.

His thoughts were interrupted by another man's yell. "Sergeant Major!"

Powers made his way to where the other two men were standing. One was in the process of losing his dinner; upon arriving Powers could understand why.

The body was battered, and most of the flesh on both legs was gone, but the two clear blue eyes stared up at the gathering darkness with a peaceful look about them.

They'd found Emma Plunket.

CHAPTER 16

Land Between the Lakes
7:34 P.M.

Powers had the four men in a tight perimeter, back to back. The low ground of Fords Bay was growing darker as the sun went down, and soon the night would surround them. They had two sets of night vision goggles, but Powers didn't feel safe here, goggles or not. Besides their M16s, they also had an M21 sniper rifle with a laser night scope. Cartwright stirred next to Powers, his eyes riveted on the cliff face.

"What's the matter?" Powers asked in a low voice.

Cartwright gestured up toward the cliff. "We're being watched. I can feel it. We've been watched ever since we pulled in here."

There were enough cracks and crevices in the rock wall to hide a hundred Synbats. Powers had to admit he'd had that same feeling for the past ten minutes. After discovering the woman's body, he'd pulled everyone in tight and they hadn't done any more exploring. Each man had his M16 and sidearm, but they were at a disadvantage in the low ground. It wasn't the time to go looking for trouble, especially since trouble might come looking for them soon.

Powers opened his rucksack and turned on the PRC-77 radio.

7:38 P.M.

A young lieutenant appeared at the door of the humvee where Riley had been kicked back, trying to get some sleep. "Mister Riley, you're needed at the TOC."

Riley grabbed his M16 and double-timed over behind the lieutenant. The two generals were clustered around a radio along with Colonel Hossey, who gestured with his good arm for Riley to come over.
Riley recognized the voice on the radio as soon as he heard it.

"I say again, I've found the body of a woman along with three horses.
The bones of several other small animals are gathered here too. Over."

Trollers had the mike. "How were they killed? Over."

"It looks like they were run off the cliff. Over."

"Get the grid," Hossey advised.

"What is your location? Over."

"North side of Fords Bay. Wait one." Powers's voice disappeared
with the squelch and then came back on. "Grid one two four, six four
three. I say again: one two four, six four three. We need some reinforcements here. Over."

Riley looked at his map. It made sense. Powers was only a couple
of klicks away to the south. The Synbats weren't running. They were
hiding. Merrit had said they had no place in particular to run. The cliff
was the most secure location for them within miles. Powers had found
the Werners' horses.

"Any sign of the Synbats there other than the bodies? Over," Trollers asked.

"Negative." There was a brief pause. "But I can feel them. They're
here. We're being watched. Over."

Trollers turned to Colonel Hossey questioningly. Hossey looked up
from the map where he had been plotting the grid. "Sergeant Major
Powers is a good man. He wouldn't have said that if he didn't think
we needed to hear it. He's seen some heavy action and he's still alive.
I'd trust his instincts."

Trollers looked at Riley. "You have the location. Get going." He keyed
the mike. "We've got help on the way. Hold your position. Out. Break.
Nighthawk, this is Search Base. Over."

7:46 P.M.

The small red dot probed among the rocks. Looking through the night
scope, Powers could see both the dot and the surrounding rock clearly
despite the gathering darkness. The AN/PAS-6 night scope mounted
on the M21 was a vast improvement over all previous systems he'd

ever worked with. The point of aim of the rifle was wherever the emitted laser beam touched.

As darkness fell, Powers had decided on a tactical retreat—General Trollers's order to hold fast notwithstanding—loading everyone back on the Zodiac and anchoring twenty meters offshore. They could do the same job from the boat, and Powers felt safer with the water between him and the shore. Of course, if the Synbats had weapons, as the men had been briefed, this position was more exposed, but Powers had decided that the move was worth it. If the Synbats were on the rock wall, the creatures had the advantage of the high ground. Powers was hoping to partially decrease the vertical angle by putting some space between his men and the base of the cliff.

Something moved at the edge of the scope. Powers overcorrected and then swung back. A Synbat! It was high up, about ten feet below the lip of the cliff. It slipped out of sight, melting into the rock. Powers watched carefully for it to reappear. There it was, moving swiftly! Powers placed the red dot and fired. Sparks flew as the round hit the rock, and the wall exploded with screeches.

Powers cursed as he tried to pin the creature with the laser beam. The scope mounting must be off slightly; he hadn't had a chance to zero it in, which accounted for the miss. The Synbat scrambled over the lip of the cliff and was gone before he could pin it down. A shot roared right next to him and Cartwright yelled out: "I spotted two going up. They're over the cliff. I don't think I hit." He slapped his M16. "Can't aim this thing worth a fuck with the goggles."

"Damn," Powers muttered to himself. All they'd managed to accomplish was to scare the Synbats out of their lair.

7:48 P.M.

Louis turned away from the fire and looked out to the east as two shots cracked the night air. They were camped with the rest of their "regiment"—all forty-three of them along a wood line. The sixteen horses were picketed in the trees. They'd been hearing numerous helicopters and vehicles moving around ever since the sun started to go down.

"That didn't sound like no musket," Jeremiah said.

"What were them yells?" the regimental sergeant at arms, Buford P. Lister, asked no one in particular.

The screeches after the first shot had caused the hair on the back of Louis's neck to stand up. "Don't know."

"Don't care," threw in Billy Pates. The man was what Louis would label the regimental fool. He made everyone around him look intelligent. Pates lifted his canteen cup to his lips. "As long as we got some of this here firewater, everything'll be all right."

And for a while everything did seem all right. For at least ten minutes. Louis was sitting through the third rendition of one of Buford's jokes when Jeremiah plucked at his sleeve.

"What?"

"Listen."

Louis looked at his brother in irritation. "To what?"

"The forest."

He gave it ten seconds, tuning out the noise of the camp. "I don't hear nothing."

Jeremiah nodded. "That's what I mean. It's quiet. Can't hear no night animals. Remember earlier today? That thing that attacked us? This is just how it got before it came on us from the trees. It's coming back."

Louis wanted to smack his brother over the head. The damn fool had always acted weird. "You don't even know what it was. How the hell can you know it's coming back?"

"It's the devil. He's come to claim our souls."

"Ah, goddamnit, Jer. You're going off your rocker. You listen—" Louis paused as a horse whinnied and then another. The animals were pulling at the picket line, straining back.

The men who had mounts left the fire and moved into the trees, trying to calm the horses. Louis's horse, Jezebel, had almost pulled her halter loose; he was retying it when he noticed his brother standing nearby, musket in hand, ignoring his own horse, just staring at the woods.

"Want to give me a hand here, Jer?" he asked, the irritation plain in his voice.

"There it is!" his brother yelled, throwing the musket to shoulder and firing. With the deep roar of the powder going off, all hell broke loose. Figures exploded out of the dark, firing rifles at the disbelieving men. Buford Lister and Billy Pates were among six that went down in the first ten seconds, their screams tearing the air.

Jeremiah and Louis ran, Jeremiah reloading on the run, Louis grabbing his musket and kit as he raced by the fire. A few more rounds ripped through the air around their heads and then the firing ceased. They halted two hundred meters away in a field and turned back, Jeremiah with musket at the ready, Louis reloading. Other shaken men of the 7th Cavalry were scattered around, breathing hard from the run and yelling senseless questions.

Soldiers from other campsites came running up to ask what had happened. But no one headed back into the tree line where the 7th U.S. Cavalry had been camped. The last of the screams died out.

8:14 P.M.

Eight hundred meters away, the three humvees of ODA 682 were rolling down a trail, the occupants oblivious to the destruction occurring close by. The headsets for radio and intercom, along with the rumble of the diesel engines, effectively deafened the entire team.

Riley had heard Powers report that he'd fired on the Synbats and that the animals had scaled the cliff and were running. Other units were closing in. The TOC was trying to throw together a hasty net to try and sweep up the Synbats.

The radio crackled. "This is Nighthawk. I've got multiple contacts on LLTV, vehicle and dismounted. I've also got horses on my screens. Impossible to find the target. Over."

"All elements, this is Search Base. Mark yourselves for identification by Nighthawk. Over."

Riley slid down into the humvee and reached into an outer pocket on his rucksack, retrieving a black watch cap. He turned the cap inside out, exposing the fluorescent tape sewn there, and put it on. Standing back up in the hatch, he knew that the tape would show up clearly on the low-light television (LLTV) of the Spectre gunship and the thermal sights of the OH-6s.

"This is Nighthawk. I've got small arms firing. Grid one two five, six five three. I say again. Small arms firing. Grid one two five, six five three. Over."

Riley shined a red-lens flashlight down on his map. "Take the next right, John." As the vehicle turned, Riley released the safety on the trigger of the .50 caliber.

CHAPTER 17

Land Between the Lakes
8:33 P.M.

Doc Seay and Martie Trustin were working on the wounded under the glare of headlights from various pickup trucks and rigs. Riley had the rest of his team deployed in a loose perimeter, supplemented by almost a hundred men with Civil War muskets. It would have almost been humorous except for the four bodies laid out under ponchos nearby and the wounded who were being tended.

Riley had already called the situation in to Search Base. Other than holding a perimeter to prevent the Synbats from coming in again, he was at a loss as to what to do. Going after the Synbats wasn't possible because they had no idea where the creatures were. By the time they'd gotten here, the Synbats had already disappeared and no one was sure in which direction.

Riley had ignored the numerous questions thrown his way by the reenactors. There wasn't anything he could say, except to tell everyone to stay inside the parameters of the open field.

Military vehicles were now rolling into the field as reinforcements arrived. General Trollers and Colonel Lewis hopped out of one humvee and hurried over to Riley's location.

Trollers's eyes were flashing in the glint of the headlights. "Where did the Synbats go?"

Riley shrugged. "I don't know, sir. They hit coming from the west, but I haven't been able to find anyone who could tell me which way they left."

"What about Nighthawk?"

202 SYNBAT

"It's picking up multiple targets. Our people are marked, but these reenactors are all over the place."

Trollers turned to Colonel Lewis. "Let's clear these people out *now*."

"Yes, sir."

8:57 P.M.

Few wild animals have had a more devastating encounter with man than the bison, commonly miscalled the American buffalo. From an estimated peak strength of thirty million to a low of five hundred at the turn of the century, the herds have slowly increased to a present size of approximately thirty-five to fifty thousand.

With a half moon rising in the eastern sky, the herd of fifty-three bison at the Buffalo Range at Land Between the Lakes had just increased by one. The mother finished licking the newborn calf to clean it off, and it immediately suckled up.

The bachelor groups of massive males, some weighing almost two thousand pounds, ignored the maternal efforts. It would be two more months until breeding season, when they would mingle again with the cow-calf herds to initiate the reproductive process.

This particular evening one of the males, an old bison that had seen the turn of many seasons, was alert, but not because of the events going on inside the fence of the range. There was something outside that disturbed him.

He turned his massive head from side to side, shaggy long hair drooping to the ground. His nostrils flared as he took in a deep breath of dark air: There it was again, just on the edge of his smell range, coming from the east. Synapses clicked in the bison's brain as it tried to recall ever smelling that particular odor.

The bull waited with growing agitation. The smell was getting closer— an incoming tide of danger. Other bulls were aroused, shaken by the old one's movements. A ripple of unease ran through the herd. Instinctively the mothers pushed their young calves to the center and the males spread out in a semicircle, facing the Trace that ran along the fence on the east side of the range.

The old bull's beady eyes narrowed, searching the dark tree line on the far side of the road. Something tentatively left the safety of the darkness and crept out onto the road. Another joined it. The intruders were drawn by the smell of fresh blood from the birth. The bulls began snorting and stomping at the earth, huge horns swinging back and forth.

The newcomers crossed the road, skulking up to the fence, sensing that the barbwire was the range of their safety. They looked over the thousands of pounds of horned protection between them and the newborn calf.

Tonight would not be the night. The intruders turned and slunk back into the woods in search of easier prey.

It took the herd almost an hour to calm down. Soon all but the old one were asleep, the newborn curled up with its mother. The old one walked slowly along the fence. He was troubled. This was something bad and he didn't like it. He knew that those predators would be back.

10:15 P.M.

Riley put his team on 50 percent alert. There was a long night ahead and tomorrow would be a critical day. His men needed rest. He doubted that the Synbats would attack Search Base, but at this point he was past trying to figure out what they would and would not do.

He'd received Kate's last message from Powers when the NCO had returned to the base camp after his adventure at the cliffs. Although Ward was no longer an issue, Merrit certainly was. How much of what she said could be believed? Riley hadn't been overly impressed with the videotape. Although it was certainly possible that the Synbats had been trying to trick Merrit into opening the cages, it was more likely that she had overreacted. Riley shook his head. The issue wasn't Merrit; the issue was the Synbats. He needed to concentrate on what he knew for sure.

He lay back on his rucksack outside the glow of the lights at the TOC and took stock of the situation. About half of the reenactors had been moved out, but there were stragglers here and there. It was also unknown how many other people were still in the park. Tomorrow would be the big clearout and then tomorrow night the shoot.

It was all looking too easy. The Synbats had been one step ahead of him from the start, mainly because he'd thought of them as animals, never as intelligent opponents. Now that he knew the truth, it was time to correct that operational fault. To anticipate the enemy's moves was a tenet of operational planning. Riley decided to review the facts in his mind, see how they fit together, then try to project a course of action for the Synbats.

As he started to concentrate, a figure appeared in the darkness. "We need to talk."

Riley unwrapped himself from his poncho liner and followed Colonel Hossey over to the DIA van. A single man sat at the communications console, monitoring it. A small figure bundled in a blanket in a chair was the object of Hossey's search. He tapped her on the shoulder, waking her. "We need to talk to you."

"Stop!" she cried out. Merrit blinked the sleep out of her eyes. "Another contact with the Synbats?"

Hossey led the way to the door. "No. I want to discuss what's going on. Let's go outside and talk."

The sky had cleared up somewhat and a few stars poked through. The weather report called for intermittent showers through Saturday. The temperature was down into the low fifties and Riley could see his breath puffing as they talked.

Hossey started out with the one remaining question Riley had about the past events. "How did the Synbats escape?"

Merrit looked at Hossey, then glanced around furtively. She spoke in a low whisper. "There was a power failure on Sunday night—actually early Monday morning. In response to the loss of primary power, the security guard lowered the status on the containment on the Synbats. Then those three escapees that Colonel Lewis is using for his cover story arrived at the lab. I don't know why, but they killed the security guard and then broke into the lab. We found all three of their bodies the next morning. The security guard was gone, but they found his body in a van driven by the sister of one of the escapees."

"Shit!" Riley exclaimed. "You mean you already had four dead people when we showed up here Monday morning?"

Merrit moved closer. "The security guard was killed by the convicts, but the three of them were killed by the Synbats."

"Great. That's just fucking great." Riley clenched his fists. He wanted to hit someone or something very badly.

"We thought the collars had terminated them by the time you showed up," Merrit reminded him.

Riley closed his eyes and did a slow count to ten, trying to control his anger. He knew that Merrit was not responsible for making the decision to withhold information from his team.

Hossey summed it up. "So right now the Synbats have killed a whole bunch of people and we've managed to get only one of them, losing a helicopter in the process."

Riley pointed at the TOC. "Doesn't anybody in there realize that it isn't just luck that these things have been a step ahead of us the whole time? The Synbats have had some sort of plan, while we've been pulling stuff out of our hat in reaction to them."

Merrit was confused. "I thought you had a plan now."

Hossey tried to make her understand. "We do, but we're still leaving a lot of initiative up to the Synbats. I've tried telling General Trollers that it isn't as simple as it appears, but he sees it differently. He feels that the attack on the Civil War reenactors was a sign of desperation because Sergeant Major Powers flushed them out of their lair. Trollers thinks they're on the run now. What do you think about the attack on the reenactors?"

Merrit was quiet for a few moments. "I don't think they would have attacked without a purpose. Every move they've made so far had a reason. I think they probably considered the reenactors part of the force that was after them and attacked to strike back. Those men were armed and acting in a military manner. I think it's reasonable to assume that the Synbats couldn't tell the difference between real and simulated."

"But the bottom line is that they are intelligent creatures, right? And they know they're being hunted," Hossey interjected, cutting to the heart of the matter.

"There's no doubt of that," Merrit replied.

"As intelligent creatures who want to survive, what do you think they will do now?"

"They have to find a new lair. They'll need a source of food for the young and someplace to hide for several days at least."

"Then the plan for tomorrow should work?" Hossey wanted to know.

Merrit shook her head. "I really don't know. They know they're being chased, but they certainly can't know the extent of the net around them. As I said before, I think they will try to hide. They already did that once at the cliffs."

"What about escape?" Riley asked.

"To where?" Merrit replied.

"I don't know." Riley thought for a few seconds. "Maybe we ought to go look at the cliff where they were hiding and get an idea of what they were doing. That might help us figure out where they might try to hide next."

Hossey quickly warmed to that idea. "We'll send you in at first light."

10:30 P.M.

The regiment's horses had broken free of their picket line during all the commotion earlier in the evening and disappeared. Now the army people were telling them to vacate the area immediately and go home. Louis spent a fruitless five minutes arguing with some army major. He was damned if he'd leave behind eight valuable horses, six of which weren't even his.

The major had been sympathetic but unyielding. He gave Louis a vague promise that they'd be notified when the park was reopened after the escapees were captured, and then they could come back in and recover their animals. When Louis had asked when that might be, so he could decide whether to stay in the area or go home, the officer had told him to go home.

"Fuck it," Louis muttered. He turned to Jeremiah. "Let's get out of here."

They walked back to the main parking area where their rig was parked. The brothers slid the ramp into their trailer and shut the back doors, making it ready for travel. They got in the cab and Louis started the engine.

"You ready?" he asked. He received no response at all from his brother. Jeremiah had not uttered a word since the attack. As far as Louis was concerned, the sooner they got home the better. The army was full of shit about the escaped prisoners too. Why the hell would escaped prisoners have been up in the trees? And there had been something weird about those "escapees" from the faint glimpses he'd had of them. They hadn't looked quite normal. Louis didn't envy the regimental commander who had volunteered to fly up to Chicago out of Nashville and notify the families of the four dead men.

They followed the army guides who waved them out of the camp and onto Lick Creek Road. Army vehicles, machine guns mounted on top and headlights blazing, were parked all along the road. Louis reached the Trace at the Golden Pond Visitor Center, then followed a soldier's lighted baton and turned right onto Route 68.

At the bridge over Lake Barkley, roadblocks manned by army personnel were set up in center span, blocking any traffic from going out. On the far side of the bridge, the Kentucky State Police had roadblocks facing the other way. Passing the last of the army people, Louis breathed a sigh of relief. He could see helicopters with searchlights flying over the water on either side of the lake. They were damn serious about sealing off the park.

They rolled through Cadiz, then headed east along 68; at I-24 they would turn north for home. Louis decided to drive straight through and get his brother away from this place as fast as possible.

CHAPTER 18
WEDNESDAY, 8 APRIL

Land Between the Lakes
4:12 A.M.

Three shadowy figures were standing in the tree line, two with something on their backs. Merrit knew she should be feeling fear but for some reason she didn't. Instead she felt almost peaceful. She started walking across the grass toward them, her hands held high, indicating that she didn't have a weapon and meant no harm. The Synbats held their position, their golden eyes unblinking.

Merrit wanted to talk, but she knew they wouldn't understand the words. How could she explain what was happening anyway? They were the hunted and she was one of the hunters. The Synbats finally moved, slowly turning to head back into the deep darkness of the forest. Merrit halted where she was. They all disappeared, except one, which looked over its shoulder at her. She stared. It was no longer a Synbat but a human face—a man. She recognized the face with a start; it was her father. She started walking toward him, drawn by something beyond her control. As she got closer he changed back into the Synbat and the mouth was wide open, fangs bared. She turned and ran.

Robin Merrit almost fell off the chair as she awoke, her head jerking up from the desktop where it had been resting. She was damp with perspiration. Her unfocused eyes swept over to the door of the van, half expecting to see her father standing there. As the fuzz faded from her vision, she recognized Colonel Lewis silhouetted against the glow of lights from the communications console.

"Are you OK?"

Merrit blinked. "Yes."

"You cried out. Get some more sleep. I talked with Colonel Hossey. You'll be going in with Riley at first light to look over the lair at the cliff."

"All right." As Merrit lowered her head, thoughts of the Synbats filled her mind.

7:27 A.M.

"Tango Two Seven, are you in place? Over."

"This is Two Seven. Roger. We've got you covered. Over."

Riley swung his arm over his head, toward shore. The four Zodiacs pulled on line, an M60 machine gunner in each prow, covering the advance. Three other Zodiacs, with men from another team, stayed offshore to give supporting fire if needed. Two A teams were positioned on top of the cliff to give covering fire and stop any Synbats that might try to escape in that direction, if by some chance they had returned to their lair.

Overhead, General Williams was flying in his command and control (C & C) Blackhawk helicopter, monitoring the radio net. Riley had a PRC-77 strapped to his back, with the headset tied off to the front of his combat vest on the left shoulder.

He reached up with his left hand and pressed the transmit button. "We're moving in. Over."

There were no signs of Synbats as the boats beached and Riley's team secured the area. He had his men clear fifty meters in each direction, making sure that at least the level ground was free of the creatures. The Synbats could be hiding on the rock face, but he had to count on the men in the boats and on top of the cliff to take care of that.

Satisfied that he had a relatively safe beachhead, Riley pressed the transmit button on the handset. "Clear down here. Bring in Merrit. Over."

A fifth Zodiac beached. Doctor Merrit stepped off, and Riley and Powers greeted her. The sergeant major pointed. "The dead horses are up here. We removed the woman's body last night. She was found over there."

They moved to the base of the cliff. Riley pulled out a machete and hacked at the undergrowth, gradually revealing more of the horses.

He noted that Merrit was either getting used to the sight of death or she was detaching herself from reality as she spoke. "The four Synbats that escaped were very cunning. I'd guess they drove the horses from the campsite where the Werners were killed to this point, then off the cliff face. Then they must have split. You chased two of them to the west, but the other two must have stayed here, hoping they'd escape the search. In fact, the two you chased were probably a diversion to lead you away. I'm sure they kept both sets of pods here." She bent over the horses, the stench apparently not affecting her, and pointed. "Look at these cuts in the rib cage. I think they planned on planting the pods inside the horses' bodies. That would ensure an adequate supply of food when the pods hatched, at least for a while, even if the other two had to leave this location and lead you away if need be."

The radio squawked. "This is Tango Two Seven. We're going over the edge. Over."

Riley looked up as ropes were thrown over the lip of the cliff. Men with submachine guns slung over their shoulders backed over the edge and slowly started rappeling their way down, sticking the snout of their guns in every crack and crevice that could possibly hide a Synbat.

Riley doubted they'd find anything, but it was worth checking out. He returned his attention to the base. "Since we took this site away from them, what do you think they'll do now? Find a similar area and do the same thing?"

Merrit nodded. "Their primary concern will be a food source for the young. Although they are omnivorous, they will most likely be looking for meat, because that would be the most readily available food source in quantity."

Riley pulled out his map and spread it on the ground, squatting down and looking it over. "Where would you go if you needed meat, Dan?"

Powers knelt next to him. "Plenty of deer out here."

"But they'd have to hunt it. I don't think they can run down a deer, and I'm sure they won't use their weapons for that. It would give away their position." Riley shook his head. "No, I'm talking something easier than that."

Powers stabbed a thick finger down on the map. "I'd go there."

5:34 P.M.

The day passed with aircraft and humvees traversing the park with loudspeakers, advising all people to leave the area. The exodus slowed to a trickle by afternoon. For the past two hours, all the roadblocks had reported negatively when asked if people were still leaving. There had been no sign of the Synbats throughout the day. No sightings, no trails, no contacts—nothing.

General Williams was fighting his primary battle not with the Synbats but with the news media, who were gathering like locusts around the perimeter, demanding to know what was going on. Two news helicopters from Nashville had tried penetrating the aerial perimeter and been turned back by gunships. The cover story was holding so far, although there had been interviews with some of the Civil War reenactors, which had confused the situation somewhat.

The thump of helicopter blades echoed across the sky and a flight of OH-6 Special Operations helicopters flew by. The single-rotor helicopters were flown by the Nightstalkers—members of Special Operations Task Force 160. The two-man aircraft had advanced night vision and thermal sights on board and a 7.62mm minigun slung off one skid. For tonight's mission, the aircraft would fly in pairs, searching the area in a grid pattern that the operations officer had spent the entire day carefully laying out. Come dark, they would fire on any two-legged, two-armed image that didn't have fluorescent tape marking it as friendly.

6:54 P.M.

Powers scanned the pasture. The bison were stirring. The disturbance started from the far side and spread until the entire herd was alert. As Powers watched, the animals gathered together in a tight defensive perimeter, as far from the fences as they could get, the massive males on the outside, the females and the young on the inside.

The radio was a low, annoying buzz in his ear as the TOC coordinated the various elements that would begin the aerial search in six minutes. Powers and his team were hidden on a small hill overlooking the buffalo range. They'd been there for six hours, ever since Powers and Riley had convinced Colonel Hossey that the penned-in animals would make a tempting target for the Synbats and that the abandoned barn on the side of the field might make a good hideout for the creatures. Powers felt more worthwhile waiting here than sitting around at the TOC.

The sun was about down and the twilight made for very difficult viewing. Powers pulled his night vision goggles down over his eyes and turned them on. The range, fenced with barbwire, bordered the Trace on the side opposite Powers and his team.

"Be ready," Powers whispered. "Something's got the buffalo spooked."

On either side of him, men turned on their rifle night vision scopes; invisible laser beams licked out across the open field, probing the far tree line.

Two low-lying silhouettes broke out of the tree line on the far side of the road. Powers could barely make them out through the goggles, but he didn't want to take any chances. He gave the order while the shadowy figures were at the edge of the Trace. With a crack, two rifles sounded in concert.

Powers limped back down the hill and hopped into his humvee. His driver cranked the engine and they roared around the dirt trail circumventing the range.

The headlights illuminated the scene as the driver brought the humvee to a halt. Powers leapt from the vehicle, rifle at the ready. There were two bodies. The first dog—a scraggly Airedale—lay dead, shot through the chest. The second—a golden retriever, its coat almost black from dirt—lay panting, blood trickling from the bullet wound in its left foreleg.

Powers shook his head as he dismounted. The retriever looked up at him with wide eyes and whimpered. "What were you doing, dumb dog?" Powers whispered as he lowered his rifle. The dog's ribs showed and its fur was matted with brambles and dirt. It had obviously been running wild out here for quite a while.

Powers checked out the wound; the round had gone straight through and missed the bone. He tenderly wrapped a compress around the leg. Tying it in place, he scooped up the dog and placed it in the back of the humvee. So much for their buffalo idea so far. Powers drove back around and returned to his overwatch position. Maybe larger predators would be coming later.

8:34 P.M.

"Are you sure they can see this? It seems so small." Merrit looked dubiously at the fluorescent tape sewn onto the top of the watch cap that Riley had handed her.

Riley nodded. "The sights in those aircraft not only can see at night, but they also give quite a bit of amplification. As long as you wear that, they'll know you're one of the good guys. That tape shows up like a beacon."

A Blackhawk helicopter settled onto the field. Riley tapped Merrit on the arm. "Let's go."

Riley shouldered the radio, tucking the end of the antenna down into his shirt, and picked up his rifle. He gestured for his team to move out, then he escorted Merrit onto the aircraft, seating her facing forward next to him. The aircraft lifted in a smooth rush of power.

Riley grabbed a headset that was hanging from the roof and put it on. "This is Chief Riley. We're all set."

The pilot answered. "Roger. I'm Captain Patrick. We're going to fly above the gunships, and we're on their freq so you can hear them talk."

As the chopper gained altitude, Riley's men rigged rappeling ropes on either side of the cargo bay. The ropes were attached to large O-bolts hanging from the ceiling, then were carefully coiled in deployment bags, ready to be used if they had to get out of the aircraft and a landing zone wasn't available. After checking the rigs, Riley turned to his team and gestured as he yelled above the sound of the blades and engines. "All right. Lock and load." Eight magazines were slammed home and the bolts pulled. The rifles were held between the knees, muzzles pointing at the floor. They were ready.

9:14 P.M.

"Eagle Center, this is Nighthawk Three One. I've got movement. Location point eight klicks east of checkpoint three seven. Request permission to break pattern to investigate. Over."

"This is Eagle Center. Permission granted. Over."

Riley found checkpoint three seven on his map and spoke into the intercom to the pilot. "Let's slide on over there, sir." He felt a surge of adrenaline. First contact of the evening. Maybe the last.

"Roger," the pilot acknowledged. The Blackhawk swooped to the west, overflying the OH-6 gunship pilot. Riley could see the green and red running lights of the smaller helicopter below.

"This is Nighthawk Three One. I've got multiple targets moving west. They're under the trees. Over."

"This is Eagle Center. Roger Three One. Break. Nighthawk One Six, break pattern and support Three One. Three One and One Six switch to tac frequency one-niner-five. All other elements hold in place and move to an altitude of five hundred AGL. We might be going hot here. Over."

Looking like fireflies, the other gunships drilled up into the night sky to five hundred feet and held position while the two designated gunships paired up. Riley had his pilot switch frequency and listened to the two pilots coordinate as they closed in.

"Do you have them? Over."

"Roger. I've got you and them clear. Do you have me? Over."

"Roger. Got you in sight. I've got a clear field of fire at two hundred degrees. Over."

"I've got a two-seventy. Eagle Center, we've got multiple targets on thermals. Image is broken. They're moving under the trees. Request permission to fire. Over."

There was a brief pause and then General Williams's voice came over the airways. "This is Eagle Six. Do they look like they might be people? Over."

"Eagle Six, this is Nighthawk Three One. We can't tell through the thermals. There's too much residual heat coming off the trees to get a clear picture. If we can get them out in the open we could check them with our goggles. Over."

"Do you have any open area in the immediate vicinity? Over."

"Roger. About five hundred meters to the south we've got a field. Over."

"Use your miniguns to move your target to that field and get a positive ID. Over."

"Roger."

A line of tracers roped out of one of the helicopters. Again and again it fired small bursts, herding the target in the desired direction.

"This is Three One. They're moving south. Over."

"This is One Six. I'm in position at the tree line. Over."

Riley talked to his UH-60 pilot. "Move us above One Six; over the field, so we can see the tree line." Riley took a set of night vision goggles and slipped them on. He put another set on Merrit. "Watch that tree line."

Another burst.

"This is Three One. They're just about there. Over."

"There!" Riley grabbed Merrit's arm. "See them?"

In the green glow of the goggles, shadowy figures were slipping out of the tree line. "What do you see?" Riley asked Merrit as he strained to make them out.

"I don't know. They're moving fast."

"This is One Six. Hold guns. Hold guns. I've got targets in the open. I make out six deer. Over."

Williams's voice was disappointed. "This is Eagle Six. Resume search pattern. Over."

"Take us back up, sir," Riley spoke into the intercom. The Blackhawk climbed into the sky and they settled down to wait.

Three more times they moved in as gunships picked out heat images under the trees, and each time the result was negative. As the night chill settled in and the residual heat dissipated, the thermal sights began to function better, identifying targets under the trees without having to move them out into the open. No Synbats—just deer and other animals.

By midnight the helicopters were beginning to retrace areas that had already been searched. There was the possibility that the Synbats had moved through search areas and been missed, but it was a slim one. The operations officer had even planned the refueling schedule to make sure that contiguous areas were monitored and there would be no gaps.

At five after midnight, Riley's Blackhawk swooped down and flared, wheels settling onto the grass. Riley leapt off the left side and then turned to help Merrit. His team off-loaded wearily. The aircraft lifted with a surge of wind to head for the forward arming and refuel point (FARP) that the 160th had set up in a nearby field.

"Make sure your caps are on, tape facing out," Riley ordered. Despite being at the headquarters, he was taking no chances. He walked over to the TOC with Merrit. It was not a happy group that stood in the large tent listening to the radio reports and tracking the search on map overlays. The entire park had been covered. The lair had been gone over in excruciating detail. No live Synbats had been found in the park. The perimeter defenses had reported negatively. Nothing.

"What do we do now?" Williams directed the question at General Trollers, the senior man on the ground.

Trollers was as exhausted as everyone else. "We've done about all we can do." He turned to Merrit. "Is there anyplace you think they could be hiding from the thermals?"

Merrit seemed lost in thought. "I have no idea."

Riley was listening to this exchange with a growing sense of frustrated anger. He wasn't sure what the source of his anger was. Surprisingly, he couldn't focus on the Synbats as the enemy. Even though they'd killed two of his men and all the others, including the young girl, he was beginning to realize that the Synbats were pawns in this game just as much as he was. The one at whom he could best direct his disgust was Trollers. Hossey and Williams were like Riley; they'd been caught up in the fix-it phase. Trollers, however, was responsible for the start of the project. But even Trollers was just a figurehead, Riley knew. Ultimate blame had to rest with a system that saw the need to develop something like the Synbats.

Trollers laid out the facts, almost as if he were trying to convince himself. "We've checked the park. We're almost positive there are no live Synbats inside the boundaries. Our perimeter was secure and there's no way that any of the Synbats could have made it down to Route 79, or to one of the bridges, before we sealed them off. We'd have spotted them in the water from the air if they'd gone that way." He looked around the tent. "So where are they? Could they be dead and that's why we're not picking them up on the thermals? Or could they be hiding in a pond or a cave or somewhere that the thermals can't penetrate?"

Williams was looking at the map. "As far as we know there are no caves in the park. If they were in the water, they'd have to be breathing and we'd pick up some slight heat difference at the surface."

A fuel truck loaded with JP-4 lumbered by on the road heading for the FARP, where the helicopters were being refueled. Riley watched the truck roll out of sight. Then the idea came to him, as if it had been sitting there all along in his frontal lobe. He turned to the others. "They're not in the park anymore."

Trollers turned to him angrily. "How? How could they have gotten out, mister?"

Riley looked the general in the eye. "They rode out."

"They what?"

"The Civil War reenactors," Riley explained. "They had horse trailers. Did your people search them as they were leaving?"

General Williams blinked and then slowly shook his head. "No. We were in too much of a rush to get them out of the park. We never thought of that."

Riley wanted to kick himself for not realizing it earlier. He'd even been standing there while some of the reenactors had loaded, and he'd watched the cars and trucks drive away. If they had been looking for humans, they would have searched the trailers, but everyone had been thinking of the Synbats as nonreasoning animals. Riley vowed that this was the last time he would make that mistake.

"We need to contact the civilian authorities and try to track down those trucks."

Trollers wasn't buying into it. "You're saying they stowed away on one of those vehicles?"

Riley laid it on the line. "We have got to accept that these Synbats are intelligent and will do almost anything to survive. Whether you believe Doctor Merrit or not, they have capabilities we don't even know about. They're out of the park."

"How can you be sure of that?" Trollers demanded.

Riley stood his ground. "I'm not, but it's the only thing that makes sense. We have to listen to the evidence we do have. As far as we can tell, they aren't in the park. That means they got out somehow, and the most logical explanation is that they rode out. That would explain the attack on the reenactors. They forced our hand, making us move the Civil War people out quickly."

It was too much for Trollers. "You're saying that these things figured out that the park was surrounded and the only way they could get out was to sneak out in a vehicle? How could they have known that?"

"The same way they knew to attack Search Base," Riley replied. "The same way they split up and tried to lead us off in the wrong direction. We're dealing with something we don't understand, General."

Being talked to like that by a warrant officer wasn't high on General Trollers's list of favorite things. "Don't tell me what I have to do, mister. I've done—"

"Sir, I have a suggestion." Hossey tried calming everyone down. "We can still keep the perimeter around the park and continue the search here. If the three adult Synbats have managed to hide somewhere in the park, I think they'll have a much harder time staying hidden once the young ones are born. We'll find them then. But if they are out, we need to get on line with the civilian authorities and check it out."

"Do you know how hard it's going to be to find all those vehicles and then find out if the Synbats were in them?" General Williams looked at the glowing red numbers on the clock above the radios. "We have about six hours before the backpacks initiate. If the Synbats were on one of those trailers, they could have hopped off anywhere along the way. We'd need a miracle to find them now."

Trollers rubbed his forehead. "All right. I'll get my people in Virginia working on the vehicle angle. Everything else here stays in place and we keep looking."

CHAPTER 19
THURSDAY, 9 APRIL

Chicago, Illinois
6:17 A.M.

Ken Bradley was enthused about the new job waiting for him in Atlanta. He'd been out of work now for two months and things were finally looking up. He was less than enthused about this last task he had to accomplish before he and his family hit the road. In his old Ford LTD he cruised the roads to the west of Soldiers' Field, crisscrossing the numerous railroad tracks that ran through there, looking for the right location.

Ken had tried, ever since getting the job, to find someone who would take his daughter's dog, Holly, but there wasn't much demand for an eighty-pound mixed-breed mutt with a half-chewed ear. They'd picked her up as a pup at the pound and Ken had wanted to take her there to be put to sleep. When news of that plan had been overheard by Kristen, she'd thrown the tantrum to end all tantrums. He'd promised not to do it.

Ken randomly took a back alley between several warehouses, until he was out of sight of the traffic on South Indiana Avenue. Then he stopped, got out of the car, and opened the back door. He unbuckled the dog's collar and threw the strap onto the front passenger seat.

"Come on, girl."

Holly eyed him warily and didn't move.

"Come on, you dumb mutt." Ken reached in, grabbed her front paws, and pulled, but eighty pounds of reluctant black Labrador and German Shepherd can be very difficult to remove from a backseat. Finally

219

he resorted to climbing in behind her, putting his back to the other door, and pushing her butt with his feet. Acknowledging defeat, Holly leapt out the door and stood in the garbage-strewn alley looking up at him.

Ken slammed the door and got into the driver's seat. Holly stood expectantly just outside, nose pressed up against the glass. He turned the car around and headed for South Indiana. In the rearview mirror he could see Holly following.

"Damn," he muttered, pressing harder on the accelerator. Holly disappeared as he sped around the corner.

Just before reaching his house he rolled down his window and threw her collar onto the street. Now at least he could honestly tell his daughter that he hadn't put her dog to sleep. He'd make up some story about a family with their own little girl who wanted the dog.

In the alley, Holly finally stopped and looked around. The shadows beckoned darkly on all sides. She raised her head and cautiously smelled the air. With a low whimper, she slunk off into a small opening in the wall of an abandoned warehouse.

6:30 A.M.

Chicago police officer Billy Shields was driving down I-90 watching the rush-hour traffic start to pile up when he spotted the horse rig stopped on the side of the road. Shields pulled past the rig, noting that the back doors of the trailer were open slightly. He parked in front of the truck, called in the stop to dispatch, and got out.

The driver's door was open. Shields stepped up and poked his head in. There was no sign of anyone in the cab. He wondered if it had broken down and the driver had walked to the next exit to get assistance. Shields walked around back, boots crunching in the gravel. He grabbed the back door and swung it open.

The officer had seen more than his share of wrecks, some where the victims had to be scraped off the road, but he'd never seen anything like this. Two men lay in the straw on the floor of the rig, bodies literally torn apart. One man was completely disemboweled, his guts strewn about like strands of spaghetti. The other's neck was almost completely severed, the head lying cocked at an impossible angle.

Shields had his gun in his hand, but he couldn't remember drawing it. He scanned the rest of the interior of the trailer, the muzzle tracking with his eyes. Nothing but bales of straw and horse feed. He hurried back to his patrol car, trying to keep his breakfast from coming back up.

Land Between the Lakes
7:24 A.M.

"We've got them!" General Trollers exclaimed as he read the fax. "A Chicago cop found a rig with two bodies in it. Two brothers who'd been attending the reenactment. Both bodies were badly torn up."

"Where?" General Williams asked.

"The south side of Chicago, parked on the side of an interstate." He grabbed an atlas and thumbed through it, an expectant crowd looking over his shoulder. "Damn, they sure made it a long way." His finger rested on a blown-up map of Chicago. "Here—just before I-90 crosses I-55."

"Any sign of the Synbats themselves?" Hossey asked.

"No. The locals are treating it like a double murder."

Riley thought of his own home in the Bronx. He looked up at Colonel Hossey. "They're in the city."

The tent went silent for a minute as everyone realized the implication of the Synbats loose in a heavily populated area.

Trollers turned to Colonel Lewis. "Let's get some aircraft moving. We can get there in a couple of hours."

"And then what, sir?"

Trollers blinked at Riley's blunt interruption. "What do you mean?"

"What are you going to do when you get there, sir? You've got an urban jungle to look in. The Synbats have thousands of places to hide and millions of people to feed on. We've tried everything to find these things so far—dogs, helicopters, thermal sights, Spectre, vehicles, traps—and nothing has worked. What makes you think any of that will work now?"

Trollers threw back the challenge. "What do you suggest? Just leave them alone and let the pods initiate?"

"No, sir. I suggest we alert the local authorities about what the threat really is. We can't afford to keep it secret any longer." Riley gestured about him. "If you think we had a high body count here in this park, wait until they have some time in the middle of Chicago."

"We can't alert the local authorities." Trollers's voice was firm.

"We can't afford not to," Riley shot back. "The Synbats will be spotted sooner or later. Hopefully sooner. The longer they're out there, the more they'll kill. And once the pods activate—" Riley glanced at his watch— "which is right about now, we'll never be sure we got them all."

"Alerting the locals is unacceptable. We'll go up there ourselves and try to contain the problem. We'll tie into the local media and law enforcement, and at the first sight of the Synbats, we'll federalize the whole case."

Colonel Hossey shook his head. "That's illegal. Hell, even what we did here in the park is illegal. The Posse Comitatus Act forbids the use of federal troops in domestic action unless directly authorized by the president."

Lewis looked at Hossey as if the colonel had grown another head. "Get with it, man. Do you know what will happen if word of the Synbat project is leaked to the public, or even to the military affairs subcommittee in Congress?"

Lewis pointed a thick finger at Riley and Merrit. "You get your butts on up to Chicago ASAP. I'll have papers and ID waiting for you when you land. I'll make sure your cover is good. We have plans for things like this."

En Route to Chicago
10:34 A.M.

The pilot had the throttle wide open and the Blackhawk was shuddering along at 175 miles an hour. Riley sat in the back, uncomfortable in the civilian clothing he had rapidly donned prior to takeoff. A second Blackhawk would follow them in thirty minutes carrying Lewis, and would link up with the head police representative in Chicago. Riley and Merrit were going directly to the horse trailer.

Riley glanced across at Merrit, sitting in the jump seat opposite him. She hadn't said a word since they'd taken off. Riley had been considering the information Westland had given him for the past hour, and he finally leaned forward to talk to Merrit. "Do you think we'll find them?"

"Chicago's a terrible place to find creatures that don't want to be found," she said. "I'm worried about what will happen when they need to feed not only themselves but the embryos that do survive." Merrit shook her head. "The local authorities and the media should be alerted."

Riley had already fought that battle and lost. "I've worked in the military long enough and been on enough classified missions to know that many times the desire for security overrides common sense. Trollers's number-one concern is that word of this project doesn't leak out. He's already got a pretty substantial body count and the only thing he seems worried about is how he's going to cover it up. Nothing you or I say is going to change him on that."

"You can't give up that easily," Merrit pressed.

"Hey, *I* didn't create these things," Riley snapped. "And I'm not giving up. Why do you think I'm on this damn helicopter? I'm the garbageman who has to come around and clean up your mess. Two of my men have died so far doing that, and I don't want to lose any more. What do you want me to do? Go to the press? Walk up to whoever's meeting us in Chicago and say—'Well, hey, you've got three genetically designed killing machines loose in your city and they just had a whole bunch of babies'."

Riley paused and took a deep breath, trying to control the rage that was pulsing through his veins. "It really doesn't matter much anyway, does it? At the rate they went through people in Land Between the Lakes, I have a feeling that your Synbats are going to be front-page news rather quickly."

Merrit's eyes flashed at Riley's last sentence. "They're not *mine!*"

"Hey, you made them," Riley pressed, watching her carefully.

"I was wrong to go along with what they wanted." She began to cry. "I'll pay for it. I will pay for it."

"Hey," Riley said, grabbing her shoulder. "Take it easy. We'll get them."

"It's already too late," she said, the words blown away by the whine of the turbine engines.

Riley leaned back in the web seat and rubbed his eyes. He was tired and troubled, not only about what had happened and was going to happen, but about deeper issues.

"We'll be landing in two minutes," the pilot announced over the intercom.

Riley shook his head and looked out the window. The skyscrapers of downtown Chicago loomed to the immediate north. Urban sprawl extended as far as the eye could see. Somewhere out there were the Synbats. They could be anywhere.

A police officer stood in the parking lot, directing them down. Riley could see several police cars parked around a semi with a trailer. The pilot landed on the indicated spot.

Riley leaned over and grabbed Merrit, rousing her. "Let's go!"

She looked out the door and didn't move.

"Come on," Riley yelled. "Let's move it."

She slowly got to her feet and followed him off the aircraft.

A hard-looking man with a high and tight haircut and wearing a rumpled suit was waiting for them. "I'm Sergeant Scott."

Riley extended his hand. "Special Agent Riley, and this is Doctor Merrit."

Scott nodded. "The lieutenant's waiting for you by the trailer."

"I thought it was found next to the interstate," Riley commented as they walked over.

Scott laughed. "Yeah, it was, but we had to move it. You fuck with rush-hour traffic, you fuck with the city. We towed it over here. We got photos, and forensics went all over the site, so don't sweat it. The lieutenant can show you all that stuff."

As they approached the rear of the trailer, a short, slender woman stepped out of the back. She had black hair, cut tight against her skull. She wore gray slacks, flat shoes, and a sleeveless blouse that showed off the olive skin of her arms. She reminded Riley of the girls who used to hang out behind his high school in the South Bronx and smoke cigarettes. She was as dark skinned as he was, and her face crinkled up as she came out into the bright sunlight. She eyed Riley and Merrit with little pleasure.

"You the feds?"

Riley pulled out the ID the pilot of the chopper had given him, identifying him as a special agent of the FBI. "Agent Riley. This is Doctor Merrit. She works with my team."

The woman didn't offer her hand. "I'm Lieutenant Giannini, Chicago homicide. This is a real pile of shit."

Riley stepped up next to her. "Can I take a look?"

Giannini shrugged. "Yeah. I wouldn't take the doc in, though, unless she's got a strong stomach." She pointed at a black van with Coroner stenciled on the side. "I gotta move the bodies soon. Would've had them outta here by now if the chief hadn't called and said you were coming."

They ignored Giannini's comment and climbed into the back of the trailer. Riley took in the bloody scene. He glanced at Merrit; she seemed detached, gazing at the bodies without expression. He walked through the trailer, noting the droppings near the front end among the straw. The Synbats must have ridden up there, hidden in the bales. No sign of the backpacks—not that Riley had expected to find them. Something had caused the two men to stop and open up the back. Had they heard something, or seen something in the rearview mirror? Maybe they spotted the Synbats trying to get out.

Riley hoped that the Chicago Police Department would assume that the feces were from horses and not investigate too thoroughly. He kicked some straw over the pile with his foot before he went out the back to rejoin the female detective. "You find anything in there?"

Giannini shook her head. "Just the two stiffs." She flipped open a notebook. "Wallets ID them as Jeremiah and Louis Sattler. The rig is Louis's." She closed the book. "The chief said you have some idea who did this and that I'm to cooperate with you." Her shoulders squared up and she looked Riley in the eye. "So what do you have, and why are the feds taking this over?"

"I work with the bureau's serial-killer task force. We've been tracking two men who we believe are responsible for some killings down in Tennessee. We think these two might have hitched a ride in this trailer and come up here."

Giannini reached into her pocket and pulled out a pack of gum. She popped two pieces in her mouth without offering any. "Quit smoking last week. It helps a little." She chomped on her gum for a few seconds. "All right. What about you, Doc? What do you do for a living?"

Merrit turned slowly and looked at the police officer. "I work with Agent Riley. I do psychological profiles on killers."

"A shrink," Giannini nodded. "OK. Well, it don't matter much to me. The chief said this is your case now. I'd prefer not to have any of the citizens of my city killed, so I'll help you as much as I can. What now?"

Riley looked around. "Where was the truck found?"

"I'll take you there." Giannini gave some orders to a few uniformed cops and then led the way to an unmarked car. Riley got in the passenger side and Merrit sat in the back.

"These two guys—they must be pretty damn mean. I've seen some fucked-up bodies, but these about take the cake." Giannini glanced over her shoulder at Merrit. "I hope my language doesn't offend you, Doc."

Merrit appeared not to have noticed.

"Well, anyway, the weird thing is, are these guys cannibals or what? I mean those poor stiffs in there were missing some flesh."

Riley nodded as they pulled out of the parking lot. "Our suspects have done the same thing before to other bodies."

"Uh-huh." Giannini roared down the on ramp to the freeway and expertly cut her way through traffic then she clamped a small blue bubble onto the roof and pulled off the highway. "This is it. The truck was parked off the road right here."

Riley got out of the car and looked around. Buildings pressed up on all sides of the highway. "Do you have an estimate on time of death?"

Giannini watched the cars speeding by. "Rough guess is about an hour before the bodies were found. The coroner might be able to give us a little more accurate time." She popped her gum. "Hell, your suspects might've hitched another ride and be in another state by now."

Riley thought about the backpacks and the thousands of hiding places in the city, along with the ready supply of food. "No. They're here."

Giannini frowned. "How do you know that?"

"I can feel it." The words were out before he realized what he'd said.

Giannini looked at him closely. "A fed with feelings. That's a new one on me."

Riley ignored the comment. "Let's drive around a little."

They got back in the car, and Giannini took them off the interstate and cruised the surrounding neighborhoods. With a sinking feeling Riley took in the vast number of abandoned buildings and warehouses.

"What are you looking for?" Giannini asked.

"Just taking a look," Riley replied. "I've never been here before."

"You sound like you're from New York," Giannini noted.

"Yeah. The Bronx," Riley replied, his eyes flickering over the neighborhoods as they drove through.

"You Italian?" the detective asked.

"No. Irish and Puerto Rican."

"Hmm" was Giannini's only comment.

"What's that over there?" They had almost forgotten that Merrit was in the backseat. She pointed between the two of them.

"That's Soldiers' Field, where the Bears play," Giannini told her.

"The bears?"

Giannini looked at Riley with a raised eyebrow as she turned the corner and headed toward the large stadium.

"A professional football team," Riley explained.

"Stop here," Merrit said. Giannini stopped the patrol car at the start of an overpass that crossed a Gordian knot of railroad tracks running next to the stadium. A park stretched out on the far side of the overpass, leading to Lake Michigan. The landscape was well groomed and Riley doubted that the Synbats would be able to stay hidden long in there, although it was the only open area he'd seen since landing.

"What about the park?" Merrit asked, her thoughts obviously echoing his own.

Riley winced as Giannini swung her head from Merrit to him. "You think two nutcases would try to hide out in the park after slashing a couple of people?"

"They like nature," Riley explained lamely. "But you're right. They wouldn't go in there."

"Why are you so sure they haven't moved on? You said they moved here from Tennessee. Seems to me they'd be used to moving, and if they got any brains at all they wouldn't want to hang around here."

"Maybe they have," Riley said wearily. He was tired of playing games. He needed to dump the cop—she was asking too many questions. "Let's go to your headquarters. My boss should have arrived by now."

Giannini pulled a tire-squealing U-turn. The rest of the drive was made in silence.

Colonel Lewis was waiting in the police chief's office, neatly attired in a three-piece suit. He had been wooing the police chief and making sure that all information on the killings was kept from the media. The chief was more than happy to have the case taken off his already overburdened officers. A gone file was a cleared file.

"Anything you need, we'll be glad to give you a hand," the chief said as the meeting broke up. "I'm assigning Lieutenant Giannini full time to be your liaison. You tell her what you want and she'll get it for you."

Riley glanced sideways at the detective and saw her jaw set in a tight line. Lewis gave Riley directions to the safe house he'd established in the city, then Lewis took Merrit with him, leaving Riley with the detective to give her the list of information they required. Giannini led the way to a small cubicle that was piled high with file folders.

"Grab a seat," she said as she slumped down behind her desk. She sat there for a long minute, her dark eyes quietly assessing Riley, then she grabbed a notepad and pen. "All right. Give me the laundry list of what you want. Your boss must have some pull to get the chief to be so cooperative."

Riley had been thinking about what he needed the entire time they were in the car. "We need to know about any killings, particularly if the circumstances are similar to what we had in the horse rig—mutilated bodies and all that."

"Of course," Giannini replied, making a note.

Riley ignored her sarcastic tone. "I'll be by twice a day to get all this stuff. We also need to know about missing persons, broken down by areas last seen."

Giannini frowned. "That won't be easy. People have to be missing for forty-eight hours before we list them officially. By then it's usually 'cause they don't come home and someone reports them, so it ain't like we got this long list of where they were last."

Forty-eight hours. Riley cursed silently. That was a dead end. "All right. We also need to know if anybody reports seeing something strange."

"Something strange." Giannini put down the notepad. She didn't bother masking her tone anymore. "Like what strange? This is Chicago, for chrissakes. There's always something strange going on."

"These two guys were last seen wearing animal skins—fur and all that," Riley explained lamely. "If someone reports something like, say, a werewolf or something, I need to know ASAP."

"A *werewolf?*" Giannini took a deep breath and looked at the ceiling for half a minute. "All right, Agent Riley. Why don't you level with me? Who the hell are you? You're not FBI, that's for damn sure. They always wear three-piece suits and carry clipboards. And even *they* know that missing persons reports are forty-eight hours old. No disrespect intended, but you don't know diddly about law enforcement. And you don't know diddly about Chicago. I can't help you if you don't help me."

Riley continued, ignoring the questions. "The fugitives will probably come out of hiding at night, if they come out at all. They won't be going to motels or bars or any of that—they don't like people much." He met her glare. "That's the kind of strange I'm talking about."

Giannini's lips were pursed together and her voice dropped the temperature in the room. "All right. Strange. You got it. Anything else?"

Riley stood. "No." He handed her the card that Lewis had given him. "This is my number. Call me if anything happens."

"Uh-huh."

9:04 P.M.

"We've got two unmarked panel trucks downstairs at our disposal," Lewis said. "We've got eight portable phone lines. It's just a question of waiting."

"Waiting until the Synbats kill someone," Riley replied.

"Or get spotted."

"What about reaction from the police when we open fire in the city?" Riley asked as he watched the members of his team lay out their sleeping bags on the wood floor. Their weapons were racked against the wall ready for use. They were occupying a warehouse in south Chicago that was used by federal agencies such as the DEA and the FBI whenever they conducted operations in the area. The other personnel from Riley's team had arrived several hours ago, all looking uncomfortable in their civilian clothes. They'd all been issued papers and cards identifying them as federal agents.

"Don't worry about the police. That's my job," Lewis said. A half dozen of his men were also in the building, ready to react. They had a command post set up not only to man the phones, but also to listen in with scanners to all emergency frequencies.

Riley shrugged. It *was* Lewis's problem, and as far as Riley was concerned, he hoped the lid did blow off this whole operation. He was concerned for the safety of his men.

Doc Seay was the acting team sergeant; he'd taken Riley aside a half hour ago to brief him on the close-out down in Tennessee. The local media had bought the story of escaped prisoners. The deaths of Knutz and T-bone had been explained away by placing them on board the helicopter, which had been described as crashing during a training exercise. Seay said that Colonel Hossey was more than a little upset with the DIA, but the commander of the Special Operations Command at Fort Bragg had personally flown up and intervened between Hossey and General Trollers.

Another mess had been swept under the rug in the name of national security. Riley preferred to think of it more as career security for most of the people involved.

"I want your men ready to move out with five minutes' notice," Lewis ordered Riley. "If we get anything off the scanners, we're going in right away."

"Yes, sir."

11:35 P.M.

Holly's nose was buried in a cardboard box of rotting vegetables thrown away by a produce truck on its way out of the city. The dog ate ravenously, teeth crunching on some carrots, when she suddenly paused and lifted her head. She looked from side to side, eyes straining to penetrate the shadows in the deserted street. A lone streetlight more than a hundred meters away cast a feeble glow, reflecting off broken glass. The roar of traffic from the more populated part of the city was muted here.

It wasn't the noise or the light that had caught Holly's attention, though. Above the smell of her decaying meal, she'd caught a whiff of something else, something that her mind said was danger. She slunk farther into the darkness near a dumpster and crouched down, peering out. Then she heard the noise of glass breaking. Something was moving, coming closer from the dark end of the street. Deep, raspy breathing echoed off the warehouse walls.

Holly's head twitched from side to side. A low whimper started deep in her throat but her mouth clamped shut in an instinctive sense of self-preservation.

A figure lurched into the dim light, thirty meters away. The sight of the drunk relaxed Holly slightly. But in a second she was tense again as two figures appeared behind the man, moving fast. She barely had time to register their presence before they were on the hapless human. He uttered one brief yelp of surprise before his throat was torn out. The figures began dragging the body away toward the darkness.

Suddenly, one of the creatures halted and turned, golden eyes peering back up the street, searching. Holly froze, her breathing halted, instinctively knowing that she was in danger. The blood-covered muzzle of the creature turned in Holly's direction and bared large fangs as it growled.

Holly bolted for the opposite end of the street, deep-throated howls following her escape.

CHAPTER 20
FRIDAY, 10 APRIL

Chicago
7:04 A.M.

"Anything?" Merrit asked.

"Nothing," Riley replied as he slid his 9mm pistol in the shoulder holster under his denim jacket.

"What's the plan for today?"

Riley pointed to the desk where Lewis was sitting, going through the reports gleaned from all sources. "We're going to the area where the Synbats left the rig and start searching outward, checking all the abandoned buildings. It's a shot in the dark, but it beats sitting here all day."

Merrit looked over at Riley's men, who were eating fast food brought in by one of the DIA agents. "How are you going to do that?"

"Civilian clothes. Armed only with pistols. We've got our FBI IDs, and Lewis will take care of the locals."

"It might work." Merrit pointed at the city map posted on an easel. "I don't think they've gone far from where they got out of the rig. If the timing on the brothers' deaths is correct, the Synbats had only a few hours at best before the pods activated. Once that happened they had to find a place to hide."

"How long before the young Synbats are able to move about?" Riley asked.

"Two to three days," Merrit answered. "A week before they'll have any chance at self-sufficiency by killing small game, such as rats, dogs, or cats, and scavenging garbage. They'll be eighty percent grown in a month. Able to mate in two months. Full grown at four months."

"When will they be a threat to humans?"

Merrit shrugged. "That's hard to say. Individually I would say in a month. But I'd hate to run into a pack of week-old Synbats working in concert."

"If we stumble onto their lair in the next four or five days, then we ought to get all the young ones, right?"

"We should, unless they've split forces and have more than one hiding place."

That stopped Riley for a second. It's what he would do if he were in the Synbats' position. "You think they'd do that?"

"I hope not, but they split up in Tennessee in order to survive," Merrit reminded him. "There's no reason why they wouldn't do it again."

Riley backtracked. "If we get all three adults in the next four days and eliminate them, the young would starve?"

"Unless the old ones have left an adequate supply of food for the young ones."

"Damn," Riley cursed. "They already tried that once with the horses back in the LBL, so I guess they'll do it again."

Merrit nodded. "Now you're beginning to see the magnitude of the problem. Not only that, but don't forget that the adults are capable of breeding again. With only a ten-day gestation period, we could see another generation of Synbats born early in the week after next."

"I know all that," Riley remarked irritably. "I'm more worried about the fact that they always seem to be one step ahead of us. We need them to make a mistake, or we need a hell of a lot of luck, and I don't like working that way. The problem I'm having with all this—" He paused as Colonel Lewis strode up.

"Lieutenant Giannini just called. She says she has something you might be interested in. I'll take your men and start the search while you go downtown." He tossed a portable phone to Riley. "Stay in touch. Clear?"

"Yes, sir." He turned to Merrit. "Let's roll."

8:55 A.M.

Giannini was dipping a doughnut in a cup of coffee when Riley and Merrit appeared at her door. She waved the dripping pastry at them, gesturing for them to come in. "Grab a seat."

Riley glanced around, then stepped back out to drag in an extra chair, while Merrit took the only one available. A silence ensued, broken only by the sound of the detective eating her breakfast. Riley looked around, taking in the files piled here and there and the overflowing garbage can. There were a few plaques on the wall and Riley read the nearest, a commendation for bravery while breaking up a bank robbery. Riley returned his gaze to Giannini and she was looking at him. Their eyes locked for a long second.

Giannini broke contact first, pointing at the grungy coffeepot sitting on top of her filing cabinet. "Want some?"

Merrit shook her head, but Riley stood and poured himself a plastic cup full of the dark liquid. He took a sip and grimaced at the gritty taste. "What have you got?"

Giannini kicked back in her seat, sipping out of a cracked mug. "Nothing solid. Just been wandering around the station house that covers the district where your killers disappeared. I was there earlier this morning when the shifts changed." She grinned, laugh lines appearing around her dark eyes. "You want to find out what's happening on the streets, you just hang around the locker room."

"The locker room?" Merrit asked.

"Yeah," Giannini said. She smiled again. "Don't worry, they ain't got nothing in there I haven't seen before." She put down the mug. Merrit didn't react to the remark. "Anyway. There were two guys talking about some old bum who'd been nagging them when they were trying to walk their beat. He was all upset 'cause his shopping cart got stolen."

"So?" Riley prompted.

"Well, the bum said that he'd left it parked near his 'home'—some of these people are very territorial—and a—get this—a 'gorilla'—that was his word—stole his cart."

Riley sat forward. "A gorilla? What did it look like?"

Giannini shrugged. "That was all they had."

"Can we find this bum?" Riley asked.

She shook her head. "I doubt it. There's probably dozens of homeless in that area, and the two guys didn't remember much about what the fellow looked like. I know the place they were talking about, though. It's about eight blocks from where the truck was left."

"Can we go there?"

Giannini stood up, strapping on a large-caliber revolver in a shoulder holster.

Fort Campbell
9:00 A.M.

Sergeant Major Powers read the latest message from Riley, then tore it into little pieces and burned it in his trash can. The other members of the battalion headquarters staff were just arriving after having spent the last several hours conducting physical training, getting cleaned up, and eating breakfast.

With a slight limp, Powers went to the door and made his way to the Group headquarters building. He knocked once on the commander's door and entered. Stopping the appropriate two paces in front of the desk, he saluted and waited.

Colonel Hossey looked up from the papers spread across his desk. "What's the latest?"

"They're set up in Chicago. Riley thinks the Synbats have holed up there in an abandoned building. He feels they will most likely not find them until the Synbats themselves make contact."

"Shit," Hossey muttered. "Anything else?"

"No, sir. I know where Riley and his men are located and the phone number at that location."

"All right. I want you to keep two teams on alert status, ready to roll with fifteen minutes' notice. Live ammunition, civilian clothes— you know the deal."

"Yes, sir."

"I'll have a Blackhawk from the aviation platoon ready to fly. You call out to the airfield and talk to the pilot in command. Make sure you can get hold of him."

"Yes, sir."

"Carry on."

Chicago
9:30 A.M.

"This was the street the two officers were walking," Giannini said as she pulled the unmarked car over to the curb, next to a hydrant. "The homeless person could have come out of any of these side streets."

Riley looked around. It reminded him of the South Bronx, his home. There were numerous small shops on the ground floors of the buildings, just opening to greet the day's customers. The upper floors contained apartments. The side streets led to other apartment buildings and businesses. Several of the buildings were abandoned, some burned out.

"Let's take a walk," Riley said as he opened his door. Giannini and Merrit followed.

As he walked the sidewalks and filthy alleyways, Riley lost hope of ever tracking down the Synbats. There were just too many places for them to hide. He looked up at all the broken windows peering over his head like so many eyes; the creatures could be hiding behind any one of them.

Even if he did stumble across the Synbats, Riley was none too sure that he and his men could stop them. Knutz's and T-bones's M16s hadn't been found, which meant that the Synbats most likely still had them, along with the combat vests containing extra ammunition. Despite Ward's claims that the Synbats had not been taught to reload, Riley didn't want to test them on that.

After two hours of wandering, Riley could sense Giannini's impatience. They'd exchanged barely twenty words the entire time.

Finally, Giannini halted outside a local delicatessen. "Let's get some lunch."

Riley acquiesced, and they went into the small store. He was surprised when Giannini spoke in Italian to the proprietor. The two seemed to know each other and conversed rapidly as the old man sliced the meat and cheese for the sandwiches they had ordered. When the three large submarines were laid on the countertop, Riley insisted on paying, and Giannini didn't even pretend to argue. They took a table near the front window as the lunchtime crowd started to surge in.

"You from around here?" Riley asked.

"No. I used to work this area, though, when I was first assigned to the force." Giannini took a large bite of her sandwich. Riley was amused to see Merrit dubiously eyeing the massive amount of bread and cold cuts.

"How long have you been a cop?" Riley asked.

"Fourteen years."

"Like it?"

Giannini cocked an eyebrow at Riley and answered with her mouth full. "You writing a book or what? It's a job." She swallowed. "Yeah, I like it. Makes each day interesting. I'd go crazy if I had to get up every morning and do the same shit every single day." She turned to

Merrit. "So, Doc. Any idea where your killers might've gone? You've been awfully quiet."

"They've found a place to hide," Merrit said.

"Yeah?" Giannini shook her head. "Doing what? They got to eat, don't they? And what're they waiting for? Do they need money? Maybe they're looking for a job. Maybe they're ripping people off. You haven't given us shit to work with. All you want us to do is tell you if anything unusual happens. Yet we just wasted a morning walking around the streets looking for God knows what. You must have some idea what you're looking for." She turned back to Riley. "How about giving us a description of your suspects other than that they're wearing animal skins."

For the briefest moment, Riley was tempted to chuck it all and tell her. He remembered his bitterness about not being told himself, yet here he was doing the exact same thing.

"We don't have anything more than that," he said quietly.

"Bullshit!" Giannini spat out, slamming her sandwich on the table. "Then what the hell is *she* doing?" she asked, pointing at Merrit. "Making a psych profile out of thin air?"

"I'm . . . I'm basing it on the crime scenes," Merrit stammered. "I'm tracking their actions and trying to get an idea of who we're after."

"I told you I've been on this job for fourteen years, and I've never been involved with something as weird as this," Giannini said. "The chief may have bought off on all this crap for his own reasons, and that's fine and dandy, but that don't mean I have to. I checked with my source in the FBI and he says there's no Special Agent Riley listed in his computer. I called the coroner's office and they told me the bodies of the Sattler brothers were taken away by people from the federal government and they have no idea where they are now. There wasn't even an autopsy."

Giannini leaned forward. "So who are you and what's going on? And don't give me any of your supersecret federal bullshit. That stuff only works in the movies. I'm a cop and this is my city and you're fucking with it."

Riley hadn't moved the entire time she was speaking. When she ran out of steam he leaned toward her and lowered his voice. "I'm not going to give you any bullshit, all right? If I tell you what's really going on, it's not going to be like in the movies, because the people you're dealing with don't play games and don't make speeches. They could kill us both. You've got fourteen years being a cop; well, I've got quite a few years playing another game altogether and it's got its own set of rules. I didn't make the goddamn rules and I don't like them and sometimes I don't even see a reason for them, but that doesn't mean I can just do whatever I please.

"There's a price to everything. You should know that—you're a cop. You break the law and you pay the price. If I tell you what's really going on—since you obviously know that the cover story is bullshit—then you'd damn well better be ready to pay the price when the hammer comes down." He opened his denim jacket and pulled up his T-shirt, briefly exposing the puckered skin where high-velocity bullets had exited his body. "I've paid the price before. Are you willing? Are you really willing?"

Giannini's voice was flat. "I'm willing."

Riley stood. "Let's go to the car." They threw the remains of their lunch in the garbage and made their way to the police car. A cable TV van had blocked them in while the workers were playing out cable into an open manhole. Giannini had to get the truck to move before they could pull into the traffic.

"Find someplace to park and Doctor Merrit will tell you about what we're after."

Giannini parked underneath the elevated highway and, with the roar of traffic overhead, Merrit begin relating in a monotone the story of the Synbats from inception to breakout. Riley picked up the action from there until arriving in Chicago. When he was done, Giannini stared at him. "If it wasn't for seeing those bodies in that trailer, I'd be looking around for Candid Camera right now. This is the craziest stuff I've ever heard." She blinked. "You're not bullshitting me, are you?"

Riley shook his head. "No."

The detective slumped back in the car seat. "Holy shit," she muttered. She stayed silent for a few moments before finally turning back to Riley. "So, you're army, Special Forces?"

Riley nodded.

"And these things beat you and your men down there in that park?"

Riley nodded reluctantly.

"Then how the hell do you expect to catch them up here?"

"Because we didn't know what we were up against in Tennessee. I was lied to, just as you were lied to by me. And that's why I'm telling you the truth now. My men are here in the city. First sign of the Synbats, we're going in hard."

"First sign will probably be some dead bodies, if what you say about these things is true," Giannini said.

"I know that," Riley replied.

The lieutenant turned to Merrit. "You made these things?"

Merrit didn't hear her; she was lost in her own thoughts. Giannini repeated the question.

"I was part of the team that developed them."

"Jesus Christ!" Giannini exploded. "What the hell were you thinking when you did that?"

Merrit turned away and stared out the window. "I'll pay for it," she whispered.

"That's not the issue right now," Riley interceded. "The fact is that the Synbats *were* created and they're out here in the city somewhere."

Giannini sighed and sank back in the driver's seat, peering out the windshield. "All right. I can't tell anyone that I know this, right?"

"If you do, you'll be out of circulation as soon as Lewis finds out," Riley said.

Giannini considered that for a few moments, then switched tack. "You think the gorilla that stole the shopping cart might've been one of your creatures?"

"It's possible," Riley answered. "It's also possible that the man was just drunk."

"What would they want a shopping cart for?"

"I don't know," Riley said. "But I guess we'll find out. Sooner or later they'll kill, and you'll hear about it. Then we go in and nail them."

Giannini looked at him. "And what if you don't? Huh? What if you don't get them, and they multiply?"

"We'll get them," Riley insisted.

"Uh-huh."

6:45 P.M.

Outside the windows dusk was settling over the city. Riley had dropped off Merrit at the command center an hour ago and checked in with Lewis. They'd found no sign of the Synbats during their daylight covert search. Riley had continued on down to police headquarters on State Street. Giannini greeted him with the news that there was no news.

"I've checked everything. Nothing that could be your creatures."

Giannini looked up at Riley from the police reports. "Let me ask you something."

"What?" Riley replied warily.

"The feds lied to you—just like you lied to me, until I got on your case. Now you're up here trying to clean up this big pile of shit these same people laid in your lap." She rubbed a hand wearily across her forehead. "And you said you've been doing this for a long time and this isn't the first time you've been involved in something like this. Right?"

"Yeah," Riley admitted.

"So why are you doing it?" Giannini demanded. "Why are you doing this? I don't know you, but I get feelings about people. You have to, to be a good soldier. And I feel that you're a good person. You wouldn't have told me what's going on if you weren't. So why are you still doing it?"

Riley crumpled up the plastic coffee cup he'd been holding and threw it into the overflowing trash can. He sat down in the old wooden chair and propped up his feet on the scarred front end of Giannini's desk. "I do it 'cause I think I'm reasonably good at it. The places I've been and the things I've done—someone's had to do it. I like to think I do it better than some yo-yo who would get his people wasted."

"You could've been good at something else besides what you do," Giannini said quietly.

"Yeah," Riley admitted. "But the army got me off the streets of the South Bronx. All my buddies from school—and I'm talking grade school, 'cause most didn't make it to high school—they're in jail, dead, or might as well be dead. But I got a ticket out. The army's been good to me. I got a high school diploma and an associates' degree from the army. I've been able to travel all over the world and—"

"Visit exotic places, meet interesting people, and kill them," Giannini cut in.

Riley sat up in his seat, his dark eyes meeting hers. "Yeah, I've heard that crap before. And I've *done* it. But let me ask *you* something. Have you ever lived in a foreign country?"

"No," she admitted.

"Well, I have. I've been all over the world. I've seen a lot of countries, and the people in them. And the people—they're not so different. People are the same everywhere. There's good ones and bad ones. Most just want to live their lives without the government fucking with them."

The front legs of Riley's chair hit the floor with a slam. "Yeah, this is total bullshit—tracking down these Synbats. The fact that they were made. The fact that they tore apart a bunch of people, including a young girl. Yeah. All right. I agree. But what do you want me to do? Overthrow the government?

"I'll tell you one thing—one thing I truly do believe," he continued. "We live in the greatest country in the world. Yeah, we got our problems. Who doesn't? The *world's* a fucked place. You've walked the streets. You know what people are capable of. Doesn't it follow that some of these people end up in the government? But people like me and my team and the thousands like us make up for the occasional sociopath who makes it to the Beltway. I have to believe that. It's all a balance of powers, right? So far, it seems to have worked all right."

Riley stood. "You got to believe in something. Right now we have one goal: Kill these things as quickly as possible."

Giannini stood also. "I'll help you find them. *You* kill them."

Chapter 21

Saturday, 11 April

Chicago
9:04 A.M.

Riley took the portable phone from Lewis's hand. "Yeah?"

"We got something." Giannini's voice was calm.

"What?"

"A cable company crew is missing."

"Missing?"

"They were supposed to be in by six last night. They didn't show up. Two men."

"Where were they?"

"One of our units found the van—no sign of the crew. Indiana and Cullerton. Near where we were yesterday. We'll go there. Be at my office in fifteen minutes."

Riley hung up. Lewis was hovering nearby. "What's going on?"

Riley took a second to collect his thoughts. He remembered the van outside the deli yesterday and the pieces fell into place. "They're underground."

"What?" Lewis asked, confused.

"The Synbats are underground," Riley repeated, slamming the 14-round magazine into his pistol and sliding it into his shoulder holster. "We're going to need night vision goggles. Thermals probably won't be worth much down there. I'm going to check it out. I'll give you a call to bring in the rest of my team if it looks like a good lead." He turned to Merrit. "You ready?"

"Yes."

Riley wasn't too sure of that. Merrit looked exhausted, her face drawn from lack of sleep. He was used to working with people on the edge of physical exhaustion but there was something in Merrit's manner that worried him. Whatever was draining her went beyond the physical.

As they walked out of the building, Riley turned to Merrit. "How good is the Synbats' night vision?"

"Good," Merrit replied.

"Good?" Riley repeated, grabbing her arm. "Ward said they were day creatures. What exactly does *good* mean?"

"About three times better than human," Merrit answered, looking down at Riley's fingers pressed into her arm.

"Great," Riley said, releasing his grip. "Just great."

9:55 A.M.

Giannini pointed at the open manhole with a portable work railing around it. "The shift chief says they were supposed to be down there laying cable. Should've been back in by six last night. We got the call early this morning." She turned to the vehicle parked nearby. "No sign of foul play. The van was unlocked and their tool belts are missing."

"Anybody been down there yet?" Riley asked.

Giannini shook her head. "No. The shift chief wanted to go look but I sent him home. I figured I'd give you the honors."

Riley got on his knees and stuck his head in. "What's down there?"

Giannini shrugged. "Sewers, I guess."

All Riley could see was a metal ladder descending into a dark shaft. "Let me borrow your flashlight."

Giannini went to her car and returned with a large four D-cell light. Riley turned it on and pointed it into the manhole. The ladder continued for about thirty feet and ended on a dirty concrete floor. There was no sign of the cable crew.

Riley looked at Merrit. "What do you think?"

Her eyes were fixed on the dark hole. "It makes sense. It's a perfect place for them to hide. They can stay down there during the day and come out at night to forage for food. They can also travel underground without being noticed."

Riley swung his legs over the edge and put his feet on the rungs. "What're you doing?" Giannini asked.

"I'm going to take a look."

"Alone?"

"You can come," Riley replied.

Giannini sighed. "All right. You go first."

"I want to go," Merrit said suddenly.

Riley looked at her briefly. "Not right now. We're just going to check it out. If we spot anything we're going to have to call in some help."

"You need me to deal with the Synbats," Merrit insisted.

Riley tapped the pistol in his shoulder holster. "I can deal with them. You wait here."

Riley clambered down the ladder, the echo of his movements bouncing off the walls. He reached bottom and looked around. A tunnel, about eight feet high by four feet wide, extended off in two directions. The walls were pitted concrete. Giannini came down next to him and peered about. "They could be a long ways from here."

"Yeah." Riley pointed at the bands of cable stretching along one wall. "But the two men must have been working somewhere close by. If the Synbats attacked them, we should see some sort of sign."

Riley's pistol was in his hand and Giannini pulled out her own. He played the light on the floor, which was covered with patches of mud. "There," he said. Two sets of footprints moved off to the left. "Let's go."

Riley led, feet squishing into the black ooze. The glow of the flashlight preceded them by only ten feet, leaving the rest of the tunnel in darkness. Something glinted up ahead, and Riley focused both pistol and light on it.

"What is it?" Giannini hissed.

Riley moved forward, pistol at the ready. A work helmet with the cable company logo lay on the floor along with a wrench. Riley played the light around, checking out the area. He stopped in shock. "Jesus Christ!" he muttered. "You don't want to see this," he said to Giannini as she stepped up next to him.

She pushed forward. "What?" When she saw what he had found, she froze, then took several deep breaths to get herself under control. What remained of the two workers was little more than two severed heads and a pile of intestines and bones. Their slashed uniforms were stuffed behind the two heads, which stared with unseeing eyes, the faces fixed forever in an expression of terror.

"What did those things do to them?" Giannini demanded.

"The Synbats killed them and then butchered them for the meat." Riley moved the flashlight to the left. The familiar tracks of the Synbats showed clearly in the mud, along with four straight lines that disappeared down the tunnel.

"Those are the Synbats' tracks." Riley squatted down. "The straight lines must be the shopping cart. Two men—two sets of marks. They killed the two men, cut them up, then loaded up the shopping cart. They had to make two trips to get it all."

"Goddamn," Giannini muttered, her eyes riveted on the remains. "Goddamn."

"Let's get back up top," Riley said, grabbing her arm. "We need more firepower before we go down that tunnel."

11:30 A.M.

Giannini had the street cordoned off, and Riley's men were crowded in the back of the large truck parked next to the manhole. Merrit stood alongside Riley as he briefed the team.

"We've got a definite set of tracks. Trovinsky, I want you up front with me. We'll all wear night vision goggles. Strict noise and light discipline: I want to kill them, not scare them off. Remember—they're armed."

Riley pulled a small foil-wrapped object from his pocket. "We're going to mark our route and each other using IR chem lights." He cracked the package and pulled out the light stick, which in the dim light of the truck showed nothing. Using the night vision goggles, though, the chem light would show up brightly. Riley looped a piece of cord through the hole at the end of the chem light and slung it over his back. The rest of his team did the same. "That will mark you from behind. Make sure you turn on the IR light on your NVGs. That will mark you from the front. I want everyone to stay tight. You see the Synbats, shoot to kill. We've got to get all three adults. Any questions?"

There were none. Riley pointed at Merrit. "You stay right behind me." He looked out the back of the van and saw Giannini leaning against her car, out of earshot. She had been shunted aside by the colonel upon his arrival, and had not taken it very well. "Let's do it." Riley hopped off the back of the truck and headed for the manhole.

At the bottom of the ladder, Riley waited while the other seven members of his team and Merrit climbed down. Earlier Lewis's men had removed the remains of the two cable company men in body bags.

As the team gathered round, Doc Seay tugged on Riley's sleeve. "What do you think?"

"About what?" Riley asked.

"Are we going to get them all?"

Riley peered down the tunnel. "We'd damn well better."

Riley looked around—everyone was in place. Trovinsky quickly led the way down the tunnel, following the twin set of wheel tracks. Riley followed right behind, feeling hemmed in and vulnerable. Their numerical advantage—just a little more than two to one—wasn't going to help much in these tight quarters. Technology wasn't going to be much of an advantage either. They had the goggles, but if Merrit's information was correct about the Synbats' ability to see in the dark, then the goggles were more of an equalizer than an advantage.

The tunnel curved to the right and Riley splashed through the thin layer of mud, eyes on Trovinsky's back. The point man's head was down, watching the tracks. Despite their best attempts to keep quiet, the noise of the team moving through the tunnel was easily audible. They came to the first junction—a tunnel cutting at right angles across their front. The tracks turned left. Riley cracked an IR chem light and left it at the intersection, marking the way back.

Something glinted in his goggles directly ahead. Riley tapped Trovinsky on the back, halting him. "Cover me," he whispered.

Trovinsky moved over to the far right side and knelt on the scum-covered floor, ignoring the goo that soaked through his pants. The rest of the team spread out and waited. Rifle at the ready, Riley advanced. The object slowly took form in his goggles—the missing shopping cart. He halted briefly and carefully checked out the area. The tunnel continued on as far as he could see. Near the cart was what appeared to be a crack in the wall, about two feet wide and starting two feet up, extending to the ceiling.

Riley stepped next to the cart; the metal on the bottom gave off a sheen of dried blood. He stopped and listened carefully for about thirty seconds. The only sound was the nervous movements of the members of his team behind him. He leaned forward and, weapon first, peered into the crack. It widened to about a yard and went straight down twenty feet. There were no rungs on the sheer concrete wall. The bottom was another concrete floor, in a small alcove that appeared to open off to the left. No sign of the Synbats.

Riley turned and gestured with one hand. Doc Seay shrugged off the small daypack he was wearing, pulled out two lengths of rope, and came forward, handing them over. Taking the shorter, twelve-foot length, Riley quickly fashioned a field-expedient Swiss seat, wrapping it around his legs and waist. He unclipped a snap link from his combat vest and looped it through the rope at the front of his waist.

Riley then tied off the longer rope to the bottom rail of the shopping cart and wedged the cart lengthwise against the opening. Stepping over the cart, he clipped the long rope into the snap link on his Swiss seat, looping it once around the metal. He leaned back, one hand holding the long rope tight against his chest, the other holding his M16. With a nod to Seay, he pushed his hand away from his chest and descended in short bounds, reaching the bottom in a few seconds.

Riley quickly knelt at the bottom and scanned. He was in a small chamber, about five feet around, with an opening directly in front of him. There was no sign of the Synbats other than some dark spots on the dirty concrete floor, which Riley surmised were blood. Pulling the end of the long rope free of his snap link, he edged forward and looked through the opening. Another tunnel stretched off to either side. It was in a horseshoe shape about seven and a half feet high by six feet wide. On the far side, large conduits and cables, held in place by metal stanchions, ran the length of the tunnel. The walls were made of crumbling concrete and the floor was concrete, occasionally covered with damp dirt. A smell of decay was faintly noticeable in the air.

Riley edged out into the tunnel and checked the ground. He couldn't see any Synbat tracks. One thing he could tell for sure: This tunnel was not part of a sewer system. There were two small rails on the floor about two feet apart, as if some sort of small train system once ran down here.

After a few moments, Riley turned back into the opening and slung the M16 over his shoulder. He took hold of the rope with both hands and, clinching with his feet, pulled himself back up to an anxious Doc Seay.

"What do you have?" Seay whispered.

"Another tunnel," Riley answered in a normal voice. "I don't know how far it extends, but it seems to go quite a ways. I couldn't spot any tracks. Before we go any farther, though, I think we need a map of this tunnel system. We're wandering around in the dark, and that's to the Synbats' advantage." Riley pulled up the rope and untied and recoiled it.

"Let's get back to the surface."

1:56 P.M.

The back of the large van was now Lewis's field headquarters. Radios covered most of one of the walls and a small table occupied the center. Around the table stood the colonel, Riley, Merrit, and Giannini, peering at a set of old blueprints.

"Your suspects," Giannini said, giving Riley a small look, "are in an old set of tunnels that were once used as a freight system." She tapped the blueprints. "I got these from the Board of Underground in the City Transportation Department, but all they show is the sewer system and the subways. The system you went into is below those."

"You don't have plans for these freight tunnels?" Lewis asked incredulously.

In reply, Giannini flipped open her notepad. "I talked to this old guy at the Board of Underground for an hour after you all asked me to check on this. He told me there are no plans on record for those tunnels."

"Well, how far do they go?" Riley asked.

Giannini flipped a page. "When they were first built, they stretched under the city for a little over fifty-nine miles."

"What?" Riley exploded. "Fifty-nine miles!"

Giannini nodded. "I couldn't believe it either. Let me give you a summary of what this guy told me." She flipped back a few more pages. "All right. Let's see. Construction on these tunnels began back in 1898 and they were opened in 1904. They were orginally built to carry coal to buildings downtown and reduce congestion in the streets. Apparently the soil down there is some sort of blue clay that's real easy to dig through. They'd have shifts working all night digging out the tunnels and then the day crew would pour concrete to make the walls."

She glanced up. "Here's something interesting. Did you ever read *The Jungle* by Upton Sinclair?"

Lewis shook his head irritably and Riley just waited. He knew Giannini was pushing the colonel.

"Well, the main character in the book, Jurgis Rudkus, worked as a digger in these same tunnels." She shook her head. "It's funny, I've read the book, but I never thought those tunnels actually existed. Anyway, the last tunnel was built in 1954 for the Prudential Building, but it was never used. The system was shut down in '59. That was the year the Chicago Tunnel Company—the people who built and ran the tunnels—went bankrupt."

"Can we try and find some records from that company?" Riley asked.

"Nope. I asked."

"Who's responsible for the tunnels now?"

Giannini gave a weary smile. "The city. Who else?"

Riley sank down into a folding chair. "Does anyone have any idea where they go?"

Giannini pulled off the top blueprint and displayed a street map. "No one knows the full extent of them. Over the years, parts of the system have been blocked off or destroyed. When they built the subways, they cut through some of the freight tunnel system, especially when they built the State and Dearborn Street subway."

Riley looked at the map. "That's just north of here. You say these tunnels served downtown. Do you have any idea how far they extend in that direction?"

Giannini's finger made a loose circle, enclosing not only the Loop formed by the Chicago River and Lake Michigan, but crossing the river both to the north and west. "They're not only here in the Loop but they go under the river too."

"Does anyone use these freight tunnels?" Merrit asked.

"Yeah," Giannini said. "The city leases some of them to Edison, the power company, and to some cable companies, but they only use a very small portion—a couple of miles at most."

"So we have about sixty miles of tunnels down there where the suspects could be hiding," Riley summarized. "And we have no map of the system, so we have to go in blind and just wander around, hoping we run into them."

Merrit pointed at the map. "They stole the cart here, to the south. The cable crew was missing here, and as far as you can tell, you went almost a half mile in the sewer before you reached the point where they descended to the freight tunnel. I'd say that their hiding place is very far removed from where they go up to the surface."

"Detective," Lewis asked, "do you have any more information on the tunnels that might be of use?"

Giannini looked at her notebook. "Just some odds and ends. There are openings from the tunnels directly into the subbasements of many buildings—that way the coal could be run directly into the buildings. Almost all of those openings have been closed off; as a matter of fact, this old man told me that many of the owners of buildings in the Loop don't even know they were connected to this system or that it even exists." She shrugged. "That's about all I have."

"Thank you," Lewis said. "We'll contact you if we need anything else."

Giannini left without another word, glancing at Riley on the way out.

Lewis faced Riley. "Any ideas?"

"We need more people, sir. We've got more than fifty miles of tunnels to look through. That's going to take awhile."

"The Synbats might not even be in the tunnels themselves," Merrit noted. "They simply might be using them as their road system and actually be hiding in the basement of some building. I'm sure they've found a relatively isolated place to set up their base to take care of the young."

"All we can hope for," Riley said, "is to find some tracks and get lucky."

Lewis sighed. "All right. I'll call General Trollers and try to get some more people up here. Meanwhile, you start from where we know the Synbats were last and work your way north toward downtown."

3:23 P.M.

"I've got tracks!" Trovinsky hissed, his low voice echoing off the concrete walls.

Riley moved up next to him and looked down at the thin layer of mud that covered this part of the floor. Two distinctive pad prints showed up clearly, heading down the freight tunnel.

"All right," Riley said. "Let's go that way."

He'd split his team in half, taking Trovinsky, Caruso, and Carter to the left and sending Doc Seay with three men to the right. The two four-man teams would break down once more to two-man teams when each hit the next intersection. Riley told Seay not to break down below two men, and even at that level he felt uncomfortable facing the Synbats. The FM radios would not work in the tunnels, so they had to rely on IR chem lights to mark their trail. Riley's greatest fear was that one of his teams would be attacked and he might not even know it.

The tunnel rose slightly and Trovinsky paused as the mud disappeared from the concrete floor. He pushed onto the next section of mud and then halted. "They're gone."

Riley looked over his shoulder. The mud was undisturbed. "We didn't pass any turnoffs. How can they be gone?"

Trovinsky looked about. "Remember when they took to the trees back at the Land Between the Lakes?"

Riley nodded.

Trovinsky pointed at the large tubes holding power and cable lines that were bolted to the side wall. "I bet you they're going along those."

"Shit," Riley muttered. "All right, let's keep moving. If they didn't double back on us, they've got to be ahead somewhere."

5:56 P.M.

Doc Seay paused and signaled for his men to take a break. They'd been moving for more than three hours and had covered about three miles of tunnels. They'd spotted Synbat tracks once—the faintest impression in an isolated patch of dirt—but only once. They'd already passed sixteen side tunnels, but Seay had kept his party intact and on a straight course, due north by his compass. Looking at his map in the infrared glow of his goggles, he estimated that they were directly underneath the Loop and close to the river. For all he knew, they might have even gone under the river; it was hard to tell down here.

As Seay was contemplating his location, Bob Philips suddenly hissed for his attention. "Listen," he said, pointing to the next intersection.

Seay cocked his head, ears straining. At first he heard nothing, but then he slowly became aware of an intermittent, very low clicking sound bouncing off the walls—something striking the concrete floor. With hand and arm gestures, he indicated for his team to take defensive positions, oriented toward the intersection ten feet away.

The noise suddenly stopped. Seay held his breath and then the noise started up, louder and quicker this time, but heading away. Seay sprinted to the intersection and caught a brief glimpse of something low to the floor turning the far corner and disappearing.

"Let's go!" he yelled, and his men were behind him, sprinting down the tunnel. As they rounded the corner, Seay again caught sight of what had been making the noise, but it was too far away to make out clearly— almost fifty meters down the darkened corridor.

Seay flinched as a row of red tracers exploded past his right ear, the flat crack of the bullets echoing off the wall. "Cease fire!" he screamed as he rolled away from the rounds. The sudden silence was as abrupt as the shots. Seay slowly got up and turned to face his men. The team's junior engineer, Bartlett, stood there, rifle held in his hand, looking sheepish.

"Jesus, Bartlett, you just about took my head off!" Seay admonished. "Did you even see what you were shooting at?"

"I saw something running," Bartlett said.

"It looked too small to be a Synbat," Bob Philips commented. "Maybe a dog."

"A dog?" Seay asked. "How did a dog get down here? Maybe it was one of the baby Synbats."

"Merrit said the young ones wouldn't be able to move for a while," Philips noted.

"Merrit's been wrong before," Seay said. He pointed down the corridor. "Let's move out, but from now on, no one, and I mean no one, shoots across the formation." He turned his bulky goggles to peer directly at Bartlett. "Clear?"

"Clear, Sarge."

8:12 P.M.

Saturday was Lester Karney's favorite workday. It was the one day when the City Hall was empty. Lester was thirty-eight, going on sixty. His body was whipcord thin, and his face lined and pitted from the ravages of alcohol.

Lester pushed his cleaning cart down the second floor main hall-way to the freight elevator. He rolled the cart in and punched the button labeled B3. With a steady rumble the elevator descended, past the ground floor and the first two basement levels to the subbasement. The doors whooshed open, revealing a dark corridor that led to the furnace room and storage areas. Lester flipped on the set of naked lightbulbs that lined the corridor and left his cart just outside the elevator doors. He slipped a paper bag from underneath a cleaning rag and stuck it in the large back pocket of his coveralls.

Lester walked past the double doors that opened into the furnace room, then took a sharp left turn in the corridor. He shook his head as he passed carton upon carton of papers piled haphazardly against the hallway walls. If the fire inspector ever came down here, there'd be hell to pay. But Lester knew that no one official had come down here in a long time. He'd poked through some of the boxes once and found papers dating back thirty-five years.

He heard the clink of a bottle around the corner and smiled. He entered a room lined with boxes, with a dilapidated desk in the center. Seated behind the desk was a skinny black woman of indeterminate age, her face crinkled up in a smile. "Sit down, Lester, baby."

Lester sat on the corner of the desk, pulled out his own bottle, and clinked it to hers. "Bottoms up."

He took a long swig. "So how goes the third floor, Liz?"

"Same as two," she replied, cackling. It was their little ritual every Saturday night. Lester took another slug and then set the bottle carefully on the floor next to the desk.

"You're in a little bit of a rush tonight, ain't you, Lester?" Liz said as he came around the desk.

"Been a long week, sweetie," Lester replied as he wrapped his arms around her from behind.

"Mmm," Liz replied, arching her head back and meeting his kiss. Lester lifted her out of the seat and turned her around. With smooth movements, he pulled her coveralls down around her feet. Pushing her down on the desktop, he began unfastening his own clothing.

He grabbed her legs and stretched them up into the air as he plunged into her. The two lost sight of the dinginess of their surroundings as they fell into the animal passion of the moment.

The clink of the bottle falling over on the floor was lost on Lester, but not Liz. Her eyes cracked open and looked past the form of the man on top of her. They grew wide as they took in the other occupants of the room. She screamed and Lester thrust even harder until he suddenly arched back, his face frozen in a grimace, his body shuddering. Liz screamed again and Lester smiled down on her for a brief second before a hand wrapped around his throat and another hand, holding a knife, cut across it, severing his jugular vein. Blood exploded out, pulsing over Liz, who was pinned to the desktop by Lester's dying weight. She pushed at him futilely as a grinning face dominated by two massive fangs loomed over Lester's body.

Liz closed her eyes and began praying to the God her mother down in Alabama had beaten into her. The prayers were interrupted by pain, and for a few seconds her agonized screams echoed unheard through the basement of City Hall.

Fort Campbell
9:00 P.M.

Hossey crumpled up the message that Powers had transcribed and stuffed it into his pocket. The sergeant major stood at Hossey's side as he looked out the window of the 5th Group headquarters, peering at the stars in the clear night sky.

"What do you think, sir?"

"I think this is a bunch of bullshit, Dan," Hossey answered. "I think Lewis is in over his head and Trollers is playing politics."

"They aren't going to find them, sir," Powers said. "Sixty miles of tunnels . . ." He shook his head. "Shit, in Vietnam we hit tunnels and it was always bad news. And we weren't going against anything like these things."

Hossey rubbed the back of his neck. "I know. I know. They need more men."

"I've got B Company standing by, sir," Powers offered.

Hossey sighed and pointed across the street. "See that car, Dan?"

"Yes, sir."

"What do you think?"

He took in the two men sitting in the front seat. Powers sighed in turn. "DIA."

"Yeah. The minute we alert Bravo, they'll be down on us. I'd need the choppers to lift them up to Chicago, but when I talked to Captain Devens ten minutes ago out at the airfield, he said that two of Trollers's people were out there. They'd never get off the ground."

"Shit," Powers muttered.

Hossey left the window and went back to his desk. "But if we can't do the job, I know someone who can. And they're a bit closer than we are."

"Who, sir?"

Hossey absently reached up and rubbed a finger across the Ranger tab on his left shoulder. "I talked to Colonel Luckert of the 1st Ranger Battalion earlier today and his Alpha Company is at Camp McCoy in Wisconsin right now. He told me I could use them."

For the first time that evening a smile crossed Powers's face. A company of Rangers. The smile disappeared, though, as he thought it through. "They'll bust you, sir."

"Yes. They will." Hossey picked up the phone. "But if I don't do it, people may die. I don't have much of a choice. I'm putting them on alert to move in."

Chicago
10:56 P.M.

Riley peeled off his mud- and sweat-soaked combat vest and threw it down on the floor of the van. Lewis was sitting in front of a communications console, watching him without expression.

"Get some sleep," Riley ordered Doc Seay, who simply nodded and slipped out the back of the van. They'd spent the last thirty minutes briefing Lewis on the results—or more appropriately, lack of results—of their search today. The back door of the van rattled closed behind Seay, and Riley was left alone with the colonel and his night shift of DIA agents.

"Do you think Seay's man fired at a young Synbat?" Lewis asked.

Riley tugged his 9mm pistol out of the vest holster and started breaking it down, cleaning the parts. "I don't know, sir. It doesn't matter, does it? Bartlett didn't hit anything."

Lewis looked at a map. "As best as I can tell, you and your men covered about eight miles of tunnels."

"That leaves only fifty-two miles to go," Riley said. "And that doesn't count the fact that they could be hiding outside of the tunnel system and simply using it for traveling."

Lewis slapped the map down on the desk. "We've *got* to get them tomorrow. We can't keep our cover come Monday."

"I know that, sir," Riley replied. "We need more people."

Lewis rubbed his eyes. "I know we need more people. I told General Trollers that not twenty minutes ago. But he insists that we keep this under wraps as much as possible."

Riley smoothly slipped the barrel back into the pistol. "If we don't get more bodies working on this, we'll keep it under wraps until it blows up in our faces. And then we'll have a panic. We have only about four or five days before the young are able to forage on their own. That's if Merrit is right, and at this point I'm not too sure about that anymore."

Lewis didn't respond.

Riley finished putting the gun together and slipped it into his shoulder holster under his shirt. "I need to get some sleep, sir. We'll go back in at first light. If you had more men you could have someone down there now searching," he added unnecessarily.

Riley pulled up the back door of the van and hopped out, closing it behind him. As he walked toward the rent-a-car, a figure appeared out of the dark shadows to his left. He twisted, hand snaking toward his holster before he recognized who it was.

"Not good news, I suppose," Giannini commented as she slipped a piece of gum into her mouth.

Riley relaxed slightly. "No."

"Let's get a cup of coffee," Giannini said as she led the way to her unmarked car.

Riley followed and slumped into the passenger seat. There were no words spoken as Giannini drove through the dark streets of downtown Chicago. She pulled up in front of an all-night cafe. "Wait here."

She went inside and reappeared a few minutes later with two cups of coffee. She handed one to Riley and pulled the lid off hers. "So what now?"

Riley blew on his coffee. "I don't know. We go back down in the morning after getting some sleep."

"Is there any way to maybe gas the tunnels to get these things?" Giannini asked.

"I've thought about that, but it's too dangerous. If we use some sort of chemical agent, it's going to get out of the system and into the buildings through the basements and onto the street through the interconnecting tunnels. The only answer I see is to get a whole lot of people down there and go through the entire system. Even then, there's a chance they could keep moving and stay out of sight."

"We've got thousands of police officers we could use," Giannini said.

"Trollers would rather see half the city dead before doing that," Riley responded. "I keep trying to tell you that security is the number-one priority for these people. I wouldn't even be surprised if my men and I were pulled out of here after tomorrow and Trollers let this be *your* problem."

"But how would they explain away the Synbats?"

"They wouldn't have to. There'd be no connection between them and Trollers."

"They have your men's M16s."

"Lost on a training exercise," Riley answered.

"But how would the existence of the Synbats be explained?"

"It wouldn't be," Riley said. "Trollers doesn't care about all that. All he cares about is that he gets his slice of the budget pie and that his career stays unblemished."

"Christ, I can't believe this shit," Giannini grumbled.

"Yes, you can," Riley replied. "Don't tell me you don't have people in your department who aren't more concerned with covering their asses than the safety of those below them."

"Yeah, we got people like that. But not at this scale. We're talking a bunch of dead people already, and the body count's going to get higher."

"You'd be amazed at some of the things your government is capable of," Riley said with undisguised bitterness.

"I don't care," Giannini said. "What I care about is stopping these Synbats. If you don't get them tomorrow, I'm going to my chief."

Riley shrugged. "You can do that, but I wouldn't be too surprised if he isn't on Trollers's and Lewis's side."

"Then I'll go public," Giannini countered.

Riley sighed. "All right, let me tell you what's going on. I'm in contact with *my* commander down at Fort Campbell. Lewis doesn't know that I am. And my commander has already alerted some troops in Wisconsin to be flown here to help in the search. So if we come up with nothing tomorrow, *I'll* be the one to go public. I think when a dozen or so helicopter lifts of heavily armed Rangers land in Chicago and go into the tunnels, the story will be out pretty quickly."

CHAPTER 22
SUNDAY, 12 APRIL

Chicago
7:04 A.M.

Appropriating a handful of Lewis's men, Riley had split the force into four three-man teams. The IR chem lights they'd used the previous day were already extinguished, so today each team had spray cans of IR-reflecting paint that they would use to put arrows on the tunnel walls to indicate their direction and what had been searched. The basic plan was to fan out at the first intersections, each team trying to keep a northerly direction. Using pace count, they would go north approximately two and a half miles, which should bring them to the vicinity of the Chicago River. Riley's best guess was that there would be only a limited number of crossings under the river; if they could search those, they might be able to tell if the Synbats were contained under the Loop or if they had moved into other parts of the city.

The most difficult part of the whole operation was the fact that they had no map of the system. They had passed numerous exits from the tunnel the previous day but most had been walled off—either in the tunnel or at the end of the exit tunnel where it entered a building. Seay had found two openings into building basements, but he couldn't tell exactly what building he was in without drawing attention to himself by going up to street level, so he'd moved on.

As Riley moved through the freight tunnel with Caruso and the DIA man, Killian, he considered the odds of success about fifty-fifty. Riley's greatest hope was that they would stumble upon the place where the

elder Synbats had cached their young. Then the Synbats would stand
and fight rather than flee.

The tunnels were cool—a constant fifty-five degrees—and uncomfortably damp. The small IR light on the front of the night vision goggles
cast a glow that extended thirty feet ahead; beyond that was darkness.
The tunnels were eerily quiet, making it difficult for Riley to imagine streets full of people just fifty feet above.

10:12 A.M.

Holly's head snapped up and her nostrils flared as she sniffed the air.
The dog's little den of ratty newspapers and cardboard boxes, tucked
away in a corner of the deserted third subbasement of a warehouse
building, had been her home for the last twenty-four hours, since leaving
the area south of here where she'd seen the two strange creatures. Now,
it appeared that this place was not safe either.

There was fear in the air; she could sense it, coming from more than
one source, and the feeling writhed its way into her mind and along
her spine. She rose and abandoned her position, heading for the rick-
ety wooden stairs that led up to the daylight.

11:30 A.M.

Giannini leafed through the bulging missing persons folder with little
enthusiasm. From hard experience she knew that most were runaways—
from young girls to harried husbands—people who wanted a new start
even if it was up a dead-end alley. Some were victims—a disturbingly
high number—but no one really knew how high. Even with all the
entangling webs of modern society, the number of people who simply disappeared each day left little doubt in Giannini's mind that there
were voracious hunters out in the world preying on humans. Up to now,
though, all those hunters had been human themselves. The thought
that a nonhuman predator was now under the streets of her own city
chilled her.

The offices outside hers were mostly empty. Detective work was
at a low on Sunday mornings. Helplessness made her physically ill;
she was not used to being in a situation where she could do nothing.

She fought the desire to go out onto the streets, tear off a manhole cover, and descend into the depths. If these Synbats were as dangerous as Riley had told her—and as confirmed by the bodies of the two cable company men—then she would be making a foolish move. On top of that was the possibility of running into Riley or his men. She had a feeling that they would shoot first and ask questions later.

There was nowhere else for her to go, no one waiting for her at home. She'd gone through her second divorce two years ago and decided not long afterward that she preferred being alone than with someone who added little to her life. Her job was enough—at least for now.

Giannini stood up and strode out of her office, heading up to the police communications center, where at least she could sit and watch, waiting for something to happen.

1:30 P.M.

Merrit, seated in the back corner of the van, was ignored by Colonel Lewis and his men. Not that they had much to do. There was always the possibility that the Chicago PD might call with some news, but so far the Synbats had made only one mistake—killing the cable company crew. No other havoc had been discovered yet, and might not ever be discovered.

Merrit leaned forward and her low voice cut through the heavy silence of the van. "Colonel, what's happening back at the lab?"

Lewis was surprised. "What?"

"What's happening at Biotech?"

Lewis shrugged. "They're checking the computer records to see if they can make any more sense out of what happened Monday night, although from what the girl we found told us, it looks like the escaped prisoners were the cause of the Synbats getting out."

"What about the project records?"

Lewis's voice grew guarded. "They'll be taken care of."

"What does that mean?"

"It means that we spent a whole lot of money on this project and we're not going to throw it all away. It might serve some useful function in the future."

Merrit nodded and sat back in her folding chair, her blank expression masking the thoughts going through her head.

3:00 P.M.

Riley paused as a feeling he hadn't had in more than a year eased into his conscious mind. He was being watched. He didn't know how he knew it, but he had enough experience to trust the feeling. Sixth sense is one or more of the five senses that aren't being used primarily and are picking up something that swirls around in the subconscious. Only a truly alert person has that feeling move to the conscious mind.

Riley held up his hand and the other two men halted, Killian a little slower than he would have liked. Riley held still, his eyes shifting in short arcs through the goggles, searching the dripping concrete and the cables and pipes on the right side of the tunnel. Next he concentrated on his hearing and listened, tuning out the water plopping onto the floor, the slight fidgeting of the two men behind him. What had caused him to become alert?

A minute passed. Another. Still, Riley was motionless. He heard someone—Killian, he supposed—shift position with a rustle of clothing. Five minutes and Riley had not twitched. He knew that Caruso could appreciate the importance of patience. Riley had taken the team out to the Fort Campbell golf course one day and had them lie down among some bushes on the edge of the green. They'd spent the entire morning there, not moving. In that time none of the golfers that passed by had spotted them, despite the fact that they were in clear sight. One man had even gone after an errant ball less than twenty feet away from them and not realized that ten sets of eyeballs had watched him.

This tunnel, though, was no golf course, and Synbats weren't golfers. Riley slowly took a deep breath and exhaled it. If the Synbats were out there, and if they could see in the dark as well as, if not better than, he could, then they could see him and his two men standing here. So what were they waiting for? They had Knutz's and T-bones's M16s, unless, of course, they had used up the ammunition.

No, Riley corrected himself. They wouldn't shoot. Not if their lair was somewhere close by. They had to dispatch any potential threat quietly and not draw attention to themselves.

If he was one of them, what would he do? Riley asked himself. He spun around and dropped to one knee, startling Caruso and Killian. His M16 was at his shoulder and he scanned the top of the cable pipes on the right side behind them. A quick movement caught his eye and

he fired, tracers streaking by barely two feet from Caruso's head. The
other two men dove for the floor and Riley fired two more three-
round bursts.

Red tracers roared from behind and Riley flattened himself as the
Synbat that had been in front of him fired. A surprised yell told Riley
that one of his men had been hit. He rolled on his stomach and returned the fire with a quick three-round burst. The bullets ricocheted
off the concrete and whined into the darkness.

"Caruso?" Riley hissed.

"All right, chief. Killian's hit."

The silence was unsettling. Were the Synbats retreating, advancing,
or holding position? "Caruso, you cover back down the way we came.
If they come, they'll come along the pipes. I'll cover the other direction. Clear?"

"Yes, sir." There was a short pause. "Killian's bleeding bad, sir."

Riley edged back to the other two. Keeping his head pointed up,
scanning the tunnel, he reached down with one hand to the DIA man's
body. "Where's he hit?"

"Chest, as far as I can tell."

Killian was lying on his right side. Riley's hand slid into a mangled
mess of blood and torn flesh on Killian's back. The high-velocity 5.56mm
round must have entered in the front and then tumbled through the body,
tearing bone and flesh as it exited. Riley moved his hand up to the
neck to check for a pulse. It was barely there. With one hand Riley
kept his rifle pointed up the tunnel and with the other he pressed down
on the wound, trying to stop the blood. As he did so, he remembered
his intense medical training; he was ignoring the entry wound, and blood
was ebbing out there also, taking life with it.

To bandage both would require relaxing his security. Could the Synbats
see him? Were they watching and waiting? He felt for the pulse again.
Nothing. Shit, Riley cursed to himself, putting both hands on his weapon.
His eyes searched the darkness—nothing that he could see. He flipped
the selector switch on his weapon to semiautomatic and pulled the trigger.
The bullet whined ineffectively down the tunnel.

"There," Doc Seay said. "Did you hear it?"

Trovinsky nodded. "Yeah. This way." He turned right and splashed
down a tunnel, weapon at the ready.

*   *   *

"Throw out a chem light," Riley ordered.

Caruso complied, cracking the light and throwing it down the tunnel. It lay on the floor, the reflection glowing in his goggles.

"Steady," Doc Seay whispered. "Steady."

He crept forward, Trovinsky on his right, the DIA man pulling up the rear, walking backward.

Another shot echoed out, reverberating down the concrete walls. Closer now.

Caruso's finger twitched on the trigger before he saw the glow in the middle of the forehead of the lead figure in the tunnel.

"Help's here, sir," he whispered to Riley.

"We're here," Riley called out. "We made contact. They might be up on the pipes."

The three figures came closer, weapons at the ready until they arrived. Riley recognized Doc Seay. "Got a wounded man here, Doc. Trovinsky, take Caruso and go down the tunnel another twenty feet. I think the Synbats are gone, but make sure."

"Right, chief."

Doc knelt down next to Killian, and his experienced hands ran over the body. "He's dead, chief."

Riley slumped back against the tunnel wall.

"What now?" Seay asked.

Riley pulled out the can of IR paint and sprayed Killian's corpse. "We leave the body here and search for the lair. It's got to be close or else they wouldn't have attacked."

There was no sign in the immediate area that Riley had hit anything with his firing. He'd expected as much. With goggles on, it was impossible to use the sights on the rifle, and aiming became a best guess.

"Let's move," he ordered. Riley led the way down the tunnel, in the direction he'd been heading when he'd first sensed he was being watched. In sixty feet, a side tunnel crossed his path.

"Doc, take your men and go right to the next intersection, then come back. I'll go left and meet you back here. The Synbats have to be very close."

Riley and Caruso turned left and moved down the freight tunnel. Riley paused every ten feet and listened carefully but heard nothing.

He sniffed the air and caught the faint odor of decay. He flipped off the safety on his M16, switching to three-round burst. Sixty feet in he could see an opening to the left. Signaling for Caruso to cover him, Riley pressed himself against the far wall, decreasing his angle to the opening. It was a rectangular doorway, once covered over with boards, but several of the boards had been broken, and an opening beckoned darkly. The smell was coming from there.

Riley stood directly across from the opening and waited, sweat running down his back despite the cool temperature. Muzzle first, Riley poked into the opening. A short corridor—about eight feet long, with the ever-present rail tracks—showed in his goggles, the tracks disappearing into a bricked-up wall. The floor was littered with offal—loops of intestines, cracked bones, and torn flesh—both human and other. The remains of the two backpacks taken from the lab were lying among the bloody mess. The amount and type of body parts left no doubt in Riley's mind that the body count caused by the Synbats was now higher.

Riley looked up to the ceiling and then around the walls of the small enclosure. He'd found the lair, but the Synbats were gone.

4:23 P.M.

Four battery-powered flashlights burned in the lair, illuminating the ghastly contents. Merrit knelt beside the plastic cylinders of the backpacks and carefully examined them. She unrolled a poncho on the floor and sifted through the remains, sorting them into different piles. Colonel Lewis—on his first foray into the depths—and Riley stood behind her, watching her bloody work. They all had cravats tied around their faces, trying to block out the awful smell of the chamber—all except Merrit, that is. Riley had decided to stop worrying about her. They were close to their quarry and he didn't want to be distracted by the weird doctor.

"Any idea how many live baby Synbats we have?" Riley asked, his voice slightly muffled by the cloth.

Merrit held up a softball-sized skull. "This is a Synbat skull." She held up another. "This is a cat." She pointed to an obviously human skull. "You know what that is." She tapped the Synbat one. "Look for these."

Riley got down on his hands and knees and went to work. Lewis watched for a few minutes and then joined in. After half an hour they had searched the entire floor. Fifteen baby Synbat skulls lay on the poncho.

"Thirteen survived," Lewis noted.

"Unless they hid some of the remains," Riley commented. He wasn't going to take anything for granted concerning the Synbats.

Lewis stood and looked at Merrit. "Where do you think they've gone?"

Merrit shrugged. "I have no idea, but I think they'll stay down in the tunnels. They've served their purpose well so far."

"We're no closer now than we were before," Riley said. "All we've done is—"

"I know what we've done!" Lewis's voice betrayed the pressure of the past week. "I know it all right, Mister Riley. That was my man we had to drag out of that tunnel just now. But I don't make the rules— I follow them. All I can do is *suggest*, and I've suggested several times to General Trollers that we bring in more troops. He isn't buying it. I'll recommend it again; that's all I can do." With that comment, Lewis stalked out of the chamber to follow the route that Riley had marked back to their entry point.

Riley and Merrit stood in the silence of the Synbat-made crypt, each lost in thought. Merrit was the first to break the silence. "We have to do something."

"I know," Riley said. "The question is, do what? I agree—the Synbats are still down here. No reason for them not to be. But if we keep wandering around like we have been, they have all the advantages and time is on their side. They're like rats down here, able to breed rapidly and hide and—"

"Let me go after them," Merrit interrupted. "They'll come to me."

"What do you mean?" Riley asked.

"They'll come to me," she repeated. "They come to me in my dreams— they're trying to communicate with us. All we have to do is listen. I can bring them to you."

Riley stared at her speechless as she continued.

"I know it will work. The Synbats were the closest—" she paused, searching for words—"the best minds I ever worked with. In Texas we could only work with cats, but even then I could sense the processes, the functioning." She reached forward and grabbed Riley's arm. "They got in my head in the lab—you saw it on the video. They'll do it again here." She gestured about. "You'll never find them in these tunnels. They can move about at will—coming up to the surface at night for food—even crossing under the river to other parts of the city. They're already multiplying. Mine is the only way to get them and finish them."

Riley's brain latched onto something in Merrit's ramblings—besides the fact that he now knew what was missing from her psych profile. He gently removed her hand from his arm. "I've got an idea. Let's find Giannini."

7:23 P.M.

Giannini had listened without comment to Riley's recounting of the day's events. It was as bad as she had feared. As he wrapped up with Lewis's orders to deploy men around the lair on the off chance the Synbats might come back, she finally spoke. "If they're half as smart as you say they are," she said, pointing at Merrit, "they won't go back there."

"I know," Riley agreed. "That's why I think it's time to do something drastic."

Giannini frowned. "Like what?"

As Riley outlined his idea, her frown deepened. When he was done she sat in silence for a long minute, then shook her head. "You have no idea what effect your plan will have on the city. You also can't be certain you'll kill the Synbats."

"I think there's a good chance we'll get them. And even if we don't, it will drive them out of the tunnels into the open."

"Can your men do it?" Giannini asked.

"I can do it," Riley replied.

"You're forgetting something," Merrit said. "Even if you get all the Synbats here, that doesn't necessarily end the threat."

"What do you mean?" Riley asked.

"There's enough information in the computer at Biotech for someone else to come in and restart the whole project," Merrit explained.

"Let's take one problem at a time," Riley said. "Right now, all I'm concerned about is getting rid of the Synbats that are alive. The theoretical ones in the computer in Tennessee can wait."

"No," Giannini said firmly, surprising Riley. "They can't wait. You told me you've been doing this stuff for years, and that kind of attitude is why you have to keep on doing it. I saw what these things can do to people and I can't find any justification for such a project. If someone can get into that computer down there and do this all over again, then it's our responsibility to make sure it doesn't happen."

"*Our* responsibility?" Riley repeated. "What are *you* going to do?"

"I'll do whatever I have to," Giannini retorted.

Riley suddenly smiled. "All right. Good. You don't mind doing some breaking and entering on a Sunday evening, do you?"

"Not if it helps to stop these things," Giannini replied, standing up.

Fort Campbell
7:45 P.M.

Colonel Hossey read the radio message from Riley one last time and then slowly put it down on the desktop. He looked up at Sergeant Major Powers. "Are you prepared to do this, Dan?"

"Yes, sir."

"If you get caught, it will cost you your career."

Powers shrugged. "Fuck it, sir. Can't always hide behind that pension."

Hossey nodded. "Looks like Dave is getting ready to step in some deep shit up in Chicago too. I'd hate to lose my two best soldiers."

"Don't worry about us, sir. We can handle it."

Hossey stood up and shook the sergeant major's hand. "Good luck. And Dan—for both our sakes—we never had this conversation."

"Roger that, sir. I was going to say the same thing." Powers spun on his heel and was out the door.

Hossey picked up his phone and dialed the number for the 2d Ranger Battalion headquarters at Hunter Army Airfield outside Savannah.

CHAPTER 23

Giannini watched in fascination as Riley poured the gooey mixture into the PVC pipe he held between his knees and waited until it settled a foot short of the end.

"Will that stuff explode?" she asked.

Riley nodded as he took a large wok and pressed it down into the center of the mixture, creating a concave depression. "Fifteen pounds of fertilizer to a half gallon of gas. Guaranteed to ruin your day. Before I became an officer and a gentleman, my specialty in Special Forces was engineering—or demolitions, depending on whether we were building something or tearing it down. You'd be amazed how relatively easy it is to make expedient demolitions if you know what you're doing and are willing to scavenge." He held the pan in place for a few minutes until the mixture kept its form. "The caps we stole from the construction site will set it off." He pulled out the pan and placed the pipe next to the seven others he'd already made. "They'll be hardened by the time we get to the target."

He glanced over at Merrit, who was standing at the window to the front of the abandoned warehouse, staring aimlessly out into the street. Riley met Giannini's gaze, and she lifted her eyebrows and shrugged. He'd told her about Merrit's actions in the lair and Giannini had agreed that the woman had crossed the line away from sanity. But she'd also had to agree with his realization that they could use Merrit's help since she was the only Synbat expert.

"Let's get moving," Giannini said. "We can put them in my car."

267

The two of them loaded the charges and then hustled Merrit into the backseat. Giannini started the engine and they headed out.

Fort Campbell
7:50 P.M.

On the southern end of the main post of Fort Campbell is an area known as Old Clarksville Base. Surrounded by a one-lane tar road and a rusting fence, it presently contained the headquarters for the 160th Special Operations Aviation Regiment and, nestled in one corner, the post's ammunition storage facility.

Decades ago, though, Old Clarksville Base had served another purpose; it was a nuclear weapons storage facility. Massive bunkers were built into the sides of ridges throughout the area, along with numerous concrete pillboxes that had once held marine guards. Plant life now camouflaged the structures.

Sergeant Major Powers had the lights of his pickup truck pointed at the front of one of the abandoned bunkers. He worked swiftly, unlocking the massive padlock that secured the iron bar on the front of the bunker doors. The rusted metal protested as he slid back the bar. The large door swung open with a groan.

Powers pulled a mag light from his fatigue pocket and shone it around the interior. If Colonel Hossey found out about the existence of this cache, Powers knew that the old man wouldn't hesitate a moment before busting his ass to Leavenworth. Upon first arriving at Fort Campbell a year and a half ago, Powers had inherited the cache from a retiring sergeant major with whom he had served in Vietnam. It was knowledge he would have preferred to have been without, but now it was paying dividends.

Powers spotted what he needed. He tore open the crate of C-4 plastic explosive and took out the white packets. He rapidly retraced his steps and relocked the bunker, then hopped into his truck and drove away.

Chicago
8:50 P.M.

"How are we going to get all this to where it needs to go?" Giannini wanted to know as she peered through the windshield.

"Same way the Synbats moved what they wanted to move," Riley replied.

Giannini pointed to the police barriers blocking off the street and the large, darkened van sitting near the small tent that covered the entrance to the manhole. "How are we going to get it in *there?*"

"We're going to carry it," Riley replied with a smile.

"Aren't they going to see us?" Giannini asked.

"Who? Lewis's men? They got their asses so far up their computer screens, they aren't bothering to look outside. That would be like real work. No problem—we can do it."

"Why don't you just go to Lewis with this plan?" Giannini asked. "Seems like it's something they'd like—get rid of their problem in one fell swoop."

"I could," Riley admitted. "And they most likely would like it. But they also might dick around with it too long. We have to go *tonight.* Tomorrow's Monday and this place will be crawling with people, even at night. I can't take the chance of Lewis calling Trollers and having one of their damn conferences to discuss it. We have to end this now."

"What about the men watching the lair?" Merrit asked suddenly, surprising both of them.

"No problem. Doc Seay and the other six members of my team, and the three DIA men—they'll clear the tunnel by 0200 tomorrow morning." Riley looked at his watch in the glow of the streetlights. "That means we've got five hours to move all this stuff, get it set, and clear out before the shit hits the fan." Riley stepped out of the car. The two women opened their doors and got out.

"I'll help," Merrit said. "I'll go with you."

Riley pulled out the first charge. "Why don't you just stay up here and keep watch?"

"No," Merrit insisted. "I can help."

Riley shook his head. "I don't think you should—"

"Hey," Giannini growled, a charge on her shoulder. "Let's stop jawing and do it."

Riley grabbed a second charge and handed it to Merrit. "Follow me."

Vicinity Bumpus Mills, Tennessee
9:00 P.M.

Sergeant Major Powers was whistling as the headlights of the pickup truck guided him through the Tennessee countryside. By the dim glow of the dashboard, he could see the miscellaneous pile of supplies on

the passenger seat. He smiled. There were several large bags of in-
cendiary mix that he had worked up prior to picking up the C-4. Three
parts flour and one part aluminum shavings, the mixture sat next to
the more lethal concoction of C-4 and blasting caps. It'd be an ugly
scene if he had an accident right now.

It had been a long time since Powers had to work out a problem like
this, and he was enjoying the challenge. The repercussions would come
tomorrow. Tonight was action, and action was the fuel that Powers ran on.

As he turned up Route 139, Powers's time sense slowed down and
he mentally prepared himself for the night's events. After thirty years
in the army and Special Forces, it wasn't hard. His smile grew wider.

Chicago
11:30 P.M.

"How much farther?" Giannini asked as she pulled at the front end of
the battered shopping cart.

"Another four hundred meters," Riley answered.

They'd turned the cart sideways and dropped it down from the sewer
level to the freight tunnel level, then carefully lowered all eight pipes
by rope before going down themselves. For more than an hour now
they'd been moving due north. They had taped flashlights to the front
of the cart, and the glow extended about twenty feet ahead. Giannini
and Merrit were on either side of the lights, pulling, as Riley pushed
from the rear. It was hard going, since the small wheels would get stuck
in the mud or suddenly spin around, causing the cart to tip from side
to side. Anxiety would rise as the cart threatened to tip over and spill
its volatile contents.

Riley's eyes flickered about, searching. The three were making enough
noise to alert any Synbat within a half mile. The light was also a dead
giveaway, but he had access to only one set of night vision goggles
and they'd never make it in time with Merrit and Giannini stumbling
around blindly in the dark. His M16 rested in front of the cart in the
child's seat and his pistol was snug in its shoulder holster. Giannini
had discarded her jacket, and a rather large Colt Python was riding
under her left arm.

"How we doing for time?" Giannini asked.

Riley glanced at his watch. "We're just a little behind."

Biotech Engineering
11:45 P.M.

The DIA guard had been pulling the ten to six graveyard shift for the last three days; the novelty had worn thin within two hours of the first shift. The entire building had been stripped bare and all the equipment and supplies piled up in the main foyer. They were due to be picked up tomorrow morning and taken away.

The guard leaned back in his chair and flipped the page on the paperback he'd started the first night. As his eyes registered the first word something flickered across his line of sight. He started forward, but a cloth tightened around his mouth and he reflexively sucked in a large breath. He was unconscious within five seconds.

Like taking candy from a baby, Sergeant Major Powers thought as he grabbed the guard by his armpits and dragged him out of the building and across the parking lot. Powers tied him to one of the light poles and blindfolded him for good measure. He figured the guard would be out for at least six hours, but Powers didn't believe in taking chances.

Powers recovered his pickup from its hiding spot a quarter mile down the road and drove it up to the lab, parked next to the front door, and began unloading his equipment.

Chicago
12:45 A.M.

The tunnel began descending slightly and the air grew increasingly damp. Small droplets of condensation plopped off the ceiling onto the floor, forming a small rivulet of water. Riley kept them going until the tunnel began rising slightly. "This is it."

Merrit looked around. "You're sure we're under the river?"

Riley nodded. "Pace count and direction add up. We just went down about five extra feet, and I'd say it's pretty damn damp in here."

"Now what?" Giannini asked. "You know what to do?"

"You think I'd take you all the way down here and not know what to do?" Riley asked as he lifted the first pipe out of the cart.

"Hey, I've seen stupider things done," Giannini replied as she pulled out her revolver and ripped the tape off one of the flashlights. "I'll cover the way we came."

Riley paused and handed Merrit his pistol. "Take the other light and cover in that direction."

Riley pulled a mini-mag light off his vest and clenched it between his teeth as he worked on the first pipe. He carefully took a nonelectric fuse and wrapped a length of detonating cord eight times around it, then he placed it inside the small opening on the base of the pipe and pressed it into the ammonium nitrate–gasoline mixture. Using normal TNT as a blast factor of one, this mixture had an effectiveness of only .42—thus Riley's insistence on using a larger amount than his calculations told him would do the job.

Finished with the first pipe, Riley placed it back in the cart, fuse end facing down, concave end up. He carefully threaded the det cord through the blood-stained grate at the bottom of the cart and coiled it, keeping it out of the water on the floor. He did the same to all eight pipes. Then he tied all eight fuses along another length of det cord, and left the last piece dangling.

When he was done, he tied a large flat cake pan, layered with a half inch of explosive, about a foot below the bottom of the cart. He primed the charge with another fuse and det cord.

Giannini would occasionally glance over her shoulder and watch Riley work, his hands expertly twisting the explosive rope into knots and handling the fragile detonators. She searched for something humorous to lighten the mood a little and then gave up, focusing on the dark corridor that stretched up and out of sight.

Riley stood slowly and held both pieces of firing cord in his hands. "I'm ready to wire this up to the ignitors."

"Why two?" Giannini asked.

"You *always* have a dual firing system." He held up the piece of det cord tied into the pipes. "This is the primary. It should set off all eight pipes at once. If that fails," he held up the other cord, "then this one is set to go off five minutes later. It blows the explosive on the pan below the pipes. That explosion ought to be enough to initiate the fuses in the pipes."

"Then what?" Merrit asked, diverting her attention for the first time.

Riley pointed at the pipes. "Those are called shaped charges. I don't know exactly how it works, but the concave shape on the top of the charge focuses the blast."

"Don't you have to put it against whatever it's going to blow up?" Merrit asked.

"No. You need stand off for the blast to focus." He looked up at the pitted ceiling. "I don't know how thick the concrete up there is, but it can't be more than a few feet. There's a layer of dirt on top of that, and then the river. There's enough explosive here to go through at least five feet of reinforced concrete—and this stuff isn't reinforced—and about ten feet of dirt. It will do the job."

"Let's stop talking and get out of here," Giannini suggested.

Riley looked at his watch. "It's almost two. Seay will be moving his people out in a couple of minutes. I'm going to wait until then to hook this up to the ignitor."

2:00 A.M.

Doc Seay and the other six members of ODA 682 stood up and moved out of their defensive positions as the second hand swept by the twelve, marking the hour.

"Let's get out of here," Seay ordered.

When the DIA agent in charge started to protest, Seay shrugged. "You can stay here and die, or you can go to the surface with us. It's your choice."

"What do you mean 'stay here and die'?" the DIA man asked.

"Stay here and find out," Seay replied cryptically as he and his men set off down the tunnel. The three DIA men looked at each other briefly and then quickly set out behind the Special Forces soldiers.

Biotech Engineering
2:01 A.M.

Powers placed the bags of mixture throughout the first floor of the building, taking special notice of the equipment stacked in the main foyer, particularly the computers. Next to each bag he placed a small charge of C-4. He primed it with a blasting cap and linked them together with detonating cord. Then he ran the det cord back to the front door and hooked it into a radio-controlled fuse ignitor.

The C-4 would explode the aluminum and flour mixture, which would blow out, causing a total vacuum on the inside of the building. Air pressure on the outside of the building would implode the structure, effectively destroying everything inside. Powers would have preferred to simply blow up the building, scattering it over the countryside, but the amount of C-4 required to do that was more than had been available in the bunker. The expedient dust initiator mixture would have to serve.

Powers used the guard's key to descend to the lower level and do the same thing, hooking the charges into another remote fuse ignitor on the same frequency as the one above. He took the elevator back up and made his way out of the building.

Chicago
2:04 A.M.

Riley finally used the last two items they had laboriously carried here— two small lockboxes with timers inside. He hooked the det cord from the tubes into the fuse ignitor on the bottom timer, then connected the one from the backup system. He looked up at Merrit and Giannini, who had gathered in close.

"My watch reads 0205," he said. "Seay's clearing the tunnel and will be out in thirty minutes. It will take us about forty to get out." He moved the hour hand on the tube clock back to eleven. "I'm setting the primary to blow in one hour." He moved the backup to 10:55. "The backup goes off in an hour and five if the primary doesn't blow. You all ready to move out?"

Both women nodded.

Riley pulled a pack of four double-A batteries from his pocket and tore off the plastic cover. He pushed two batteries into the backup clock, and the second hand started moving. Then he pushed two batteries into the primary clock, and immediately pressed buttons on his wristwatch, setting the stopwatch for one hour. He placed each clock into a lockbox, then locked them shut with two keys. He handed the keys to Giannini. "You take these."

"What do we need them for? I don't even understand why we're locking the damn things."

"I'm locking them because if there's a one-in-a-hundred chance that the Synbats come across this setup, I don't want them messing with the ignitors."

"They could just pull out the wires," she noted.

"They could," Riley agreed. "But there's only so much you can do. We've got fifty-nine minutes. Let's roll."

They set off down the tunnel, Riley in the lead, Merrit in the middle, and Giannini bringing up the rear.

Biotech Engineering
2:20 A.M.

Powers sat in the cab of his pickup truck and looked at the lights glowing in the foyer of the building. He reached into the cooler between the two seats, pulled out a soda, and popped the top. He took a deep draft, swished it around, and then swallowed. After a brief pause, he belched.

He pulled the handset for the remote fuse ignitor out of his parka pocket and leaned it on the steering wheel next to the soda, then took another long drink.

"Let's see if the master can still whip up a good dust initiator," he said to himself as his forefinger played with the power button on the control. He flipped it on. There was a bright flash inside the foyer, then nothing happened for a millisecond. The windows in the buildings suddenly imploded with a whooshing sound as everything was sucked into the vacuum caused by the blast. Another brief pause and the ceiling collapsed with a thunderous crash.

When the air cleared, the mission had been accomplished. The only thing they'd be trucking out of Biotech the following morning was a load of debris.

Powers put away the control and slowly drove off, steering with one hand as he continued to drink his soda in celebration, looking forward to the cold brew waiting back at Fort Campbell.

Chicago
2:35 A.M.

They were more than halfway back to the manhole, Riley in the lead, holding the flashlight with his right hand under the hand guards of the M16. His left forefinger was on the trigger as the light played over the walls, left to right, forward, and then back, in a continuous pattern. Behind him, Merrit stumbled along, exhausted, holding his pistol. In the rear, Giannini crabbed sideways, flashlight in one hand pointing back, revolver in the other. There had been no conversation since leaving the demolition site; each person was lost in thought or trying to tune into the hostile environment that enveloped them.

They hit one of countless cross tunnels, and Riley quickly scanned left and right, then unerringly continued straight on, due south. The walls seemed closer now and more forbidding. The darkness beyond the feeble reach of the flashlights was absolute.

Another cross corridor and Riley stepped out into the intersection. Taking a quick glance left, he swung to check right, and as he moved, a Synbat slammed into him from that side at full charge. Large, sinewy arms wrapped around him and he immediately dropped both weapon and flashlight to fight for his life, trying to keep the fangs from closing on his neck.

Directly behind, the second Synbat ignored the greater threat of Giannini and her pistol—its eyes focusing on Merrit. It leapt over the struggling forms of Riley and the first Synbat and landed on the doctor, slamming her to the ground. Merrit screamed as fangs tore through her shirt and into her stomach. Giannini swung her light around, pistol locked on the two figures struggling in the center of the beam.

"Get out of the way!" she yelled at Merrit.

Riley's left forearm was levered against the Synbat's throat. Saliva splashed on his face from the fangs just above him. He could feel distant pain as the Synbat swung at him with its powerful hands. He slammed his right fist into the creature's gut, with no apparent effect.

The second Synbat looked up as Giannini took a good firing stance, flashlight locked with her free hand under the barrel of the pistol. The clear shot disappeared as Merrit reached up and wrapped both arms around the Synbat.

"Let go!" Giannini shouted.

But Merrit held on as the Synbat reached down and twisted her head, breaking her neck. Giannini fired three times; two of the magnum slugs hit the Synbat, killing it.

The shots echoed in Riley's ears as the Synbat on top of him bit down on his shoulder. He heard, rather than felt, bone snap. The Synbat rolled, pulling Riley on top of him as a shield.

"Shoot!" Riley screamed as the Synbat's head dipped for a second attempt at his neck. He swung his right arm outside the Synbat's grip and jabbed his rigid fingers directly into the creature's face. The creature howled as three of Riley's fingers pierced its right eye. Riley felt the bones snap in those fingers as the Synbat reared back, and then it was gone.

Giannini fired her three remaining shots as the creature sprinted away into the darkness. She immediately knelt, snapped open the cylinder, dropping the empty casings to the floor, and slammed a speed loader against the empty holes. She stood and shone the light back down the corridor. "I think I hit it."

Riley forced himself to a sitting position, his back against the wall, feeling the bones in his right shoulder grate together. "How's Merrit?" he gasped.

Giannini backed up and knelt next to the doctor. "Dead. Neck broken. I told her to get out of the way, and instead she grabs the damn thing."

"She wanted to die," Riley said, breathing heavily.

"What?"

"We kill these—and if Powers destroys the lab—the only link to making the Synbats is her. She knew that. Now she's gone too."

Giannini shook her head and played the light over Riley. "Shit, you're a mess. Can you move?"

"Think so," Riley said, gritting his teeth. He grabbed her outstretched hand and started to get to his feet when his left knee suddenly buckled. "Son of a bitch," he muttered. "I didn't feel that get hurt." He reached down and tenderly felt around. "It isn't broken. Must have strained something when the Synbat jumped me."

"Here, I'll give you a hand." Giannini helped him to his feet and then wrapped his left arm over her shoulder. "Can you walk like this?"

They took a few tentative steps forward, Riley placing most of his weight on her whenever his left foot came forward. "Yeah."

They started moving. "But if another Synbat shows up, we're gonna be dessert," Giannini commented.

"We killed one. One's wounded. That leaves only one healthy Synbat, and I think it will stay with the young," Riley said. "But if we don't get out of here soon, we'll have more to worry about than the Synbats."

3:02 A.M.

"What the hell are you doing up here?" Lewis demanded, staring at the group of men clustered around the manhole.

"We're waiting for Mister Riley, sir," Doc Seay replied.

"Why aren't you at your positions?" Lewis asked.

"Because they were no longer tenable, sir."

"What?" Lewis asked incredulously.

"They were no longer tenable, sir." Seay looked at his watch. "As a matter of fact, the whole tunnel system is going to become untenable in a few minutes."

Lewis stared at Seay and sorted through his military mumble-jumble. His eyes grew wide. "Where's Riley?" He looked around at the gathered figures. "What's he doing?"

"He's blowing a hole in the roof of the tunnel where it crosses under the Chicago River," Seay said.

Lewis's mouth dropped open as he realized the implications.

Seay didn't add that he was getting increasingly worried about Riley and the two women. They were late.

3:07 A.M.

The primary clock flicked to twelve and the electrical impulse fired a charge, which ignited the det cord. The det cord didn't burn—it exploded, initiating all eight fuses simultaneously. The fuses set off the gasoline-ammonium mixture from bottom to top, causing the force of the explosion to focus on the roof of the freight tunnel.

Riley had been quite modest in his claims. A car-sized hole instantly appeared in the roof of the tunnel, the force of the blast easily carrying through the concrete into the soil above. The hole grew smaller and smaller until it punched through into the bottom of the Chicago River. There the force of the man-made explosion finally lost its power to that of Mother Nature. The pressure reversed and the water came in.

A dull rumble sounded through the tunnels. Giannini paused; Riley stumbled and almost fell. "What was that?"

"You know what it was," Riley said.

"How fast will the water come in?" she asked as they continued on.

"I don't know."

"How far do we have to go?"

"I don't know," Riley said. "Just follow the arrows we painted."

3:08 A.M.

"Fuck," Riley cursed as he stumbled and fell, taking Giannini down with him. "I'm feeling light-headed. I think I'm losing too much blood from my shoulder."

"Your shoulder?" Giannini asked. She shined the light on him, pulled aside the torn cloth, and gasped as she saw the mangled flesh. Blood had soaked his entire side. As she lowered the light she could see that the dark stain reached all the way to his boots. "Why didn't you tell me?"

"Because we didn't have time and I thought I could make it," Riley whispered, closing his eyes and trying to get control of his spinning brain. He'd felt this before, on the chopper flying out of China after being shot. He knew that he was minutes from passing out.

"Go on without me," he said.

"Bullshit," Giannini replied as she fumbled with his combat vest, looking for a bandage. She found one in his first-aid pouch and pressed it on his shoulder. A hiss of pain escaped his teeth.

3:09 A.M.

Only an occasional car passed over the Kinzie Street bridge at this hour, and in the dark its occupants wouldn't have noticed that in the water to the south of the bridge a whirlpool had formed. Swirling, it sucked down small pieces of debris from the surface of the river and bore them down twenty feet to the hole in the river bottom. The water was gushing into the hole at a rate of more than 100,000 gallons per minute. The freight tunnel under the river was completely flooded and the water was searching outward, north and south, east and west, the level lowering as the number of tunnels increased. But there was no end to the water that could come. All of Lake Michigan waited to flow into the river and then into the tunnels, until every last square foot of space below river level was full.

3:10 A.M.

"Come on, let's go," Giannini urged, pulling on Riley's left arm.

He pushed up on his good leg. "All right." The two set off down the tunnel. There was a low, constant roar sounding through its length, yet no water had appeared. Above the roar came another sound—a riveting howl.

"What was that?" Giannini asked.

"A Synbat," Riley replied.

"Where?" she asked, the flashlight in her free hand jumping about, searching around them.

"Not close to us," Riley replied. "I think it got wet feet and is trying to figure out how to get all those little ones out. Let's hope it doesn't succeed."

They continued on, Riley closing his mind to everything but taking one step forward, and then another. Giannini's hand was sweaty on the flashlight. She felt uncomfortable not holding her gun, but they needed the light to find their way out. She spotted another of the bright red arrows they'd painted on the wall on the way in. The entrance couldn't be too far now. Another intersection beckoned.

She was startled by the roar as the water caught them from behind, knocking them off their feet. Losing her grip on Riley and almost dropping the flashlight, she struggled to her feet against the water swirling about at thigh level. There was no sign of Riley.

"Shit!" she cursed as she plunged her hand under the water, feeling around. Nothing. She stuck the flashlight in her belt and used both hands, flailing about in the water, searching. Something brushed her left hand and she grabbed hold. Gripping with both hands, she pulled Riley up, sputtering and hacking. His eyes held no sign of recognition.

"Don't lose it on me now," she pleaded. She pulled out the flashlight and pointed the way ahead. The water was dark and oily-looking with floating debris. It wrapped around her upper thighs like a cold, slimy blanket. "Come on!" she exhorted Riley, trying to get him moving. She could feel the water slowly creeping higher as she moved.

3:12 A.M.

Seay took one more look at his watch and slung his M16 over his shoulder. "Let's go," he ordered, swinging his feet into the hole leading down. The rest of ODA 682 followed without question, leaving Colonel Lewis and his DIA men to contemplate the dark opening.

Seay clambered down to the sewer and quickly made his way to the opening leading to the freight tunnels. Shining his light down, he could see water in the chamber below. "Trovinsky, you come with me. The rest of you stay up here and be prepared to do some hauling to get us back up."

The other five members of the team formed a human anchor point for the rope as Seay and then Trovinsky rappeled down. The water was waist high when their feet finally found purchase on the floor.

Seay immediately headed to the left, due north, pushing his way through the water.

3:16 A.M.

The water was up to Giannini's chest, and they were barely making progress. Riley was a sodden weight on her arm, his legs moving slowly under the water. He'd bled through the bandage she'd put on his shoulder, and blood floated out behind them on the scummy water.

"Go on without me," he whispered.

"So, there's life in there after all" was her only comment.

"You aren't going to make it with me, and you don't have much time," Riley insisted.

"It isn't much farther," she grunted, leaning forward into the water. "I wish you hadn't been so good at your demolition job," she added. "A smaller hole might have done just as well."

"Haven't heard the Synbats since that howl," Riley muttered weakly. "I think we got them."

"I think we got *us*," Giannini retorted. A swell of water broke against her face and she sputtered as some got into her mouth. "Shit, do you have any idea what kind of crud is in the Chicago River? If we don't drown we'll die of hepatitis."

They reached another intersection. She stopped for a second, leaning Riley against the cable pylons on the side, and stepped up on one of the pipes, peering ahead. No sign of where they were. The arrows were all underwater by now. She had no idea which way to go.

She reached down and grabbed the back of Riley's vest to keep his head above water. He was losing consciousness. She took another step up on the stanchion holding the cables in place. The water was five and a half feet deep, leaving only a foot and a half of space below the concave ceiling.

"Come on, Riley. Don't give up on me now." She felt the strain on her arm as the water tried to drag away his body. "Give me a little help here, bud," she exhorted. Riley's good hand reached under the water and gripped her belt, fingers curling up. "That's it," Giannini said as she looked anxiously about. "That's it." She slid her feet along the pipes, another foot closer to the exit, however far away it was.

A light flickered to her left. "Down here!" she screamed, firing her revolver into the water for emphasis. Two men, only their heads visible above the water, turned the nearest corner.

"We'll get you!" Doc Seay called out as he led the way. He swam up and grabbed hold of Riley.

"He's hurt bad," Giannini gasped.

"Let's get out of here," Seay yelled. Trovinsky gave a hand to the exhausted woman. Seay hooked his arm under Riley's chin and breaststroked his way back to the opening, only one turn away, where the rope was waiting.

6:34 A.M.

Three stories down and two blocks east of the Chicago Mercantile Exchange, in a side tunnel of the freight system, the bodies of eleven baby Synbats and an adult with an injured eye floated listlessly in the pitch black waters. Under the Mercantile Exchange itself, a boarded-up entryway for the freight system was the watery grave of the one uninjured adult. She'd made it there, hours previously, fighting the water, a baby cradled under each arm.

Her hands were bloody where she'd pried at the boards closing off the tunnel from the building's subbasement. Her left arm was jammed into the small opening she'd created, fixed there by the pressure of a jet of dank water pouring into the hole. She'd squeezed the two babies through the hole before succumbing to the water.

As the morning wore on in buildings throughout the Loop, people were slowly discovering the rising tide of river water in the basements. The water rose over the power cables, and electricity started going out; by midmorning the power company was forced to shut off service to the entire area affected by the flood. No one knew where all the water had come from, until someone noticed the whirlpool in the Chicago River just south of the Kinzie Street bridge. Even then, no one was sure how the water was getting from there into the buildings.

EPILOGUE
WEDNESDAY, 15 APRIL

Fort Campbell, Kentucky
9:00 A.M.

Riley looked up as the door to his room opened and Detective Giannini walked in. "Well, this is a surprise," he grinned, glad to see her, especially after all the official visitors he'd had over the last few days.

"A good surprise or a bad one?" she asked as she came up to him.

"A good one."

She glanced at the newspapers lying on the table next to his bed. "You been keeping up with the story?"

Riley had been following the daily developments of the Chicago Flood from his hospital bed. He'd noted that the first diver sent down to check things out had been an ex–navy SEAL. He wasn't surprised when the official statement was issued: Although there was no definitive answer, the flood must have been caused by fatigue in the roof of the freight tunnel where it went under the river. And he certainly wasn't surprised when the president declared downtown Chicago a disaster area and the Army Corps of Engineers moved in to clean up the mess. He had little doubt that someone from General Trollers's staff was intimately involved in that effort, and that when bodies were discovered—human or Synbat—they would be whisked away quickly.

He'd faced some hard questioning from one of Trollers's stooges after the rescue. Lewis had been relieved of his post and had disappeared. They interrogated Riley about the explosion at Biotech, but he had professed ignorance, and the matter had been dropped. The prevailing theme seemed to be that there was enough mess to clean up without having to dig for more. In any case, too many people at Fort Campbell and in Riley's chain of command knew what had happened for Trollers to make an overt effort to punish Riley.

"Yeah, sounds like a three-ring circus," he commented.

Giannini sat down in a chair facing the bed. "I drove down—left last night. My boss thought it would be good if I disappeared for a while, so he put me on paid admin leave. I wanted to see how you were doing."

"I'm all right. I think they're keeping me in here for the same reason your boss put you on leave. My shoulder will take awhile to heal, but everything else is functioning well."

"The feds questioned me for a while, but the emphasis was mainly on threats about my future if I ever let out what had really happened." Giannini leaned forward. "I heard rumors they've found some bodies down there, but the army's taken over everything."

Riley nodded. "They'll keep it covered up."

"Yeah."

There was a long pause, then Riley looked over at Giannini. "Hey, listen—" he hesitated.

"What?" Giannini asked.

Riley fidgeted in the bed. "Well, I just wanted to say thanks for all you did."

"You mean saving your life?" Giannini asked with a smile.

"Well, yeah, there's that," Riley admitted.

"Yeah, there's that," Giannini mimicked, then she turned serious. "Think we got them all? There's been no reports of anything unusual on the streets."

Riley had been thinking about little else for the past forty-eight hours. "If some of the young ones escaped, you'll be hearing about it real soon."

"Unless the engineers drain the tunnels real quick and the Synbats go back underground," Giannini noted.

Riley shook his head. "You can bet the army will take its time getting the water out."

Giannini slumped back in the chair. "They're estimating that the loss to businesses in the Loop is going to run into the hundreds of millions."

"I don't think Trollers is very much worried about that."

"I just can't believe something like this can be covered up," Giannini said.

"You can always go to the press," Riley remarked.

"Yeah, and get my head handed to me. I'm not as dumb as I look."

"I don't think you look very dumb," Riley said.

Giannini sighed. "I guess all we can do is wait and see what turns up."

A long silence ensued. Riley tried to sit and Giannini hopped up to help him, putting a couple of pillows behind his back.

"Thanks," Riley said. He ran his good hand along the splints holding his broken fingers. "Hey, listen . . ."

"Yeah," Giannini said.

He fidgeted for a moment longer, then looked up and met her steady gaze. "It sounds kind of stupid, but I don't even know your first name."

Giannini smiled and settled back into her chair. "It's Donna."

Chicago
10:20 P.M.

Holly slunk under the fence surrounding the construction site for a new skyscraper that was to grace the Loop. She moved toward the pile of metal rods and assorted lumber that she was making her new home when she suddenly froze, the hair on the back of her neck standing up. She recognized the scent immediately, and her eyes strained to pierce the darkness and find the source. Moving slowly, belly low to the ground, she made her way forward, the faint smell growing stronger.

Something scuttled around in the opening between two trailers. Holly froze and waited. It moved again—now there were two. They were a foot and a half high, and moved with jerky movements. One of them turned toward her and grimaced, displaying fangs that already were larger than Holly's. The two began moving toward her, separating to trap her between them.

Holly's tail twitched and she half-turned to run. Then she stopped. This time she wouldn't run. She exploded out of her stance and charged, taking the young Synbat on the left completely by surprise. Her teeth closed on its neck and she furiously shook the hapless creature until its spine snapped.

The other Synbat ran. Holly dropped the first one, the body sliding

onto the ground like a rag doll, and went after the second. It hit the
fence and scooted under, Holly less than five feet behind. It headed
for the park, but Holly caught it halfway down the street and took it
down from behind, teeth clamping down on the back of its neck. As
the small hands pounded at her side, she let go briefly, but chomped
down again, this time with a death grip.

In thirty seconds the last Synbat was dead. Holly placed a paw on
its chest and raised her bloody muzzle to the moon.

The Author

Bob Mayer, a West Point graduate, spent several tours of duty with both the Infantry and the Special Forces. He served two years as the commander of a Special Forces A team and two years as the operations officer for an SF Group overseeing military deployments across Europe. After leaving the Army, he moved to the Orient to write and study the martial arts. His first novel, *EYES OF THE HAMMER*, takes a Special Forces team into Colombia to battle drug lords; his second, *DRAGON SIM-13*, follows Riley and his team to China. His fourth novel, *CUT OUT*, continues the Special Forces series. Mayer is currently in the Reserves as an instructor at the Special Forces Qualification Course at the John F. Kennedy Special Warfare Center and School at Fort Bragg. Mayer, originally from New York City, now lives in Clarksville, Tennessee.